Endurance

Tor Books by Jay Lake

Endurance

Jay Lake

A Tom Doherty Associates Book
New York

This is a work of fiction. All of the characters, organizations, and events portrayed in this novel are either products of the author's imagination or are used fictitiously.

ENDURANCE

Copyright © 2011 by Joseph E. Lake, Jr.

A Tor Book
Published by Tom Doherty Associates, LLC
175 Fifth Avenue
New York, NY 10010

www.tor-forge.com

Tor® is a registered trademark of Tom Doherty Associates, LLC.

Library of Congress Cataloging-in-Publication Data

Lake, Jay.
 Endurance / Jay Lake. — 1st ed.
     p. cm.
 "A Tom Doherty Associates book."
 ISBN 978-0-7653-2676-8
 I. Title.
 PS3612.A519E53 2011
 813'.6—dc22

                    2011021613

First Edition: November 2011

Printed in the United States of America

0 9 8 7 6 5 4 3 2 1

This has grown beyond my daughter's story,
but this book is still dedicated to her.
Her struggle is her own, her triumphs are her own,
though I share in them both. I can only hope
to wish her strength and love in her life.

Acknowledgments

This book would not have been possible without the wonderful assistance of people too numerous to fully list here. Nonetheless, I shall try, with apologies to whomever I manage to omit from my thank-yous. Much is owed to Dr. Kevin Billingsley, Kelly Buehler and Daniel Spector, Sarah Bryant, Michael Curry, Dr. Daniel Herzig, Bronwyn Lake, Ambassador Joseph Lake, Shannon Page, Dr. Paul Schipper, Ken Scholes, Jeremy Tolbert, the Umberger family, Dr. Gina Vaccaro, the Omaha Beach Party, Amber Eyes, and, of course, everyone in my blogging and social media communities. To those whom I may have neglected to mention: That omission is my own and does not in any way reflect upon you.

I also want to recognize the Brooklyn Post Office here in Portland, Oregon, as well as the Fat Straw coffeehouse and Lowell's Print-Inn for all their help and support. Likewise, the doctors and nurses of the Knight Cancer Center at Oregon Health Sciences University for keeping me alive so I could write this book. Special thanks go to Jennifer Jackson, Beth Meacham, Melissa Frain, and Terry McGarry for making this book not only possible but real. Also, I want to thank Irene Gallo and Dan Dos Santos for another striking cover that shows Green as she lives—in angry motion.

And of course my brother and his ox. Errors and omissions are entirely my own responsibility.

Endurance

The High Hills

I SAT AMONG the late autumn-blooming clover amid a sloping grave-meadow and picked at my memories as if they were old scars. Fat, slow, red-bodied bees bumbled about me as they passed through scattered shafts of sunlight limning the damp, chilly air. Their indifferent drone was desultory. Empires would rise and fall, gods pass from bloody birth to fiery death, every woman who ever lived slip quietly into her final sleep, and still bees would find their flowers.

That was a lesson for me. I was certain of it. Sick of lessons, I ignored the thought.

Recollection served my mood little better. As they always have, the people of my life crowded close in these quiet moments. Federo, locked inside the bandit-god-king Choybalsan, that haunted look in his eyes at the last. Septio, the only man I'd then bedded, his neck snapped within the loving circle of my arms. Shar, the desperate woman who'd lived with my father into the final days of his ruination. Mistress Danae, whose addled mind and ravaged body survived as a shadow among the graves. Cities full of flame and despair, knives in the dark, my fear racing faster than even the flying of my feet.

"*Stop!*"

The single word echoed among the silent graves scattered across this empty hillside. Tiny birds whirred up from the long, golden grass into the cerulean bell of the sky. My belly twinged as the child within stirred. She was still so little, this poor god-struck bastard of mine. I placed my hands upon my abdomen and crooned softly. I don't know if the ancient ghosts whose abode this was heard me. Perhaps it didn't matter. My baby returned to sleep and took the bitter sting of memories with her.

In time I emerged from my enclosing song and looked about. Inattention has never been a habit with me, not from my earliest years. Even so, the unquiet dead were no threat, the nearest possible ambush was hundreds of paces away downhill, and this place *smelled* of safety. Most of the bees had moved on to other stands of clover on their day's rounds. The pallid northern sun had climbed higher into the patient vault of the heavens. The day was as warm as ever it would be at this time of year—almost enough to make me wish for a hood or a hat, rather than simply sitting bareheaded in the wind that carried the first sharp-edged tang of winter. The scent of the clover remained strong, mixed with the dusty-rock odor of the ridgetops.

Even now, I still believe that the High Hills were as timeless a place as I'd ever known, at least since the never-ending summer amid the rice paddies of my earliest youth. No ox stood placid and wise to watch over me. Instead, I watched over myself and my child. These forgotten grave-meadows were safely outside the purview of the several gods who had made themselves so dangerous to me. Nothing here but ghosts, dwindling gently with the slow passage of years as we all must do.

The grave nearest me offered a smidgen of shadow, but Ilona had said the old king who lay there rested uneasy. It was not so good to place myself close under his touch. A shame, too; his grave was pretty enough. The sepulcher had been dug back into the hill, so that only the face stood clear. That visible portion of the monument boasted a cladding of red stone, carven into small pillars and a carved entablature. The elaborate frieze had long since worn to a tale of shapeless heroism among faceless warriors. Brass and bronze banded the pillars, and served as tarnished ornaments to the tiny stoa. The grave was a miniature of a classical Smagadine temple, rendered through the imagination of some Stone Coast mason who'd likely never even sailed as far as Lost Port.

An idea of a memory of someone else's history. Just as with my own life, from my happy beginnings down all the years since. But also as with my life, in a curious manner all the disparate elements and desperate divisions came together to form something greater than could be inferred from the constituent parts. In the case of this grave, the harlequin whole of the architectural truth served to hold a dead man and his unquiet ghost. The mound that rose behind the facing was pretty, a gentle swale of turf dotted with tiny, wound-pink flowers.

But unquiet. So unquiet.

The ghosts whispered when you walked among them if you had ears to listen. Ilona had suggested that as I had been god-touched, my hearing was plenty sharp for what was needful here. I'd certainly had my share of arguments with the divine, from the Lily Goddess to Blackblood to Endurance himself.

My god. The one I'd created.

That thought still had the power to stagger me, months later here in my exile.

I wandered along the slopes. Yarrow hissed against my calves. Clover crushed beneath my feet added a sharp rush of bruised green to the already-heavy scent of flowers. Smaller, less forward blossoms peeked eye-bright from among the larger stalks.

And through it all, the graves. Some little more than hummocks of grass, covered in brambles or roses or stranger things, depending on the will of the original mourners and perhaps the sensibilities of the ghost lurking within. Others were more elaborate, such as the final home of the redstone king I'd just left behind. Certain of their fellows were merely collapsed hollows— dents in the earth where I could lay myself down and walk awhile among the strange dreams of the lords of the dead past.

Each carried a whispering voice. Certain of them spoke like wasps under a distant eave: barely a buzzing whine, hints of meaning concealed within the cycling tonality. More resembled chatter after a temple service. Arguments, bargaining, the rhythm of a joke being recounted; the sense still not quite fully formed to my ear.

A few were awake, aware. Some called my name with voices as forceful as life.

"Green."

"Come here, girl."

"You dare too much."

"You do not risk enough."

Still, they were merely ghosts. Like so many of life's oppressions, the power of such clinging souls is only that granted by the victim. I had already faced worse than any of these would ever wield against me.

"Sleep," I called, invoking the formulation that Ilona had taught me. "Sleep, and rest upon your beds of dreams."

I had no idea if that phrase eased the ghosts, but my use of it seemed to ease Ilona. That was good enough for me. I picked a careful path down toward the stand of dogwoods that marked the lower boundary of this high grave-meadow. These High Hills possessed a view that on a sharp-aired day might contain Copper Downs itself. As ever, I prayed that no one in Copper Downs could see me here.

Ilona's cottage crouched among the untended apple orchards like a rabbit in a cornfield. More of a cabin, in truth, it was a compact structure of sturdy logs caulked with clay and covered in a neutral gray stucco, topped with a slate roof. The first time I'd come here, I'd been half dead in my flight from the war camp of the late Federo. Ilona had nursed me back to health and sent me onward without ever revealing her name, let alone much else. When my business in Copper Downs had concluded as much as it was likely to at the time—given an overabundance of fatalities and a shortage of competent governance—I'd traveled back to this place in hopes of a welcoming hearth.

Today Ilona met me at the door, wearing the orange dress of hers that I loved so. I never was able to disguise my interest in that dress, and the way she filled it out. This was well enough. We had not become lovers as I had hoped, but we had become very good friends indeed in the five months I'd stayed here with Ilona and her daughter, Corinthia Anastasia. Given my ragged hair and the scars I'd carved into myself to seam my cheeks and notch my ears, I knew that I was not one to tempt a woman close simply for the sake of my beauty. Still, I never stopped hoping that the fires within my heart might light her path toward me.

Perhaps it did not matter in any case. For the first time since my days with Samma in the aspirants' dormitory back in Kalimpura, someone cared to watch over me while I slept. And I felt safe enough to allow it. Such a rare trust at any time in my life then or since, I yet treasure the memory.

Everyone else was afraid of me.

I set that thought aside and accepted Ilona's swift, welcoming embrace. "Where's Corinthia Anastasia?" As I spoke, I let my lips almost brush her pale ear lest she had somehow forgotten my interest.

Ilona's hands tightened on my shoulders. "She's gone down to harvest onions. The stand along the Little Bright Creek has grown in nicely."

Nothing up here was more dangerous than me; both Ilona and I knew that. The lynxes prowling these woods would not bother the child. The wolves stayed away from Ilona and any who smelled of her, through some old bargain I did not understand. I was fairly certain the ghosts had something to do with that. Even so, any number of things could happen to a girl wandering alone.

Bandits still roamed the lands Federo had for a time controlled in his incarnation as the nascent god Choybalsan. Most of his army had returned to their fields and farms on disbanding. Some had been burned out of their homes, or turned away for misdeeds and old grudges. A few simply preferred to carry on in predatory packs, knife-armed and ruthless. Most were smart enough to stay away from this part of the High Hills, but not everyone got the word. We'd found that out the hard way twice since I'd come here.

The hard way for *them*, I should say. I burned the two flames to the souls of each dead man, and made them decent graves in a beech grove far enough from the house that we would never be troubled by their unquiet shades.

We.

That word snuck up sometimes. When it did, it frightened the life out of me. "I'll check on her," I told Ilona, my left hand straying to cradle and protect my belly. Too many children had been stolen in my earliest youth. Starting with me.

"Green." Ilona put a finger to my lips. "The war is passed. *You* ended it. If my daughter cannot gather onions for a few hours, then our problems are much larger than we know. Let her roam and let her learn." The older woman grinned. "Besides, she runs fast, and is a fine hand with the boning knife."

Ever since my previous stay here at the cottage, Corinthia Anastasia had made it her ambition to be a Blade like me. Though I was secretly flattered, I had absolutely refused to teach her anything about the business of violence and intimidation. This of course had not stopped her independent experiments in the matter.

"Fair enough." I shuddered to think how far I'd run, only a little older than the girl was now. At least Copper Downs had been no nest of child thieves and youth gangs, as Kalimpura was. We tended to other vices here. The idea of Corinthia Anastasia trying her hand at political assassination made me vaguely ill. Yet slaying the Duke had seemed so needful to me at the time.

Another lesson there, I was sure of it, but I *was* heartily sick of lessons. Even now, I must laugh to admit it has ever been my habit to follow the long path to understanding. Instead I grasped Ilona by the hand and drew her across her own threshold. The overlay of my deep brown skin against her pale ruddiness was a blessing, a pair of contrasting gems, each highlighting the beauty of the other. *If only she would see it.* "Surely we can find some way to pass the time alone together?"

"Yes. You may chop the potatoes, and I will check how the quail stock is coming."

I gave off a halfhearted attempt to squeeze her close again and went to look for a knife that was not intended for killing.

Corinthia Anastasia returned breathless and reeking of onions, with her feet caked in mud, and rain upon her face. "There's a dark brown man down the hills looking for Green!" the girl shouted as she burst into the small cottage. "I was going to give him a good kicking to, but I ain't got my knife-toed boots!"

"You don't *own* any knife-toed boots," I said sharply from my place at the table. I was shredding carrots with a too-short, too-safe blade. The non-weapon made my fingers twitch. "And even if you did, your mother wouldn't let you wear them."

Ilona abandoned the pot over the fire and knelt close to her daughter. The line of her thigh pulled my eyes, until I looked away again, torn between embarrassment and lust.

"Who is looking for Green?" Ilona demanded, her voice low and fierce. "Did he see you?"

"No, Mama." Corinthia Anastasia stared at the floor. "I followed the Little Bright all the way to Briarpool hunting onions, and the man was down there talking to the Saronen brothers. I listened from the bushes, which I think maybe Eller Saronen saw me. But maybe not. He didn't say nothing if he did."

Ilona's eyes met mine over her daughter's head. No accusation glittered in her expression, but this problem was mine, following me into the High Hills. No question. I draw trouble the way a honed edge draws blood—fast and all too easy. I turned to fetch my long knife, the fighting blade I would choose every time over most Stone Coast swords, at least in the hands of most Stone Coast swordsmen. Ill-trained brutes, one and all, in this part of the world. With my long knife and the two short knives, I could bring a swift end to almost anyone's regrets.

"*Wait,*" said Ilona in a voice straight from the Factor's house. We had both been trained there, at the hands of women focused on molding girls into a certain kind of female. Ilona had grown too plump for the role and been cast off, while I had slain my way out some years after her time.

As with so much of my life, that was another memory not bearing close examination, for behind it lay so many deaths. And worse, the broken terror of Mistress Danae, who *did* sleep among the graves of the High Hills. The horrible fractures in her mind were slowly being replaced with the horrible fractures of stronger wills long dead but yet restless.

Ilona turned back to her daughter. "Describe the man."

"He was dark, like Green." Corinthia Anastasia touched her own face, as if the freckled paleness of her skin were in doubt. "Brown skin, brown eyes, black hair. He talked funny."

"A Selistani?" I blurted. "Here in the High Hills?"

"More than one, I'd say." Ilona's voice was dry but loving. "*You're* here, after all."

I collected both my thoughts and my better judgment. At that time, I was still blind enough to believe the Bittern Court was *not* after me here, protected as I was by the width of the Storm Sea. With equally foolish certainty, I assumed that the Temple of the Silver Lily would not pursue me into the exile they'd laid upon me, either. *Not with* male *agents, in any case.* "What did these Saronen brothers tell the searcher?"

Corinthia Anastasia shrugged. "I don't know. I left after a while."

Ilona cast her eyes toward me once more. "They will not speak of you," she said with confidence. "Still, your time of shelter here is nearing an end."

I touched my growing belly. Within, my daughter stirred. Uneasy, already. Five months I'd spent up here, right into the margins of winter. I'd grown so. I blew out a long, slow breath before replying. "I'd hoped to wait until the baby came."

"That day is three months away, on the other side of winter yet to come. You barely show even now, and your body has not yet begun forgetting the things it needs to forget in order to learn what it must know for the baby to arrive."

Despite myself, I bristled. "I can still run and climb."

"Exactly." Ilona smiled.

"You'll always run and climb," Corinthia Anastasia added with a sturdy loyalty.

"As may be." Her mother's voice snapped though her eyes were still merry. "Now wash those onions. And for Green's sake, keep your eyes and ears open."

That evening while I sewed another day's bell to my silk in the manner of the people of my birth, Ilona sat beside me on the split-log bench outside the little cottage. A starveling moon rode thin-bellied at the bottom of the eastern sky amid ragged, icy clouds. Corinthia Anastasia was already snoring faintly in the wall bed I normally used. The notion of simply sharing Ilona's cot seemed warmly inviting, but distinctly improbable. That border had not yet been crossed. Perhaps it never would.

Still, our thighs pressed together. Her scent filled my nose—musky, rich, traces of salt and spice and that sweet-sharp honey of a woman with love on her mind. The evening air carried the cutting odor of windfall apples on the rot, overwhelming the host of small changes night brought to the forested hills. Ilona twined my fingers within her own, causing the silk to shiver and chime, but turned her eyes away from me.

"I shall not tell you to leave. But I am certain you will soon need to return to Copper Downs, regardless of either of our intentions." She sighed. "You cannot bring them so close to the edge of their own disasters, then walk away."

"Of course I can. That is not my city." Even I did not believe that. Inasmuch as I *had* a city, Copper Downs was it. Or so I understood at the time. In my earliest youth, I had been stolen from a rural backwater, where a settlement of a hundred people would have been considered a vast, brooding metropolis teeming with sin and darkness. As to the only other candidate for my city, I'd been banished formally from Kalimpura, Selistan's capital and home to the temple of the order that had trained and sheltered me. Otherwise, none of the wretched towns and villages I'd visited on either side of the Storm Sea had any claim on the loyalty of my heart.

"You slew their Duke. By some lights, that makes you responsible for them."

There was nothing wrong with her command of history, but Ilona's grasp of politics seemed to be lacking. "I was *eleven* years old. No one sane would have handed me the throne, then or now."

"That is not my point, as you well know." Her grip on my hand tightened. The baby stirred within my belly. She moved so much, for such a small thing. "This is not a matter of ruling, this is a matter of repairing what you have broken."

I glanced downslope in the direction of the beechwood grove and the bandit graves. "*That* repair is already beyond the work of a lifetime. And

I did not inflict the break, only the final blow to what was already rotted. It took the people of Copper Downs four hundred years to dig the hole they find themselves in now."

She followed the line of my gaze. "You are no bandit yourself, girl."

Tugging at Ilona's hand, which suddenly seemed heavy, I brushed the fingers to my lips. All I wanted was to stay here. To love and be loved. To put away my knives and open up my fists and simply cook and clean and live. *Quietly.*

"I will not go back," I whispered, trying to swallow the quaver in my voice.

Ilona squeezed my hand once more. "As you will, Green. You are always welcome here." She stood, the hem of her dress brushing my thigh. "Tomorrow, will you take some food up to Mistress Danae?"

"She will not be approached by me."

"Perhaps. In any event, you can leave it at one of the sheltered graves up on Lady Ingard's Hill."

"You think it good for me to be among the dead," I muttered. We had discussed this before.

Ilona smiled and swept into her house.

I sat in the wan moonlight awhile. It had paled Ilona's skin, rendering her nearly into a ghost. My own fine dusky hue simply darkened until I was almost no one at all. Not Selistani, not of the Stone Coast, of neither divinity nor womankind.

Just a shadow girl hidden in a shadow world. As ever, for me, both then and now.

In time, I stretched upon the bench and took my rest. I couldn't bring myself to displace Corinthia Anastasia. If Ilona had wanted me in her bed, she would have invited me. Still my hips twitched and rolled as I settled in toward sleep. The scent of rotting apples was my lullaby, the night mists my blanket.

Morning brought a pale sky almost brittle blue. The early sun lifted my fey mood of the previous evening into the autumn air. I shook off the veils of gloomy anticipation that had settled upon me, stretched my aching limbs, and ventured forth among the frosted golden grass to capture a hare for breakfast. They were numerous enough in the meadows above the neglected apple orchards, and slow with the summer fat they had not yet lost to winter's coming.

Prowling slowly among the late wildflowers, I realized that Ilona had the right of it. Even if no one had come asking after me, I could not stay here in the High Hills. The declining weather would strike a wound in me as deep as any blade might hope to cut. Even the chill coastal fogs of Copper Downs froze and shrank my soul with little more than a graying damp that numbed the fingers. Snow up here would pile eaves-high on the north side of the cottage. The streams froze for months.

This was no place for a child of the sun.

I touched my belly again. Just a bump, not so much more than an overlarge meal might leave me with. Other women showed far greater than I, six months pregnant. Ilona had said I'd probably carry well nearly to the end. I am not a large woman, and was not even quite to my full height at that time, but she placed much faith in the strength of my frame and the fitness of my body.

"Will you grow here and be happy?" I asked my baby. I didn't know if I meant the High Hills, Copper Downs, or the world at large. And with Septio dead well before her birth, what would my baby miss about her father? I had been raised by and among women, but Papa had been there first, along with my grandmother.

At that moment two hares emerged from a gorse bush. My chase was on. It is a simple enough affair. You close in sufficiently to overtake them; then, when you judge the moment correct, you break right. A hare will randomly break either right or left, but you cannot outthink an animal with little sense of its own. I always break right. Half the time I have my chance, and I never worry overmuch.

So I ran, scooping up a good-sized rock as I did, watching for the twitch of their stride that meant the escape attempt was coming. I broke right with one of my targets, while the other headed left. Short knife in my off hand, I went for him with a swift toss of the stone. I tripped on something in the grass. Still I caught him, but I *lost the blade*.

Stunned by my throw, my prey managed to kick, clawing my neck and arms, though I kept my face away until I could break his neck in return. I rose, found my weapon glistening in the damp grass, and paced back a few steps to see what had grasped at me from the earth.

Nothing, in truth. Nothing but my own clumsiness.

I patted my abdomen again. "You do me no favors, little girl," I told the baby. "I cannot feed or protect either of us if you steal my balance away."

———

Once I had returned to the cottage, I dressed the hare in the work area out back. The pelt I left for Corinthia Anastasia to prepare for tanning. The offal I dumped in the cracked clay pot we kept outside against such uses, for later disposal. The prepared carcass I carried inside to place in Ilona's smaller iron pot with a goodly portion of well water, some of the previous night's onions, a very generous pinch of salt, and a pair of gnarled carrots that I shredded. As Ilona still slept, or at least rested, I set about making the day's bread. My earliest lessons with Mistress Tirelle back at the Pomegranate Court had included cookery, and those memories were among the few that I treasured from the years of my enslavement. Dried rosemary and fresh chopped garlic went into the dough along with the leavening, and I worked it just so. The loaf would not rise and bake in time for the breakfast stew, but we would eat well this afternoon, especially with butter or honey.

As I folded the dough back into the crockery bowl to rise, Ilona's hands snaked around me. I stiffened and almost pushed her off out of sheer reflex before stopping myself. *Fool!* She hugged me tight, just below my breasts, before pressing her head against my shoulder.

"Much cannot be," she said, voice muffled.

"Much can never be," I replied. The moment spun between us like a dropped wine glass. "This is not to despair." I grasped her forearm with my left hand and squeezed it. If only she would turn me that we might hug or kiss! Still, I didn't move for fear of upsetting the mood.

"I worry for your child."

This feeling I understood. Ilona rarely showed me anything save practical strength, but I also knew how she regarded Corinthia Anastasia with a deep and helpless love. The same maternal aspects that drew me to Ilona were brought out in rare force by the prospect of her own daughter.

My own child . . . Well, a bastard at the least. Neither fully Selistani nor entirely Stone Coast; not with poor lost Septio's seed long since quickened inside of me. If only I'd understood then what lay ahead.

Despite a lack of invitation, I summoned the nerve to squirm about in Ilona's arms and take her in the embrace I'd been craving so long. She pressed her body against mine, and we leaned into the kiss, finally.

Then Corinthia Anastasia spilled out of my cupboard bed with a giggle. I broke away from Ilona, my breasts aching, to turn urgently to my bread. A blind man would have known my heat was up from the scent flooding the air.

My would-be lover stroked my hair a moment, before stepping away with a secret smile into her daughter's needs.

Ilona frowned. "I think it important that you make an effort to speak with Mistress Danae."

In truth, I would much rather have spoken with the Dancing Mistress, had she not vanished into the distant country of her kind. Teacher, trainer, friend, sometime lover—I missed her fiercely, especially when I ran through the woods, working my body hard. And I felt little guilt concerning the Dancing Mistress, for everything that had passed between us both good and ill had been wrought equally by the pair of us. Whereas Mistress Danae's current, broken state was entirely my fault, if not my actual doing.

I had never much minded my dead. Which was fortunate, given their restless numbers. It was the living who had the power to haunt me.

"Yes," I said, summoning a smile.

The little bundle I would take up onto Lady Ingard's Hill was nearly complete. The butt of my garlic-rosemary loaf, still hot from the oven, steamed at the top of the pile within. Mistress Danae would quite possibly eat better than I today.

She had been just one of the Factor's constellation of women, captive to whatever money or penalty or stranger currency of trust the old schemer had used to buy each of them off one by one. She had taught me my letters, and through them much of the history and philosophy of these people who had fathered my child.

I could not imagine spending a lifetime working at the training of unwilling children into pliant women. At my most mercenary, it was obvious to me that teaching anyone to read and think ran directly counter to an expectation of unquestioning obedience. Even beyond the brutal practicalities of educating a hostile student, what of the damage to each teacher's own soul when they bent an unwilling child to their devices?

As I tied off my bundle, I wondered if I would manage any better with my own daughter. Surely her personality, her needs would run counter to my desires for her. That was the fashion of children everywhere. Whom was I to trust? Whom to believe?

"It must have been difficult, to be Mistress Danae," said Ilona from behind me.

"Not so difficult as to be the girl under the lash," I replied with more bitterness than I intended. Ilona had shared my early fate, though her path was different. How could she bear such sympathy for our tormentors?

"You have no idea where she began." Ilona's voice was soft but carried a strange edge.

I turned to her, bundle in my hand. "I used to wonder if the training mistresses were failed candidates themselves. But Mistress Tirelle always made such grave threats against me that I could not believe it."

"You were surely a special case, Green."

I forced another smile to my face. "Always. But now I must depart, if I wish to be home again prior to sundown. Then I will ready myself to return to Copper Downs before more of those men come finding you up here."

Ilona leaned forward and kissed my forehead. "That is well enough, dear. You will always be welcome."

"Save me some bread for tonight, then."

"Perhaps not *that* welcome." Laughing, she saw me off into the day's weak light. I waved to Corinthia Anastasia, who was weeding in the little garden along the south wall of their cottage. She threw a clod at me by way of response, then bent again to her work.

I headed uphill through the orchards, careful as always not to take the same route twice to minimize any visible trackways.

Mistress Danae had moved up on to Lady Ingard's Hill shortly after my arrival at the cottage in the late summer. Ilona reported that she'd been lurking down among the Adamantine Graves before then—all the ridges and upper slopes in this part of the High Hills were dotted with necropoleis—but my presence, even unseen, seemed to have disturbed her.

I'd since watched from a distance as Ilona took food and supplies up to Mistress Danae, and twice had stalked my old teacher for the practice, but the sheer cruelty of that was quickly apparent. She was wounded, frightened, and scarred so deeply that no words or deeds of mine could ever heal her. All I would do was reopen the injuries to her heart and mind. Now, perhaps, I might be wiser and so behave more kindly to my fallen teacher, but I was still very young then.

When I'd brought down the Duke of Copper Downs four years past, all of his powers had unraveled at once, like a storm cloud at dusk. This included the money and spells binding the guards he'd placed on the Factor's house. I'd been safely away by then, sprinting toward a ship and flight from the erupting chaos in the city. The girls of the other courts and any of their Mistresses who happened to be within the Factor's bluestone walls were slain by his guards in a rampaging orgy of rape and flame. Of them all, only Mistress Danae had escaped with her life.

The gods had granted her no favor in this.

I wondered if one of the Lily Goddess' sisters had spared Mistress Danae for some future purpose. Desire, their mother-goddess, watched over women, it was said. *Protected* was too strong a word, though. Women were so obviously unprotected in this world, unless they stood very close indeed to a divine altar, or ran with the Lily Blades.

Mistress Danae had been protected from nothing, in the end. Not even the elements up here, that I could see, though Ilona said she'd passed the last four winters on these mountaintops. Somehow my former teacher survived. That required more than Ilona's little packages.

All this on my mind, I climbed the shallow cliff that led to the slopes of Lady Ingard's Hill. Once long ago a road had wound up this face. Its piers and footings were still somewhat in evidence, though most of the collapsed stonework had long since been hauled off for other purposes elsewhere.

Mistress Danae had climbed this as well. How, I wondered? She had the use of her arms and legs, but the few times I had seen her, the woman had been so visibly confused as to seem trapped senseless within her pain.

I slipped over the crumbling edge into the meadows above. I had no idea who Lady Ingard had been or why this was her hill; my extensive history lessons in the Factor's house had not once concerned the ancient graves of the High Hills. The usual scattering of turved mounds and little stone death-houses covered this whole area. A squat tower rose near the ridge of the hill, half a mile's walk upslope from me, like the king on a chessboard.

Ilona had left her gifts for Mistress Danae there before. It was the only real building up here, as most of the graves were either sealed or shattered. The tower stood roofless and doorless so in the winter it would likely be even more miserable than the leeward shelter of one of the mausoleums.

I headed upward in long, ambling switchbacks across the slope. The air was clear and sharp, as if it had abided upon some higher, colder mountain before blessing my lungs. Grasses nodded in the wind. The fat red bees also did their patient work here. I startled up quail, rock doves, and swift little green snakes as I strode among the graves.

As always, those were interesting in their own right. Much like the miniature Smagadine temple I'd noted the day before, these mausoleums, monuments, and cenotaphs constituted a condensed history of architecture and ornamentation of Copper Downs. Several sported tiled domes of a style that were almost certainly imported from Selistan somewhere down the long ages. That lent a flush of pride to my sunstruck southern heart.

Very few of the graves were marked to tell who lay within. This seemed odd to me—most cemeteries I knew of featured little biographies of their inmates, as if knowing the year a baby had died would make the child more real to a passerby of a later generation.

Markings or not, these graves were decorated in a manner that had clearly once been lavish. Jewels and metal chasings had for the most part vanished uncounted generations past. Carvings remained. Details. Images cast in tile, or painted underneath a sheltering roof. That a person was buried here at all stated "I am wealthy" in the manner of distant Copper Downs long before the rise of the Dukes. These graves dated from the time of Kingdoms, and some from the Years of Brass prior to that, when the mines beneath the city were active and stranger things had walked the streets than did today.

At least for the most part, given that Skinless and Mother Iron inhabited the city now.

Wordless, the graves still offered their tales. This one featured small bat-winged children, like demon messengers, with a hint of torment on each tiny, wind-worn face. That one's pilasters were bundles of sheaves, wrapped in vines, as if the dead had been overlords of some great swath of farms or vineyards. In this manner, each crypt told its silent story. Some were little more than threadbare memories; others shouted from beyond death's veil.

The whispers I ignored. I was not here to treat with ghosts. Nothing of my experience with the Factor after his death lent me any desire to pursue their fickle company.

I paused a few dozen yards from the battered tower. Up close, the structure looked as if it might at one time have been besieged. Why anyone would invest a grave site with force of arms was beyond me, but fire scars surrounded the narrow tunnel of the door, while shallow dents in the stonework testified to the impact of projectiles hurled in blunt anger. Nowadays moss and tiny grasses grew in those hollows, a scattering of eye-blue flowers lending them a melancholy air. The top was eroding, only a third of the crenellations remaining. The remainder of the circle of stone dipped like a dancer beneath her partner's arms.

"Mistress Danae," I called in a gentle but carrying voice. My judgment was that it would not be meet to shout, either for the dignity of the place or for the sake of her fragile mind. "Green is here." I took a deep breath and uttered a word I'd long ago sworn away amid blood, pain, and murder. "Emerald. You knew me as Emerald. Of the Pomegranate Court."

I received no answer but the wind, which took little note of my name—either of my names. A bird trilled nearby. Clouds sighed slowly across the sky, dragging their shadows behind them here upon the ground. Flowers and seed-heavy grass stalks nodded. In time, I tried again with cupped hands and raised voice. "This is Emerald, Mistress Danae. I am here. Ilona sent me."

Then I picked up my bundle and trudged to the tower's broken entrance. I could leave the food in the shadows within the shattered door, look about for any sign of her as news to bring to Ilona. After that I would be free to return to the necessities of my life, those violences and demands that I'd had no business bringing into these High Hills and laying upon my hostess' quiet hearth.

The tower's interior was a domain of bats and spiders. Something occluded the open roof above, though my eyes could not make out what within the shadows. A crosswork of sticks and branches, up here so far from the trees? The dirt floor was scuffed and tamped down, confirming Mistress Danae's at least occasional presence.

I had bent to lay the bundle just inside the door when I realized the floor was not dirt, but rather soil scattered over stone. Washed in by generations of rain, spread by the tracks of animals, and finally carried upon the feet of this broken woman I sought.

Tracing my fingers through the layer of grime, I found marble beneath. Of course this was a tomb—everything was in the grave-meadows of the High Hills—but instead of a mound or a mausoleum, whoever was buried here had caused a tower to be built in his name. This left no doubt that he was a man.

"Erio," croaked a voice in the inner darkness. I jumped so hard I banged my shoulder against the rocky jamb of the doorway.

"Erio?" I slipped my long knife free from my thigh scabbard.

"That is who abides here." The voice . . .

"Mistress Danae," I gasped, fears of ghosts slipping from me with an overwhelming sense of having simply been *silly*.

"She has died."

My eyes were already adjusting to the shadows within. A small, pale figure huddled bent-limbed and askew not four yards from me, at the back wall of the tower, surrounded with lumpy mounds of scavenged belongings.

"Ilona sends food, and needful things. Stockings for your feet at night, and a small comb." After a moment I added with a shyness that surprised me, "I baked the bread for you."

Some insect whined close to my ear for a moment before she replied. "Danae is dead."

"I–I'm sorry to hear that." I didn't know what more to say. My failure of words shamed me. I could not thank this woman, or apologize to her, or heal her in any way. A gulf opened in my heart then, as I realized once again that some wounds were too deep to treat. "Mistress Danae was kind to me when I was young."

Her voice flashed, the broken, growling quaver momentarily fading to return me to afternoons in the still air bent over the classics of the city's literature. "You are still young."

And you *will never be young again,* I thought, but halted the words before they passed my lips. Thus is the foolishness of youth, to think such things, as if I would be immune to the ravages of time. As yet uneducated by the years, I bent down to lay the bundle on a piece of broken masonry. "Whoever you are, take this offering in peace."

"None of it is mine."

That was almost an aphorism from Alimander's *Booke of Thought,* which she and I had spent several weeks studying. "Nothing belongs to any of us but the breath in our lungs," I replied, quoting the ancient philosopher back to her.

This was an old game, and it must have caught at some corner of her memories of herself. "If we do not hunt, we do not kill."

I supplied the next line of that quatrain. "If we do not kill, we do not eat."

"If we do not eat, we do not live," she answered.

The closing line was "If we do not live to hunt, why do we live?"

"I don't know, girl," Danae said. "I do not know why we live." That was when I knew beyond doubt that she *was* my old mistress of letters, and that, furthermore, she knew exactly who I was.

"I am so very sorry," I whispered. My eyes stung with unshed bitterness. But for my deeds, she would still be hale and whole. "I lit the white candle and the black for everyone I could name within the walls of the Factor's house, and also more for those whose shades were beyond my knowing."

She made no answer. I waited, as the bright meadow at my back came further alive with the morning. The eddying breeze brought a grassy smell to war with the rotting funk of Mistress Danae's lair, while some troupe of insects began a cycling, buzzing hum.

Eventually, I turned to step into the sunlight.

"Wait, girl."

I paused, unwilling to face her again. Mistress Danae did not need my sharp gaze when trying to draw her own words forth. Instead I stared down across the shoulder of the meadow at the rucked-up forest of the lower slopes. A flock of birds—starlings?—circled above a towering oak, as if something moved beneath. A haze of mist lay in the valleys farther below. Somewhere out of my line of sight Briarpool glimmered, and the Greenbriar River, which eventually spilled into the sea just west of Copper Downs. All through those woods and hills were mossy walls, stretches of paved track-way, tumbled towers. What was now almost a wildland had once been a daughter city of my adopted home.

I could see the sweep of the land, the benison of history given over once more to the wilderness. Whatever impulse or power had drawn the people of Copper Downs north into these High Hills had long since released them back to the chilly margins of the coast. The wonder of the struggle between the Dancing Mistress' fading people and the power of the old Duke was that it had not prevailed over a much deeper time.

Or perhaps it had done so. Were humans driven from this land by pardines, some years after the grave builders had given up on their hilltop refuges?

My thoughts brought me back to where I stood, facing away from a woman who could not speak to me but had something she needed to say. I was not expected to answer her, that much was clear. Knowing this would take some time, I settled into a more comfortable crouch to ease a twinge in my back. This allowed me to remain faced three-quarters away from her while keeping her at the edge of my sight.

I did not fear attack. No matter how feral or desperate Mistress Danae might be, that slight, bookish woman could not overpower me. Rather, I wanted to see what she would do.

My patience was rewarded as she eased out into the middle of the tower floor. She was not hiding her movements from me, I think, so much as from herself. I closed my left eye to block the greater part of the sun, and cocked my head slightly to bring my right into shadow where I could see her better without quite watching her.

At the pace of a flower opening, Mistress Danae shifted her bundles of rotting straw and cloth and began to sweep the dirt on the floor with her left forearm. She was making a place at the center of the little round room. If the tower truly was a grave marker, that was most likely the occupant's resting place.

Was he one of the uneasy dead with whom Ilona spoke? My hostess and protector had a secret life among the graves of which she would sometimes hint in fragments, but had never shared directly. For my own part, I had too many dead of my own to want to open congress with that world.

Erio.

That was the word she had first whispered to me. "Erio" must be the name of whoever slept away the centuries here.

Eventually she cleared a spot about the size of a coffin lid. Marble gleamed faintly in the shadows, the stone catching the sunlight from my doorway. I watched sidelong as Danae polished the exposed stone for a while. When her voice cracked to life again, though almost an hour had passed, it seemed no surprise. "Erio wishes to speak with you."

One hand patted the empty spot.

I knew what happened to those who slept among the graves. Besides Mistress Danae, Ilona was the only permanent resident up here. She acted as a sort of guardian, though these dead seemed quite capable of maintaining themselves. Others came and went, I had been told, seeking the wisdoms of the past by taking a night or two or ten among the graves, until the whispering ghosts drove them out again.

What no one ever seemed to understand about the past was that the people who lived there were just as petty and thoughtless and misinformed as those today. The dead had only the advantage of the veil of years to make them seem noble and wise.

Still, this was why Ilona had sent me up these hills one last time before I made to take my leave of her. To learn what might be here for me to learn.

Moving very slowly, though nowhere near Danae's creeping pace, I stretched to my feet and sidled once more into her shadows. I was careful not to turn head-on, but rather kept myself sideways to her. That seemed to alarm my old mistress less. At the cleared spot, I lowered myself to the marble and stretched out as if for a nap. The stone was far colder than I had expected. I rolled to one side and placed my ear against the ground.

From outside, the autumnal insect hum built louder. Winter lurked already in this patch of ground to which I had pressed my face. Though I had not seen them in the dim light of the tower's interior, I could feel incised letters against my cheek.

Mistress Danae's hand brushed my ankle, only for a moment; then she scuttled back to her resting place with a speed that must have felt blinding in her silent, years-long stupor. I closed my eyes and let the dank quiet of the tower wrap me. Already the noises and scents of the day outside seemed to be fading. It was as if I had taken ship, and the meadow was a receding shoreline.

"Why do you tarry here, little foreign girl?"

The male voice was so close, so normal, that I startled. My muscles twitched as my free hand brushed the hilt of my long knife. Mistress Danae squeaked some small, animal terror, but did not flee.

"I was bid to lie down in this place." As I spoke, my lips brushed against the slab of the grave. I felt foolish.

"You are needed in your city."

A man, definitely. Speaking the Petraean of Copper Downs with a curious accent, but clear enough. He sounded old, tired, and distracted. Or perhaps bored. Surely death was the most uninteresting part of life?

I denied Copper Downs again. "It is not my city."

"You who birthed a god and slew one on the streets?" He laughed, though the sound of it was airless and frightening. "You have made the city your own, and the city has made you into its own."

"No," I told him, kissing his grave with every word. "Your people stole me away. I gave myself back to myself."

"You will learn. All you have worked for is in the balance once again."

"All I have worked for is *ever* in the balance," I protested. "There is no going back, no setting things to rights. Not the way people play at politics. I will not be the fulcrum on which the fate of Copper Downs rests." It occurred to me to wonder why I was arguing this point with a ghost.

"You do not carry the seeds of choice."

No, I carry another seed. How deeply did this ghost-Erio see? How deeply did he spar with me? "The choices are always mine."

His tone grew more plaintive. "Go. Please. I speak as a king of old begging one of the queens of latter days. Return and see what they are making in your absence. Set things to rights. I fear for our city."

My blood curdled. "I am no queen, and never would be one."

"Go." Now his voice was hollow, lost, more like the whispers I'd learned to ignore while walking among the graves. "Go, go, go, go . . ."

A cold silence followed.

"Erio is the strongest of them," Mistress Danae finally said, though it took me a moment to recognize that it was she who had spoken.

I sat up slowly and looked toward her shadowed face. "Is that why you live here?"

"I would rather borrow his purpose than have none at all."

Those words wrenched at my heart, but I had nothing else to offer her, so I rose and stepped back into the world of daylight.

All the way down through the meadow the graves called to me, some pleading, others crying, as if Erio's spirit yet clung to me and drew them forth in their broken numbers. Mistress Danae was no different from these, except for the accident of breath still in her lungs.

I prayed that when I died the Wheel would swiftly take me up and pass me onward. Their fate seemed immeasurably sad.

Scrambling down the cliff from Lady Ingard's Hill, I fell almost two body lengths. I knew how to take such a drop, and managed to protect the baby, though I wrenched my left shoulder doing it, and surely collected some bruises. I might not yet be showing much of my pregnancy to the casual eye, but my balance was clumsier than ever it had been. Ilona had already let out my leathers once, which embarrassed me to no end, even just between the two of us.

The Dancing Mistress would have known what to do. For a moment I mourned my absent teacher and friend; then I limped down through the woods and into the apple orchard, careful as always to make no path where I could help it.

Approaching Ilona's cottage, I heard adult voices. *Living* voices. That put me very much in mind of Corinthia Anastasia's report of someone searching for me down at Briarpool. I crouched lower, moving now as I might have running with Mother Shesturi's handle. Blade training was never far from my mind; though I had been lazy enough in my months up here, I still maintained my form. Even with my poor balance and aching shoulder.

I drifted into a stand of brambles that would afford me a view of the house. A dark-haired man stood in the open doorway, his back to me. I could hear Ilona's voice from within. Her tone did not sound panicked or afraid, though the rise and fall of argument was clear enough. And the visitor's accent held the familiar rhythms of Seliu. The searcher from Briar-pool was here! Carefully I scanned for guards, for watchers, for reinforcements.

Had this one come alone?

From the tenor of the conversation, their contention seemed likely to continue, so I slipped to my left and carefully circled the house from about a dozen rods into the trees. I would have to cross the gardens outside the south wall, or considerably widen my arc of travel, but otherwise I could flush out whatever wards the visitor had set. It was the work of twenty minutes or so to creep full circle. I found nothing except a fox and a few angry jays bickering amid the fall corn.

Now was time to face whatever hunted for me. While I was skulking in the woods, the intruder had gained access to the interior of the cottage. Not gone, certainly, for I would have marked his departure, but Ilona had admitted him within. Or she had been forced.

Abandoning caution, I sprinted for the door and burst through, short knife held low in my right hand. Ilona jumped up from the kitchen table, dropping her second-best crockery bowl to shatter in a shower of beans on the flagstone floor, while Chowdry stood to meet my attack.

I turned my blade in to the wood, unable to stop from slamming bodily into my old friend and sending him flying across the table. Grabbing the edge to right myself, I gasped several short, sharp breaths to regain my usual calm.

"What in the name of the Wheel are you doing here?" I shouted in Seliu.

Chowdry picked himself up and wiped beans from his hand and arms. He bled from several cuts. Ilona rose to stand beside him, her skin flushed. My heart missed several beats at the fear and panic in her face, though she smoothed her expression swiftly enough. "He was looking for you, Green," she said slowly, picking up my meaning without understanding the language.

"Endurance asks for you," Chowdry said by explanation, answering in Petraean for the sake of politeness.

Onetime sailor, cook, and reluctant pirate—or at least coastal raider—I had left this man in charge of the cult I had accidentally founded in the process of bringing down the bandit god Choybalsan. Many prices were paid that day. One of them was that I had *made* this man who he was. How *dare* he come to fetch me?

"I do not answer to you," I snapped.

"And you are not answering to the god either," Chowdry replied mildly. "But he asks for you anyway. Your work in Copper Downs is in danger."

"That is the second time I have been told this thing today," I muttered. "It is not my city, and there are tens of thousands living there. Surely someone among them can step forward."

"You sulk, Green," Ilona said mildly in her most maternal voice, as if chastising Corinthia Anastasia. "It is unbecoming."

I whirled away from both of them to regain my composure. "S-sorry about the bowl," I told the fireplace.

Chowdry touched my shoulder, a brief gesture of comfort or camaraderie. "I know how you are," he said in Seliu. "I was wrong not to wait outside where you could see and hear me."

"You don't assassinate someone for the sake of a bowl of beans and a conversation," Ilona added, though I knew she had not taken the meaning of Chowdry's words.

"I have killed for less," I said in my smallest voice, and screwed my eyes shut against the tears. My breath shuddered in my chest, and I was shamed that the two of them could hear it. When I turned back, the compassion in their faces stung me even more. "Why did you come up for me, Chowdry? Your man at Briarpool was already looking."

He glanced sidelong at Ilona before answering. "I am not knowing of Briarpool. I am sending only me. I knew you would listen to no one. You never do. Especially not me. But I can be arguing with you. Anyone else is too frightened."

Ashamed all over again, I leaned forward and snatched my short knife from the tabletop. I was *not* a difficult woman! "If you were not frightened, you weren't paying attention. And who was looking for me at Briarpool?"

"More Selistani have arrived in Copper Downs from across the sea. Kalimpuri high-noses with their city ways, wearing their money as if it was being power. They prepare for someone greater. I do not yet know who."

I was momentarily distracted by the political issue that implied. The number of Selistani back in Kalimpura who spoke Petraean was quite small. Who was coming, with the power to scour the merchant families and counting houses for those people? Not Mother Vajpai, or anyone from the Temple of the Silver Lily. Wealth and influence we—they—had. But not sufficient to compel unwilling persons on an adventure across the Storm Sea. Our writ was mighty, but definitely limited to the bounds of Kalimpura's city walls.

Oh, how much I later paid for lacking sufficient foresight then.

"It is time for me to leave here." I nodded at Ilona. "If such people are seeking me, I cannot stay. But I resent being pushed into the service of the city once more."

"There is no pushing here," Chowdry said. "All I am asking is that you come to speak to Endurance."

"The god is mute," I gently pointed out. I had made him so myself.

"The god is wordless. He still has much to say at times." The pirate-priest smiled. "Born of your deeds, how could he be otherwise?"

I had to laugh at that. To my immense relief, Ilona chose to laugh with me. We bent to cleaning the scattered slops and ceramic fragments, while I furiously wondered what was so bad that both the god Endurance and the ghosts of the High Hills should care that it be me who stepped into it.

Return to Copper Downs

Coming down out of the hills with Chowdry, I decided to follow the route I'd taken while fleeing Choybalsan's army at the beginning of the summer. This was a rough track, so I carried only my knives, some small essentials for cooking and sleep, and of course my belled silk with the needles, thread, and cache of bells. That line of work had been broken too often. I would not abandon it yet again. I did roll the cloth carefully so as to pad the bells that I did not jingle as I walked.

I stayed away from the Barley Road and the banks of the Greenbriar River, and instead traveled along the ridges following goat tracks, tracing the crumbling high road of former times where possible, and indulging in a fair amount of plain old bushwhacking. Following me, Chowdry was not so pleased.

"It was taking a long day to find your cottage from the city as it is," he complained in Seliu as we rested in the shelter of a wisteria. The weather was sunny but sharp, somehow the worst of both summer and winter in one difficult walk. We shared our bower with a mass of late-season mosquitoes, but I was more interested in being out of the biting wind than in fleeing from the insects. Besides, they were more attracted to Chowdry than to me. He continued his litany: "Now we are walking several days for no reason."

"You're spoiled," I announced with a grin, watching him slap at himself like one of the rough-trade Blade Mothers after a bad night in the rack. "When I met you, you were crewing the rankest little coaster ever to sail

Selistani waters. You would have been glad of fresh squirrel over an open fire and a dry place to sleep."

"I am not seeing fresh squirrel here," he grumbled.

"You will. But first understand that I have my reasons. I am coming with you. Surely that will be enough, for now. As neither of us answers to the other, nothing else is possible."

The look Chowdry gave me suggested that he had different theories on who answered to whom, but then he shook his poor humor off and smiled. "Then I am to be cooking the squirrel this evening, so long as you are to be killing it."

"Perhaps," I told him.

We made camp that night in a rotten-roofed barn that still sheltered one dry corner. I managed to bring in two squirrels, some windfall peaches, and a collection of herbs and green onions from a long-neglected garden near the foundations of the vanished farmhouse.

Once the supplies were in place, I pushed Chowdry aside and began to do the cooking myself. That was one of the few undiluted gifts of my childhood training. I was able to do far too little of it. What I made was not even stew, for we had no stock and no time to prepare it. Rather I heated a piece of old iron on our little fire, smeared it with squirrel fat and the juice of several on- ion stalks, then fried the squirrel meat together with the peaches, seasoned nicely enough in the Stone Coast fashion.

Even such primitive cookery was a pleasure. I was glad enough of the good food, and even more glad of the company. Otherwise this would have been the first night I had spent completely alone since arriving at Ilona's cottage these months past.

As we cracked the bones in our teeth, I turned my thoughts to what lay ahead. "Tell me more of why Endurance wishes me back in Copper Downs."

"You are already saying how the god has no words." He toyed with a squirrel thigh, picking seared meat from the bone and flicking the bits into his mouth as he watched me for a reaction.

"Well, yes. A mute god seemed . . . safer."

"I am not to be saying you are wrong. Still, this makes troubles."

"You never meant to be a priest," I offered.

That made him laugh. "I am never being a priest. I am servant to a god. Others dance in robes and light incense and make up new books of ancient ceremony. I do what Endurance asks of me." He paused, his mirth falling away. "Demands of me."

I allowed my voice to soften. "In what manner does the god compel you?" I had already enjoyed far too much experience of divine influence in my own life. Though I only suspected it then, more was all too definitely to follow.

"Dreams," Chowdry said slowly. "Pictures. Thoughts without words. So I *know* that such a thing should be done, without it being said. This is not like Utavi ordering a sail to be reefed back aboard *Chittachai*. Or you, pushing me where I would never be going of my own."

"Do you dream with Endurance in Seliu?"

He gave me an odd look. "There are no words, I am already telling you."

Somehow this became very important to me. "But *where* are you in dreams? In a field under our hot sun?" My father's paddies, where Endurance the ox had lived and died. "Or on the cold streets of Copper Downs?" This northern city was a strange place for any Selistani.

Almost helplessly, he replied, "I am with the god."

Having stood far too close to Blackblood for the comfort of any sane person, and been called by the Lily Goddess, I could take his meaning. Gods happened in a place where the everyday world was an incidental detail. As if one could see and hear *everything*. Which, while possible for the divine, was very difficult for the merely human. As an ant might be confused to view the world as seen from a person's eyes.

"I understand," I told him, patting my silk, which awaited this evening's sewing of the bell.

Gratitude flashed across Chowdry's face. "So you see, I cannot be saying exactly what the god wishes of you. Only that the god wishes you to return to his domain."

"Is he afraid?"

That provoked a thoughtful silence. Finally: "That I cannot say either."

I let the matter drop then, and tucked into the last of my fried squirrel with peaches. I had eaten far worse.

Two days later we arrived at the place I'd had in mind on choosing this difficult path back to the city. The last of the inland hills petered out several miles from my goal. They terminated in a final upthrust knee of rock, soil, and trees from where I'd observed the condition of Copper Downs under occupation at the time I'd previously made this journey.

I wanted that hawk's-eye view again, from the branches of the great oak spreading amid a stand of bayberries. Not to seek out the disposition of armies, for surely they had not gone that seriously wrong, but just to take the mood of the city. I would count the chimney smokes and look for evidence of either riot or festival. In Kalimpura, those two were nearly synonymous. These Stone Coast folk celebrated with a reserve that was almost depressing.

I had thought also to be able to number the masts in the harbor, which was perhaps the best indication of the health and welfare of any trading city. In that I was disappointed—memory did not supply the view, and in reality too much of the city intruded for me to accurately gauge the density of shipping. At least the day remained clear, instead of misty along the waterside as this season so often could provide. The scattered clusters of hutments and wayhouses at the outer edges seemed normal enough, but that told me little.

Chowdry sat and watched me watch as the sun trundled along the trackway of the sky. Finally, as I paused from my study to sip at my waterskin, he spoke.

"You hunt the city far more carefully than you hunt our dinner."

"It is bigger game," I said, meaning that for a joke. The humor rang flat in my own ears. Nothing in his eyes suggested that he took it any better.

"They fear you and love you."

"Who?" This line of conversation was making me want to change the subject.

"The people. Of this city. Also, more Selistani live here now. They buy passage, or jump ship."

"*What* would possess any of our people to emigrate here?"

"You and I came here," he said quietly. "Endurance is here. The first new Selistani god in generations, birthed far across the sea from his proper home. Some wish to learn his mysteries and carry his name back."

I listened carefully to the catch in his voice. "You do not favor that, do you?"

"I do not know what the god is. The *god* does not know what the god is. Not yet. We are much too soon to make promises in another country. Even our own country."

That made a great deal of sense to me. I exhaled slowly, trying to release some of the uneasiness he raised in me. I knew too much of gods already, far too much. I could not unlearn, but I could most certainly avoid more of such dabbling.

So I thought then, at least.

To distract myself, I turned my attention back to the city.

We camped on the hill one more night. Chowdry cooked this evening as a gentle, chilled rain descended. That dinner was wasted, as this time the smell of squirrel made me violently ill. I was reduced to gnawing roots while feeling both hungry and nauseous at the same time.

"It is your child," Chowdry said in Petraean, oddly.

"My child?" I didn't think I'd shown that much yet.

He switched to Seliu. "The baby inside does not like some foods. My sister, every time she is pregnant, must have plantains, but cannot stand mangoes."

"Wonderful," I muttered. Losing my balance *and* my appetite to my daughter. What was in this for *me*?

I had to check that thought. Poor, doomed Septio lived on inside me. And through him the seed of the god, if Blackblood was to be believed. Time away from the streets and temples of Copper Downs, and especially the dark, hidden world of Below, had lessened the grip that those same gods held on my imagination. I suppose I'd expected to turn inward, become focused on the child, as women were said to do. So far the baby and I had gotten along well enough not to notice much.

Until these last few days.

I ran my hand over the leathers tight upon my abdomen. Beneath my touch, I fancied that she eased.

Still, I didn't eat any squirrel.

"Green," Chowdry said, drawing my attention back into the moment.

"Mmm?" I looked at him fondly, this thin man with the perpetually worried expression who'd so unexpectedly inherited divine responsibility.

"I am to be returning to the city tomorrow. If you are staying up here to eat shoots and berries, that is your business. But the god wishes your attendance. Do not wait too long, I am begging of you."

He was almost cute about it. I smiled, feeling a wash of tenderness. "Do not fear, old friend. I shall soon be there."

Chowdry appeared even more worried at my words, but he said nothing more.

The next morning, the old pirate took his leave of me with the dawn. He followed our backtrail, stumbling down to the Barley Road well away from camp. I watched Chowdry trudge through the morning mists off the river, until he caught up to a farm family driving their pigs to market. I could not mark him out after that amid the people and the intermittent rain.

I spent the next hour or so examining not just the city, but also myself. What had I been about the night before? The way I had spoken to Chowdry was so unlike me. This pregnancy was making me untrustworthy. I resolved to cultivate a healthy suspicion and maintain distance from people around me, lest unthinking kindness blunder me into greater trouble.

Certainty. The path forward always lay through certainty. The Lily Blades taught that—always be certain, always be prepared to change one's mind.

That in turn moved me to hone my long knife, test the sharpness of my short knives, and spend several hours sprinting up and down hills and speed-climbing damp-barked trees, all out of sight of the road below. I was slower than I should have been, and did not move quite as I might have liked, but I could still kick, dodge, and roll almost as expected.

The key, of course, was not to get into fights in the first place. As I worked myself, I thought of Mother Vajpai. She could take down almost anyone in a straight match but rarely needed to do so. As dangerous as her body was, her mind was the far deadlier weapon.

Another lesson, surely. One I should have attended to more closely in the days that were to come.

It occurred to me to wonder who I was planning to fight *with*. Body or mind, I had no serious enemies roaming the streets of Copper Downs. Endurance could hardly wish me ill. Blackblood was, well, complex, but not precisely an enemy. I no longer feared Skinless, as that silent avatar of the god seemed to hold a mute, deep regard for me.

Finally I shook off the mania of preparation for combat and cleaned my campsite. While I'd worked my body the wind had blown in a few flower petals that might have been lilies, so I burned them with reverence and gave the ashes back to the air as I buried my fire. It was close to midday before I gathered my belled silk and my few other belongings to scramble down toward the Barley Road in order to join the travelers following Chowdry into Copper Downs.

Entering the city was like cooking in a familiar kitchen. I knew the pans by touch, did not need to look for the cutting knives. So with these streets. The fall harvest was being brought in to the bourses and markets for auction to the cellarmen and canners and warehousemen. That meant an unusually large number of carts with confused horses and even more confused country lads atop the drover's bench. Still, they laughed at one another and shouted rude names in booming voices instead of jumping from their seats to brawl.

I marked their progress and watched for other signs of commerce. Did the bankers' boys trot past at double time with their lacquered boxes slapping against their chests? What of the runners from the Harbormaster's office and the shipping exchange? How many clerks hurried along the streets mixed among the ladies' maids and shrieking children with their stick-a-hoops?

I was surprised at the brown faces I saw. A fair number of my countrymen lived here now. Only one in a hundred, perhaps, but that was still ten times what I could recall from even last summer, let alone the years of my training when I might have been the only Selistani in the city aside from the hand-ful of resident trading families and a few passing sailors.

Rarely did I pause to think on the color of my skin—there always seemed to be more urgent matters which needed attending to—but it pleased me to see faces as brown as my own. My child would not be so alone in this place as I had been.

Endurance's temple stood not in the Temple Quarter, where the houses of the gods generally were to be found, but rather was a building amid the Velviere District. I avoided both those areas at first. In due time I would need to see to the god I had helped birth, and call on Blackblood as well. For now, I had a different destination in mind.

The breweries were busy as ever. So far as I knew, not war nor famine nor fire nor outright bankruptcy had ever succeeded in stilling this city's thirst. The Stone Coast was not wine country, not at all. Distilleries were common enough, and some of their product was magnificent, but beer was the bub-bling heart of these northern people.

I was headed for a quiet alley amid the breweries, where I might find a certain tavern. Last I knew, Chowdry had been cooking there most nights, though his duties to Endurance had probably taken him away from the Tavernkeep's kitchen more often now. This nameless place was the heart of the small community of the pardine people in Copper Downs. My old Danc-ing Mistress was the first of that race I'd ever known, but I had yet to meet one I did not like and respect. Even the Rectifier, a violent and difficult old rogue with an unfortunate tendency toward murdering human priests, was charming in his strange way.

However, when I turned the corner into the brick-walled alley with its familiar cracked flagstones now damp and slick, the area before the tavern entrance was full of people. Humans, not pardines. And Selistani at that. Chattering, almost angry, a buzz of voices arguing in Seliu.

Startled, I tugged up my hood and dipped my face. I was far too easily recognized with my scarred cheeks and notched ears. Until I understood what mischief this restless crowd was about, I did not want them to know me.

I eased into a crowd of men in white linen kurtas, a few women in colored sarongs scattered among them. My black leather would have been more conspicuous if they'd been paying much attention to me, but these people were focused on a woman standing in the doorway of the Tavernkeep's establishment, arguing both with someone inside and with several men outside.

Moving closer, with a cold stab of my heart, I recognized the one at the heart of this brangle. It was the Bittern Court woman, whose name I had never known. How wrong I had been in my sense of being safe from her. Nameless, she was only a power to me, a persecutor. This woman had pursued me to exile back in Kalimpura, while calling for my head over the matter of Michael Curry's assassination. I owed the Bittern Court no loyalty and even less affection for their conflicts with the Temple of the Silver Lily, not to mention their attempts to persecute me. To see *her*, *here*, could only be very bad news indeed.

No wonder I'd felt a need to sharpen my knives this morning. I would be lost to the Wheel before I would place myself under this woman's influence.

Pulse pounding, I backed slowly through the crowd, pushing toward the open street beyond. Someone bumped me, then shouted out my name in Seliu. This was not the time to confront whatever had brought people across the Storm Sea in search of me. I ran, sprinting out of the alley, down past the Cooper's Brewery, and away on the stones of the city. I might not have been as fast as before, but I was still faster than those behind me.

Winded, but safe, I paused for breath in an empty lot near the old wall, now simply a dividing line between the Greenmarket and the Ivory Quarter. Crumbling bricks rose forty feet to a walkway that joined four surviving towers. It was pretty enough, in a desolate way, and a tribe of indigenes had made their stick-and-daub homes atop the walkways and tower crowns, so that the whole thing looked as if it had been colonized by enormous raptors.

A firecart offered meat sticks, while the strange little people who lived atop this section of wall passed in abundance on their own errands. No Selistani were in evidence.

I fished out a copper tael from my limited supply of coin and bought a length of some birdflesh. I didn't ask what fowl, and the man did not say. It tasted mostly of charring, and a bit of sage, but that was enough for me in the moment. My hands were busy and I looked as if I might belong there.

Truly, I needed to stop wearing black leather. That was like a fart at a temple service—marking me out and making people stare. I resolved to purchase a colored wrap at the very next opportunity, and decide later how to be safely anonymous on a more consistent basis.

I pondered whether Chowdry had known that the Bittern Court woman had arrived across the sea from Kalimpura. Persons of her status did not voyage alone, either. He'd said important people had arrived from Selistan, some mission or embassy calling here at Copper Downs. It was beyond unlikely that I would not be involved in their purposes.

Had Chowdry brought me back to Copper Downs only to betray me?

Or had the Selistani stranger asking after me at Briarpool been searching on behalf of the visitors?

Perhaps it did not matter so much, except as concerned future trust between me and Chowdry. Enough that I was here. Enough that a woman who'd tried to claim my life back in Kalimpura had made a challenge in one of my safest places. Not particularly welcomed there, from the look of things, but still, *she* had come to *me*.

I fingered the hilt of my long knife. This was Copper Downs. We had no Death Right, and not so much in the way of governance these days. She would be hard-pressed to hire locals to kill *me*, unless they were complete fools. Anyone she had brought with her would be lost here until they learned both the streets and the local customs. I knew Below, and they did not. I could take her far more readily than she could take me.

This was *my* home ground.

Simply slaying the Bittern Court woman out of hand, either quietly or publicly, had much to recommend itself as a strategy.

My child moved at that thought, and I caught myself. I had only days ago dreamt of a quiet life of cooking and peace, and here I was now plotting another death. That for the sake of my convenience.

I needed help, I realized. I could not pursue this on my own, not if an entire embassy had arrived from Kalimpura. Endurance might be of some aid, but my trust in Chowdry was provisional until I could understand what he had known before he came up to see me at Ilona's cottage. Not just what he had known, but more to the point, what he might have failed to tell me.

Any mission of note from Kalimpura would be accredited to the Interim Council. While the councilors were venal bastards to a man, they were venal bastards with whom I could work. Furthermore, they *did* owe me.

I headed for the Textile Bourse, seat of the Interim Council ever since my slaying of the Duke had vacated the palace on Montane Street. The Lyme Street building was a fraction of the size of the old palace, and crowded to the rafters with clerks and ministers of government, but it had thus far kept them free of the taint of the old regime, free to create their own, novel disgraces.

The building had not been fully repaired since the day last spring when we brought the god-king Choybalsan down from the roof. Almost six months past, now. His lightnings had shattered much of the facade. As for the damage to the street, I'd accounted for that personally. The cobbles I'd broken had since been filled in with gravel to keep the street traffic flowing while presumably someone sought funds for more permanent repairs. The shattered windows were boarded over, while the front door was replaced with stout, iron-banded oak. The flowers that had sprung up full-grown with Endurance's theogeny were long vanished.

The banner of the city still hung overhead, a copper shield in four parts, surmounted by a coronet and a ship. As I'd assumed, the Interim Council had not relocated during my time in the High Hills. That was confirmed by the two very large guardsmen at the door. They were the sort of accessory that served as a timeless classic in the halls of power.

I paused at a little teahouse I did not remember from the days of struggle. That was not so long ago, yet it felt like half my life had passed since. Just outside the teahouse, on the edge of the street itself, small round tables of lacquered wood perched on twisted metal legs, inviting me to take my ease in ironwork chairs. A twinge in my back reminded me that I hadn't sat like a civilized person since leaving Ilona's cottage. Nor had I enjoyed any tea, let alone the rarer vice of kava, a habit I longed to acquire in detail some day just for the sake of the steamy brown richness of the stuff.

The streets were no place for me to linger, but neither could I dash into the Interim Council with nothing more on my mind than a panic at seeing a tradeswoman from across the sea. I compromised by taking a chair in the shadows next to the rippled glass window. That position carried an excellent view of the Textile Bourse while keeping me relatively anonymous. For once today, the black leathers would work in my favor.

I had begun to understand why the mothers of the Temple of the Silver Lily had so disliked my Neckbreaker guise. The affectation was beginning to gall even me.

A short woman with cinnamon-colored skin placed a basket of well-buttered cardamom rolls in front of me. Where were *her* people from? Suddenly I was hungry beyond measure. The *smell* had drawn me, I realized. I nodded at the woman, whispered "Kava, with cream" in my gruffest tone, and fell to.

What with one thing and another—riot, revolution, godhead—I have rarely found time to practice my baking. I am a good hand with breads, thanks to Mistress Tirelle, who did her best to make the most of what could be made of my enslavement in the Pomegranate Court. It was not just my empty stomach or the demands of the baby, I was sure, that led me to find these pastries the most delicious I had ever eaten.

I knew I should have meat, greens, some fruit. The Temple of the Silver Lily had been quite clear on the care and feeding of pregnant women. But this soft, crisp-edged bread that came apart in my hand, steaming of butter and spice, and melted on my tongue, was divine. I did not even notice when the woman brought me my kava, until its insistent smell wedged past my obsession with the baked goods.

After the cardamom rolls, even the kava seemed a bit tame. Still, the rich bitterness overtook my palate much as a fine wine might do. A good third of an hour had passed before I finally came back to myself. I had intended to sit, and plan, and consider my statements on broaching the Interim Council. Instead I was brushing crumbs and shining dark droplets of kava off the front of my leathers.

"I must have needed that, badly," I said aloud.

The cinnamon-skinned woman was back. "More?" she asked, with an accent I could not place any better than I could place the unusual color of her face.

"My thanks, but no. I need to move on. Those were the best rolls I have ever eaten." I considered subtleties of texture and flavor. "A wash of egg white, yes, with sea salt and a pinch of sugar to go along with the cardamom seeds?"

She looked surprised. "You are baker?"

"Not really." I smiled at her. "I trained for a while, to be a palace chef." That wasn't even a lie, exactly, though it was only a fraction of the truth.

With a dubious glance at my clothing, the woman nodded. "You need work, maybe we use early morning. You wake before sun?"

I was sorely tempted by her offer, if nothing else to learn the secret of these magnificent rolls. The distractions of food were always of interest, even if unwise at times. And cooking had ever soothed my troubled heart. "Unfortunately, I often do wake early. But I have work enough, though I thank you." Saying I had work *was* a lie, though not in spirit. I slipped her one of my last silver taels as gross overpayment, decided to trust my quick thoughts and quicker tongue, and, much relieved, stepped into the street to stride firmly toward the Textile Bourse.

Even those few rods of distance were haunted with more memories than I had realized. To this day I am still learning the power of place to summon recollection; back then I had scarcely begun to understand it.

Here I had fought alongside Skinless and the Factor's ghost and most of the pardines to be found in Copper Downs that day. Here my old enemy and older friend Federo had died when the god Choybalsan finally left him. Here Endurance had been birthed from the wild power and passion of the moment. Here was where I had last seen the Dancing Mistress, my dearest friend.

By the time I mounted the steps to the damaged portico fronting the first floor of the three-storey stone facade, the contented peace that the teahouse had brought me was fled as swiftly as mist on the water. I faced the two brawlers in their ill-fitting uniforms, which I did not recognize. One of the dormant regiments? Copper Downs had never been good at armies.

Each was more than a head taller than I, and they had the sort of muscles that scared off would-be footpads just on principle. If this pair didn't know who I was, they would soon learn. A lesson that would profit them little, though I'd be glad of the workout.

"I am Green," I announced. "Here to meet with the Interim Council."

Instead of the brutish resistance I'd expected, they both pressed back against the stonework of the building. A quick glance exchanged between the two men served as the drawing of straws. The loser stammered, "You're expected, miss. Ma'am. G-Green." The winner opened the door and waved me inside.

Expected? A curious choice of words, under the circumstances.

Within was the same chaos of clerks and desks and stacks of paper that I remembered from the days of summer, though lit by oil lamps in the absence of sunlight from the tall, street-facing windows still boarded over. They moved in a swirling mass orchestrated by the formidable mind of Mr. Nast. The man doubtless directed his minions personally even while asleep in whatever closet he propped himself within to take his rest.

I knew where I was heading. No one seemed inclined to either stop me or lend me aid, so I stalked through the wide room to the stairs with one hand on the hilt of my long knife. The path opened before me as if drawn by the finger of a god, and closed behind me with a murmur. The familiar black and white marble of the steps, mostly covered with more documents in their files and stacks, bore me upward.

Near the top I turned and looked down at several dozen staring faces. I was tempted to bare steel, or simply yell some nonsense at them, for surely they would scatter like chickens before the cook's axe. Instead I satisfied myself with a sharp nod.

Oddly, several of them returned it, and more broke into smiles. I almost felt welcomed.

Upstairs stretched a long, familiar hallway lined with offices and cluttered with even more desks. Here the more senior clerks and functionaries were not so shy about halting in their work to goggle at me, some grinning like cats in a buttery. I tightened my grip on my long knife and stalked with exaggerated deliberation toward the council chamber at the end of the hall. Lily Blades understood violence as theater, and theater as violence. As I approached the stained-glass door illustrating the wonders of felt, Mr. Nast stepped out.

Pale, pinch-faced, severe as any Justiciary Mother, he had changed little. Mr. Nast also betrayed no surprise at my presence in his hallway. "Just on time, you are."

"I was not summoned." In a perverse way, I liked this man, but he also brought out the argument in me—which was in all fairness never buried far from the surface.

"As it pleases you to believe." He bowed. I saw something stiff in the movement, and tried to remember. Had he been shot during last summer's fight outside this building? The crossbow bolts had flown wildly. "Though it may stretch your credulity to hear such from me, I find myself gratified to see you well."

"I should say the same of you, sir." I bowed in return, then released my weapon's hilt to clasp his hand. "You are brave, and honest, even in the face of impossibility."

A shadow that might have been regret flickered across his face. "The council meets," he said. "They expect you."

"So the trained bear at the door said." *But why?* No one but Chowdry knew I was returning to the city just now. While I could imagine various treacheries of the old pirate, conspiring with Nast and the council was not among them.

Nast quirked a small smile, then rapped on the door.

"Now what?" shouted someone within.

He pushed through. "The Lady Green is here."

The Lady Green!? How in the name of all that was unholy had I received *that* promotion? I followed him into the meeting room.

Three of the five who'd sat within the last time I came calling on this council were dead now. Federo, at my hands. Stefan Mohanda, also at my hands in his guise as the Pater Primus of Blackblood's temple. And Mikkal Hiebert, killed in the fighting I'd brought down upon them all.

The two survivors surely had my role in the recent council successions much on their mind. Roberti Jeschonek, of the sea captains, who had taken over chairmanship of the Interim Council amid the disruption following Federo's death; and Loren Kohlmann of the warehousemen and brokers. They were seated with three other men. None of the new councilors were known to me.

This room was much the same, with its brass lamps, and high narrow windows with more stained glass depicting the husbandry and processing of wool, all surrounding the long table I'd slammed my knife into on my last visit. *That* scar was still visible in the glossy finish of the mahogany.

None of them seemed surprised to see me, either. My heart sank.

Jeschonek rose as if to counterbalance that fall. "Green. Welcome back to the city. I trust your retreat to the High Hills was restful and in good order."

"And it would be still if someone hadn't dragged me back." I eyed the new men suspiciously.

"May I introduce Councilor Lampet? He sits for the great families of the Ivory Quarter and the Velviere District." Lampet was small, dapper, and entirely bald, wearing a suit of silks and wool with a too-precise mustache. I hated him instantly, both for his looks and for the wealth whose interests he represented here. "To his right is Councilor Kohlmann, who you already know." Thick-bodied and brutal-faced, Kohlmann simply nodded at me.

"Whom," you twit, I thought, letting my returning stare remain blank and ungracious.

"On this side of the table is Councilor Ostrakan, of the bankers." Ostrakan could have walked down any street in this city unnoticed. A talent he shared with some of the most dangerous of the Lily Blades. I marked him out as the greatest action risk in this room of supposedly thoughtful men. I also noted that Jeschonek was giving me a moment between introductions to assess each man.

"Finally we have Councilor Johns, who represents the trading interests. Including those from beyond our shores." *That* was intriguing. Johns appeared as Petraean as anyone in the room, but his portfolio bespoke foreign influence reaching into Copper Downs.

I nearly laughed at that thought. I *was* foreign influence reaching into Copper Downs, for all that they'd bought and paid to bring me across the sea as the smallest child. And, of course, the Bittern Court here now on my trail.

"We amuse you?" asked Lampet. His voice was as oily as his appearance.

Kohlmann stirred, then clearly thought the better of warning his colleague. I credited the man with sense, but held myself tight, very glad of the roll and kava that now steadied my nerves. "Hardly," I told him. "You would be surprised what amuses me."

"No, we would not," Jeschonek said seriously. He glared at Lampet. *"None of us."*

"So tell me." I drew one of my short knives again, laid it down across my previous scar upon the table. I allowed my gaze to pause on Councilor Johns. "What is that woman from Kalimpura's Bittern Court doing here in Copper Downs?"

Johns answered, to no surprise of mine. "She did not come alone."

I had sudden visions of an invasion of the Street Guild or worse; Kalimpuri enforcers in Copper Downs. This was news that I could wait out, though. No point in showing eagerness to this cage of snakes.

After a moment, Johns spoke as if I'd asked anyway. "The Prince of the City has voyaged to Copper Downs from Kalimpura to grace us with his person, leading an embassy from his people. He has required your presence in attendance upon his mission."

At that I did laugh, long and loud. The five of them stared, variously puzzled, bemused, or alarmed.

Finally I asked them: "You do not understand anything of Kalimpuri politics, do you?"

"We understand a delegation," Jeschonek said. "With monied traders, men under arms, female assassins, and coastal pirates in the Prince's train. Someone has gone to a great deal of trouble to seek you out."

I was struck by his mention of female assassins. Had some of the Lily Blades sailed across the Storm Sea in the company of the Bittern Court woman and her fellow conspirators? That seemed almost inconceivable, unless a person of great will had bound them together. *Not* the Prince of the City, a pretty fop meant to distract the foreigners, who could not likely command a pair of buttery maids. At least not beyond his bedchamber.

Was this what had worried the ghost Erio? An assortment of thugs and figureheads from over the sea would hardly be a threat to anyone in Copper Downs but me. I could not imagine the ghost urging me down from the High Hills for this.

Later, I was to wish mightily I had possessed a greater imagination in the moment.

"What do you plan to do about this inconvenient embassy?" I asked.

"Appoint you to answer them," Jeschonek replied flatly. Lampet seemed pained, while Johns appeared thoughtful. The other two kept their own counsel behind calmer faces.

"I am out of the business of managing the affairs of cities. Especially this one." I touched my belly. "With child, tired, and young, I hardly qualify."

"Few here speak Seliu," Johns answered. "And fewer of them do we trust."

"If you trust *me*, you are twice a fool." I picked up my weapon.

"It is too late not to trust you." Kohlmann's voice grated low. "You have already overset the affairs of Copper Downs, and brought us a new god in the bargain."

Twice, I thought. *I have overset your affairs twice.* Few enough knew the truth of my assassination of the Duke when I was but a girl. That news certainly had no need to spread now.

"Trust whom you will. I am not your lackey." I grinned without humor. "Perhaps you should send one of the other women on your council."

Kohlmann bored on. I had not marked the councilor to be the power in the room, but this business clearly stirred some passion within him. "They seek you regardless. You may as well respond in our name. I will accompany you as surety."

"You could not stand against a Blade Mother." My voice was flat. "If this embassy would claim our lives, we are already forfeit. So I do not see what further protection you might offer."

"The protection of legitimacy. And witness. You they might seek to capture as one of their own gone astray, but such an assemblage of envoys should consider thoughtfully before striking down a councilor of Copper Downs."

"These are people with a *ship*," I told him, as if he were simple. "If they are hunting me, as you think, then all they need do is lay chains on me and sail away. Who would care then what corpses lay cooling in their wake?" After a moment, I added thoughtfully, "At least, that's how I'd do it."

Kohlmann blinked twice. I was fairly certain that constituted an outburst, coming from him. "They have too much of their trade and good name invested in this embassy. The Prince of the City would not cross the Storm Sea on some petty raid."

He had the truth of that. The Prince had far too many receptions to attend. "Fair enough. You've seen farther into this than I. But you *are* coming with me."

"When?" Kohlmann asked.

Just for the sake of twitting him, I replied, "I will meet you here on the morrow, an hour past dawn." With a sharp nod, I bid them good day and saw myself out. Nast, in the hallway beyond, gave me an almost genuine smile and pressed something into my hand.

"Sir?" I asked quietly. This man and I had our differences, but we'd always shared respect. Unlike some people I knew, he'd be unlikely to shove stinging nettles or a bag of scorpions upon me.

"You are back in Copper Downs, without patronage," Nast said in that thin, pinched voice. "The clerks have collected a purse to ensure you may live decently."

He was right, so far as it went. My bonds were still held by Nast on my behalf, but they were hardly spending money. I could buy passage across the sea, but not pay for a basket of rolls with them. I allowed my doubt to sharpen my tone. "Is this your way of reducing the terror that I will doubtless once more wreak upon your city, or do your people actually care so for me?"

"A tool can serve two purposes. You will not go hungry, and a few less windows may be broken. We shall all rejoice on both counts." His face pinched into what might have been a smile. "The more, ah, impulsive . . . among my staff also hold you in high regard. They seem to credit you with much to their benefit."

"Thank you," I said simply, and glanced about at the clerks and their assistants crowding the halls, oh-so-carefully not watching me in return.

Gossip eddied in currents behind me as I left them all behind. A small smile lingered on my face.

My experiences in the teahouse left me very much wanting a decent, protected place to sleep. The weather was already too close and miserable to curl up on a rooftop or find a reasonable straw heap. I could not risk the sort of cough I'd catch in the chilled damp of winter's encroachment. The Tavernkeep's establishment was impossible, of course, with this new embassy in the city and looking for me there. I did not feel ready to approach Endurance in his temple. Which left me with remarkably few options, short of simply renting a room like any traveler who ever came to any city on the plate of the world.

Even with some funds now beyond the few silver and copper taels I'd carried with me from Ilona's house, that did not appeal. Too much like an animal going to ground in an unfamiliar burrow.

So I did what I'd so often done in my later days in Kalimpura. I headed for the docks and found a winesink where I could occupy a bench in a dark corner. Along the way, I bargained a patched blue and green robe from a ragpicker for half a copper tael—I refused him a kiss—to wear over the silly leathers. For the moment, I stayed with the black for my evening's excursion. There are some places where appearance matters.

At random I chose a tavern called the Bilge Pump. Low ceilings, scattered tables battered by years of rough use and daily fights. A fireplace sat cold, though coals were heaped on the grate for later in the evening. The place smelled of bar fug—spilled beer, the old salt of sweat and bad food, and something rotting amid the cracks in the floorboards.

In other words, a typical sailors' bar, filled with the chatter of a dozen languages, and men of all sizes who shared a common look in their eyes and set to their stance. Working a deck with wide horizons will do that to a person.

No women but the serving girls. Ordinary enough for a waterfront bar. In my leathers with my ragged hair, so long as I kept my face tucked down, I could still pass for a boy. The scars helped that.

Not much longer would I remain a lad, not as the baby grew, but for tonight the disguise would hold.

I kicked a drunk off a bench and placed my back to the wall, my little bundle beside me. Ordering a plate of pickled eggs and a tankard of their darkest ale, I set myself to the old game from Kalimpura. I simply listened.

In those days, as in my years since, I was hot for news of the child trade. While that evil had never been struck from my list of worries about the world, now I listened simply for the sake of hearing someone else's troubles. So many voices, so many faces, so many races. No wonder I'd always liked the waterfront.

The Petraean was easiest for me to pick out.

". . . docked me three weeks' wages, all for a lousy joke . . ."

". . . in truth? Bloody odd doings on the posh deck, if you ask . . ."

In Smagadine, which I could barely follow: ". . . cheese sellers. I cut them . . ."

In Hanchu: ". . . you count, you count more, still they cheat you . . ."

Back to Petraean: ". . . raising the port fees again. Then demurrage atop that. The poor bastard was . . ."

In Seliu: ". . . not in the city, they say. But there was that fuss today . . ."

My eyes popped open, though I kept my head still so as not to betray my interest. I *knew* that voice. I certainly knew that language.

I took my time, trying to pick out the stream of Seliu again, but they had fallen silent. Or possibly changed languages. The voice didn't pluck at my ear in Petraean, though. Behind my tankard, I discreetly scanned the room.

Two men were leaving. Dark-haired, perhaps dark-skinned as I was, though that was hard to tell as they were backlit by the late daylight in the doorway. One turned and my heart went cold.

Little Baji. Sailor off *Chittachai*, and onetime crewmate of Chowdry.

That coastal trader couldn't have crossed the Storm Sea on a bet, not even with the hands of a god behind it. He had to have come with the Prince of the City's embassy.

Did that mean that Captain Utavi was here, too? Now *there* was a right bastard.

I considered quickly whether Chowdry's entire trip with me from our hasty departure from the trader off the Bhopuri coast had been a setup. Was the man a spy, trailing me from the beginning by the simple expedient of placing himself under my wing?

That was difficult to credit. Chowdry, even the new Chowdry the high priest of Endurance, was never a deep man. Such a game would be beyond his reckoning or his desires, either one.

But Little Baji could perhaps turn his old crewmate through old loyalty, or the threats of familiarity. Chowdry *had* said that there was an inrush of Selistani over the past few months. That seemed swift to me, for word of

Endurance's theogeny could barely have crossed the Storm Sea and back in the time since.

Little Baji was no immigrant, though, or ship jumper. Not if I understood his words correctly.

I considered leaving, finding another place to spend the evening and possibly the night. But here I could watch the door, and was surrounded by dozens of men with no interest at all in either me or the people who seemed to be hunting me.

Soon enough the baby let it be known that she did not like pickled eggs, not the slightest bit. I held my gut behind my teeth and cleared my throat with more of the ale. The stuff grew less foul as I drank deeper and deeper of my allotment. For this I was glad. The drink seemed to carry some of my worries away with it, as well.

Some lessons in this life are difficult to learn, even upon repeated application. Then as now, I have discovered a certain, all too common foolishness at the bottom of a tankard. Morning found me with my cheek stuck to the table. The Bilge Pump was nearly empty. A tired slattern waved a mop at the floor. Several men snored about the room, while a handful of very dedicated drinkers continued to keep the bar from tipping over. A window I hadn't realized existed was thrown open, dawn's light lancing in from the left edge to lacerate my eyeballs.

I pried myself from the wood and found somewhat to my surprise that I hadn't been robbed. A long night of steady drinking with a bare blade clutched in hand seemed to have done the trick.

Precisely what trick I could not say.

The baby was not happy either. I stood to find a place to wash, and to my surprise spewed the remains of last night's eggs and ale. The poor woman with the mop gave me a long, despairing stare. Guilty, I fished a silver tael out of my new purse and gave it to her. The coin left a surprising number of its fellows behind for my future use. That amount would be a week's wages in this place, and could have rented me a rather decent room last night with a warm bath. This morning the coin purchased merely my conscience for the vileness I'd left on her floor.

Stumbling outside, I realized I'd hardly been the only one sick in the place. Ah, well.

I resisted the expediency of jumping into the harbor to clean up. For one thing, it would probably have made my mess worse. Also, the morning was quite chilly in that strange way when the sun shows his cloudless face distant and cold, reserving all his fires for himself. Cold seawater seemed a terrible idea. Instead I slipped into an alley and took to the rooftops. Even stumbling tired on the backside of a drunken evening, I could manage that. People didn't ask so many questions around a rooftop cistern as they did at a watering trough or a public pump. I was not willing to face Kohlmann grubby and ale-soaked, and all the less so anyone from Kalimpura.

When I did find water, I was careful to splash it out, so as not to foul someone's morning tea. As I was alone on the roof anyway, I stripped to my skin and made a decently thorough washing of the business as I resolutely ignored the cold. While naked, I examined my belly. It had developed a definite bump that suggested I either needed more exercise or less sex.

The leathers seemed too tight and sweaty to me, so I slipped into the patched robe without them underneath. I might have wished for something more formal—stately even—but this would do for the moment. I made a bundle of the rest of it, which in turn reminded me I had not sewn a bell last night. No time now, but I promised myself two bells this coming evening. Checking my knives, I began a rooftop run back toward the Textile Bourse.

The councilor would be expecting me soon. Arriving in the flush of a strong workout would mask the last of the ale scent on me. The burn in my muscles could only improve my outlook.

So I ran harder.

The problem with running the roofs is that it is a lot of work. I'd been living in the woods for the last five months, and much of the time before that aboard ship. Every alley must be leapt. Every street must be climbed down into and scrambled back up from on the other side. All in a foolish robe that kept tangling in my legs until I bound it up in a clout.

Certainly the bakers' boys and vegetable sellers of the early morning saw me. I was not attempting stealth, or speed. Just seeking the reward of strong effort, and making myself difficult to follow.

In those objectives I was confident that I succeeded. I finally stopped on the flat roof of the silk weavery two blocks down Lyme Street from the Textile

Bourse. Their biggest loom stood almost as high as the eaves within the inner court, though the mechanism was heavily shrouded against the morning damp. Already someone was at work within on a smaller loom, the clack of the shuttle audible below me.

My breath heaved awhile, and in time, so did my stomach. I had little left to spew, and deeply resented the necessity. So the baby did not like pickled eggs. Fine. Perhaps she did not like ale, either. Or vigorous exercise.

Wiping my mouth, I placed my free hand on my belly once again. "You and I will need to reach some agreement, little friend," I said quietly. "We cannot live together if you will be so demanding."

I was certain to be ignored, but I had to try.

Finally recovered, I spied up the street to see whether Kohlmann was assembling an ambush for me. Two guardsmen stood as expected before the Textile Bourse. A honey wagon moved down the street collecting slop buckets from those buildings not connected to the ancient sewer system. Mange-ridden and dirty white, a three-legged dog nosed through garbage in the gutter.

Quiet yet busy, as only a city at morning could be.

The baby moved. Demanding . . . what? "Easy," I whispered.

Was this how mothers spoke to their children? I had no idea then. With no memory of my own mother, and having been raised by a number of indifferent and cruel mistresses, how could I know? The thought frightened me. Perhaps I would become Mistress Tirelle, a sword-edged check on my daughter's ambitions.

And when had I decided she would be a girl, anyway?

The thought comforted me. I was not ready to raise a man. I might not know mothering, but I believed I understood something of being a woman. Otherwise I'd want Septio back, which was pointless. Not even his ghost remained. And besides, I'd hardly loved him in any way that mattered.

I settled in on my rough, empty stomach and watched for Kohlmann. After a while the buttery-yeast scent of baking prompted rumbling in my gut. Despite the recent spewing, my desire for those cardamom rolls grew almost to a fantasy. I ignored my hungers until the councilor emerged from within the Textile Bourse and scanned the street.

No one suspicious or alarming had passed by in the meantime, so I climbed down behind the silk weavery. As it happened I would walk right past the teahouse on my way to meet Kohlmann, so I tapped on the shuttered window. The cinnamon-skinned woman cracked it open to peek out at me. She shook her head, but smiled anyway. A moment later she came out a side door with a napkin folded around several of the rolls.

"You take." A shy slyness glinted in her eyes.

I dug for my purse, now rolled into my leathers.

She shook her head. "Ah, no, you take for gift."

"Thank you for the kindness," I told her. With a sharp nod, I trotted off through the crisp morning to meet Kohlmann.

"Hello, Green." The councilor stood at the bottom of the steps. Glowering guards loomed over our heads at the top of the flight. Kohlmann was dressed this morning in severe suit of dark wool, which made a rather unfortunate contrast to my patched and now-sweaty robe.

"Good morning," I replied, then found myself overcome by the scent of food in my hands. Greedy, I opened the napkin to reveal three cardamom rolls still steaming from the oven. "Would you like one?"

"No, thank you. I have already broken my fast."

I could not determine from the dryness of his tone how serious he was, so I took Kohlmann at his word. The rolls went down very quickly, warm and solid within me, offending my gut not at all. I wiped my hands on the napkin before tucking it into the end of my bundle of leathers, intending to return it later.

"You are not approaching this embassy from Kalimpura with the august trappings of your position," he said.

The leathers were sweaty and tight and reeked of waterfront bar. I wasn't about to tell Kohlmann this, but I definitely didn't want to put them back on, either. Not before a good cleaning, and possibly some work letting out the seams a bit further. "I intend to appear as a supplicant," I told him, lying cheerfully. "The Prince of the City will appreciate such a humble approach."

"Hmm." His expression left little doubt as to his opinion of my story. "Are you otherwise ready?"

To face the Bittern Court woman? Always. And never. How ready could one be? "Let us go. Where is the embassy housed?"

"They have taken a mansion in the Velviere District."

That was second only to the Ivory Quarter as a fine address within the city of Copper Downs. Oddly, though perhaps not a coincidence, the Temple of Endurance was in the Velviere District, being built on the site of one of Copper Downs' ancient mineheads that long predated the houses of the wealthy.

While I knew much concerning the great families and remnant aristocracy of Copper Downs from my days in the Factor's house, I didn't have enough information to associate them with their particular properties on a street-by-street basis.

"I trust you will lead us there."

"Of course." Kohlmann nodded to the guards; then we set out together.

The councilor was precisely my sort of conversationalist. That is to say, taciturn. Nonetheless, as we walked along Lyme Street, I indulged my curiosity in one matter on which he might usefully enlighten me.

"I did not recognize the uniforms of your guards back there. I don't recall the Textile Bourse being secured under arms last summer."

"Councilor Lampet has taken it upon himself to organize a Conciliar Guard." The distaste in Kohlmann's voice was unmistakable.

"The old Ducal Guard wasn't bad enough?"

"They have been reconstituted." He snorted. "The city guard was never more than a jest under the Duke; news criers and lamplighters without any authority. Federo always argued against forming them into something greater. Over the past months we've seen more private guards, and subscription militias. There needs to be some authority."

"The Harbormaster has troops," I said, dredging up an odd fact from the days of my education.

Another snort. "Absent the Duke, do you imagine Paulus Jessup recognizes anyone's authority but his own? The Interim Council is fortunate that he continues to remit the customs revenue and put down dock riots. A less scrupulous man in the Harbormaster's position would be running his own waterfront kingdom by now." He paused, then slowly finished what had obviously begun as a private thought. "No, Lampet has the right of it. Shame it had to be Lampet, though."

My memory of the old days was that the Ducal Guard enforced the general peace, as well as governmental and judicial edicts. The city guard lit the lamps, cried the hours, and hurried the drunks home. The regiments, which mostly consisted of old banners in dusty halls filled with rusted blades, were the defense of a city that hadn't seen or needed an army in four centuries. The wealthy, as always, had private guards, but not rising to the level of street militias.

Now the situation was apparently much more like that in Kalimpura.

Except without the interlocking apparatus of the Guilds, the Lily Blades, and the Death Right to keep violence contained to what was needful, or at least could be bought off.

In the course of the conversation and my subsequent thoughts, we'd passed down Montane Street and into the Velviere District. Where much of the city, at least its relatively monied portions, ran toward two- and three-storey buildings standing wall-to-wall, the Velviere District consisted of widely separated structures set back on their own lots. Many of the residences were truly mansions. Some businesses were located in the area, of the quiet, tasteful variety that displayed no signs and quoted no prices. If you needed to ask, you were in the wrong place.

The streets were wider, too, paved with fine gravel that was regularly oiled and rolled to keep it smooth and quiet. Nothing like the varied cobbles, bricks, ruts, and mud of much of the rest of Copper Downs. The blocks here were for the most part lined with broad elms, oaks, and other deeply shaded trees. No roof-running in this neighborhood, nor any lurking in alleys. Even the walled compounds—perhaps half the properties here were such, as opposed to the Ivory District, where virtually every home was walled—had setbacks with wide lines of sight. It was as if the architects had planned for war and assassination, even during the centuries-long stagnation of the reign of the late, unlamented Duke.

Not a place for sneaking. So we walked as if we owned the street. Kohlmann did, at any rate. I strode alongside him, trying to look dangerous in my robe and realizing that in its way, this was almost as silly as my leathers. When had I become so conscious of my appearance? I felt as foolish as poor Samma, the weakest of my fellow Blades back at the Temple of the Silver Lily. Besides, no one who looked like me lived in a neighborhood such as this. The dark color of my skin cried "thief" to these people, not "servant." Never "one of us."

Kohlmann paused at an intersection. I thought we might be at Richard Avenue, but wasn't sure. The streets were shady and quiet as some Arnaud painting from the last century; *Idylls of the City* perhaps. The whitewashed walls to left and right, the branches overhanging from behind, the smells of fruit trees and kitchen fires. All it lacked was a small dog and pair of washing girls in wimples and kirts.

"Around this corner we will see their gate." His voice was even more quiet and serious than usual. "Whatever guards they have are sure to recognize you. Are you ready for this meeting?"

I was surprised at such concern. "I am always as ready as I need to be."

Which was another way of saying I was ever unready, but Kohlmann let the statement pass with a nod.

In truth I felt a bit of a fool with my bundle underneath my arm, but I just couldn't face donning the leathers again. I did not imagine needing my knives here, not in the presence of a formal embassy, and my body continued to rejoice in the comfort of the loose robe.

We walked around the corner to spot one of the Prince's men outside a gate halfway down the block. His guards were peacocks, snickered at by the Lily Blades for their pink and blue silks and sweeping, showy swords that anyone could block with a stick and a moment's thought.

Of far more concern was the woman next to him on guard. A Lily Blade. As we approached, I recognized Mother Argai. A sometime lover of mine, and longtime sparring partner. I fancied she'd always liked me, even when the tides of rumor and gossip had run strong against me among the Blades.

The Prince's man stared straight ahead, facing a whitewashed stucco wall across the street from him, but Mother Argai looked me over quite frankly. As Kohlmann and I approached, she spoke. "I see you've become a ragman's apprentice, Green."

Seliu, of course. Kohlmann could have no idea what she'd just said.

"I pass about in the manner of this city," I replied, another cheerful lie. "How is it with you?"

"You know. Always pulling girls out of deeper trouble."

Something played in her eyes. Not a lie. More of an urgency. As we closed on her, I answered with: "I try to find trouble before it finds me. And today I bring a powerful friend as witness." *What is she not telling me?*

Mother Argai nodded once. "This is a damp, miserable place. Mind you don't make your grave here, or your shade will be chilled down all the years to come."

"And the same to you," I replied in my brightest voice. If she was trying to help, this woman had a strange way about her.

The peacock man decided to recognize me. He slipped a sidelong glance at Mother Argai, then turned to strike a bell before opening the carved blackwood gate that admitted into the grounds of the mansion. Bas-relief scenes of a sylvan paradise swung away from me, until the leaping pardines in their glens stood at an odd angle.

"Now I will ask if *you* are ready," I told Kohlmann in Petraean.

"It is not my friends who guard the gate," he answered mildly. I could see the muscles bunching beneath his suit, and realized I wasn't the only one spreading lies this morning.

A trio of Selistani servants saw us from the porch, and turned to hurry into the main house. It was large, positioned back among the trees, in the Haito style. White walls with great reddish-brown cross beams, tall doors and windows, little external ornamentation. Almost a child's cartoon of a home, though five centuries past this had been the very pinnacle of architectural taste in Copper Downs.

A good education never went to waste. If I did die here, at least I would have the comfort of knowing I'd passed on amid high style.

By the time we'd walked up the granite flags to the large but simple porch, a protocol master from the Prince's court had bustled out the front door. I did not recognize the man, but in his flowing orange silks and rounded red velvet hat, he made the peacock at the gate look a drab hen. Despite my deep mistrust, it still warmed my heart to see in this place a man of my people in the trappings of wealth.

Wealth or not, they had started their day early. Back in Kalimpura, the court would not even accept a letter much before the noon hour. Let alone admit callers. Either the Prince disliked this northern clime overmuch and wished to hurry through his business, or they were poised for action.

"Green," the protocol master said warmly in accented Petraean, though I knew we'd never met. "And Councilor Kohlmann." Credit to him for recognizing the local powers-that-were on sight. "Greetings from our humble house. With the Prince of the City in residence, you have here returned to the grace of Kalimpura. May you be welcomed home again."

Those words stopped me. Kohlmann pulled up short alongside at the foot of the steps, so we were both looking up into the protocol master's nostrils. I had studied much of diplomatic niceties and court practices in the Factor's house, and knew well enough what the protocol master was telling me.

"I was banished from Kalimpura under pain of death," I said, also in Petraean for Kohlmann's benefit. "By order of the Temple of the Silver Lily, for whom *you* do not speak. If I am indeed back within the city's purview, Mother Argai at the gate behind us would be protected by the Death Right should she strike me down from behind in this moment. I will not be welcomed within at the cost of my life."

Kohlmann stirred, but I touched his arm. He knew well enough we were on my ground now. Literally so, as this place was for the nonce by twist of law part of Kalimpura.

"I do not speak for the Temple of the Silver Lily, as you say." The protocol master took trouble to appear pained, a deliberate rebuke to my gracelessness. "But I do speak for the Prince of the City. You are under his protection in this place."

My next words were chosen very deliberately. "Do not bandy foolishness with me. The Prince of the City is a fop with no real powers save a title to impress the foreigners. Someone else is behind this embassy, and I believe I have already seen her face here in Copper Downs. Should the Bittern Court seek my life, I do not know what the Prince's protection might be worth, beyond a pretty speech at my funeral. I prefer to remain under my own protection, and that of the city of Copper Downs." I turned to face Kohlmann, giving the councilor his cue.

The big man's expression promised more questions of me later, but he played into his part like a temple catamite on feast day. "As a representative of this city's duly constituted government, I assure Lady Green our full protection." He divided his attention between me and the protocol master.

Whatever "full protection" meant. No good ever came of trusting the Interim Council, but the statement ought to give the protocol master and his superiors pause. If nothing else, at some point these people needed to be able to make their way safely back to the docks and take ship. Precisely the sort of thing that even this Interim Council could manage to prevent, however hapless they might be in the face of larger pressures.

"Then we shall consider your exile in abeyance," the protocol master said smoothly, as though he had not moments before claimed quite correctly not to speak for the Temple of the Silver Lily. Ah, the forms of protocol. Like combat, without the pleasantries.

We stepped within.

The front hall boasted that same high-ceilinged architecture so beloved of the important and the self-important everywhere in Copper Downs. The house smelled musty, as if it had been long closed, though an overlay of Selistani spice was working to combat that scent of neglect with the warm, familiar sting of curry and red pepper. I blinked away the particolored sunlight streaming in the stained-glass windows above and looked to see who awaited me here.

All of them, I realized in rapidly dawning horror.

The Prince of the City was poised on a throne in the center of the hall, where by the usual traditions of Haito architecture there ought to be an ornamental pool. Behind him were arrayed a selection of the men and women of his court standing tall, their bird-bright silks gleaming oddly in the streaming morning light. To his right stood the Bittern Court woman with a glare of triumph on her face. To his left was poised Mother Vajpai—senior trainer of the Lily Blades and my longtime mentor, before I was ejected from Kalimpura by her order. Though not, I later came to understand, by her will.

As I understood matters then, these two women were the agents of my banishment. My free hand brushed the hilt of my long knife where it protruded from the bundle of my leathers. On my best day I could barely score a touch on Mother Vajpai. Pregnant, tired after a drunken night's half-sleep, and dressed in these ridiculous robes, I could scarcely claim even that much skill this morning.

"The girl Green," said the protocol master loudly in Seliu. "With a councilor of this city, Loren Kohlmann."

Kohlmann bowed at the sound of his name filtered into our tongue, with its differing inflections of case. I remained alert, tightly drawn for a battle I could not hope to win.

The Prince of the City rose to his feet. "Welcome," he said warmly in Petraean, focusing his attention on Kohlmann. "We have been awaiting your presence. Would you take some fine southern wine with us?"

Kohlmann bowed. I whispered, "Don't fall for it," but he ignored me. Standing straight again, he smiled. "I am blessed by your house," he said in bad Seliu. Then, in Petraean, "I would be pleased to take wine with you, great Prince."

Mother Vajpai stepped forward. In a voice straining with memorization, she said in Petraean I knew she did not speak, "I would see my old student." Someone behind her hissed. She added, "Awhile."

I turned toward the front door. Kohlmann caught at my arm, nearly earning a deep stab for his troubles. "This is my game," he growled quietly. "Play it my way. They will not kill you while I am present. And I will not leave without you."

Though I desperately wanted to ask the man what he would *do* if my old mistress simply refused to release me, I held my tongue. Unless the Rectifier was in the city, no one in Copper Downs could take down Mother Vajpai in a straight fight. I knew this because no one in this place but the Rectifier could take *me* down in a straight fight, and *I* was afraid of Mother Vajpai.

"We will speak of this later," I said, matching his growl with my own. Stepping forward, I let a smile slip on to my face. It was not entirely a lie—I had always respected Mother Vajpai, and liked her even, while never finding reason to believe the affection was not mutual. I understood even then that my banishment had not been engineered for petty personal reasons. The opposite, in truth, given the pressure for arranging my death or turning me out to the dubious justice of the Bittern Court.

And *that* smarmy bitch gave me a sweet, gleeful smile over Mother Vajpai's shoulder as my old teacher swept me into a hug. This raised my hackles as surely as a bared blade would have done. She'd never hugged me before in my life. "Have a care, Green," Mother Vajpai whispered. She took me by the hand and led me toward a side chamber, away from the entrance, away from Loren Kohlmann, away from all the freedom and independence of my exile.

I almost balked again, except a door ahead of me swung open and Samma stepped forth to usher me onward.

Samma.

I stopped, heart pounding. My mouth ran dry. My hands shook.

Samma. Dark-haired, doe-eyed, sharp-faced, and as always slightly contrary of expression. My very first lover, ever. Closest to my heart for the better part of a year in the Temple of the Silver Lily. Fellow aspirant, and now a Blade, or so I presumed.

Doubting every step, I turned toward her, and allowed myself to be taken away from the man who'd promised to guarantee my safety here among the leaders of my own people.

We perched on a Pilean Era settee. Armless, low-backed, covered in a thick silk brocade that would irritate bared skin, it was a piece of furniture designed for short, intimate conversations without the temptations of further dalliance. The room was likewise, a small parlor off the great hall where people were intended to meet to seal bargains or make arrangements. Narrow paintings lined the paneled walls, while two equally narrow windows opened into the shadows of the lawn to the south—cues of architecture and design intended to push the occupants to discomfort.

All of this was apropos to my being here. Short, intimate, without the temptation of further dalliance. "What are you about?" I hissed to both of them.

Mother Vajpai spoke first, as she always had and probably always would. "The Lily Goddess has sent us for you, Green."

"No." I let myself sound cross. "That woman outside, from the Bittern Court. She has longed for my heartsblood for a year now. If you came at the Lily Goddess' behest, she would not be among you."

"Surali," said Samma unexpectedly. "Her name is Surali. And she's not so bad."

"Samma." Mother Vajpai's voice held a warning tone.

"She has a right to *know*!" Samma blurted, then cowered back, overwhelmed at her own temerity in speaking. *Such classic Samma,* I thought. Never quite the nerve to stand up for what needs standing up for. She had sufficient conscience, but not the courage to act.

"You will be silent." This time Mother Vajpai's voice was much more severe. Then, back to me, "You are wanted at home. The Temple Mother has passed away, as has Mother Meiko. There is much disruption among all our orders. The purpose for your exile no longer applies. I hear you have vanquished the danger she had concerned herself with." A smile, as genuine as anything else this very controlled woman ever did. "We need you, Green."

All my careful thought, my planning, my sense of politics—it all slid away in the face of this woman who had almost been a mother to me in her way. "Who do you need?" I asked nastily. "Green the killer, who couldn't be trusted? Green the goddess-touched, who wouldn't cooperate with the priestesses? Green the obsessed, who roamed the docks looking for child traders? Or perhaps Green the sensual, fucking every woman in the temple who would hold still long enough!?"

My voice had risen at the last, and the crude obscenity caught at her, as I'd known it would.

Her voice was as sorrowful as her face. "We need Green, who had grown to be heart to all the Blades, though we did not understand that until after we had let you slip away."

I was forced to remind myself that Mother Vajpai always maintained absolute control of herself. The emotion was a weapon surely as any spinning kick or hand strike. Seizing my own will, I replied, "You did not let me go. You drove me away. Because of your friend out there. *Surali.* If you find me ungrateful or suspicious, you might inquire of her as to why."

Mother Vajpai sighed. I watched Samma carefully out of the corner of my eye. If they were playing with me, she would betray the game. And my old lover did look nervous. She flexed her hands, as she always did before a sparring match.

So this is how it is to be.

Still, I could not bring myself to strike first.

Mother Vajpai began to speak again, but I interrupted her. "It is time for me to leave. I have soldiers waiting." Let her wonder about *that*. Lily Blades were famously fierce fighters, but we were never expected to stand against men-at-arms in battle formation. That training for us would have been too much for the Street Guild and the other swordsmen of Kalimpura to stomach.

"This is the will of the Lily Goddess, Green," Mother Vajpai said sternly. Her tone of voice struck deep in me. Had I been raised from birth within the Temple of the Silver Lily, as Samma was, and most of the other Blade aspirants were, it might have disarmed me as readily as a spin-kick to the side of the knee.

As it was, she just renewed my anger. My hand brushed my abdomen. "I know what happens to children there, Mother. I know what happened to *me*."

"Copper Downs happened to you," snapped Mother Vajpai. Her eyes widened as she grasped the significance of my touch. "Ah . . . Do not bring a child into the world here."

"Now we know—" Samma began, but Mother Vajpai hushed her with an urgent hand motion.

Now we know what?

Now we know it is time to leave, before more of this game is given away.

It was a mistake to have met privately with them. I could only give thanks to the Lily Goddess that they did not have Mother Argai or another experienced Blade in here. These two I might be able to escape, though I could not hope to best them.

I should not have been surprised at such a betrayal from Mother Vajpai, but Samma . . .

With that thought, I turned toward the door.

"Green." The commanding voice again, shifting slightly as she moved. "The Lily Goddess commands this."

I feinted toward the door's latch, saying, "The Lily Goddess . . ." But I was already in motion. A swift spin on my right heel, half a step, a three-fingered jab to Samma's abdomen to bring her to her knees for a crucial moment.

Mother Vajpai had taken the bait. She crashed into the door I'd just been touching, then came off it again with that preternatural speed I'd always respected and feared in her. By then I was up on the window ledge, swinging a cast-iron lamp base at the mullioned glass. I followed it through in a squeeze so tight the jagged edges tore my robes. My bundle of leathers and belled silk flew free, while the short knives I had tucked within bounced into a bed of peonies just below the window.

I jumped after them even as Samma began to shriek.

Mother Vajpai was quicker, and could either see through walls or knew me *very* well. Possibly both. She was already in a leaping kick when she cleared the window casing, trailing shards of glass in a glittering fog. I stood to meet her—no time to reach the long knife at my thigh—and took her lead foot in my shoulder instead of my neck or chest.

That spun me around with a crack that sounded like a broken bone. I rolled into a cartwheel and came to my feet on the graveled path beyond the peonies. Mother Vajpai was after me again, this time with *my* long knife in her hands. I had not even seen her draw it from my scabbard. And I'd never fought her without rules.

No rules?

I stepped into the sweep of the blade, let it score my left biceps, and slammed my head into the hollow at the base of her throat. Then I bit her, digging my teeth in over the pulsing artery.

She had the wrong knife now. One of the short knives she could have reversed, and simply stabbed me. Instead Mother Vajpai was forced to club my left shoulder from behind with the hilt. I felt her blood bloom hot and salty in my mouth and my fingers scrabbled at her short hair, trying to force her head back.

"Halt!" shouted someone in Petraean. The unmistakable hiss of a crossbow bolt narrowly passed us by.

As if we were sparring she slapped me out. The long knife thudded to the gravel path. Mother Vajpai moved swiftly back three strides, pressing a hand tight over her wounded neck. The spaces where her fingers met were marked with carmine lines like claws.

I nodded to her—the courtesy of the training room was not easily broken, even now—and spun to see Kohlmann standing on the path with a crossbow in his hand. He already had it recocked. Where had he gotten the thing? By the Wheel, the man was both fast *and* strong. I marked that against future need. The Prince's guards were spread out behind him with weapons drawn, while the protocol master looked to be at mortal risk of apoplexy.

Samma stumbled out of the house behind them, her face sick with what might have been regret. Or perhaps just nausea, given where I'd kicked her.

"I believe I am ready to depart," I told Kohlmann in my most even voice.

The guards looked to the protocol master—*not* to Mother Vajpai, I noticed—who nodded wearily. I turned back to face my old teacher. The vicious glint in her eye nearly sent me away without speaking, but I could not just let loose of this.

"Had you asked me as an equal," I said softly, "you might have heard a different answer."

Her reply came as I reached for my scattered knives, abandoned leathers, and belled silk, voice pitched so soft and low that only I could hear it. "I am sorry."

Walking away from her, Kohlmann kept his body between me and the house. Looking past him, I saw why. The Bittern Court woman—no, *Surali*. Surali stood in the doorway with an expression that could have curdled kava.

She was the key to this drama. What threat had the Bittern Court held over the Temple of the Silver Lily to force all that must have unfolded?

Moot now. I could not afford to care. Not even bothering to meet Samma's eye, I walked down the path with Kohlmann.

"They will not shoot us down," he said.

That did not deserve any answer whatsoever, so I gave it none. As we passed the gate, he fired the crossbow's next bolt into the trees, then handed the empty weapon to the peacock-guard. Mother Argai gave me a strange look indeed, one that after a moment I deciphered as grudging respect.

"Green," Kohlmann said as we walked easily back down Ríchard Avenue. By the goddess, this man was a coolheaded one. "We must speak of this as soon as possible. You very nearly launched a war back there."

"Councilor," I began as we turned the corner onto Knightspark Street. Out of sight of Mother Argai, I put every ounce of my strength into running. I let the pains in my back and the open wound in my arm and the ache in my shoulder and roiling of the baby and the dissolution of my stomach all pour into the pavement, feet slamming one after the other as the loosened silk jingled. He shouted once, but did not give chase.

I did not care. All I wanted was to be free for a while. Even Below would have been too limiting. So I *ran*. I ran as if the wind were at my heels. I ran as if I *were* the wind. I ran as if my very life depended on it, though blood slicked and stinging, my arms and my back threatened to collapse like poorly handled soufflé.

I ran until I was sick and I ran some more, crossing what seemed like half the city and back again until in my turnings I reached the Temple of Endurance.

The temple was under construction on the grounds of the old minehead in the Velviere District. I'd run so hard and unthinking I'd spiraled around it twice before stopping at the modest gate that had been knocked into the ancient boundary wall. The minehead had originally been walled off without any entrance at all, in order to permanently block the site from the fine homes and buildings surrounding it. I knew the location, but when I'd left Copper Downs, they were still arguing over the size of the hole.

What I saw now as I panted out the hard knot in my gut was a pair of green lacquered pillars standing against the old stone of the protective wall, topped by a crossbar that looked more Hanchu than anything to me. Between the pillars tall oaken doors stood open. Wide enough to drive an oxcart through, I realized.

An older man—not Selistani—in an undyed linen robe of a simple cut sat on a chair before the gate, a walking stick across his lap. He looked at me incuriously as I stood bent with hands on my knees, gasping. My lungs burned as the air puffed away from me in thin, white shreds.

Finally I found my breath, straightened, and approached him.

"Been in a fight, have yer?"

I grimaced. "A master of the understatement, I see. Please, I seek admittance."

"Temple's open." He didn't shift his position or lay his stick aside. I could have stepped around the man easily enough, but this had the feel of a test.

"The temple is open, but I have not been invited to enter."

A smile dawned upon his face. "Now, that is a different matter."

"I am Green," I told him. "Summoned by the god."

"A silent god has spoken to you." His words were flat but his eyes twinkled.

I'd already had this stupid argument, with Chowdry, and I knew the secret answer. "Endurance is mute, not silent." I leaned closer. "Besides, *he was* my *ox*!"

The old man spun his staff so close to my face he might have taken a tooth out, then rose from his cane chair. "We know who you are, Mother Green. We are glad of your return." A swift, mocking bow. "Welcome, and bid fair to enter."

I walked past him a couple of strides, then turned. The man was gone, only his chair remaining. Stepping back, I ran my fingers across the fraying cane. Cool, and still beaded with the morning's frost now dripping to water.

Another one of this city's avatars, or possibly a ghost. Building a temple atop a minehead, when the local tulpas haunted the dangerous galleries and tunnels of Below, had not been the wisest judgment ever made. I tried to remember if this had been my idea.

Somehow I had the feeling that it was.

The last time I'd passed this way, the area within the walls had been a forest of brambles and broken machinery. Those were difficult days indeed. Now the lot was cleared. A low fence stood around the open shaft, apparently to keep people from wandering into it and breaking their necks. Though there was a ladder below, it would be a long, fatal fall for the inattentive or unlucky. Oddly, Chowdry and his acolytes had not blocked or guarded the opening, as I might have done in their place.

Most of the metalwork and timber baulks about the property had been taken down or hauled away. A hasty wooden structure about two rods square obviously serving as a temporary temple stood to the south of the shaft, while foundation stones and colored posts laid around the shaft showed where a more ambitious structure would someday rise.

The small building was set on piers, raised far enough above the ground that three steps led to the porch. Chowdry sat there with hands folded, watching my approach. Several faces peered from within.

"You have come," he called in Seliu.

"I am here."

"Would you like aid with those wounds?"

I staggered forward and sat beside him, my loosened bundle of belongings slipping to the ground. The time was not yet right for me to enter the god's sanctuary. Though I served the Lily Goddess, Endurance was my god in the most literal sense. I still wasn't prepared to face him just then.

"The blood on my mouth is not my own," I said. "But if someone can see to my arm, I'd be obliged. Everything else will heal. Oh, and you had an avatar at the gate when I came in. Saucy old bastard."

"You are being as a lamp to moths for the spirits of this place." Then, in Petraean, over his shoulder, "Fetch Sister Gammage out here, with her needles and bandages."

Chowdry held my hand as Sister Gammage—an older Stone Coast

woman with a squint and not very many teeth, but a steady hand with a needle—cleaned and sewed my arm. I could almost forgive Chowdry for Little Baji being in the city, but was not prepared to ask the questions that rose from that unfortunate business.

After they were done I allowed myself to be led to a large tent among a stand of them behind the temple where hot water was being poured into an enormous copper bath. Chowdry brought my silk and leathers before excusing himself. Sister Gammage chased everyone else away, persuaded me to give up my knives for a little while, stripped my damaged robe from me, and helped me slip into the water. Once there she brought me a flowered tea I did not recognize—which is saying something, given my early training—and left me to soak in peace.

Soak I did until I slept. The water was so hot my muscles did not knot.

I rested two days in another tent, in truth sulking while people chattered, laughed, and labored outside. Sister Gammage or Chowdry brought me lentils and watered milk, for the baby. My gut would suddenly tolerate nothing else. Where had these food sicknesses come from?

Also at my request I'd been provided with boys' clothing. The robe was a silly idea, proven pointless. I refused to return to the leathers, was all but ready to be shut of them completely; so brown corduroy breeches, canvas shirt, low sturdy workboots, and wide, flat cap seemed far more practical. There was even a quilted cotton jacket adequate at least to the autumn chill. I could run roofs, tumble through dirt, and, best of all, attract no attention whatsoever while dressed as an everyday youth of this city.

Well, except for my dark skin and the slashed scars upon my cheeks, but one thing at a time. Perhaps some profession here wore masks or veils I could adopt without causing comment. Beekeepers? Temple virgins?

In the meantime, I hid my leathers and my good fighting boots in a bundle beneath a pile of stones between the tent complex and the wall. I wrapped them carefully in waxed linen, then tent canvas, and scattered herbs within the folds to keep off the molder. I did not know how long I might need the Blade costume to wait in secret for me, but it required care much as anyone or anything else might.

Best of all, no one bothered me. Whoever was looking for me—the Interim Council, the Kalimpuri embassy—Chowdry and his people were having none of it. I had not yet been to see the ox god, but I was certainly under his protection. Much as I had been as a small child, and likewise down the years since.

This situation was not so restful as being at Ilona's cottage had proven, but it was peace enough to be worth my while. Still, I knew events moved in the city. The ghost Erio had been worried about what might happen here soon. Regardless of my usual opinion of the ancient dead, that one had been lucid, focused, and afraid of *something*.

Mostly the baby needed me to rest. I tried to keep relatively still and calm, let my back ease up, my shoulder heal, all my bruises fade, and the stitches on my arm be reduced from weeping pink fluid to a horrid scratching that smelled faintly of the gin that Sister Gammage splashed on the wound every few hours.

Gin and hot baths, they seemed to be the entirety of her book of healing. Well, that and stitches. Definitely my kind of woman.

On my third morning, the lentils did not satisfy, and my own laziness was beginning to irritate me. When restfulness became a problem, it was no longer a solution, as the Lily Blades liked to say. I rose, gathered my belled silk and adjusted my boy's clothing, then headed out to find better fare. I needed to be well-fed before I could square accounts with my ox god. The baby did not seem to mind, and my appetite was drawn to the crackling smell of sausages on a fire nearby.

"Mother Green!" said a cheerful young man who looked Selistani and sounded Stone Coast. He appeared vaguely familiar—one of the drawers of water for my bath two days ago? He also held a large, flat pan covered with the sizzling meat.

"I am no one's mother," I snapped. *Not true, of course.* And it was better than "Lady Green." "But I have a mother of a hunger."

"Take a place." He pointed to a long wide wooden table under a thin canvas roof where a dozen young people, mixed Selistani and Petraean, sat wearing undyed linen robes, chattering happily as they ate their way through scrambled eggs, sausage, and chunks of brown bread.

This was so utterly unlike the refectory at the Temple of the Silver Lily that I had to gawk a moment. All the aspirants there had lived with intense discipline, not just the Blades. Here the atmosphere was more that of a fair, or a camp. Children playing at ritual for a lark, not serious acolytes. Not at all like my poor Septio had been, either.

I shook off my mood and laughed. "Sit? No. *You* sit!" I gently shoved him aside from his pan and took over the cooking. They had a decent selection of spices, and I called for cheese and white wine to enrich the eggs. If only I could have remade the bread. . . .

A hot stove in front of me, a pan in my hands—these things much improved my spirit. Cooking absorbed my energy and calmed my spirit awhile. I fed Endurance's young acolytes until I could resist the smell no more, then loaded my own crockery plate and found a place among them while the boy resumed cooking, somewhat educated and chastened both.

I ate so much that eventually most of the acolytes stopped talking and watched me shovel food in. The baby seemed happy, and so did my stomach. I would not waste the opportunity.

Finally I pushed aside my fifth serving. The young cook began to clap. After an embarrassed moment, the rest of them did so, too. There was nothing for it but to rise and take my bow. At least I was properly fed. "I have been called before the god," I told them, and headed off through the tents toward the small wooden temple.

As I walked past the foundation markers of Chowdry's larger ambitions— for I was sure Endurance did not so much care about his temple—I realized what my friend the priest had meant about the god calling him. Two days I'd lain in my tent, but when it was time to rise and go forth, I had risen and gone forth unquestioningly.

I stopped at the front, still not quite ready to mount the steps. The facade was a very plain, rough-ripped wood framed up competently enough. The interior would be cold in winter, for there was no chinking between the planks, and I did not think they had placed anything behind it. I wondered if Chowdry planned to lay a course of bricks or daub-and-wattle over the exposed wood.

"Enough," I said aloud as I slipped my cloak of bells over my shoulder. How else to approach the ox that had carried my grandmother to her funeral at the beginning of my days? I had nothing to be afraid of.

Did I?

That answer came to me as I mounted the steps: Endurance had been Papa's ox. Not mine. Somehow I was returning to the presence of my father, who'd sold me as a girl, and must have died long since of whatever rotting of the mind had already claimed him when I'd found him once more these four years past.

The image of Shar, his second wife, sprang unbidden to my mind. So ragged, so afraid of me.

With that thought, I passed within, the music of my birthplace jingling with each stride. The doorway was obscured by a curtain of beads. The room beyond could have held thirty or forty close-packed worshippers at most, and smelled of incense and people's feet. This was the whole of it—there was no space for priestly chambers or tiring rooms or secret dungeons. A life-sized marble statue of an ox kneeling on the ground occupied the far end, opposite the door. Straw scattered about the ox and the rough beams over my head finally cued me to the nature of this temple.

It was a *stable*.

Endurance's followers had put him in a stable.

I had to laugh at that as I approached the statue. Back in the half-remembered days of my youth, Endurance had lived outside. By the time of my ill-fated visit four years ago, someone had built the ox a small hut to shelter in. But a stable?

Ribbons had been tied to the ox horns. Some had slips of paper dangling from them, others curls of ash. I leaned forward and turned a scrap in my hands.

help aunt jem for her crab disese

Prayers, then. Given most directly to the god. Some sped on their way with a little offering of flame. Narrow, long trays of sand held dozens of burnt incense sticks just below the statue's nose. That struck me as a bit odd—I did not think that Copper Downs worshipped so. This *was* a Selistani god. Plates of fruit and dried-up bread were scattered among the incense holders, around the god's knees.

I settled into a comfortable tailor's seat. The belled silk gathered around my thighs and flowed to the floor at my back. In this place I did not even have my short knives, but Endurance was not the Lily Goddess. My offerings to him were drawn neither from strength nor violence.

This god I had seen in direct manifestation, the day we had brought down Choybalsan and poor Federo. I *knew* Endurance. He had risen unbidden from my own memories to take form in a numinous moment of theogeny.

Closing my eyes, I leaned forward until the top of my head rested against the nose of the ox. I let the smell of incense and feet—and this close to the fane, rotting fruit—wash around me.

The heat came first. Those halcyon days of my earliest youth, when the sunlight was a hammer to smash flat anyone's ambitions. I felt it pass through me like fire through a hay barn.

I strained for the smells that went with that heat. Scorched air. The dank water of the rice paddies. Clay banks at the edges. Plantains and bougainvillea. Ox dung. My father's musky sweat.

When I found those I began to weep. Pinarjee, Shar had said his name was Pinarjee, but my father had sold me away, sold away my name and turned his face from me. He'd never even told his second wife of my existence.

A shadow fell upon me. Once again I was small enough to fit beneath the standing ox. The white hair of his flanks met in a troubled gray line like a storm cloud down the center of his belly. I could have reached up and grasped onto it as monkey infants cling to their mother's fur.

I let the shade protect me from the heat. I let the ox's earthworn smell protect me from the memories of my father. His solid presence shielded me from all that had passed before and all that was yet to come. Surely he saw better than I, but Endurance did not warn me of the future. Looking back now after all that happened, I suppose I would not have turned away even if he had.

In time—short or long, I could not say—a sense of need began to fill me. Not my need, for I was safe and happy returned for a little while to the last carefree days of my life. The god's need. The calling that had descended first upon Chowdry, then me.

Without words I knew I was Endurance's champion. The god was not jealous of my oaths to the Lily Goddess across the Storm Sea. They simply did not signify to him here in this place. He had warded me, and I would ward him.

"From what?" I asked, the words escaping my lips.

The tropical sun blazed even hotter, fire in the sky fit to blister my skin.

From what comes, I thought. No, Endurance thought, and gave the idea to me.

I knew enough of gods to understand that their lot was not easy. Neither was my own.

The shade of his belly grew cooler, deeper. Though the world around me threatened to catch fire, I was safe. For now.

"So you ward me yet."

With those words, I opened my eyes. The silk was heavy on my shoulders. Smoke curled before me. All the prayers had been blackened to ash. The fruit on the plates was desiccated, the breads curled and hard. Even the incense sticks had been reduced to worm-gnawed dust, already collapsing. Time had been stolen from around me to feed the vision I had just been granted.

"You wanted me back in Copper Downs," I told the statue of the god. Rising, I rubbed his forehead for luck, right between the horns. "I suppose you have me. Whatever it is you fear."

Thoughtful now, I doffed the belled silk, carefully folded it, and placed the tinkling bundle between the ox statue's forelegs. My inheritance would be more safe here with Endurance than under my own arms in the days to come, and I had missed sewing the bells before. Always, I caught up. Besides, this would be another binding between me and the ox god.

When I walked back outside, the young acolytes were gathered before the entrance. Many carried their tools of construction or survey, so for a brief moment I thought I saw a mob. Then I realized that no, they simply awaited me.

"I have prayed to the god," I said.

"We know," replied the grinning young man who had served me sausage. His expression was serious now, though the humor never seemed far from him.

I realized that my face itched. When I touched my scarred left cheek, my finger came away bloodied.

A while later I sat at the now-empty eating tables with the young man, whose name proved to be Ponce. He served as a factotum to Chowdry in the management of the temple building project. Ponce's enthusiasm for the work of Endurance bubbled, even as a light, gusty rain pattered off the canvas stretched above us and quested in from the open sides.

"How does this god call to you?" I was quite curious. My own connection to the god was clear enough, but also deeply personal. Uniquely so.

"Endurance is, well, new." A seriousness flashed across his face. "More concerned with peace, or a calm center, than most gods. Here in Copper Downs we have a god for fishermen and a god for death and a god for women and a god for the rules of fate. The Temple Quarter is like a market full of stalls. Each sells some shade or scent of prayer, some form of protection or enlightenment or passion or redemption. Endurance just . . . exists. His purpose is a gentle wholeness."

"There is something to the muteness, is there not?"

"Exactly! You understand." Then his cheeks flushed, that red which only Stone Coasters can find in their embarrassment. "Of course you would understand. You birthed the god."

My hand touched my belly. All the morning's food lay heavy upon me, but not hard, and the baby still didn't seem to mind. "I birthed nothing," I told him. "At most I was midwife. Endurance is a vessel for a much older power that needed a place of safety to abide."

The long-lost heart of the pardines, stolen by the late, immortal Duke, released by me to settle into Federo and twist him beyond recognition, then once more released by me into the god Endurance. From forest to field, by way of the stone streets of Copper Downs.

I prayed in that moment that I should never have to touch such power again. Another contact would twist me more than it already had, and I did not want to think of the effect on my child. Would that my prayer had been granted.

Finally Ponce spoke again. "Endurance is peaceful. The city needs peace. Some of my Selistani brothers and sisters see the god differently, but for those of us from Copper Downs, that is enough."

"A god who does not demand so much," I said absently.

"Oh, no. Endurance demands everything."

After that, I went to help them with their foundations.

Chowdry remained absent through the morning, as did anyone else more senior than Ponce. I wondered what they might be about, but did not trouble myself too much. Instead I helped measure foundation courses around the hole of the mine opening, and even took my shift wielding a spade to turn what earth could be turned until someone with stouter tools and longer arms was available to break the rock beneath.

I wondered what the plan was for the permanent temple. I hadn't the heart to tell Ponce how misplaced their stable-altar was. Endurance had been a creature of open fields and sunny skies, not confined to a dank, straw-floored enclosure. Surely Chowdry knew the truth.

But then, here in Copper Downs, maybe they understood a stable better than they understood a rice paddy. This cold, meager northern sun encouraged no one to remain outdoors overlong.

To each people their own meanings.

As I levered some good-sized stones away, Ponce approached me. A black-robed lad followed, younger than me, with a badly shaven scalp and a look of incipient panic about him.

I paused from my labors, holding my mattock tight in lieu of a real weapon. It could smash a skull better than my bare fist. "Greetings again."

"This boy is Nunzio," Ponce said with little of his usual good humor. "He is from the Algeficic Temple."

That gave me pause. My baby's father had been a priest of that temple and its patron, Blackblood. I did not want my daughter anywhere near the pain god.

Nunzio refused to meet my eye. Instead he seemed to find his own feet very interesting. Still, he blurted out his message. "Y-your p-presence is requ-quested at the temple."

"By whom?" I asked, amazed. "I killed off most of your priesthood myself. Surely the survivors have no use for me now." The late Pater Primus, Stefan Mohanda, had nearly done for me. In both of his roles, as Blackblood's high priest and as a member of the Interim Council. Though I did not resent the pain god personally, I had no love for his people. I was forced to concentrate on not slapping the mattock against my free hand. This poor acolyte could see that as nothing but a threat.

And rightly so.

Ponce paled at my words, but said nothing. Nunzio made a visible effort not to run away. "They—he—it wishes to speak to you." He quailed. "By name."

I almost refused him then and there. Little good could arise from such a visit, while I could imagine a number of disasters ranging from priestly vengeance to a renewal of the erratic attentions of a rather dangerous god. Blackblood took up pain from his male followers and their sons by way of sacrifice. In return, he prepared them for an easier path to the halls of the dead. I recalled what Septio had told me about how the god's priesthood was recruited—from those suffering boys and men not yet worthy to be taken up.

What had befallen Nunzio that he served as an acolyte of this most difficult of gods at such a young age? I could almost pity this boy.

To my surprise, I found that I did.

"Return to your temple." My voice was gentle. "I will be along in time. Your duty is faithfully discharged."

After Blackblood's acolyte left, Ponce looked at me with a clearly unaccustomed seriousness. "He is not the only one to have called here searching for you."

Curious, I asked, "Why did you let him find me, and not others?"

"Chowdry left instructions as to who could see you, and who could not. The Interim Council has sent messengers, and once Councilor Kohlmann in person. We have said we do not know where you are." His grin returned. "Which was true. You might have been sleeping, or bathing, or eating. How did I know, from out front? Likewise, several Selistani have been asking after you."

I wondered how they kept my countrymen among the acolytes from speaking to Surali and the embassy. That, I decided, was the god's problem. It would only become mine at need. In any case, these young people seemed frightened of me, or at least my reputation.

"But you were to admit the servants of another god?"

Ponce shook his head. "Not as such. I asked Endurance for guidance."

Since my experience in the temple this morning with the ox god's wordless will, I could better understand how Chowdry and this young man were so willing and able to take direction from their mute deity. "I would visit Blackblood soon, I think." It seemed the right path now, and action was better than hiding in this temple. "The visit will be better made in full daylight. Will Chowdry return this morning?"

The young man shrugged. "I should depart whenever I was ready, were I you."

"Yes. I will."

He paused, something else clearly on his mind. "A worry, for you, if you please, Mother Green."

"Just Green," I said firmly, my free hand straying to my belly.

"It is long past now, but there have been . . . attacks . . . in the Temple Quarter."

That seemed almost silly. "I am hardly concerned about street thugs."

"Not on women. On their gods." He withdrew from my attitude. Later I regretted that I had spoken so dismissively, for I might have learned more sooner.

Dressed as a boy, I went forth, keeping my chin tucked down and my hat tilted forward. The Street of Horizons was familiar enough. Odd, clever architecture and a sense of vanishing perspective. Whatever long-dead architect had first laid out the Temple Quarter had been inspired, at the least.

The area was busy, though with a liveliness that took me some time to unravel. The great iron pots that lined the street were in better repair than on my last visit here. People seemed to throng rather than scurry. Choybalsan's fall had lent renewed, healthy energy to this place that had been little more than an open-air tomb during the days of the Duke.

Gods had not been so popular in a city ruled by an immortal with stolen magic.

Yet there was a tension in the air. Not the furtiveness of the old days. More like nervousness. As if a thousand people on the street at once could be mugged together. Ponce had mentioned attacks, but on the gods themselves? Who would dare? Who *could* dare?

It was a staggering thought, even to one such as I, who had brought down a god on the streets of this very city.

In any event, something poisoned the air just enough for discomfort, like water from a well in which a dog has drowned long ago. The city worried, through the collective fears of its people.

The Algeficic Temple was familiar as ever. Faced in black tile, its tall metal doors were still bent where the god's avatar Skinless had forced them closed, trapping the last of Blackblood's previous generation of scheming priests within. Clearly they had been opened since, but not repaired. On the right rose a very old building, blocky and tan fronted by squat pillars. On the left, a white stucco temple topped with a gold-colored pediment. Though I knew the names and histories of most of the gods here, much as with the families of wealth and power, I did not know their houses.

Even while I worried a bit about how Blackblood's renewed priesthood would welcome me, this was not a day for skulking caution. I had been bidden, I was arrived.

I marched up the uncomfortable steps and pushed into the darkness beyond.

The hall within was as silent and dusty as I remembered, though there seemed to be new stains on the floor besides the ones I'd caused on my last pass through this place. Perhaps a crisis of succession, argued in the most pointed manner? Dark banners still hung from the clerestory thirty feet above. The mercury pool quivered in the center of the space. A living scrying mirror, though such things had never spoken to me.

I had slain here, and nearly been slain myself. Death and healing, and the touch of Skinless, that horrific avatar of the pain god, had all taken place in this hall.

Five men in familiar dark robes stepped out of the shadows toward me. Each wore a woven leather mask. *Ambush!* I thought, and palmed one of my short knives. Then the priest at the center raised his hands cautiously.

"Please, Mistress Green, we beg you not to strike us down."

Straightening from the fighting crouch into which I'd dropped unthinking, I declared loudly, "I intend to strike no one. And come only at invitation." I couldn't stop myself from adding, "I believe I have meddled enough already in your priestly affairs. Don't you?"

From the way their robes shuffled and their masks were cast down, these priests did not find my little joke to be so funny.

"The god has spoken for you," the leader continued. "I am Pater Primus." At the expression that crossed my face, he swiftly amended himself. "The *new* Pater Primus. It is as much a title as a name."

"An ill-favored title, if you ask me," I grumbled, but I understood that I was being graceless. This awkward banter covered a bad case of nerves on both our parts.

"As may b-be." The priest turned to his fellows. "She is exempt from our practices."

"We will not challenge," muttered one of them.

"And I will not challenge you," I replied. "But where shall I approach the god? I have been down in his basements before, and do not long for another visit."

"Best you stand before our altar at the back of this hall."

"I will not be taken up," I warned him.

The Pater Primus' voice was pained. "No one here would be foolish enough to try to make a sacrifice of you, Mistress."

Not now, at any rate.

I took that as all the permission I needed, and pushed past them toward the god's fane.

Much of my prior experience here had been confused or worse. I'd passed through this temple twice, for different reasons, but never by simply walking in the front door and looking around. Once through the basements and once by dropping in from the roof. As I walked among the narrow pillars toward the recessed sanctuary at the back of the great hall, I wondered what kind of god abided without worshippers. There were no benches or pews, no prayer rugs, no stalls.

Just empty, silent space draped in deepest shadow.

Except, of course, Blackblood was a pain god. He had worshippers everywhere, in every moment. He didn't need them to gather together and sing praises.

At the rear of the great hall three doorways granted access to the altar in the next room. I had no notion of the ritual use of each, and the priests were so frightened of me that there seemed little point in asking them. I strode through the central door and stood before the altar.

In a room of grave dust and death shadows, a slab of black marble drank up what little light there was. A table, really, made of a stony darkness. Here the suffering was taken up from the most desperate of Blackblood's appellants. Behind the table rose a carved wooden screen that appeared to be ebony, as best I could judge. Above them both loomed an empty throne with shackles at the arms and pediment, as if to bind the god close. Restraint in devotion?

For the first time, it occurred to me to wonder what price the pain god paid for his role in the lives of his followers. Did taking the pain up cost him pain of his own? Was that sort of balance required of all gods? The Lily Goddess had been worshipped through prayer, song, observance—all the trappings of a service—but mostly through the dedication of the lives of hundreds of women. Blackblood was worshipped through the dedication of the suffering of boys and men.

Women were not so welcome in this temple. Not even me.

"I am here." My voice fell flat, curiously without echo. The darkness seemed ready to grow teeth and devour me. I stood firm. "You asked and I came. Do not expect such consideration routinely."

Something large and invisible moved nearby. Skinless, I devoutly hoped. The avatar in its dim way had proven to count me as a friend. Were it some other servant of the god, I would have to give in to the gibbering fear that did not threaten me at all. Not one bit.

"There are no women like you." The voice was smooth and rich as heartsblood.

The god was upon his seat, had always been there, I realized, only my poor eyes had failed to see him before this moment. Where the manifestation I'd last witnessed had been a pudgy child on the point of petulance, now Blackblood appeared as a languid youth. Dissolute, louche, dangerous in his detached passions. Even so, power shone through. The chains that bound him to the chair did not seem fit to hold him back.

Still, I faced him. It was not courage I summoned, but foolishness, and the worn edge of familiarity. My words were brave, nonetheless—always that has been my strength and downfall. "Whereas gods such as you might be found in every city of the world."

"You have no concept." The hopeless despair of centuries threatened in his tone.

I peered closely at his face. Blackblood's expression seemed a study in indifference. At the least, I had expected the god to be angry with me, given my dealings with his late priesthood.

"There are many things I have no concept of," I told him. I was much better at arguing than at obeisance. "You surprise me." Nohow would I call him lord. "I might have thought to meet more anger from you."

"If I were capable of gratitude, I might have shown you that." His face remained eerily slack.

I spoke with a puppet, I realized. The body before me was not Blackblood, any more than the statue of the ox was Endurance. I knew what it was to be close to a god. Standing before divine regard was like standing before a racing tide. It was possible—with luck, strength, and some good bracing. But the struggle was never simple, and always bordered on the fatally overwhelming.

"What keeps your attention from me?" I asked, going on the attack.

This time Blackblood's focus did sweep to me, and I regretted the question. Those eyes opened wide, to become dark, swirling pools. That languid face transformed into a cruel, predatory leer. Weeping sores and suppurating wounds chased themselves across his body like roaches in a filthy kitchen.

When he spoke again, his voice was the hollow, rust-showered tolling of neglected iron bells. "You bear my child."

Calling on both the Lily Goddess and Endurance, I braced myself from dropping to my knees. His aspect was unfolding to push me down. Still, I continued to pretend to bravery. "So you have claimed."

"You will bear me a son, and he will be presented unto me."

"*No!*" I shouted, unthinking. "My daughter will not be stolen away."

His next words echoed like a dropped iron kettle. "You will have no choice." The laughter that followed threatened to flense me.

I faced him with murder in my eye. No one threatened to steal my baby. No one, in no way, ever. I might not be able to stop the child selling in Kalimpura, but by all the gods I could keep it from starting here in Copper Downs. Looking back, I realize now how blind I was to what was so clearly to come. Only my youth and my anger can excuse the foolishness that came next.

"I will not pimp my own daughter for you," I screamed into the continuing storm of his laughter. Then I was alone in the little room.

That utter *bastard* of a god. He had all but threatened me. Skinless might be a friend of sorts, if I were lucky, but his master had just set a course that promised ill will between us. I wished Blackblood every plague the divine could endure, then stalked back through the temple. The new Pater Primus stood near the scrying pool, but retreated after one glance in my direction.

It was nice to have *someone's* respect.

Blinking back tears of rage, I returned to the street. I was sick of sunlight and people and crowds and simply being *looked* at. I heartily desired to head to the quiet of Below. That was a place of dubious safety, but the threats there were ancient and indifferent to me personally. Even Below, I could not hope to evade Skinless, but at least the human servants of Blackblood would be hard-pressed to follow me there.

I sought out an entry point. The Prince of the City's embassy could not reach me there. Neither could the Interim Council. All I had to worry about were the ghosts and avatars that always haunted the lower reaches of this city.

Once I was safely out of the cold sunlight amid the dank stone and moldering air of Below, I found my mind settling. Blackblood could *not* take my child. Though I was certain she was a daughter, that did not matter. Boy or girl, the baby was mine. I had been afraid of returning to Kalimpura for the sake of not losing her, but now Copper Downs might prove as unsafe.

One stolen childhood in a lifetime was enough for me.

This mixture of sewers and tunnels and mines older than the city slumped in the open air above were as familiar to me as my own hands. At least, my usual paths were. I seriously doubted anyone had a true idea of the extents of Below. Copper Downs was thoroughly undermined as any anthill, saved from collapse into a great, deep hole only by the solidity of the bedrock and the dubious wisdom of engineering down the centuries. Millennia, rather.

The sewers were the easiest to comprehend. Tunnels shored by bricked or stone archways, inspection walks, ladders up and down. But they cross-connected with private diggings, some of which were ritualistic—I knew of an entire labyrinth, not so far from the Dockmarket, only a few rods beneath the streets. Others were smugglers' hideaways, or underground warrens from different ages of the city when the surface was more dangerous. Ossuaries, cold storage, prison cells; every manner of use one could think of for windowless, cool spaces.

Around and beneath the diggings were the mines, far more ancient than the city to which they lent their name. Played out, so far as anyone knew. Certainly there were no headings bringing out metal for the markets, and the ruins of the Ore Docks were barely identifiable just east of the current boundaries of the city, they were so old. Some of those galleries were strangely smooth, as if carved by the rush of waters. Others featured frenetic details that bespoke lifetimes of craftsmanship beneath the skin of the world. Caryatid pillars, battle scenes stretching for a quarter mile, footprints chiseled into floors to mark out the steps of a complex pavane for two dozen dancers who had probably never trod a single measure in the deep dark.

All these wonders, and far more that I'd likely never see. Each haunted by furtive figures and angry ghosts and the tulpas that seemed to compose the city's literal and spiritual undermind. The place had an aesthetic and an etiquette of its own, one hard-learned by me over careful months and years. During my time in the Factor's house, the Dancing Mistress had used Below as my primary training ground for subverting my transformation into a great lady of the courts of Copper Downs.

Here amid the endless shadows and the strange creatures that haunted the dreams of the city, she had taught me to run, to fight, to leap into the void, how to land, how to climb, how to *survive*. My time down here had prepared me to encounter the Lily Blades of Kalimpura without being cut to ribbons at the first. My time down here had readied me for so much. Even my earliest killings, of Mistress Tirelle, and the ancient, ageless Duke of Copper Downs.

So now I walked past timeless carvings of demon-haunted men and humans with demonic faces. Pillars; raw rock walls; long, gleaming forests of slime; strange little creeks that reeked of elements I could not name; skeletons in armor frosted with mold and fungi; great, damp footprints longer than the height of my waist.

Below. It was home, of a sort. And for the first time in a long while, I found myself willing to contemplate leaving Copper Downs for good. Most likely I should have stayed in the High Hills. I could tend graves as well—or poorly—as anyone. The unquiet dead were merely that. Unquiet, not dangerous. Even Erio with his strong opinions and ready words was not so difficult to bear. And none of them would try to take my baby.

I ranged quietly through Below, carrying a swath of coldfire as I made progress toward the minehead and the site of Endurance's temple. The cold, oil-and-rust smell of ancient machines was strong, as it always was near that point. I'd never found enough light down here to properly judge what I sensed around me. Old stone and older pathways sweated their long, slow memories. These places were far more ancient than the city above, extending back through time as deep as the abandoned galleries of the copper mines that wound beneath my feet.

In any case, Below comforted me; pattering bodiless footsteps and all. This was the heart of Copper Downs. Blackblood or no, this city was as much my home as Kalimpura ever would be. All I needed to do was find some way to unseat the embassy, and deter Surali with her prideful anger.

If I killed *her*, that would solve some of my problems. The Death Right case would be complex and expensive back in Kalimpura, at meaningful risk to my own neck. But if I never returned, well, I did not care much, did I?

Getting past Mother Vajpai and Mother Argai to reach Surali would be a trick. I wondered how thoroughly Samma had betrayed me. To trust her now was foolish.

No matter, I thought as I approached the central gallery of the minehead. I would just—

Then Skinless was before me.

Imagine a man almost a rod tall, completely flayed. The muscles and tendons of its widespread arms gleamed in the faint light of the coldfire. As always, it just barely sweated blood, slick, crimson sheets covering its body. Its great round eyes rolled amid their pads of fat, glistening.

"Hello," I said to this sending of my unfriend.

Skinless nodded. I saw a hard light in its expression.

"Is it your god's will that I be returned to his temple?" I asked.

The avatar nodded again. I thought perhaps I saw slow regret. Those great fists, each larger than a ham, opened and closed very deliberately.

I reached for the right words. This creature had carried me through the streets when I was wounded, had tended me awhile. We had a bond, I *knew* it, if I could only touch that point within its dim consciousness. "You stood with me on Lyme Street, when we brought down Choybalsan."

Silence. But no action.

"It was me who ended the corruption among Blackblood's priests."

More silence. More inaction.

Below carried as always its sense of arrested breathing. As if the city had filled great, stone lungs, and waited for a time when it could exhale once more. I smelled the blood-and-meat reek of Skinless, the sewer rot of the sludge gathered in corners, the nearby metal and oil of machines.

A moment, poised. Much as the Dancing Mistress had taught me when we first began to run Below. My earliest escapes from the Factor's house had all been about these poised moments. Body, mind, heart, soul.

Danger, balanced on the tip of a knife.

Like all such balance points, it could be pushed one way or another with the slightest effort. I stepped close to Skinless, inside the reach of its arms, and stretched on my toes to whisper near its dripping ear. "I am mother to this child. She will not be taken up in pain." The lie, then, for in the god's sending of Skinless to find me, I thought I knew who my enemy was. Or one of them, at the least. "Neither will I work against Blackblood, for he has spared my life and made me whole." And once more the truth, to bring the lie round again. "But you are my friend, and I will never harm you."

Skinless stared a long while. Its eyes—no, *his* eyes—glistened until they ran wet down the pulsing horror of his cheeks. Then he turned and shambled away into the deeper darkness that was the rightful state of this place.

I stood, breathing hard as the meat reek vanished with the avatar's departure. My hands cradled my belly, smearing coldfire across my shirt, though the child had not stirred. Strangely, I was not even ill from the smell. Perhaps because it was familiar?

Skinless I could no more defeat in a fight than Mother Vajpai. But I had not been certain that I could talk him out of a course once he was set upon it. He was an avatar of the god Blackblood. A tulpa. He was a *part* of the god. If he could be softspoken away, then that meant Blackblood himself was not fully resolute.

The chilling, indifferent power of that languid youth still haunted me.

I turned, suddenly hungry, which seemed very odd, to find myself being watched from the open gallery ahead. Mother Iron stared from beneath her cowl. The Factor's ghost stood beside her. She had no face to read, just a deep pool of shadow with a hint of red glow guttering within; but he appeared both sorrowful and thoughtful.

I had not expected to see either again. Which was foolish, of course. They both dwelt Below. Proto-gods and ghosts of this city.

With a flush of mixed embarrassment and fear, I snapped at them. "Were you intending to restage our fight with Choybalsan? All we would need now are some pardines."

The Factor seemed as if he would say something. Mother Iron, so very often mute, stood unmoving. Whatever they wanted, I would have no part of it. Not now. Sick of this city and all its plotting powers, I circled around the wider space and headed for the upper gallery that lay beneath the building site of the Temple of Endurance.

I climbed the rickety ladder to hear a great racket above me. Shouting and crying. A fight?

Just below the bright-lit opening at the top I paused. It still stood unguarded—which still seemed odd to me. Just because I had an understanding with the dark places and their restless haunts didn't mean anyone else was safe.

I listened for several moments. The shouting continued, and several dull thumps echoed. I smelled smoke. Something serious was afoot. Wary, I eased my long knife into my hand and scrambled the last half-dozen rungs as if my own clothes were afire.

No one was working on the temple foundations when I leapt up into their midst. To my right one of the tents was burning—the kitchen, I thought— with a handful of Endurance's acolytes working to beat out the flames. People screamed by the gate, and I saw a flash of blades. More folk tended several fallen alongside the wooden temple.

Wishing I'd moved a little swifter at the first, I raced toward the battle. Chowdry's people saw me coming, weapon in hand, and scattered until only half a dozen toughs with knives and staves remained to face me.

Reckless with anger, I did not falter in my charge. The attackers took to their heels. Feet pounding, I chased them out into Durand Avenue, screaming for their blood.

I only gave off when I realized their numbers, and turned back before they did the same. That I had not even laid a blow upon them felt shameful.

Within the temple grounds, Chowdry and Ponce awaited me.

"What has happened?" I demanded, feeling unaccountably winded for such a short sprint.

Chowdry shook his head. "One of my people is dead. More are being wounded."

"We didn't even fight," said Ponce. I realized he was crying. "It is not permitted."

"You do not *defend*?" I realized then I had no notion of the theology of the god I had created. Somehow I'd assumed anyone who took me as a wellspring would know their way around a blade. But of course, all these happy, well-fed young acolytes did not have the look of hard training, or even rough-and-tumble play.

With disgust, I understood that Endurance was drawing the children of wealth to his service. I had never meant to serve *them*. People with family names and money needed no further protection. I glared at Ponce, and once more brushed my free hand across my belly.

"There is enough fighting in this world," Chowdry replied sadly in Seliu. "I learned that from you, and from Utavi before you. We will not be taking up arms, or hiring others to do so for us."

"Then you will not long keep a temple treasury," I growled in the same language. *Idiots. Nonviolence never solved anything.* Then, in Petraean: "Who were they?"

Chowdry glanced at Ponce. The young man wiped his eyes. "Petraeans, not Seliu."

That I had seen for myself, though the cowards had not stood to the test. And besides, *Selistani* was the people, *Seliu* was the language, but I did not trouble to correct him then. How did he not know this?

Ponce continued: "They came with weapons and demanded to see all the dark-skinned w-women. When one of the girls, Amitra, scratched at them, they killed her."

"Me." I was aghast. "They were searching for me." And a girl had died for it. Who, though? Surali would have sent Street Guild, or maybe even the Prince's peacocks. The Interim Council would have dispatched men from Lampet's new regiment. My list of enemies was not *so* long—this left Blackblood. I made a serious error of thinking then, one that I have regretted ever since. I assumed that the god had made another play! Even while he'd sent Skinless for me. The late Pater Primus might have done such a thing, and I suppose in the heat of the moment I confused the priest's tactics with the god's.

I could see only my fear for my child, my fear of being taken by the gods, my revulsion at the death of an innocent in my place. I could not see what was really happening.

Thoughtless rage replaced my sick horror. I could feel it boiling within me. I was never giving this child up to *anyone*. Not if I had to carry her beyond the farthest horizon to keep her safe. Or kill everyone in this city.

"Yes." Chowdry stared at the knife still in my hand. The tip was weaving in tight circles now, lusting for guilty flesh to plunge into. "You should find a different path."

He was right. I could not simply fight my way out of this. Such a strategy had never worked so well in the past, though I was not ashamed of some of my victims. The Pater Primus, for example. Or the Duke himself. I had slain others for pride or for fear, rather than necessity or the greater good. Killing was an easy habit to fall into, especially if one's conscience had already been burned away.

I was a mother now. I needed to think differently. No longer could I just be a storm of swords. Resheathing my knife, I took a deep breath and prayed to the Lily Goddess.

I know You cannot hear me so far across the water. I know I abandoned You, and that You sent me away. But still You are a mother. I need a mother's wisdom now. Not an assassin's instincts. Please. Guide me.

When I opened my eyes again, I was touched with a deeper calm. Not the peace of the High Hills, but at least my boiling rage had leached away. I felt slightly sick. A weakness had taken my muscles.

"If you and the god Endurance will allow me to do so," I said, "I would like to see to the dead. Her life was taken in my name."

In fact, two lives were taken in my name. Spite, misplaced vengeance, or someone's idea of a warning, I could not say. And it did not matter.

Amitra was a young woman, barely older than I. Her skin was a rich and lovely brown much as my own. Her eyebrows were fiercely dark, a cloud upon her pretty face. When I reached to press her eyes closed, their deep amber was already tinged with a milky dullness. She was forever young now.

Ponce and the others had laid her out in the middle of the foundation project. The other girl, Nitsa, was placed next to her. Nitsa would have been a solid woman, already thicker-bodied than I, and with a paler cast of skin. Only a fool would have mistaken her for me.

The side of Nitsa's face was crushed and her neck broken, from the blow of a heavy stick swung hard. Or perhaps a mallet. I traced the wounds. The dark, thickened blood stained my fingertips. She must have died in the moment, for there was not so much of it.

Amitra had been struck down with a blade. Her shoulder was gashed open. That would be the first blow. I imagined the assailant, some brute with money in his pocket and a target on his mind. One of the old Ducal Guard, perhaps, who hadn't been taken up by Lampet's new thugs. It was rumored they were behind much of the street crime now. He'd followed up the first blow by stabbing her in the throat, probably to silence her screams. She'd died bloody, which meant slow enough to feel the pain and terror.

"I will wash the bodies now," I announced. "I will need white clay and red."

Chowdry knew what I was about, as would any Selistani who was from the eastern portions of our native land, or who had lived among the Bhopuri for a while. This was what my people did. I remembered just a little from my grandmother's funeral, before I was taken, and I had learned more during my time in the Temple of the Silver Lily at Kalimpura. The rest of Selistan considered us Bhopuri to be silly peasants, with our cloaks of bells and our sky burials and our huts amid the paddies, but this was the bottom of who I was.

Though I had laid aside my anger and the violence that quivered within its grip, everyone around me scrambled to my bidding as if murder were still in my eye. That was fine with me. I wanted obedience right now far more than I wanted argument.

First I removed Amitra's robes, and washed her body with a strip of linen torn from their hem. There were rites and blessings that should be said, though I did not know many of the words. But I knew that everyone needed to be helped from the world if they could. I had even made a prayer for my bandit, the third person I'd killed with my own hands, after Mistress Tirelle and the Duke.

It was only fit that I do far more here.

She had been lithe and pretty, this woman. Her skin was already cold and her body stiff. That spark which makes a person sensual or beautiful was fled from this cooling meat. Still, I could see her as she had been in life. I wondered if Amitra had come on one of the ships. Or if her family had lived here awhile as merchants. Traders perhaps?

I had no need to ask. The girl would tell me whatever stories she had.

Wordlessly I prayed to both Endurance and the Lily Goddess as I wiped Amitra's hurts and cleaned the grime of work from her hands and feet. She had tiny bruises along her breasts, lover's nips. I was glad she had embraced that part of life before she died.

When she was clean, I covered her over with her robes, except for her face. Then I took a bowl of white clay someone had laid down as I worked. It was already properly mixed with water to form a paste. I painted over Amitra's face, preparing her for whatever the white prepared a body for when the soul had left it. I had been told at the Temple of the Silver Lily that this was how the ancestors would know their own, taking her for the ghost she was. I had never been certain if this was a true belief or a jest at the expense of peasant ignorance.

The red I took to paint dots across her forehead, her nose and lips and chin. Drops of the blood of life, kisses of the gods, offerings to the demons to let her pass the gates of the hells unharmed. Again, the reason was of no matter. That was simply what was done.

Then I did the same for Nitsa. Her body was solid and hard, not so fat as I'd thought when I'd first seen her collapsed in her bloody robes. I could do little to hide her wounds, but I cleaned them as well. That took a great while. Her fingers were long and slender for a woman of her build, and strange little calluses on the pads made me wonder if she'd played an instrument. Had lovers danced to this one's music?

In time I covered her over and painted her with the white and the red. I used the clay to smooth the depression in Nitsa's temple, so her face would be even when she met her mothers.

There were no sky burials here. Endurance was in a very real sense a Bhopuri god, but Copper Downs had no such towers, nor the servant birds that came to clean away the flesh and polish the bones laid atop them.

I looked up to see that the day was almost gone. Several dozen people gathered around me in a wide circle. Chowdry, Ponce, faces both familiar and strange from my days staying here.

"Are you back with us?" Chowdry asked quietly.

Wondering where I had been, I said, "Yes."

"You did not work alone," he added in Seliu.

I looked to see a few stray lily petals scattered around me. The air smelled of wet ox. How great had my prayers been?

"The rite is not quite complete," I told him. "I will need two white candles and two black. Bring me also paper, pen, ink, and a writing board."

Someone had thought ahead, for these were produced immediately. Or perhaps, I realized with a wry twist, Endurance had made his will known again.

I placed the black candle to the left of each girl's head, and the white to the right. Then I took the board and with care drew out word-houses of the Hanchu script from the few that Lao Jia had taught me aboard *Southern Escape* when I'd first fled Copper Downs.

For Amitra I drew the word-house that meant "beauty." As Lao Jia had said when teaching me, each word-house has little rooms of meaning. And so "beauty" was woman and the western sun and an eel swimming in a river.

For Nitsa I drew the word-house for "peace." Those little rooms of meaning were sky and hearth and an open door.

I laid the papers down upon each girl's chest for a time, and prayed voicelessly once more. It was fit that a mute god such as Endurance should be met with silent prayer. As for the Lily Goddess, She had been close enough to hear me, but we did not have so many words to spare that I needed to speak aloud to Her another time this day.

When I picked up Amitra's "beauty," it smoldered into flame. The flare lit the gathering shadows of evening as someone gasped. I put the little fire to the black candle first, then spoke quickly before it burned my fingers. "Doubtless she was vain," I said, bespeaking her sins and sorrows. "As all the beautiful are." I reached for the white candle and spoke to her hopes and dreams. "She believed in something beyond this life, or she would not have been here."

When I moved around the bodies to reach for Nitsa's "peace," that slip of paper also flared of its own accord. I lit the black candle. "She might have resented others their grace." I could not know this, of course, but I had known solid girls in the Temple of the Silver Lily, and it was a fair guess. I had no need or desire to understand this dead woman's more shameful sins. Then the white candle. "She made music that others might know joy, which is one of the greatest gifts."

I shook the last of the paper away from my fingertips in a shower of sparks and ash, then walked back toward the smoke reek of the tent camp. The circle of watchers melted before me. Someone called out in a soft voice, "What shall we do with the bodies?"

"Bury them," I said. "Or send them Below to sleep with the echoes of history." My work was done.

I found my cot and slipped into a deep, dreamless silence. Even the worry of another attack was too far from my mind. The last thing I heard was a buzz of voices without, as the people of Endurance's temple took up their watch over me.

Sunlight glowing through the canvas brought me awake hard and fast. My fingers were blistered, the tips sore and ground in with clay. I took a long moment to recall why that might be.

What *had* I done? Armed men on the loose looking for me, and I'd spent half a day playing at being a psychopomp. The memory of timeless peace was close by, though. I realized that I must have been under the protection of the gods.

And goddesses.

This morning, I was protected by nothing more than my wits and my knife, as had been the case for so much of my life. I rolled out of the cot and looked to my workboots. I didn't recall taking them off last night, but some-one must have. These boy's clothes stank more than my old leathers by now, but they were not uncomfortable. I was better off without the sleek drama of an assassin's guise in any case.

Food.

I needed food. At that thought, my gut roiled. The baby made me hungry. I had not eaten at all yesterday afternoon. I was fairly certain this was poor practice for a woman with child.

Patting myself down, I slipped my long knife within my corduroy trousers and into the scabbard alongside my thigh. My short knives I tucked inside my sleeves. The arrangement was not ideal, but carrying a sheathed weapon openly would defeat the purpose of this guise.

I slipped outside the tent to find breakfast.

Half a dozen of Endurance's young acolytes stood waiting for me, along with several older men and women. Their faces were a mix of pale and dark. Neither Chowdry nor Ponce was present.

"What do you want?" My tone was more brusque than I'd intended.

"Nothing," one of the young women said.

"Well, I need breakfast. Then I must go out into the city, and make sure the tragedy of yesterday is not repeated."

"W-will you visit the wounded before you depart?"

A sharp retort was on my lips, but I swallowed the words unspoken. "Yes, but not to dress them for death."

They trailed me to the tables next to the ruined kitchen tent. The canvas cover was gone, but in the morning's unusually decent warmth I did not care. Ponce was once more frying sausages, this time over an open fire, camp style. Some of their cookery gear had been salvaged. He smiled to see me, though without his grinning enthusiasm of before. With some effort, I smiled back.

That seemed safe enough.

When he offered me the pan, my smile grew more genuine. The world was hard, lives had been snuffed out, but as Mistress Tirelle had beaten into me, good cooking makes up for a multitude of sins. Using the same simple ingredients as before, I made up light, tangy eggs with the sausage cut into them.

Also as before, once I'd cooked a sufficiency, I ate as if food had just been invented for the first time. The watching circle was different, though. Not amazed at a young woman eating like a cartload of soldiers. More like people waiting for a miracle.

Between mouthfuls of egg, I made to shoo them off. "Don't you have work to do? I am not entertainment."

Ponce touched my shoulder. "They hunger for your words."

"Silly fools," I spat in Seliu, before I recalled that almost half the people here were Selistani, and surely could understand me.

Those took no offense, but smiled shyly.

I am rarely pleased to be told what to do, and never dance when called upon, so I finished my meal in a grim silence. This did nothing to discourage my watchers. I resolved to depart the temple grounds as swiftly as possible. Let them try to follow me through the city. I could swarm the roofs or go Below and lose every one of these soft, wealthy children within a block or two.

With that thought I glanced at my older watchers, wondering if they were truly seeking wisdom from me, or keeping an eye on their younger charges.

No matter. I had to take some action. I had sulked and skulked too long, and it was never my way to let the fight be brought to me. "I shall visit the wounded," I announced as I scraped my fourth plate clean. "Then I will head out into the city." Someone else could clean this makeshift kitchen.

Now that I knew that Surali and the rest of the embassy were in the Velviere District, I counted it reasonably safe to head back to the Tavernkeep's place. There I might find some answers from my friends among the pardines, for whom the human politics of all this would be little more than an amusement. If that.

I rose, looked around, and realized I had no idea where the wounded had been taken.

"The temple," said Ponce helpfully. He made to lead me there, though I knew perfectly well where it was. We trailed acolytes and elders as a duck trails her hatchlings.

Chowdry was within, alongside a Stone Coast woman in a formal dress of the last decade's style among the wealthy. She was covered in blue silk falls with a shallow bustle; not the richest mode anymore, but the clothing signaled her status as a respectable, decent matron—Mistress Leonie would have approved of my quick analysis. The woman was also a doctor, judging from the black case opened wide with the metal instruments of her trade spread across a square of white silk.

I was struck by how pretty she was. A nose too broad for the tastes of the elite here in Copper Downs, but snubbed and sweet upon her lightly freckled face. Gray eyes flashed, and brown hair streaked gray seemed to match.

In another time, at another moment, I might have approached her with a smile. Instead I looked to the men and women lying on pallets on the floor.

Five of them. Three were sleeping, and seemed to have their color, so I did not fear for a sudden death. One was awake and staring at me with bright enough eyes that her fate did not concern me so much either. The fifth had been receiving the attentions of Chowdry and the doctor. He looked sickly pale, especially for a Selistani.

"I am here." First I went and knelt by the bright-eyed watcher. Taking her hand in mine, I smiled, and thanked her quietly. The three sleepers I stroked slowly across the brow one after another. Each sighed in their turn. Finally I sat beside the severely wounded boy.

"What of him?" I looked at the doctor.

"A hard blow to the belly with the butt of a staff." Her voice caught at me, stirred something within. "He has ruptured inside. Bodily humors that should never mix are being drawn together."

I reached my hand toward his gut. Chowdry gasped. Looking up again, I snapped, "I am no miracle worker. I just sorrow for his pain."

In the end, that was all I could say to them. The wounded were wounded in my name. I had a fight to carry forth to my enemies.

Out on the streets, I walked like a boy. Which is to say, not the supple, confident lope of a Lily Blade—a stride we had cultivated carefully both for its efficiency in a night-long run through Kalimpura and for the air of power even a small woman could project—but, rather, the cocky strut of a young man balanced between pride and embarrassment, angry at the prospect of being discovered for an impostor in his manhood.

More Selistani were on the streets here than I remembered there being even a few months ago. Far more than had been resident in Copper Downs when I'd first escaped the Factor's house. With my short hair and my cap low, so long as I kept my face down, even with my darker skin I was just another working lad. I had not yet found a way to hide my scars, and continued to be torn as to whether I should even try to do such a thing.

Still, I swaggered a bit, not enough to attract challenge. A fine line in its own right, and a distracting little piece of playacting while I muddled over the meaning of yesterday's attack on the Temple of Endurance. More to the point, I muddled over my sudden devotion to funerary rites.

I had laid out bodies before. We did it for our own in the Temple of the Silver Lily, Blades for Blades, justiciars for justiciars, and so forth. Sometimes the Blades did the duty for people we had slain, for one reason or another of Kalimpuri precedent, law, or custom. And we had discussed it often enough during my education.

Mother Meiko had always averred that anyone who was prepared to kill should equally be prepared to manage the entire process of dying, death and beyond. As we Blades were technically priestesses in the service of the Lily Goddess, this was sensible enough. Nuns, of a sort, though that was a Stone Coast concept with no real Seliu equivalent. Fighting nuns who ministered to their targets.

My thoughts continued while I dodged grocer's carts and shoals of dark-suited clerks. While I had not killed Amitra and Nitsa, they had died for me. So it was right that I would lay them out. But what of my intense and unexpected obsession with the ceremony?

I could only conclude that the god Endurance was showing his people what he expected of them. My first memory of Endurance was of my grandmother's funeral, so fair enough that these rites should be adapted from what I could recall of her own, overlain with later knowledge.

There was something haunting about the idea of future generations of Copper Downs being laid to rest with a ceremony that had its roots in Bhopuri death customs. "For you, Grandmother," I whispered. A tiny and much-belated funerary offering. Still, I could not help but think that she would understand and approve.

My feet had led me to the breweries near the docks. Even my wandering mind could not ignore the odor of yeasts and hops and spillage, and the spoiled barrels placed out on the loading docks, from which the poor could drink unmeasured at their own risk for half of a split copper tael or some shred of barter. Horses, too; the district always had that smell of horse, those monstrous great beasts that drew the brewery wagons about the city.

Beer I was fine with, horses I mistrusted deeply. The broken screw that had borne me on my fateful trip with Septio, leading to his death and my pregnancy, had been a wicked animal with a special hatred for me in its liquid eyes.

An ox, now, there was an animal with which you always knew your place. No question of standing with an ox. They never got above themselves, and generally were not independent thinkers. Little wonder that Endurance had manifested as he did. I shuddered to think of the moods of a horse god.

I strode casually past the mouth of the Tavernkeep's alley. I was pleased to note that no crowd of Selistani filled the narrow roadway as they had on my previous visit. Wandering around the block, I chanced to duck unnoticed behind a hops wagon, then scaled to the roof of the warehouse that should back onto the tavern. From above I scrambled across the tarred sheet metal expanse of the warehouse's flat roof, then dropped to the sloped tile of the tavern itself.

That building was three storeys tall, though I'd never been above the second floor. It surely also had a cellar for beer barrels and the distilling of bournewater, the mountain liquor of the pardines that looked like rain and stole away the sense of any human who imbibed more than a few sips. All I could do from above was watch the entrance and the alleyway. There I could see who might be watching for me.

Blackblood's men, for one. And people from the embassy. Not that the Prince of the City cared, but I had come to understand that Mother Vajpai and Surali were at odds, just as they had always been back in Kalimpura. Both of them had business with me. So possibly two sets of watchers from the embassy, poised for me and for each other. And by now, Kohlmann and the Interim Council might well have their own people tracking me.

Erio didn't need to have been concerned for Copper Downs. All the old ghost needed do was be concerned about me and the troublemakers I attracted.

Too many cared where I was to be found. Too few cared for the right reasons. I would not give up my baby, and I would not give up myself. So with my long knife balanced across my thighs I crouched up on the roof, the cistern behind me to break my outline against the sky. There I hunted my hunters as patiently as if they were rabbits in the meadows of High Hills.

A surprising number of Selistani came and went over the next hour. At least a dozen of them passed down in the alley, almost all men. They seemed of the meanest and poorest classes—beached sailors, displaced farmers, idled laborers. Most were burned dark by the sun, without the pale, oiled sleekness of the aristocracy and the merchant castes. Almost without exception they wore faded and patched kurtas, very nearly the uniform of the country of my birth for those who could not afford more, but whose modesty forbade a dhoti or a mere clout.

I would not put it past Mother Vajpai to set a clever spy for me, but I doubted that Surali would even think to hire such a person as these to her service.

Only one Stone Coast woman came in the hour, and she quite clearly was bringing supplies, in the form of two herb baskets across her shoulders. She left twenty minutes later, her baskets somewhat the lighter.

Also, three pardines.

That proved to me that the Tavernkeep had not shut his business, and that the pardines had not drifted away in the face of the human invasion brought on presumably by Chowdry's cooking.

And of course, that was where he had been so often lately. The realization struck me as funny. Chowdry was working his shifts for the Tavernkeep. A temple camp full of the round-bellied children of the wealthy, and still he trudged here every day to make curry and samosas and whatever else struck the fancy of either Chowdry or his patrons.

Did the pardines' subtle distaste for the human not extend to the Selistani lately come among them? Or was their patience simply long enough to wait out this latest insult? That was a question for which I had no useful answer, though I could spin theories enough. Besides which, it was only my curiosity talking. No stakes rode with the issue.

That I could think of.

It occurred to me that lately my judgment of what was important had been flawed.

In any case, no one lingered with their eyes on the tavern that I could see. I spent time scanning the few windows opening on the alley. All were dark and still. A watcher or three quite possibly lurked within, but my entry there would not be reported without me knowing it.

Feeling quite pleased with myself, I put away my long knife and moved two rooftops over to a loading bay out of sight of the Tavernkeep's door. There I made a rather showy descent before an audience of a ragged orange cat and several pigeons. The baby had not overset my balance so much that

I couldn't slide down a pipe or bounce off an awning. The landing stung my feet and shins a bit more than I thought proper, but the watchers did not complain or mark me out.

Inside, the Tavernkeep's place did not seem so homey as it had before, yet it still welcomed me. Low ceilings with their heavy wooden pillars, a bar to my left with a kitchen beyond, stairs at the back, a large, cold fireplace on the right-hand wall. He had no windows here, only the door, so it was dark except for oil lamps burning with some imported scent that had little in common with the usual acrid smokes of this city.

Tables were more closely crowded together than I remembered. The widely spaced circles favored by the pardines, each with its deep stone bowl, were the same; but smaller furniture had been brought in for the Selistani who now patronized the place. A number of my countrymen were scattered about the room with the air of long-term occupants. Card games overflowed, as well as several sets of the Hanchu gambling tiles that could be found in any port town, along with the inevitable clack of dice. Those who have almost nothing always seem willing to play the highest stakes.

The smell of them—that scent of food and the choice of soap and the sweat of each race of man—was so familiar that it almost made me ache. I fought the urge to step back into the alley. I could not flee my own people. The embassy aside, they were not part of my troubles.

In a sense, I was responsible for them, too. Much as I had brought Chowdry to Copper Downs, so my deeds had brought the rest of these men.

I did scan carefully for Little Baji, whom I had recently glimpsed here, as well as anyone else who seemed familiar, or simply out of place. If any of those present were watching for my entrance, they had adopted a magnificent pretense of complete disinterest.

Turning my attention to the rest of the room's occupants, I saw that a pardine stood behind the bar puzzling over some mechanism. A pump handle, I thought. It was not the Tavernkeep, but a rangy, younger male with ginger fur, two heads taller than I. He looked to have lost more fights than was properly pleasing to him. Several of their tables were occupied as well. Tails flicked attentively, but not at alert. Ears were perked, but not tense. I could read this crowd. One feline face met my gaze and nodded.

Someone who had fought beside me at Lyme Street, though I could not bring a name to mind.

I nodded back. A human gesture, not native to them according to my old teacher the Dancing Mistress. These pardines had chosen to live in exile from their forest home and mountain fastnesses here among the human sprawl. In doing so, they had made their own accommodations to fit within our ways.

In truth, I was hoping for the Rectifier, though not with much expectation. The old miscreant was difficult, and had nearly fought me to the death on Lyme Street that most fateful day when we'd brought down one god and raised up another, but I had never counted him as an enemy. In the troubles dogging me now, his sort of wisdom might be very much to the point. Surely he was disinterested in these factions much as any of his people would be. More likely he was up in the hills hunting priests, or making some other form of trouble.

Which was of course what I needed him for. Not that I meant to attack Blackblood directly. That would be foolish in the extreme. Undermining the gods of a city was somewhat different than undermining the streets and walls. Rather, I was confident that the Rectifier knew better than I how to fight, and defeat, the will of the gods.

I was merely a tool of the gods. He was a weapon against them.

Tool, weapon, or otherwise, the only thing for it was to approach the bar. I pulled up a stool near the pardine at his work. He glanced up at me. "I cannot load this spring," he said softly. His Petraean had a hillman's accent, which made me wonder where he had learned the Stone Coast tongue.

"Shall I try?" From my time with the Dancing Mistress I knew that their fingers were not so nimble as a human being's. With claws extended, their hands were weapons. With claws drawn in, their furred bluntness was inconvenient for handling small tools and mechanisms. Few pardines sewed, for example, because of the difficulties inherent in managing needle and thread.

He handed me the pump fixture with a flash of fangs that I knew for a smile. Despite my years with the Dancing Mistress, I had none of their language, nor a tail to flick as they were wont to do among themselves. I smiled back instead, and looked for his trouble.

"What will you have?"

"A very small bowl of the Tavernkeep's finest bournewater, and if he is about, a moment of his time." Though I had eaten only a few hours earlier, I also liked the smell from the kitchen. The kick from the bournewater would give me a needed lift. "And some of whatever is cooking to the scent of lentils and cloves."

"Our best cook is not in today," the pardine replied. "But the boy back there does well enough."

"Do you enjoy Selistani cooking?" I asked, curious. The spring fitted into the sleeve with the proper snugness; he had been struggling to slip it past a little burr meant to keep the metal bit safely within once emplaced.

He answered me in poor but intelligible Seliu. "The taste is very fine."

I laughed softly and handed him back his pump fixture. He shouted into the kitchen, then went to draw me my bowl. My mouth watered at the scent of the food, but I wondered how the baby would take the spice. The oddest things bothered me these days.

At my back, the murmur of Selistani voices died. One last tile clacked, and the room fell silent. I wondered if the Rectifier had arrived against expectation. A pardine voice spoke softly, and I turned about to find the greatest shock I'd experienced yet since returning to Copper Downs this time.

The Dancing Mistress stood in the middle of the room, close by the pardine who had recognized me. I had never thought to see her again. Given the expression on her face and the stirring of her tail, I realized that my instincts had probably been for the best.

"Green," she said, then began to stalk toward me.

The Dancing Mistress moved with such intensity that I wondered if I was about to fight an old teacher for the second time in a handful of days. She would be as difficult to defeat as Mother Vajpai. At most, I could battle her to a standstill and then hope to escape.

Sliding from my stool, I prepared to palm my short knives and studied her in the few seconds I might have before violence erupted.

The Dancing Mistress looked wild, as if she were as fresh from the hills as the bartender I'd just helped. I could not say precisely why—the unaccustomed rough nap of her coat, from living outdoors, perhaps? Or the way she moved through the space around her as though filling it. Much as the Rectifier did, who deliberately cultivated a feral image, and so unlike her old mode of walking, where she slid between people and the gaps they made.

Not accommodating. Rather, asserting her control and power. Uncivilized, in the most literal sense.

"Mistress," I replied warily. When we'd met in Kalimpura, we'd fought. She had not known it was me behind the mask. I was defeated by her, and I had been in better training then than I was now. "You are home from the mountains."

Her tail flicked. A half-dozen more wild pardines spread out behind her. Pottery clicked nearby and I smelled a mouthwatering hot paneer. A weapon, of course—spinach in oily water near the boiling point.

"This is not home," the Dancing Mistress said flatly.

I knew to listen to her tone, but I knew more to watch her claws. She was far too canny to signal her movements as most human adversaries would— even a well-trained woman requires iron self-control and fantastic muscle strength to lean in one direction and kick in another, but pardines are too alien to read in that same fashion.

The claw tips showing in her furred fingers were key to what would happen next. Flexed outward, but not fully distended. She would probably continue to speak with me. For now.

"It is my home." I was quite surprised at my words.

The Dancing Mistress snorted. Her smallest laugh, escaping from her narrow nostrils. "I would never have thought to hear you say that, Green." Her tail relaxed and the claws disappeared.

Without taking my eyes off her, I extended my hand behind me and grasped hold of my bowl of paneer. My mouth was watering, and while I could still throw it at need, I could also eat. The baby was hungry.

"I might say much the same." With swift decision, I plunged on. "Why are you back in the city? I'd not figured to find you again in Copper Downs after you turned me away last summer." Recovering from her wounds in an upper room of this tavern, the Dancing Mistress had refused to see me. She'd then slipped from the city without a farewell.

"The world is not about you, Green," she said sadly. For this moment, we were only a student and her former teacher.

"The world was never about me." My voice was hard; I touched my belly lightly with my right hand, still holding my spoon. "Until I made it listen. A skill *you* taught me."

"Fair enough." She ran a hand across her close-furred scalp, as if nervous. "Why are you here?"

"The usual," I admitted.

"Gods and monsters and politics?"

"That, and I was hungry for some good Selistani cooking."

She nodded, that human gesture again. "Your man here is becoming famous."

"He's not my man. If Chowdry belongs to anyone now, he belongs to Endurance."

"You brought him helpless across the sea," she replied. "He is yours."

Anger stirred and my voice heated. "Then by your logic I belong to you as much as to myself."

That brought me a feral glitter of teeth and quick flexing of the claws. "I should not be so foolish as to try to take you up like an old weapon."

"I would not shatter in your hands," I told her, "but you might not enjoy so very much the edges you find."

"It is edges I search for now." *That* was an admission of sorts. "Though not yours. I'd heard you were safely in the High Hills."

And so I'd meant to be, but I did not say that thing to her. Instead I pursued her hint: "What edges?"

"Please," she said. "Sit with me and we will talk."

My paneer and I followed her to a table at the back of the room. As I walked, the earlier buzz of men and their games resumed. Whatever came next between us would not be at the center of all attention.

One of the big round tables was clear, near the back stairs. Her escort of wild pardines spread out along the wall where they could watch our table, the room, and each other. I found that a little strange. Such conspicuous display was never the Dancing Mistress' way.

Nonetheless we sat. My bowl of bournewater was provided, and a larger one for her. A lotus flower floated in the deep stone bowl at the center of the table, symbolizing the feasts by which the Dancing Mistress' people shared souls and bound the mourning of their dead to the communal memory.

The clack of tiles and the rattle of dice was the heartbeat of the room. We sat in the shadowed back like two actors waiting for our light.

She sipped at her drink and watched me for a while. Being raised as I had among the harshest teachers, I was quite accustomed to this. I amused myself by staring back. Nothing I saw altered my earlier assessment of her. The Dancing Mistress had the mountain way about her now. She didn't seem to have been in any serious fights lately, for her muzzle and face bore no fresh scars.

We had been lovers, briefly, and I knew her body well enough. She'd lost weight. Become, if anything, more rangy.

Eventually, I outwaited her, for my old teacher spoke first. "I am come to Copper Downs once more in search of an edge. An old, old edge."

"That brought you down out of your mountains?"

"Yes." She toyed with her bowl of drink, an excuse not to meet my eye. "The search has something to do with you, though I did not expect the matter to pass directly through your hands."

"Do you regret seeing me here?" I asked softly.

"We have not met since Federo's death." Now the mourning was clear in her voice.

But did she mourn the man? Surely not the god Choybalsan, who had made terrible war upon her people, themselves only a remnant of an earlier age of glory when men were not so strong. "His time was done," I said, "and the power that was upon him needed to pass further onward."

"It was never his power." Her eyes met mine again. Something ancient and hard lay in her gaze now. "You took that stolen power and made another god of it."

"You say that as if I were a carpenter who'd chosen to build one thing over another. Besides, I could hardly have returned the power." *Where to?*

After a long moment, as if in consideration, the Dancing Mistress said, "I have spent time alongside a very wise woman of my people."

To my left, one of her guardians—or wardens? I realized—murmured a name. *Matte*, it sounded like. "You yourself are a very wise woman of your people," I told her.

"In certain, specific ways, perhaps," she admitted, "but not about the wider concerns of life."

I did not like where this conversation was heading, though I could not yet say why. "What did you learn from this wise woman?"

"That our people gave away our power too easily." Her voice grew tense and fierce. "That in my turn I was part of that giving up. That there is much to be rectified."

The Rectifier? Surely her choice of words could not be coincidence. "Every people with a long past could say such a thing," I told her, keeping my own tone gentle and easy. "Surely that has been true since the morning of the world."

Now the Dancing Mistress was very nearly growling, and her claws splintered into the tabletop as she spoke. "This is *ours*, the soulpath of my entire people. The decision to take it up or lay it down again should be ours alone."

"You've caught a bad case of pardine politics, haven't you?" I was fascinated. I'd always understood her kind to work through consensus, a sort of oversized tribal family. What made the Rectifier so unusual among pardines was the strength of his individual passion and purposes.

"Matte has shown me certain truths I had long needed to hear," she admitted. "We are on a Hunt, of sorts. A Hunt of history."

That frightened me. I knew a little of pardine Hunts. It was a practice they had laid down, or claimed to, these past few centuries. A group would band together and share their senses, their intentions, perhaps even their thoughts, so they became one creature with a handful of bodies and cunning multiplied through all those hearts and minds. "Who is Matte, then?"

"She speaks of a doctrine of Revanchism. Our people should take back what was once ours and yet rightfully belongs to us."

Something in the Dancing Mistress' voice told me she saw a weakness in her own thinking. I drove toward it. "Speaks? Or preaches? You were always so much the champion of individual responsibility. This Revanchism is not a soulpath idea. This almost sounds human."

"*What do you know of soulpaths!?*" she shouted, slamming her hand into the table so that our bowls of bournewater slopped.

I came up out of my chair. My words had struck a nerve, and we were once more on the verge of violence. Into the silence that rang about the tavern I hissed my reply: "Nothing. I know nothing of soulpaths. I would no more play at being a pardine than you and your Revanchists should play at being human."

"I apologize, Green," she answered after a long moment. "Sit, please."

Sitting, I remained silent. This was on her now. I could not twist out whatever truth she was choking upon.

"I did not intend to take up this cause." The Dancing Mistress was quiet as well, speaking almost too low for me to hear. Once more the clack and murmur of men at their games swelled up around us, though we still very much had an audience. Any battle between us here would be the stuff of legend within the hour. I'd already had my fill of legends, and resolved anew not to fight my old teacher.

She went on: "When you brought the god into being, I thought the long struggle was over. The power seemed safely grounded in a mute and pleasant beast. I do not foresee Endurance becoming greedy for conquest, or world-weary, or even particularly dangerous. Your choice was inspired."

"Hardly a choice." This was not modesty—at the time I'd had little notion of what I was doing. I had understood even less since that fateful day.

"As may be. I left without seeing you because, well, it was over. My time here. My work. With Federo, of course, but also in the city as a whole. I was done with humans. Most specifically, you."

I ignored the twinge in my heart. "And yet here you are, back a few months later."

"Because of Matte." Now her tone was almost pleading. "I do not agree with much of what she says, but she is right in one thing. Our people's power should live, and die, with us. Not in the hands of some immortal duke, or a rogue human with the aspect of divinity upon him. Nor even a mute and pleasant ox god."

I wondered if this Matte was *offended* by Endurance. What if the god had manifested as something with sharp teeth and swift wit? A frightening thought. "It is an old theft, oft repeated," I answered her. "And the threat is now safely grounded. Your people and mine fought great wars in the past. That is one reason your power was laid down. By *you*."

"It was ours to lay down, it should be ours to take up again." Now her tone was stubborn. I was far too familiar with the sound of a woman arguing to convince herself. She had nothing to convince *me* of. "And that is why I am here once more, in Copper Downs. Where I never expected to be. Looking for the edges of the power."

"What edges?" I had the sickening notion that she was referring to my baby. I could not fight the entire pardine race. I could not even fight the Dancing Mistress. Taking ship to a port far beyond any horizon had a rapidly growing appeal.

"We are not here to make war upon Copper Downs, and especially not to find any quarrel with you, Green. But there is something taken from us long ago, by the Duke himself when he first grasped for our power. A token we would redeem for our own."

Not my child then, and not the god Endurance. I sighed heavily, expelling a tension I had not realized I was holding in until that moment. "What is this token, and what does it have to do with me?"

"Something precious to us has been brought back to the city recently. Matte has seen it while walking her soulpath in the moondark. With your return, I wondered if you might be carrying it."

"I carry nothing but a child in my belly and the knives in my hands."

That brought a smile from the Dancing Mistress. A genuine pardine smile. "You carry far more than you know, Green. But in this case, I refer to the Eyes of the Hills."

That meant nothing whatsoever to me. "You propose a puzzle to which I have no clues."

"Once, far in our past, my people made temples. We did not build, not as humans do, but we find great trees and certain caves to be, well, entrances to the soulpath. You would perhaps say sacred. A wise old pardine might give up her body there, but remain on watch through the windows in her bones as a guardian of our people. Or this one might bring a lucky stone, and that one another lucky stone to join it, until one day a pillar of great good fortune has been raised."

I thought of the sky burial towers of my earliest youth, and temples of Kalimpura and Copper Downs. "Every people has an architecture of the sacred, a house for the spirit. That is what we do with minds unable to contemplate the fullness of the divine."

"As may be. One of our spirit houses was a statue. Sculpture is a rare art among my people, but not unknown. This was an ancient mother of the pardine race, idealized long after her death but honored all the more for the hand that wrought her image. She had two eyes, one a green tourmaline and the other a cobalt spinel. These were taken by the Duke as a token of his theft of our power."

For a moment, my heart stilled, then pounded within my chest. My gut roiled, the baby rejecting the paneer and bournewater along with the Dancing Mistress' words, until only by sheer force of will did I hold down my stomach.

Michael Curry, the man I had killed aboard the ship *Crow Wing* in harbor at Kalimpura, on orders from Mother Vajpai herself, had carried a key with blue and green gems inset within a head cast in the form of a snake. It was meant to guard a treasure I never had seen. At the time I'd thought the colors were to match his eyes. The key with its emerald and sapphire chips I had thrown away on purpose, to spite the Bittern Court and their shameful politics.

Surali was here for me because of the way I had ruined the Bittern Court's intentions for the death of Michael Curry. But blue and green. Green and blue. Passing through my hands to spite the plans of the mighty. The coincidence was too great.

He must have been carrying the Eyes of the Hills behind whatever lock that key was fitted to.

"You *know*," she said.

I had taken too long to reply. Besides which, of all people this woman could read my hesitations as if they were the stirrings of her own heart.

"I do not know enough to tell you what you wish." Which was a lie of omission, but not an untruth as such. I needed to extract myself from this conversation as quickly and smoothly as possible. Unless I *wanted* to set the wild pardines upon the Selistani embassy. Far more important that I retreat and think these revelations through. This bit of business tied back to the Lily Goddess, to Endurance, to all my reasons for being in Copper Downs.

Hoping to find help dealing with Blackblood, I'd come here. Instead I'd uncovered . . . what?

Something that frightened me.

The Dancing Mistress studied me carefully for a while. I pushed the paneer and the drink away as she did so—the smell of both worked to further threaten my stomach.

"I don't suppose you're carrying the gems," she finally said. "You could not lie to me about that, and I can see your surprise. You've seen them, though. Or know of them."

"A rumor only," I blurted. "Back in Kalimpura. Off a Stone Coast ship. I followed the smuggling trade, for the sake of children. I heard things."

"Blue eyes and green?"

Her shrewdness was closing in on me. I had to give up something more, and do so convincingly enough that my old teacher would believe she'd winkled the secret from me. "A man. Named Michael Curry. They called him Malice. His eyes were mismatched, and he may have guarded the gems."

"What ship?"

Did I dare deepen the lie? Or was the truth more dangerous? Such things were too easy to check, though, if you had friends in the Harbormaster's office. "*Crow Wing*. Of the Stone Coast. I am not sure which city flagged her."

So much remained unsaid. I did not mention that I had killed him myself, or that I had thrown his snake-headed key into the harbor, or that I had cut out his eyes to fulfill the letter of the Bittern Court's death order while entirely abrogating the spirit of it.

She did not need to know these things, my old teacher. Not as feral and strange as she had become. Her struggle against Federo and Choybalsan had marked her as surely as it had marked me. But the Dancing Mistress' scars were much deeper and stranger. Especially concerning the theogeny of Endurance. Had that calling on her people's power torn away part of her own spirit?

Now more than ever I wished for the advice of the Rectifier. He was difficult and dangerous, but charmingly unsubtle. Honest to the point of insanity, I suspected.

"I must depart," I told her. "This food sits ill, and I am needed back at the temple."

The Dancing Mistress did not ask which temple. I could see a flash of calculation in her eyes as she considered holding me here against my will. Our old bond won out, or perhaps common sense prevailed. Scraping my chair back, I rose with a brief bow to her guardians. "I hope you find what you are searching for," I said politely. "And I hope even more it brings you what you expect."

"Thank you, Green." The Dancing Mistress rose as well, then stepped around the table to embrace me. I tensed, wondering if she would try to take me now much as Mother Vajpai had attempted, but in truth, all she did was hug. While her mouth was close to my ear and the scent of her was stirring the memory of something warm and sweet inside me, she whispered, "I am sorry."

I smiled and broke away to weave through the tables full of busy men. None of them would look straight at me, but out of the corner of my eye I could follow the wave of stares. At the bar I paid for my food, then leaned close to the pardine working there. "Tell the Tavernkeep that I would speak to the Rectifier should that old rogue decide to call here."

"Yes, Mistress." His tone was thoroughly cowed. Was the fact that I associated with the Dancing Mistress so overwhelming for him?

No matter. I strode out the door without hurrying. Once in the alley, I checked again for watchers, then stumbled to the little loading bay I'd used to climb down earlier and spewed everything I'd eaten and drunk in the past hour.

I was sick of being sick. After throwing up, I retreated to the rooftop, not so much to watch the street as to have time to think alone, out of the public eye. The sloping tiles were a bit of unexpected trouble. On the other hand, I now enjoyed privacy, respite, and time.

At moments like this, I very much missed the Blade handles. I'd grown quite accustomed to working in company, to benefitting from experience and wisdom and the annoyance of advice.

Alone, I was responsible for everything.

Alone, I had no check upon my foolishness or my ambitions, either one.

Alone, I was, well, alone.

Still, it helped me to lay things out as if explaining them to a fellow Blade or one of the teaching mothers. That habit has stood me in good stead ever since, just as it served me then. The problem of the raid upon the Temple of Endurance still loomed. Stuck in a line of reasoning that was later to prove foolish, I continued to believe Blackblood responsible, more by process of elimination than through any positive evidence. The attack certainly would have been the style of the old Pater Primus. And the Temple Quarter was stirring. The gods of Copper Downs had awoken in the time since the Duke's death. That was part of the lifting of the magical hold he'd placed on the entire city. Gods being who they were, I could guarantee they were becoming fractious. Having personally spoken to four gods, slain one, and birthed another, I was sadly an expert on this topic that no sane person would wish to understand too well.

Then there was the assault on the Temple of Marya sometime after my departure for Kalimpura four years ago. I knew very little about Marya as a goddess, except that she seemed to be a local equivalent to the Lily Goddess—watching over women and girls, and possessing mostly a soft kind of power. The Blades notwithstanding, this was as far as that went in Kalimpura. We were a secular force in the service of the goddess, not a divine aspect. Most cities would not tolerate an order of armed and dangerous women, charged with righting wrongs and fighting crime. It would make life too difficult for men.

Marya had no Blades serving her. Only prostitutes and working women and perhaps some of the wives of this city. So when—who? Someone had come for her, bearing whatever power it took to strike down a goddess; if rumor was to be believed, the goddess had resisted.

Even if Marya had fallen, after a time another would have risen in her place. That was the way of things among the gods. Trouble might come between, however, especially for those dependent on the goddess or her successor for protection. Those were never easy transitions.

I'd read enough theogeny during the days of my forced education to understand something of how the divine settled upon the world. Much like lightning stalking beneath the storm, divinity was power that sought grounding. I had no idea if the stories of Father Sunbones and Mother Mooneyes and their garden before time held any literal truth, but the figurative truth was undeniable. Male and female principles filled the world with the same energy they drew forth—from sex, from death, from flowering trees and falling leaves and the spume of rivers. And most of all from the hopes and fears and thoughts and prayers of the men and women of every race and kind and species in the endlessly long plate of the world.

What we people provided for the divine was a channel. A concept. A mold. Blackblood manifested as he did because his followers expected it of him. Pain was real enough, and those who suffered sought a focus for their need. Likewise my own Lily Goddess. She manifested as the regiment of women who worshipped Her could best see Her. One of us. Just vaster, wiser, deeper. As the ocean is to the dreams of a raindrop.

But as to the question of who *could* even attempt to throw down a goddess, I didn't care to contemplate it overmuch. I knew all too well what was involved in such a task, and I had been supremely fortunate in my endeavors. Whoever the god killers had been, they were gone. I was here now, my divine patron mute as I had made him. On my own, for most purposes.

As for those purposes, mine were not so clear to me at this moment. The Selistani embassy complicated things further. Especially since it had drawn the Dancing Mistress and her Revanchist associates down from the Blue Mountains in search of the Eyes of the Hills.

I believed my old teacher's claim that Matte had foreseen the gems returning to Copper Downs. The gems must have traveled here through the agency of Surali and the embassy. No other explanation made sense.

But I could see no way to tie this problem to Blackblood's moves against me.

What did occur to me was that the Revanchists being in Copper Downs was a threat of another sort. As with the Prince of the City and his retinue, they were an embassy. An inimical power with designs that would undermine Copper Downs if carried forward. I could not imagine this Matte's obsession with the Eyes of the Hills leading to a sudden outbreak of peace and quiet.

As much as I hated to do so, I needed to carry this matter to the Interim Council. I'd been avoiding Loren Kohlmann since our ill-fated visit to the Selistani embassy, but that could not continue. Such as it was, their authority constituted my greatest protection here in Copper Downs. Besides which, I had to know what their response was to Mother Vajpai's attack on me. I would lay the matter of the Dancing Mistress and the Revanchists before them—she used to sit on their council, they could hardly dismiss her significance. I might also discuss the matter of Blackblood's attack on the Temple of Endurance.

I did not particularly expect wise counsel, or even worthwhile solutions, but these were civic matters. Civic authority ought to solve them. The Interim Council had already tried to push the Prince of the City onto me once and failed.

We needed a better plan.

Scaling back down to the alley on the next block, I headed through the brewery district at a boy's loping pace for Lyme Street and the Textile Bourse.

Today the Conciliar Guards were having none of me. As soon as they saw me heading for the steps and realized who I was, both of them stepped back, while one tugged the door open.

I paused before I passed inside and looked more carefully at their uniforms. Though I could not recall perfectly, these certainly resembled the old Ducal Guard.

Waste not, want not.

Never above pricking a man with a weapon in his hand, I gave them my best feral smile. "You boys part of one of the militias?"

A panicked glance passed between the two hulking brutes. The one holding the door said, "We be the Conciliar Guards."

"Lampet's Lads," the other guard added helpfully. He was slightly smaller than standard issue, merely overheight but not monstrous. I could not recall having seen him before.

"Ah, yes. Councilor Lampet." As Councilor Kohlmann had said. The thought of that horrid little man in command of a few dozen—or hundred— men under arms was appalling.

The old days really were better, in this case. The tension between city guards, the dormant regiments, and private forces had functioned in a very loose balance. Which had distinct advantages for both the law-abiding as well as the more freelance-minded such as myself. The idea of an oiled weasel like Lampet controlling a meaningful portion of the swords in Copper Downs seemed a very poor way to *keep* the system in loose balance, even without worrying as to the councilor's own personal priorities.

Perhaps I should convince Chowdry to start a chapter of the Lily Blades under Endurance's blessing. For protection.

"I see," I told the two guards. "Carry on."

One saluted, the other did not. I pushed within to the crowded foyer.

Mr. Nast was upstairs conversing with some of his senior clerks. I nodded at him and strode to the council's meeting room. Their chairs empty, which disappointed me. Early afternoon on a Thursday, not a feast day or a temple day. It occurred to me that I had no idea what the Interim Council's work schedule was. They all had other jobs, or least other responsibilities, to which they attended.

On the other hand, I had plenty of ways of making people pay attention to me. I plopped down in Jeschonek's seat and began tossing my short knife in the air. Practice with the weapon was never misplaced, and sooner or later someone would find the courage to try yelling me out of the chamber.

Simple enough.

The chief clerk did not disappoint. Within about ten minutes he peeked from behind the stained-glass door at me. "Shall I take it as given that we have argued about your occupation of this room, and good sense has not prevailed?"

"It would save some trouble, yes," I admitted. "Quite thoughtful of you."

"I'll have a girl around with some water and fruit," Nast replied. "And I've already sent for Councilor Jeschonek."

"A happy coincidence then that I'm in his seat."

His face assumed a pained expression—surely deliberate, if I knew this man. "You *could* make an appointment. As most people do. They generally have an agenda as well, and sometimes even keep to it."

"Mr. Nast, have you ever known me to do as most people do?"

"I am sure that iconoclasm is one of your greatest charms, Miss Green."

With that, he withdrew. I impatiently awaited water and fruit, which arrived soon enough. A delicate Hanchu bowl, porcelain and painted with bamboo and plum blossoms, featuring three crisp apples and a soft peach, along with a tall carafe of water with chips straight from someone's icehouse. My stomach seemed willing to tolerate these things.

After I ate I commenced to carving my name in the mahogany tabletop with one of my short knives. It was a horrible abuse of such a decent weapon, but I wanted to motivate the council to respectful haste.

If not this time I called, the next.

Councilor Roberti Jeschonek arrived before my boredom had become dangerously destructive. He was disheveled, and seemed to have run from the docks to the Textile Bourse. I said as much.

"No, 'twas a horse, but the docks did not have an easy morning of it." He sat down in Kohlmann's chair and apparently couldn't decide whether to glare or smile at me. "Two foreign crews mixed it up and we nearly had a riot."

Which was, of course, the Harbormaster's problem. Except when it wasn't. Rather like Kohlmann, and much unlike Lampet, I could readily imagine Jeschonek wading into a dockside brawl with both fists, risking himself to bring it to an end before serious blood was shed. "You did not take any hits, I trust."

"Oh, a man always takes hits. The secret is giving back more than you get."

I laughed. "A policy that has served me well thus far in life."

A moment later one of the junior clerks darted into the room with a mug of kava for Jeschonek. The young man shot me a cautious look that in turn disguised a wink, then slipped out again.

The councilor took a long, careful sip before glancing down at where I'd been defacing his table. "That will not so easily be sanded out."

"Consider it a reminder." I dropped the knife from a foot above. It landed point-first in the wood and stuck upward, vibrating.

"No one is at your beck and call, Green. Especially not this Interim Council."

"Perhaps I could arrange the bad news to arrive at your convenience?"

He leaned forward. "What bad news?"

I tapped at the top of my knife's narrow hilt as I listed off what was on my mind. "You already know of the Selistani embassy's attempt to imprison me. They nearly fought with Councilor Kohlmann. There was another attempt upon my person yesterday, in which two innocents were killed." At the surmise in his eyes, I added testily, "*Not* by me.

"Today I find that zealots among the pardines are come to Copper Downs in search of an ancient treasure stolen from them by the late Duke. Those are an even more dangerous embassy than the Prince of the City and his little collection of fops and assassins." A stronger tap made the knife quiver with a metallic noise. "All of which ties back to a warning I received during my stay in the High Hills."

"From whom?" Jeschonek asked.

I was interested to note that the issue of my source of information was his first question, rather than wondering of what I had been warned. "The graves up there talk, you know. Many of them babble, but some are very sensible indeed."

His lips curled in disgust. "Don't tell me ghost stories."

"You are being an idiot," I snapped. Pulling my knife free, I began slapping the palm of my left hand with the flat of the blade. "You lived through Federo's ascendancy. And you did it standing as close to him as anyone did who survived. You were inside the biggest ghost story to be told here in generations. Of all the council, you and Kohlmann should require the least convincing on this matter."

"The world is filled with powers," Jeschonek admitted. "As above, so below. But the ancient dead of another era, interred a long day's ride from here, have no special insight into our affairs. I do not care so much for gods and ghosts in any event. Surely they are only a projection of our desires."

"As may be. But you have seen their effects upon this world. And Erio, a king of old who has been a student of this city a thousand years or more in his moldering grave, fears for us." His warning of imbalances within the city, and plots against me, had been sincere, if sadly unspecific.

"*I* fear for us!" The councilor slammed down his kava mug and drummed his fist against the table. "You do not have to be dead to realize what trouble may descend upon this city."

"There is no *may* to this trouble," I told him. "It is here. Use Lampet's Lads to force the Selistani back on to their ship. The embassy is of my people, but their interests are not mine and most certainly not this city's. Then compose some suitable response to the pardines, for they will come to you eventually. Possibly with tooth and claw, possibly with petitions. Draw them away before their madness sinks in, for they have become infected with politics. Or perhaps religion."

"You are infected with politics," he said. "As for religion, I've never seen or heard of someone so god-haunted as you, Green. If you were not in this city, none of these others would have troubled us."

He was right, so far as that went. The Selistani were here for me. The pardine Revanchists were here for the Selistani. Blackblood wanted to control his son. My daughter. *Fires take that bastard god.*

"You were not so eager to have me gone before," I told him in a hard, quiet voice. "Not when the city was at stake. You would never have brought down Federo and Choybalsan without me."

"No. And do not think us ungrateful." He leaned over the table. "But we cannot govern a city according to the whims of your enemies and the violence of your acts, Green. Life is settling. The troubles that dog us now follow you, not Copper Downs."

"You had a goddess nearly slain in the Temple Quarter during the brass-ape races four summers past," I told him. "Which was nothing to do with me. Despite the matter of Choybalsan, I do not set my targets so large, and would never care to meet the one who might try. Trade is unsettled, or you would not be seeing riots on the dock and yourself so busy and under duress. This city has not yet fully recovered from the death of the Duke. If it had, Councilor Johns would not have a place in this room."

"That fool of a Factor trained you too well." His reluctant smile belied his words. "But those are matters we will resolve. It is you who has small armies of assassins following you around."

"Should I return to Kalimpura, then?"

"The High Hills were far enough away for me, frankly. At least there we knew where you were." After a moment, Jeschonek added with rueful honesty, "And could find you at need." He drummed the table again. "But here is my problem with you now. We bring our own enemies into being. When the Duke held the throne and kept all our politics and religion quiet, trade came to the city and little disrupted us. There has been more riot and trouble in the past four years since his fall than in the previous four centuries combined.

"You enter the city, and forces follow to oppose you. Green, I do not know *what* you are. Surely your tale is not yet fully told. God-touched, a storm of blades, or just a freakishly determined young woman, it does not matter. But your strength draws opposition. And that is what my city does not need."

It is my city, too, I wanted to say. This I had realized when speaking with the Dancing Mistress earlier. These people had bought me away from my father and my home, but they had also raised me to be one of them.

Councilor Kohlmann stepped into the room as I was considering my next words. I was glad enough it was not Lampet, for whom I already lacked patience. "Have you told her?" he asked Jeschonek.

We both spoke at once. "Told me what?" "I was doing so."

Kohlmann gave me a long look. "It is clear to me that the Selistani embassy is a sham. They are only here for you. We cannot order them to leave, for we would be embarrassed of resources to compel them to our will. The council has voted to withdraw the protection offered to you before. You are charged instead with disposing of your personal matters without further harm to the city of Copper Downs."

"These troubles belong to you, Green," Jeschonek added. "You must take them away from our door."

"You bastards," I shouted, leaping to my feet with my short knife in hand.

To their credit, neither man flinched. My blood boiled, but to what end? I slipped the weapon away, glaring at both of them as if my eyes could slice their skin. "You disgust me. I never mistook the Interim Council to be friendly to me, but my faith in our common interests was clearly misplaced."

Kohlmann stepped back as I reached the door. He was afraid of me. *Good.* I gave him a flesh-rending smile. Even more hard words rolled in my head, but I kept them to myself and departed without further discussion. They did not trouble to call me back.

In the upper hallway, the clerks cowered. I had not realized we were so loud. When they cowered downstairs as well, I understood it was me that frightened them, not the shouting. I stalked out into Lyme Street, holding back tears that shamed me horribly.

Me.

Crying!

Not now, not for insults as foolish and petty as these.

But they were still bastards.

All I could do was walk off the tension. I needed to drain my anger before I could sensibly take further action. There was risk to me, and the ghost Erio had believed there to be risk to the city. Too many players, too many plots. I had to deal with the Selistani embassy, with the pardines, and with Black-blood's moves against me. The Interim Council would be no help. The next most obvious answer was to turn my enemies against one another.

But in my current state of agitation, I could not manage to conceive of a decent plan, let alone hope to carry it out.

I stomped toward the Dockmarket instead. Some piece of homely cheese might do me good. Likewise a crowd of indifferent people about their occasions, happy or sad as the mood took them, none bearing arms with my name written on the back of their hand. No one at the Dockmarket would care who or what I was. I could lose myself for an hour or two in their pressing mass, be distracted by chandlers or toymakers or weaponsmiths, then find myself sufficiently recovered to survey what must follow. At least the day was decent, a late gasp of autumn granting us all warm sun and clear skies without the knife-edged winter wind.

The Dockmarket was busy as ever. Trade might be down, but there were few vacant stalls. Tired old women hawked handfuls of trinkets from the tops of bollards. A clown juggled pigeons, tossing the birds like stones until they fluttered back into his hands. Fruitiers and greengrocers occupied wide spreads of stalls, their produce ranked in colorful arrays like a nursery paint box. Laughing children ran through the market clutching brown-spotted summer apples and thin coins stolen from the careless. I smelled food frying, flowers rotting, machine oil, spices, the acrid scent of blades being sharpened on a grinding wheel, the dung of a dozen kinds of animals. The sounds likewise made such a distraction. Blue-robed memory men squatting on the distorted faces of ancient, fallen idols chanted histories. Hogs bellowed their fear before the sledge took them in the skull. Chains jingled, babies shrieked, hammers fell.

This place was as close to the comforting chaos of Kalimpura as I was likely to find in Copper Downs. I slipped into the rhythms of the eddying crowds, falling into the habits of a Blade on a run—my stance, the set of my shoulders, how close I kept my weapons. Realizing this, I forced myself to relax. This was not the place of my enemies. The city of Copper Downs did not oppose me. Only some people in it, most of them foreigners.

I caught myself at that thought. *Selistani.* My own people were not foreigners.

Or were they?

A crowded space of split-log benches offered a chance for folk a-marketing to pause and consume the food they'd purchased, or rearrange the goods they'd bought. I slipped onto a sawn stump, glad for the respite. This was not the time for thinking, this was the time for clearing my head. But I needed a moment. At least the anger had subsided. Calm had not yet returned.

Though people were packed in here, the rest did me good. I'd been raised in isolation behind the Factor's bluestone walls. Even so, my years in Kalimpura had inured me to crowds. I looked up at the low, scattered clouds of the autumn sky and wondered how this market might appear to a bird overhead, or some weather god with a heaven's-eye view of the world. We would be as termites in their mound, laboring for our colorful scraps of food and cloth.

Something in that image comforted me. Kalimpuri were not so different from those of the Stone Coast, when viewed from far away.

My reverie was interrupted by a cry in Hanchu. I looked up to see a small elderly man being backed against the slats of a melon stall by half a dozen youths. The Dockmarket was not so dangerous, except perhaps for pickpockets, but these things sometimes happened. People pushed by without looking or stopping to help. It was unlikely anyone in authority would even happen along, let alone intervene.

To the Smagadine hells with that, I thought. I had a soft spot for elderly Hanchu men, thanks to my time with Lao Jia, the old cook aboard *Southern Escape* who'd shown me such kindness when I first had fled Copper Downs after my slaying of the Duke.

I jumped to my feet, trotted over, and announced myself to the thugs by swiftly kicking two of them behind the knee, dropping the miscreants to the stinking cobbles mashed with rotten vegetables and animal dung. I showed the other four my short knives. "You will have a better day elsewhere," I growled.

One opened his mouth to protest—or threaten—so I opened the muscles of his forearm. At the sight of blood, they scattered.

Turning to the old man I'd rescued, I tried to frame an apology in Hanchu. I paused a moment to take stock of what I saw. He wore a long buttoned cassock in a saffron-dyed cotton weave with turned-in seams, carefully wrought handwork from the look of it. Distinctive enough, but not the richly embroidered silk and cloth frog closures typical of the better class of Hanchu attire.

"Bid welcome," I said in my limited, stumbling command of his language. "Take your ease." Except for discussions of food and cooking, and certain expletives, that greeting nearly depleted my store of words.

"And well met," he replied in Hanchu. Switching to accented Petraean, the old man continued, "We are lost in this marvelous city, and subject to the attentions of tasteless persons. You are foreign as well. Can you perhaps help direct us with more kindness than the last I asked?"

We turned out to be the man I'd rescued and another small, elderly man who could have been his twin. No, I realized, the other man *was* his twin. They were matched, even to the point of holding their heads the same way—slightly cocked like a pair of wading birds stalking loaches in the reedy shallows. Looking back, I realize now the gods could not have sent me a sign more clear than that.

I ignored it with the self-assured folly of youth.

"My profound gratitude for the rescue," the second brother said. "As well as the courtesy. Few here know our country or our language. Your people look inward, not outward."

I turned the deep brown skin on the back of my hand toward them, and brushed it with the fingers of my other hand to draw attention to the color. "You have already seen that these are not my people, though I abide here. This is a land of pale folk with ideas that are sometimes pale as well." I'd thought

Federo a maggot-man when I met him, the very first of these northerners I'd ever laid eyes upon. "I would be pleased to aid you if I am able."

"We have lost our way to Theobalde Avenue," said the first brother.

"Your docks and market caught our eye too well," added the second. "As did the louts who can be found here."

Louts, indeed. I'd run into thugs a time or two. "I believe I know the way. Are you in haste?"

The first brother shook his head. A sly wit sparkled in his gaze. "Not now that we have your delightful company."

The other caught the moment again. "You speak fairly. We shall play the old traveler's game and offer you a trade. My name is Iso, and this is my brother Osi."

Osi smiled, as clever and secretive as his brother. "We are traveling mendicants."

The words slipped back into his brother's mouth. "Our pilgrimage is longer than our lives will last, but we carry onward."

The traveler's game was something I had only read of in old stories, though I understood that prisoners played it much the same way even now.

"I am Green," I told them. "A girl—no, a woman—of Selistan, lately resident here in Copper Downs. In time I should think to return across the Storm Sea."

Osi dipped his head. "I will give you this next thing. We confess that we knew who you were, though it was only chance that brought us to you in the market."

He had given me a new piece of information, and now it was my turn to give him more if I would come to understand why they knew me. I did not feel under threat, but it was still a bit odd to realize that these two had been looking for me. "I was born in Selistan," I said, "in the region of Bhopura." *How do I get them to answer the question I want to ask?*

Iso answered this time. They always spoke this way, I was to learn, like a volley between two shuttlecock players. He had to raise his voice above the whoop of several children nearby, but this did not seem to distress him. "We are on a journey to visit all the temples of the world, but we have not yet crossed the Storm Sea."

That was an easy response. Perhaps I could drive this conversation back to my purposes. "I have crossed the sea three times, and so I am here today."

Osi, quite promptly: "We have crossed many seas since we left the country of birth as well, along the Sunward Sea."

That was far to the east, beyond the usual reach of Stone Coast shipping. Also nowhere near the Hanchu lands, which lay westward of here. The steam-kettle vessels that plied the ocean between the Stone Coast and Selistan were built along the Sunward Sea, though, where the arts of metallurgy and naval architecture and the mysteries of bottled lightning were much better understood. "I am no one to be known in this city," I said. "For though I was largely raised here, I have never lived among its people."

Iso replied, "You are known even to us, you who are a priestess of both a foreign god and a new one raised here in this place."

Osi: "New gods are rare enough that the word spreads quickly to those who study such things."

Maybe these men can help me find some wisdom to deal with Blackblood's ever more pressing claims. "I have been within a few temples," I said cautiously. "And spoken to more than one god directly. For all the good it's done me. But I am no priestess."

"And we are no priests," Iso said. "Still we have knelt before a hundred altars, and recited prayers in more languages than a man should be able to count."

The market noise rose and fell around us like waves at the shore, but I was completely drawn in to these men and their traveler's game. "You have gone much farther than I. Home is all but lost to me, even here." Especially after Kohlmann and Jeschonek had turned me away.

"Home is wherever we lay down our bowls and take our rest." That was Osi, who laid a loving hand on his brother's arm.

"Home is wherever I can put aside my knives and sleep in peace," I told them.

"That is a rare home indeed for one of your formidable talents," said Iso.

I broke the game then, in a sense, for a rush of frustrated generosity overwhelmed me. "Would that I could offer you a place to stay and set your bowls, but my own position in this city is tenuous. I am sorry."

"We know this," Osi said, "for what you say is true of everyone to some degree. Even the wealthy man in his house with a firm count of all his coins considers his position tenuous."

Iso picked up the thought without a gap in their speech. "You are just more honest with yourself and with us."

Back to Osi: "We would beg your indulgence, though, Mistress Green."

Iso: "Priestess or no, you are said to be a consort of gods and a friend to goddesses. You may be able to tell us much to support our pilgrimage."

"The work of our lives," Osi added.

As they asked this of me, the spell of the conversation was broken. I did not feel an urge to reject these men. Whatever problems they had were not my own. I possessed too many troubles already.

On the other hand, these two must have great experience with gods and their affairs. And as foreigners, they had no stake in the events unfolding about this city. Everything coming to boil around me concerned pardines, Selistani, or the Stone Coast natives and their petty gods. These men were from a distant place, and had no stakes in the nascent battles.

Could I trust them?

Of course not. Strangers were never to be trusted. But perhaps I *could* be confident in not counting them as enemies.

"I will make a bargain with you," I said. "A version of the traveler's game, in its way."

"What bargain?" asked Iso.

Did they ever mistake their rhythm and speak over one another, or leave a quiet gap in error? I would guess not, and indeed, never did catch them out so.

"I will tell you what I can of temples and gods here, and the history of this place that I do know well, if from a narrow angle of view. In return, you will tell me what you can of how the gods treat with one another, what deeds they do among themselves. I fear the politics and jealousies that pass among them have already touched my life. I would know more of that with which I am afflicted."

"Divine favor is ever an affliction," Osi replied with a small smile. "Though all the priests deny it, who could truly prosper under the fire of such attention?"

In that moment, my sense of affinity with these two blossomed. They understood me in a way that no one here had or would likely be able to. All three of us were strange in a stranger land. I could see how communities such as the Temple of the Silver Lily came into being—people of like mind and allied intent who shared interests. To the grave and beyond, if all went well. Much as what a family was said to be, though I had never known such.

Best of all, these twins were the first people I had met since leaving Ilona's side who did not place demands on me. All they wanted to do was *talk*.

"I have seen enough of divine favor to last me a lifetime." I was surprised at the bitterness that crept into my voice with those words. "A bit more secular favor would not be at all misplaced."

Iso and Osi exchanged a long glance. It was as if they were conferring, which perhaps they were. What did I know of the bond between twins? Or siblings, even. I had been the only child of my parents. On my one visit back to my father's farm, I had seen no evidence of Shar, his second wife, bearing him more children.

"We would retire from this market," Iso told me. "Will you help us find our way back?"

Perhaps this was not a ruse. "Yes." I needed somewhere to rest that did not involve sleeping with my face pressed against a tavern table. Or bringing on more of Blackblood's attacks. "I may be a danger to you. There are those who hunt me."

Another glance exchanged, this one much quicker than before. Then, Osi: "We have learned not to fear. If we are quiet and careful, no one should know."

I walked with them out of the market. They were a marvel to watch, each moving as smoothly as any senior Blade mother, but always coordinated with the other. A dance in two parts, played out against the rolling tide of a crowd, somehow never touching or brushing against anyone else. They slowed only once, passing a cart from which brass scrap was being sold so that the eyes of one brother—Iso, I thought—could linger on the cart's cargo before he was shoved onward by one of the scrapman's boys. Osi took his own look as they moved away.

I slowed my pace as well for a step or three to see what had been of such interest. The cart was large as a beer wagon, the man atop it a veritable draft horse himself. He was selling broken brass statues, bawling out the quality of their work. I let his words wash over my ears, picking them from the hubble and bubble of the crowd.

". . . finest crafting! Apes, fresh from losing the races! You knows them sorcerer-engineers don't use second-rate stuff, not never! Melts down good and smooth, you can hammer it out, all blessed. They died in harness . . ."

My footsteps had led me out of hearing of his pitch. Brass apes. They had races here, that I'd never seen, clockwork driving the creatures to knuckle through the streets. The last bout had been while I was lurking up in the High Hills. The losers tended to be broken up. I suppose someone had salvaged the clockwork and the cam-based punchleather logic mechanisms that guided their behavior.

I led the twins away from the Dockmarket along Orchid Street, south of the Temple Quarter. The street they sought was a narrow, brick-walled alley almost devoid of doors and windows where it ran through the warehouse district. In fairness not so easy to find if you did not know your way among the stolid buildings. High, blank walls loomed on each side. Iso and Osi stopped in front of one of the few entrances, a watchman's door, one of them fumbling with the lock. I turned to scan the street while the brothers let us in.

Larceny? Or just a cautious entrance to their own unlikely castle?

When I followed them inside, I beheld an odd place indeed.

The twins had made their temporary home in a warehouse filled with maritime equipment. Anchors rusting in iron rows, their upper cross members close to breaking off. Braces and mounts for masts and their crosstrees. Great coils of rope or chain each thicker than my arm. There was even a suite of offices built into what would have been the fourth storey of the warehouse, facing out toward the street and reached by rickety stairs ascending along the high interior wall.

Everything including the building itself looked worn, used, aged. Which made me wonder who would bother to pay to store such gear.

Iso and Osi had made a nest of boat furniture and tarps near the back of the warehouse. Judging from the tracks in the dust, no one but them had been here in a while.

We sat down and one of them—Iso, I think—lit a small stove powered by alcohol. Without any comment, his brother readied a copper pot to boil water, three plain porcelain cups, and a small bowl of loose tea.

"This is our custom," Osi told me. "On receiving a friend in one's home."

"Home is where your bowl is," I supplied.

Iso nodded. "And where you may lay down your knives."

For a while I let them care for me, and marked a quiet time for myself. It was pleasant to belong, even in a fleeting way. Short of some serious scouting, or possibly divine intervention, no one would find me here.

That made me very happy indeed. This was my chance to carefully sort through the matters of the Selistani embassy, the pardines and their desires, and Blackblood. Though at first I kept my thoughts to myself, their quiet murmurs and occasional mutual touch tempted me over and over to speak.

They fed me a musky tea that tasted of flowers. I liked it well enough, but would not seek out the blend again. A small bowl of lentils, cooked soft and spiced with a dash of pepper. Both sat well on my stomach. My hunger was eased.

Watching them move, I realized these two touched each other constantly. For reassurance, or as a method of communication. It was like seeing old lovers, or some of the senior Blade mothers, where the bodies were shared much as the thoughts of these twins surely were.

Finally I spoke above the roil of my own thinking, still considering my troubles. "You are very close."

Osi—I believe—smiled. "We live by a strict code."

Iso nodded. "If we touch or are touched by one not of our rite, we must be cleansed with ritual, prayer, and fasting."

No wonder they'd moved so carefully through the crowded market. These two were not fighters, they were ascetics. As I'd seen when I first met them. "So if I were to brush my fingers across yours, this would be unlucky?"

"Unclean," Osi replied. He held up his hands, as if to ward me off. "Not to say that we doubt your hygiene or your personal practices. Just that you have not followed the spiritual journey we share."

I was not offended. Rather, I was fascinated. "So you touch one another, but no one else."

"Exactly." Iso, this time. I thought I could tell them apart now. He continued: "No matter if you are a beggar or a king. We would still pull a drowning child from the waves, but we would be forced to cleanse ourselves afterward."

"Both of you?" This amazed me.

Osi ran a hand down Iso's forearm, barely tracing the seam of his brother's yellow sleeve. "For one of us to touch is for both of us to touch."

One mind, one body. I could not truly imagine such closeness. Not even with my baby, who swam inside my womb even now. No lover had ever been so merged. We are born alone, we die alone, we live alone along the way. Had these two found a method to surpass that ultimate confinement of the human spirit to a single body?

I knew it was different for the pardines, and could say nothing of other races, or humans in other places. But these two. . . . "I find your dedication admirable."

Osi shrugged, the motion passing to Iso in perfect coordination. Iso answered, "It is who we are. We garner no praise and curry no favor, but only follow our rites."

Iso added, "We must tell you a thing. In our practice, any touch is unclean, but a woman's touch or breath is a poison to the spirit of a man."

I laughed, though that rang false against my heart. "You had best avoid the Temple of the Silver Lily, then. My goddess' halls are full of women."

"You are the first woman we have taken a meal with in more years than we could easily number." Osi's tone was very serious.

Even knowing his words for flattery, he still soothed the hard edge they had just now raised in my mood. "Because I am Green?"

Iso smiled again. "Because the gods here are strange, and more disturbed than we have found before. You stand at the heart of the matter."

Osi made with his right hand a small sign I did not know. "We have much to learn. Our temple visits are not simple offertory and prayer. You are the one who birthed a god, Endurance."

His brother: "We have never before encountered a theogenetrix."

I was tempted to say they had not encountered one now, but I didn't suppose that to be entirely true, regardless of my misgivings. "You should have known Federo. He carried the god Choybalsan as a woman carries a child beneath her beating heart." I looked at their serious faces, blinking owlishly at me in the shadows of the warehouse. "Would this have been easier for you if I had been a man who called Endurance into being?"

Osi's honesty was disarming. "Yes. Much easier. But we are challenged in our work, just as anyone who pursues a quest must be."

Iso: "So we shall lay aside some rituals, and make additional time for others."

"No god will strike you down, I think."

"We are not struck," Osi said. Something in his tone plucked at my thoughts, but I could not place it, and so dropped the subject as I already seemed to be pushing beyond the edges of their comfort.

Afternoon passed in shafts of dusty light that walked slowly across the warehouse's cavernous interior from narrow windows set high in the walls. First these battens gleamed, then those grates, and for a while a pile of brass binnacles flashed like gold. I spoke more to the brothers, and spent time in my own silences as they attended to their meditations. Though they were mendicant, and seemed to possess little, what they did own unpacked and opened and refined and subdivided into smaller and more manifold belongings. For example, a small satchel revealed a collection of tools. The handles of each opened to smaller tools and firestarters and tiny blades.

It was a very *efficient* sort of asceticism. I recognized some of their implements as having violent use. A corkscrew can open a wine bottle, but it can also stab an eye or breach a throat. Osi and Iso moved with the practiced ease of old professionals in any field. It was so simple for me to see the Blade mothers in these two men, for all their differences.

I wondered if I would ever be free of the shadows of my past. Was anyone in truth ever liberated from the bondage of memory? A question that dogs me still, all these years later.

But we did talk. Some of our discussion was of Copper Downs. I explained the Temple Quarter as best I could, and the clever architecture that made the Street of Horizons, a mere eleven blocks long, seem to be endless when looked at from either margin of the quarter. The gods, how they'd slept under the old Duke and been awoken at his mysterious death—omitting my central role in that event—and how they had since pushed for power. I'd been away in Kalimpura for much of that awakening, but my own encounters with Blackblood, the past attempt to assassinate Marya, and the very presence of Endurance alongside the traditional pantheon were taken together more than sufficient to upset the established order.

The brothers in turn talked about the doctrine of theogenic dispersion. This I knew of from my readings in the Factor's house, how the titanics who were the greater gods at the beginning of the world had fallen away and sundered into their children and their children's children, just as a shattered jar will birth generations of splinters on a tiled floor. Much along the lines of my own recent meditations.

"Just as Father Sunbones and Mother Mooneyes," I said at one point, recalling a pair of theogenic tales that spoke of the birthing of Desire's daughter-goddesses, but from a very different perspective.

"Yes," Osi said. "We listen to the rituals, and we learn the tales told in each place we visit."

Iso added, "By marking the differences in the traditions over time and distance, we can chart something of the spread of the story."

"Likewise the gods themselves." Osi, again. "Every city has a sailor's god, and one who watches over farmers. We believe these to be aspects of the same facet lost in the Splintering of the Gods."

"Your Endurance is an exception," Iso told me. "We find that ilk of gods most interesting, for they can tell us what aspects of godhead arise independently, and what must descend from the earliest times."

His brother spoke again. "Someday our devotional charts will give us a map of the theogenic dispersion. From that we can trace our way back to the site of Father Sunbones' garden. Eventually we can learn of both the miracles and the errors which occurred there."

"All thinking creatures were grown to flesh and ensouled in that garden," I mused, remembering my own reading. "I assume it for a metaphor of the richness of the world."

"Some metaphors are as real as the world itself," said Iso. "Never dismiss something simply because it is used to make a point."

I sighed, a long, slow exhalation that caught their attention. "The world is a bit too real for me right now. My troubles are very much not metaphorical."

Osi made that small sign with his right hand again. "We are not of this city, and know little of its people and their cares, but we can hear you out, if you wish."

So I explained, as much for my own benefit as theirs, about my exile from Kalimpura, more of the fall of Choybalsan, and my time away. Then I touched on the arrival of the Selistani embassy, and Mother Vajpai's attempt to kidnap me. I told them of Surali, the Bittern Court woman, and how her thirst for vengeance in the matter of Michael Curry's gems fit into the appearance of the Dancing Mistress and the pardine Revanchists, drawn by their own interest in those same gems. They liked my thought that the problems of the embassy and the Revanchists might be turned toward one another. Then I began explaining my complex relationship to Blackblood. That quieted the twins to a deep and thoughtful silence.

In time, my words ran out. They stared like a pair of cats on a fence. We watched one another awhile. Finally, I said softly, "Thus I run from one problem to another, and solve none of them."

"By your own statements," Osi said, "we take you to be a fighter."

"Yes."

Iso: "You do not run from opponent to opponent, slapping first one then another, only to leave them to cut at you from behind."

"No. . . ."

His brother, again. "It is not our way to fight. Our rites are strict." I should have known that for a lie then, by the way they moved. "But as your path is that of the application of force, you might consider applying force."

"Just as we would apply our rites and meditations," said Iso.

"Force does not mean a fight," I answered. "Force can be so many other things."

"Precisely," they replied in unison.

Osi glanced at the deepening orange light now flooding almost vertical across the upper part of the warehouse. Outside the sun was setting. "Time comes for our deeper observances. Perhaps we shall encounter you again soon?"

I stood, bowed, and thanked them. "You gentlemen have granted me a needed respite, and given me time to consider my situation. Thank you."

Each pressed his palms together as if praying. "Of this, think nothing," said Osi.

Walking away, I mused that they had given me no useful advice at all concerning Blackblood. Another time, perhaps. Or just as likely, their unwillingness to speak to the question was advice in and of itself.

I passed slowly through the streets, pretending to be a tired lad at the end of his workday. That was not far wrong, and hunger called. The baby wanted food and so did I.

The endless errand these twins pursued in life was poetic enough to fascinate. It reminded me of the Dancing Mistress' words not so long ago about how far one might flee in the world, when I'd wondered if taking a fast ship and sailing away truly was the wisest option. She'd said, "Until you reached a desert or a mountain spine your hull could not cross. There you would not speak the language, or know the money. You would wind up begging beside some purple dock amid people who speak with feathers and curse one another with flowers."

Even then, that had seemed an almost desirable fate. Wandering the world, witnessing legends of the fall of the titanics so that the splatter of collapsing godhead could be rendered across a map of the world—such an errand that would be. A quest for the ages.

Much better than breaking oneself over and over to rescue ungrateful cities from their self-created oppressors. The Interim Council could go hang.

I never would do it, though. My daughter needed me here, in a place that could be made safe. For good or ill, this city was for me. And Copper Downs had its own needs. Not to mention all the children who continued to be lost every year in that distant homeland of mine. Someday I would have to return for the little girls and boys who daily saw fates worse than mine.

Amid the wandering of my mind, I realized my feet had carried me once more to the Velviere District. That suggested that some part of me felt safer under Endurance's protection than otherwise. I could not argue too much with this wisdom, though I feared to bring the same peril that had slain Amitra and Nitsa on to their fellow acolytes.

Still, I called at the temple. The gatekeeper I had met the very first time was yet absent, but I entered the grounds to discover most of the acolytes at prayer inside of the wooden hutch of the temple.

The ox god might be my creation, but I did not feel any overwhelming need to bow to him. Instead I wandered to the cooking area, outside the ruined kitchen tent. There I found a pair of grumpy Selistani men in traditional dress stir-frying spinach and then mixing the resultant crispy leaves with some Hanchu sauce.

"A dish for a countryman?" I asked in Seliu.

One of the cooks, a tallish fellow with a small scar on his cheek, looked up at me. "Take a bowl, but be quick, before the little preachers return."

I followed his advice and apportioned myself a goodly serving of the crunchy spinach. "Are you not followers of the ox god?"

The other cook, a much smaller fellow with narrow eyes and a mournful cast to his face, answered as he tossed spinach in his hot pan. "What does it mean to follow a god, boy? There are no Selistani temples in this cold stone place. A Bhopuri ox is what we have, if we wish to pray." He nodded toward the temporary wooden temple. "*Their* view of prayer is much different than ours."

That was fascinating to me. "What of the priest, Chowdry? He is one of us."

"He spends all his time with the whitebellies."

"Excuse me?" I did not know the word.

"The pale folk here," the other cook said. "And the browns who try to act like them. Not good, honest children of the sun like us."

They both laughed. I became very conscious of their kurtas and my own corduroy breeches and canvas shirt. If anyone of my people was a whitebelly, it would be me. Raised here, speaking Petraean better than Seliu.

That was when I realized they'd meant to insult me. I looked into their snickering faces and for a sharp moment considered hurling my bowl at them, and following it up with my fists and blades. These two combined would not stand three blows against me.

Instead I placed my mostly full bowl down on the edge of the rickety table where they'd been prepping their cookery. "I thank you for the time," I said stiffly.

I stalked off into the twilit field beyond the tents, on the far side of the foundation work around the gaping minehead. The brambles had been cleared here, too, but the ground had not been stamped down or graveled over as out front, so they were coming back in sharp, green shoots. A dangerous place, like walking on spikes. Not where one would wish to take a fall.

Skinning out of my shirt and pants, I squatted to put the blocky work-boots back on. Now I wore only them and a pair of linen drawers. The bulge of my belly seemed much more pronounced than the last time I'd stood considering myself naked. I took up my short knives and began to spar with an imaginary opponent. Mother Argai, perhaps. The sight of my breasts swaying as I moved would distract her slightly. And while I was swifter than she, the woman fought like a snake, always just a little to the side and curved off from where you expected her to be.

I began to work faster and faster, dashing back and forth across my claimed area. The wall loomed not so far behind me, so I incorporated jumps and climbs. The imaginary Mother Argai chased me, I chased her. I avoided only falls, for taking a roll in my bare skin across these new brambles amid the cut-down stalks of their elders would have been beyond foolish.

This was not a real sparring match, far from it. But I had not in truth sparred since leaving the Temple of the Silver Lily. Fought in earnest, yes. Run for my life. Lain lazy in bed. All of those things. Here in Copper Downs, only two mortals could match me, and those two overmatched me. Mother Argai, over at the Haito mansion with the Selistani embassy, was probably the only fighter I could meet face-to-face and make the work-out count without embarrassment to one or the other of us.

Still, I slammed myself about, used the wall as both an enemy and a friend, swung my short knives till my wrists ached, and leapt till I had worn myself to shivering exhaustion. Finally I stopped, worried about weakness and balance, and realized this was an autumn night and the air had grown cold and damp.

I looked up to see a solitary girl watching from a short distance. After a long moment of trembling silence, she called out in Petraean, "Are you fin-ished?"

"Yes," I said shortly, then mopped my face with my shirt before tugging it over my head.

"Chowdry sent all the men to their tents and told the women to mind their own business until you were done. I was ordered to watch for you."

That I had to laugh at. "He was concerned about my corrupting the men with my breasts? If any of these boys haven't seen a nipple by now, they have larger problems than me." It wasn't as if anyone here could take anything from me I didn't care to offer. I tucked the short knives into my sleeves, more to make the point to myself than for any other reason.

"I cannot say, Mistress." She approached slowly. A Stone Coast woman, a few years older than me. Not a Selistani whitebelly. It was hard to tell in the gathering dark, but I thought her eyes might be blue. Her hair was some pale color that silvered oddly in the faint light.

"Do not call me 'mistress.'" Sweating and thinking of Mother Argai had put me in a fey mood. My loins were stirring, for no one in particular. I was curious to see her close enough to tell if she would catch my eye. Or I would catch hers. To that end, I said, "Here. Balance me so I can get these boots off and the trousers on."

The woman hurried toward me and grasped my elbow. I stank, I *knew* I stank, but it was the sweat of good, honest work. Building up my body to defend the god Endurance. I hopped from one foot to the other, standing in the loosed boots to tug the pants on while she clutched at my elbow.

"So what is your name?" I gasped.

"Lucia," she said, releasing my arm to reach down and help me with my waistband.

That was more like it. I stood straight and raised my arms out of her way. Lucia bent around me to fasten my pants.

Surely she would not have done that without some interest in me.

"Tell me, Lucia, do you think I might have another bath?"

She giggled faintly. "They would deny you nothing now."

I decided to be blunt. "Then scrub me. I shall do the same for you."

"Mistr—" Lucia stared a moment at her feet. "Green. I am not supposed—"

Touching her lips, I hushed her. "Do what you wish, but I am having a bath and would be glad of the company."

Soon enough, Lucia brought me hot water in the tent with the large copper tub. The air was buttery warm now in the light of two oil lamps and a squat-bellied stove, and smelled pleasantly of the burning. Then she brought me soap and a sponge. Then she brought me a long-handled brush. Finally, she brought me herself. The light made her skin yellow, but her hair flowed downward and her breasts gathered firm as she slipped into the water with me.

We were a long time coming out again, and quite chilled when we finally did, but I fancied her smile was just as large as mine.

Chowdry was not pleased with me the next morning. "This is not your temple of harridans back in Kalimpura," he grumbled in Seliu. "Everyone in the camp knows about you and Lucia. It will be a scandal when her parents hear."

"What?" I laughed at him. We sat with our breakfast bowls on the steps at the front of the wooden temple, ignoring the morning's chill. By the Wheel, I was no whitebelly. "You were a pirate cook when I first met you. What do you care now what some parents think?"

"This project . . ." He waved around him to indicate everything within the walls of the old minehead grounds. "It costs money. A great deal of money. Young people like Lucia are blessed with older parents who are having a great deal of money to give."

"Utavi would have your head." Chowdry's old captain aboard *Chittachai*, and as unpleasant a small-time pirate as ever skulked along a waterfront.

"Utavi is not here."

"He might be," I said. "I saw Little Baji when I first returned to town almost a week ago."

That got Chowdry's attention. "Where!?"

His surprise seemed genuine enough, which served to further lessen my distrust. "The Tavernkeep's place. Where *you* cook. Which is full of Selistani men. It would not be so great a trick to hide one or another there. And the opportunity to learn too much about you, and *me*, is great."

"Ah." His face was a study in misery. "This is why I am needing people like Lucia's parents. Their money will be keeping this temple and the god Endurance safe. That safety is my safety."

I punched Chowdry in the shoulder hard enough to make him flinch. His foolishness would not ruin *my* good mood. "Just think of them all as wallowing coastal ships carrying payroll. You know how to make a raid."

"This temple will do a poor job of sailing to the next port to escape retribution," he complained.

"Then learn more, sir priest." I leaned close. "And listen to Endurance. He's rarely wrong, I am certain of it." I stood, whistling.

"Green," said Chowdry. Something sharp lay in his voice.

I leaned forward, hands on my knees, and let him pretend not to think about my breasts. "Yes?"

"Twice now a girl has called in the name of the Prince of the City. One of your Blades, but being younger and softer than you."

Samma, of course. Though in fact she was my elder, she was one of those girls who always looked as if she'd been raised on warm milk with a good blanket. Whereas I knew perfectly well that I was a walking battlefield. "Did she present herself with swords at her back?"

Though even Samma alone would be quite dangerous to anyone in this group. She might be among the weakest of the Blades, but a Blade she was.

"No. Just nerves. And always looking over her shoulder."

"Interesting." My cocky mood deserted me with the news as I was once more caught up in figuring odds and probabilities. Why would Mother Vajpai send *Samma* to me? Few of the answers that presented themselves seemed sensible. And surely Samma had not sent herself. "What did she say she wanted?"

"To be speaking with you."

"I'm not going anywhere near the Selistani embassy again. Not without plentiful swords at *my* back." The memory of Mother Vajpai in the process of taking me down was still fresh. Samma, too. "Did she limp?"

"She walked with a cane."

Hah.

As Chowdry moved on to his tasks, I returned to consideration of my own troubles. Comfortably seated on the wooden temple's steps in warm daylight, I found that they did not seem so bad. Osi and Iso were not my friends, not in any meaningful sense, but their wise and disinterested counsel had already opened my eyes to certain nuances of the situation. If Samma truly was looking for me, I could turn her against the pardines, and perhaps the other way around.

That mutual leverage appealed to my sense of orderliness, but it also felt like a double betrayal. The pardines, even the Revanchists, were not *my* enemies. Nor would it be fair to think of them as enemies of Copper Downs. If they were fighting anything, the Revanchists struggled against the weight of history and the tangled mass of their own resentments.

If I were not careful, I could make a true enemy out of once-friendly strangers. *And in the Dancing Mistress' case, much more than that to me.*

Likewise the Selistani embassy. I was nothing to the Prince of the City. Mother Vajpai could not have turned on me so thoroughly, I simply didn't believe that; she must be playing a deeper, doubled game. Or redoubled, perhaps. Only Surali, the Bittern Court woman, was seriously out to overset me and bring me low.

Now if I could manage to focus *her* and Blackblood on one another, I might truly be free.

All that made me wish I'd explained myself to Iso and Osi better, that they might have given me wiser counsel now.

A motion in the edge of my vision made me glance up. I saw Samma walking toward me. She definitely limped badly. When she realized that I was looking at her, she halted.

"I believe I kicked you in the belly," I said by way of greeting. This was not a moment likely to incline me to charity.

"Yes. You nearly dislocated my hip." She grimaced. "I have bruised black as a coal demon's face."

"Surely you have not been loitering outside the gate?"

"I was not bid to wait here for you. I have been to a kava house three times so far to while away the hours."

That there was a kava house anywhere near our gate was news to me. I continued to peer up at her, deliberately not inviting her to sit. "You would have betrayed me, alongside Mother Vajpai. Why should I welcome you, even as a negotiator? Especially so?"

Samma looked miserable—sad and nervous, her regrets writ upon her face in the not-so-secret language of her heart. "You have no reason. B-but I have tried to bring you some."

Resting my hands on my belly, I considered that. Soon I would be too pregnant to fight properly—terribly unbalanced, for one. Then even this weak sister would take me down. Better to listen for a while, perhaps. I resolved to consider new attack strategies even as we spoke. In a way, I was maturing, though then I would have scarcely admitted to a need for such. "Illuminate me, Blade."

She almost shuddered at my words. "I departed Kalimpura less than a month after you. Aboard a ship called *Atchaguli*. Sister hull to poor *Chittachai*."

That was very interesting news, indeed. I bent forward, thinking hard. "To what errand?" I asked softly.

Samma glanced about almost theatrically. She would never do for a spy, or even a decent lookout. "Mother Vajpai put me on your track. The Lily Goddess wanted you to return to Copper Downs."

Suspicious now, I probed. "The Lily Goddess? Not the Bittern Court?"

"Th-that happened later. After I left." Her misery deepened. "Please, may I sit with you?"

I relented and patted the step next to me. Samma stumbled over and lowered herself painfully. It was like watching a woman of seventy-six instead of sixteen.

"Did I truly kick you that hard?" I asked softly, my fingers brushing along her thigh.

"You kicked me so hard that Mother Argai probably felt it."

"I am sorry." Surprisingly, I found I meant that. "I was rushed."

"I know. We wronged you."

We. "Whose idea was it to take me hostage?"

"L-let me tell it from the beginning. As I understand the tale, at least."

I could not help myself; I leaned over and hugged my very first lover ever. "Speak, friend," I whispered in her ear. She even *smelled* like home.

"Weeks I voyaged aboard *Atchaguli.* Until we caught up with *Chittachai.* The crews knew one another—Captain Padma was cousin to Captain Utavi, I think."

Was cousin. She gave away a great deal in her assumptions and phrasing. "How was *Chittachai* when you found her?" I asked gently.

"Still floating," Samma replied absently. "Then. Utavi was an ass, but he took me aboard. Made me prove myself with that poor giant of his."

"Tullah."

"Yes." Our eyes met, and hers shone with something like gratitude. She'd understood my tone. "I fought the man. A large baby, in truth."

I thought sadly on Tullah, whom I had liked. "Grown enough for Utavi's hungers."

"Mayhap. It was the captain's hungers that did us in. However else you left him, you also left him angry. I thought he'd sold you. Instead he made to sell me. The crew tried to ambush me after a while, meaning to bind me over to someone searching for you."

Now we come to the crux of the matter. "What happened?" I circled her with my arm again.

"I k-killed them all. Except for Little Baji. B-but *Atchaguli* was close by. They would know my deeds, and ch-chase me. So Little Baji and I took the boat deep into the southern sea, to wait among the shipping lanes."

Keeping myself very still, I asked, "You killed Tullah?"

"N-no. He died defending me. I did kill the others, including Utavi." She rubbed her hand at some remembered injury. Or blow.

"How did you make it from an empty ship on the open ocean to here?"

"We were picked up in the shipping lanes by *Winter Solace*. Bound for Kalimpura to transport the Selistani embassy. I came back to the docks at her rail only to meet Mothers Vajpai and Argai." Her misery seemed to deepen. "They never even let me return to shore. I suppose I know too much now."

"Too much of what?"

"Of *your* story! Of *you*!" Samma's voice pitched up sharply, the anger of a little girl. "It is always you at the heart of everything. It's *you* who the mothers gossip about and linger to say how much they miss. No one cared half so much when Jappa was killed by that drunken carter."

I did not know Jappa had died. Some impulse to guilt surged briefly inside me, but I pushed it aside. "I am sorry," I told her.

"Of course you are. Green the magnificent. Green the perfect. There was never a better fighter nor a more goddess-favored aspirant than you!" She took a deep, shuddering breath, trying to calm herself.

"None of that was earned by me." My voice pitched soft, trying to reach past her anger. Not to soothe, but only so that she could hear what I was saying. "Nor wanted. I was never consulted."

Samma sniffed. "None of us were ever consulted. We only did as we could. When old Mother Umaavani died, the goddess spoke through her last breaths. *She* wants you back."

"*She* sent me away," I said bitterly, wondering who the new Temple Mother was with Mother Umaavani passed on.

"Politics," muttered Samma. "Even now. Especially now. Whatever you did to the Bittern Court has not faded from their memories. They hate you beyond reason."

"Hate me enough to suborn Mother Vajpai and chase me across an ocean? Who has been named to Umaavani's office? And who could care so much?"

"Mother Srirani."

One of the senior Justiciary Mothers. I'd barely ever spoken to her, but she was a traditionalist, I knew. The Blades had not cared for her so much. Someone whose will could be turned against Mother Vajpai, then.

"As for who could care so much . . . well, Surali could." Samma took a breath, then blurted as if she were afraid of her own words: "That woman has been bargaining with certain parties—maybe those cat people of yours—for aid in some affair the Bittern Court pursues. I cannot say what it is. They always talk in whispers, using little codes. I don't think even Mother Vajpai knows the story. Just that her hand was forced, and the Temple Mother's, to come here and reclaim you."

And so now we arrive at why the Revanchists have descended from their quiet hills and announced themselves, I thought. A ship-borne flow of prior messages had arranged the apparent coincidence of their presence here at this time. "But Surali is not here for me? She is here in pursuit of this other bargain?"

"Oh, she will take you as bonus and be quite pleased with herself, if she can."

"So why are you here?" I asked.

"They would never let me off *Winter Solace.*"

"No, why are *you* here *now*, with me? Instead of plotting my capture with Mother Vajpai."

Samma looked pained. "Mother Vajpai came to this city in large part because the Temple Mother thought it far better you be taken by your sisters than by the Bittern Court and their Street Guild toughs."

"I thought the Lily Goddess wanted me back?"

"She does. But the goddess did not pay for this expedition."

"So you Blades serve two masters." *As usual,* I thought with nasty glee. I knew myself to be unfair. Too bad.

"We s-serve two intentions, say rather."

That line sounded rehearsed to me. I wondered how much of this little errand Mother Vajpai had put Samma up to. There seemed small point in asking. I hugged her gently again, recalling the best of our times together in the Blade aspirants' dormitory. "And you came only to tell me this?"

"Mother Vajpai and I fought," she said in a rush.

"I doubt that, as you are still walking."

"N-no! Hard words, not sparring. I-I think this bargaining Surali does is aimed at the Lily Goddess. M-Mother Vajpai does not believe me."

Samma never was one for holding strong ideas of her own, not when there was someone of character nearby to follow along with. I wondered how she'd hit upon this notion, and held to it in the face of Mother Vajpai's demurral. "Why do you know this?"

"I don't know it," she said, her voice laced with misery. "I *th-think* it. Some of the ways they talked aboard the ship. How Surali glares at me, as if she could hit me to bruise you. The old rivalry between the Bittern Court and the Temple of the Silver Lily."

The Lily Blades certainly had their own rivalry with the Street Guild of Kalimpura, which was itself closely allied to the Bittern Court. The Bittern Court controlled the docks, took in moorage fees and levied excise on goods coming and going. Enormous amounts of ready money passed back and forth in those endeavors. The Street Guild were essentially licensed footpads, keeping the general peace against freelancers in return for the freedom to conduct shakedowns and outright muggings of their own.

That latter rivalry was obvious enough—weapons carriers against weapons carriers, each with a very different notion of justice and fairness. But the rivalry between the Temple of the Silver Lily and Bittern Court went back well before my time in Kalimpura, rooted in long-ago betrayals and old hatreds of which I knew nothing.

Would they truly plot to bring down a goddess? Who thought in those terms?

Me, for one, I realized with unintended irony. I'd done for Choybalsan myself, although with a great deal of help. And *someone* had laid a trap for Marya not long after I had first fled Copper Downs.

That was who Surali was looking for. With whom was she bargaining? The Rectifier? Somehow god killing didn't quite seem his mode. He had priests to hunt, but that was a different matter.

But what of the rest of the Revanchists? My blood ran cold. Surely the Dancing Mistress had small reason to love the Lily Goddess. There had been nothing kind about her treatment at the hands of my temple sisters and Mothers.

It all fit together, but somehow was still too neat. I had trouble believing in this plot. Who could conspire across the breadth of an ocean, given the excruciating pace at which messages traveled? And some pieces of it had to stretch back years. The Eyes of the Hills, for example, if they were indeed involved.

"I find it more likely that Mother Vajpai has encouraged you to think this," I told Samma. "To bait me into her grasp once more. I will not return to her again."

"No, Green." Samma sounded almost desperate now. Close to tears. "Please listen to me. The plots in the embassy are as thick as silkworm webs on a mulberry bush."

"That is the way of Kalimpuri politics," I told her. "And everywhere else, too, I suppose. This does not mean some great effort is being made to slay our goddess. They work for advantage, that their names may be ascendant."

I was loyal to the Lily Goddess, albeit very irregular in my observances, but I was not dedicated to Her political power, or the particular fortunes of Her temple. If the Temple Mother and the Justiciary Mother and Mother Vajpai wanted to fritter their years on those disputes, it was no game of mine.

There were gods aplenty here in Copper Downs to trouble me.

"I-I brought you something," Samma said, her voice very small indeed. "By way of proof."

She reached inside her Blade leathers and pulled forth a small velvet sack that had been lying close to her left breast. I knew how she favored that one when at play, so perhaps she had drawn comfort from having her secrets there.

Samma hefted the sack. I could see it was light. Money? It was not so heavy, not at all. Some ancient sigil, perhaps. But when she tugged the drawstring, two gems spilled into the palm of her left hand: a green tourmaline and a cobalt spinel.

"The Eyes of the Hills," I whispered.

They *had* returned to Copper Downs. No wonder the Revanchists were down out of their high forests and meadows. I felt ill as I realized how much of that supposed plot *had* to be real.

Maybe Osi and Iso were right after all. Set the Selistani embassy and the pardine factions on one another, then simply clear the streets.

"Where did you get those?" I asked her.

Samma shook her head, miserable, as she tucked the Eyes of the Hills back into their velvet bag. "I h-had some gems, to barter for cash or goods or passage, as I began to pursue you. I stole these from Mother Vajpai, but left her with two other gems so she would not note the theft so quickly."

"You stole from *Mother Vajpai*?" This was not the Samma I had known.

"I'm no longer the scared girl you dumped when you became a star among the Blades," she said in a determined voice. "All we do is police Kalimpura, and spend our time there. When Mother Vajpai sent me after you alone, with Captain Padma and those t-terrible men, I think I learned some things. Maybe I grew up."

"You may not be a scared girl," I said simply, "but you are a frightened young woman."

"Possibly. But I c-couldn't just let it be. Not once I knew Mother Vajpai carried something Surali wanted real bad."

Ah-ha.

"So they argued over these?"

"Surali has been beside herself for this whole trip."

Which made me wonder all over again if Mother Vajpai had manipulated Samma into even this betrayal. A way to secure my help without asking me.

Oh, the wheels inside the wheels of this were making my head ache.

A solution of sorts came unbidden into my thoughts. "Give the gems to me."

She stank of a sudden surge of fear sweat, then closed her fist. "No. I might need to put them back."

"I can keep them far safer from Surali than Mother Vajpai can." Which was almost certainly not literally true, but I was willing to hang on to the thought for right now. "Also, I know what to do with them, to ensure that no harm comes to the Lily Goddess through the agency of these gems."

"They're powerful, aren't they?" Every now and then, Samma showed something of what the training mothers had seen in her. She slipped the sack back within her leathers.

I could not allow her to leave with them. "All by themselves, perhaps not." I grabbed hold of her wrist. "But they have the power of a symbol, and are connected to an ancient magic here in the city which has been stolen and re-stolen."

"They're not *yours*, Green." Samma tried to pull away from my grip.

Tugging her toward me, I leaned in close. "They're not yours, either. And they are *dangerous*."

Samma yanked herself almost free, rising to her feet. I came up with her, then tripped her ruthlessly by the bad leg I'd injured previously. That dumped her to the ground in front of the temple steps with a hiss of pain. I followed with a body pin of my own weight, pressing her into the graveled soil as my right hand snaked inside her leathers to retrieve the gems in their sack.

Recovering her breath, Samma kicked up with her knee, catching me painfully in the thigh. I dug a thumb into the edge of her eye. "Do not try me further." I was not pleased with myself, but I had neither time nor patience for her foolishness.

She went limp, surrendering as she used to on the practice floor and in our shared bed. "*Greeeeeeen*," she gasped in whining misery.

I rolled off her and stood, wary of some last-minute trickery on her part. "Not a word of this to anyone, not even Mother Vajpai." Especially not Mother Vajpai.

Betrayal was written large upon Samma's face, scratching open a sense of guilt which I rarely experienced. "I was trying to help you," she sniffed.

"You have." I glanced down at the velvet bag, then tugged at the drawstring until the Eyes of the Hills spilled out once more, this time into my waiting hand. They tingled with that familiar metal-in-the-mouth feeling of something touched by the divine. It was all I could do not to glance skyward and look for the lightning strike to come.

Instead I leaned forward and kissed Samma gently. "Go home. Back to the embassy, then back to Selistan."

Her lips surged against mine, an old habit of sexual hunger between us; then she tore away, saying, "I hate you." But the tone of her voice told me differently.

Watching her totter out, limping yet, I wondered if I should have sent for a carriage. When she disappeared past the far side of the gate, I turned my attention to the pair of gems in my hand. Once again, I had a feeling I'd paid too much for too little reward. Except for their size, the stones were unremarkable enough to casual inspection. Blue and green, a pair of eyes that reminded me muchly of Michael Curry. I was fairly certain no one but a priest would sense the power that buzzed against my hand like a trapped wasp.

What if I had not killed him then? Would all this be different now? What if I had not just bullied Samma, hurt her to force the girl to my will?

I dismissed all of that as fruitless. It occurred to me that my very best source of information would be the Factor's ghost, for in his guise as the Duke, he had first stolen these away from the pardines.

The flaws in that idea were readily apparent, and so I abandoned it. No, I was done with turning to those who had once held authority over me to ask for help and more help. To the Smagadine hells with the Interim Council, the Factor, and even Mother Vajpai. Armed once again with the power of a god, I would seek out Osi and Iso and craft a response of my own.

Out on the streets once more in my guise as a lad of Copper Downs, I ignored my fading guilt about Samma and instead mused on Erio's fears. Surely the Eyes of the Hills were what had caught at the old ghost's attention. His own years far predated the late Duke's appropriation of the pardine artifacts, but Erio, much like the tulpas of Below, had been focused on the city throughout the entire sorry history of the gems. Their power, both as legacy and whatever remained directly invested in them today, was now too closely tied to Copper Downs. That these gems drew the pardine Revanchists with their atavistic ways back into the city would be deeply frightening to a soul who remembered the older days of pardine Hunts and the brutal wars with the human settlers of this land.

The feral aspect of the Dancing Mistress and her cohorts in the Tavernkeep's place was surely a pathway to a much darker facet of her people, harkening to those older days. I had loved her for years in various ways, but she always held a frightening depth.

Sometimes I preferred a person of simple intentions. Samma, for example. Or me. I grew tired of outguessing the inscrutable motives of those taken up with ancient, invisible agendas. Looking back, I find it amazing how unaware of myself I was in those years.

As I turned onto Calabar Street, the air around me seemed to pop. Strange shadows danced on the walls even in broad daylight. For a moment my mouth filled with the metallic taste of power. Then a sound rumbled by, loud enough that it overwhelmed all the noise of the city. I had in the past been mere handspans away from lightning strikes, thanks to the kind attentions of Federo. This was worse.

Some around me fell, mostly through fear, as the ground did not buckle. Noting the alignment of the new shadows, I turned and sprinted back toward their source. Once I was heading that way, the column of smoke and rising, multicolored sparks was easy enough to spot.

The Temple Quarter? Had Blackblood done himself a mischief? My troubles could surely not be so easily solved.

I raced toward the Street of Horizons, leaping over people huddled by the curb, pushing past the more alert who fled in the opposite direction. This was no explosion of alchemical powders, I was certain. Nothing a man or woman could create would cause such a flash of light. This was magic, the divine, something supernatural.

I approached the Temple Quarter, my sprint converted to the ground-eating lope of a Blade run. I could see that the cloud rose from a block behind the Street of Horizons. That was a smaller road of which I did not know the name. I arrived at the scene to find a few dozen stunned acolytes and priests of several orders staring at a rubble pile out of which the last of the smoke and dust was boiling.

The remaining air was strangely clear, as if wiped of all impurities. Like the garden before time, when the birds and animals had not yet been awoken to breathe it in. The metal-in-mouth taste was strong here. I could see by the expressions of several of the watchers that they shared it.

Puffing, I pulled up to the group. *I never breathe hard. Not like this!* An argument with the baby, for later. One hand on my belly, trying not to be obvious, I asked, "Whose place was this?"

None of them even looked at me, until I plucked at one young boy's robed arm. He turned and opened his mouth, popping his lips like a carp in a pond. I realized his ears were bleeding. He must have been deafened by the explosion.

All of them seemed to have been.

I hoped they had a god of hearing to pray to.

Instead of addressing them, I pushed through to the front of the semi-circle of onlookers. "Go home!" I shouted, letting the words form large upon my lips. I touched my ears, then pointed to them, then shooed them away.

Even the older priests nodded, somewhat to my surprise. In my experience, men of a certain age simply don't surrender authority to women or boys. Their willingness to heed me was a mark of how overwhelmed they felt.

I turned around and looked again. Their departure was also a mark of how utterly unlikely I was to find any survivors.

Given the intense nature of the explosion, I knew I would probably have a few minutes to myself. Especially with the smoke plume almost vanished, which would reduce the likelihood of a bucket brigade arriving.

Looking around, I realized that the damage had indeed been contained. While windows were shattered in all directions, only one building had collapsed. Rubble smoldered in front of me, beams shattered, bricks broken and ground to dust, the contents of the inside mixed into the mess—plates, a splintered table, a length of cloth.

I moved closer. The length of cloth enclosed a human leg, protruding from under a still-intact chunk of masonry the size of a large trunk. Now I wished I hadn't sent the priests away so quickly. Still, the chunk was balanced precariously on a pile of smaller wreckage. And there was no lack of loose wood for levers.

Swiftly I wedged a seven-foot length of milled lumber into place under the high edge of the masonry. Even as I worked to that, I confirmed my impression that this place had been targeted very specifically.

Was this the Temple of Marya? That hand had been played before, after all.

Someone had tried to attack this temple several years ago, not long after the fall of the Duke. I'd heard the story when I was staying with Ilona, twice, about a long night of light and flame, and a horrid creature slain in the street, only to have the body vanish with the sunrise. This had all taken place during the brass-ape races, which were a time of debauchery and general foolishness. While I'd recognized the importance of the story, I'd discounted most of the details.

Mistakenly so, it seemed.

Putting my back into the makeshift lever, I reflected that I had been quite the fool. Working my strength into the effort, I reflected that I was continuing to be quite the fool, but for different reasons.

It took me three tries, and the lever shaking hard with a splintering crack, before the masonry slid away. I leaned into the resulting hollow to pick up a dead woman. There was no reason to believe I knew her, but even if I had, her face was crushed beyond recognition.

Still, I drew her out and laid her in the street with as much respect as I could muster. Doubting terribly, I climbed back into the rubble to look again.

It had been a strange explosion. I was no expert on artillery or the alchemical arts—far from it—but I was fairly certain objects exploded in either one direction or another. From inside to out, as it were. Or the other way around.

This looked as if someone had taken a bowl full of temple and beaten it with a strong spoon. Everything was folded and mixed. Some material had gone inward, some out. Certain objects were pulverized, others nearly whole.

I clambered over the wreckage, searching for more bodies and looking for I knew not what else. If the gods of the Temple Quarter had been roused before, an attack such as this should have them on their feet and erupting from their own rooftops. Or did even gods know fear?

Some of the bricks that appeared grimed enough to have been the old outer wall had chalk marks on them. Sigils. Spells. Random scribblings, perhaps.

As I searched through the piles, the metallic tang in the air faded. The place already had the air of an old rubble pile. Magic, taking the urgency of the moment with it, covering the site over with varnished layers of time. Climbing back down, I looked into the rubble gap from where I'd pulled the dead woman, and realized another woman had lain beneath her.

This one might still be alive.

I cursed myself and leaned back into the gap. When I worked her free, she groaned. Her eyes were rolled back to whites, which did not encourage me, but her ears were not bleeding, and there was no foam bubbling from her mouth.

Perhaps she would survive.

Dragging her out could not be helping whatever was wrong inside her body, but leaving the woman under the bricks seemed even more foolish. I began praying to the Lily Goddess—the closest I knew to Marya, whose protections had so obviously failed here.

I do not know these women, Goddess.

They are not of Your priestesses. They have probably never even heard Your name. They are hardly of blameless virtue, I am certain.

But if their goddess is not able to ease their passing, or bind their souls back to their bodies, I pray You can do this thing for them on her behalf.

If no one claims them, I will wash their bodies and paint the white and the red, in Your name. Better they should rise up and live longer, though.

Not much of a prayer, and smacked more of funeral rites than a healing chant, but it was what I could manage in the moment.

I laid the women out side by side. The first victim was beyond all hope. Even if the very spirit of the goddess took over her body, her face and neck were crushed. She would never breathe or eat, though somehow her brown hair still seemed rich as life. The second one, whose dark hair and freckled coloration suggested they might have been sisters, at least had found her breath.

Water spattered on me. I looked up for rain, but saw only silver light. The air tingled.

I realized the Lily Goddess had not only heard my prayers, She was answering them directly. In that moment, I was too exhausted to drop to my knees or show obeisance, so I sat back on my butt and impatiently awaited the divine.

Now I knew why no one had run to aid me. I was cloaked in the goddess' glamour. I had witnessed this in Kalimpura, that only a few could see Her while most others knew nothing but echoing, chilly silence.

"I am here," I announced. "You might as well get this over with."

The Lily Goddess stepped out of a place between the air and the sky and smiled sadly at me. Much as with Blackblood, I saw someone who could have been mistaken for ordinary from a distance, except Her body fairly vibrated with power. My goddess was an explosion contained in the shape of a woman. Her hair was the color of all women, Her eyes shifted from gray to green to black to blue to violet to silver, all with the twisting flash of a windborne leaf in autumn. She was all sizes and shapes and ages, from gawky girl to matronly mother to withered crone.

She was all women.

"You never manifested so in the Temple of the Silver Lily," I said softly. Always She was a wind, a rush of water, a voice possessing the Temple Mother.

Never before have I appeared to you.

Had I been standing, Her words would have driven me to my knees after all. Her lips moved, but the sounds did not quite match. That sense of power arced out of the goddess like water from a stormy sky. My loins went soft and wet, and I felt the first shudders of orgasm take me.

I knew that the tingle of power from the Eyes of the Hills I now carried was less than one of Her nail parings.

Though I tried to answer Her, my own words were muted.

You are Green.

All I could do was nod. That was like moving boulders with my neck. Pleasure arced through me, so intense it was painful, all the worse because I was not free to throw myself into the sensation.

You follow one of My daughters.

It was slowly penetrating to me that this was not the Lily Goddess. Another nod, more rocks dragged by the sheer force of my neck and head. Fluid rushed from my sweetpocket, as it could when a lover touched me just *so* for a time.

She stepped—if that could be the word—to the two women I had laid out.

My grandchild Solis is dead.

The woman with the crushed face seemed to sigh and settle. She had been lost to life already, but something more had just gone out of her. I clenched my thighs and tried to control myself, against the mad, mad pressure.

A titanic! The realization was so horrifying I wanted to flee into unconsciousness. If I could have stopped my heart to escape Her, I would have.

My grandchild Laris lives.

The surviving sister—if that was who they were, siblings—seemed to breathe easier, though still trapped in the awkward unconsciousness of the badly wounded.

The goddess turned back to the shattered temple. My breathing shuddered so hard I feared to choke. Then I prayed to choke.

My daughter is passed from the world.

The grief in Her voice was the mourning of the ocean for those mountains ground to sand along its beaches. She cried as the stars do for one of their number tumbled from the night sky to strike the earth. I wanted to die for Her loss, to lay myself down as a cloak over Her suffering, and spare Her even a beat of the anguish that threatened my very sanity.

In that moment, I saw for the first time what it might mean to be a god. Not power, but responsibility. Not awareness, but omniscience. Not emotion, but something so large it would shatter the human soul.

You know Me now.

"Yes, Mother," I whispered, as though the words were drawn from me as with burning pincers. The fires of my lust were all but forgotten.

Your Lily Goddess is one of My daughters.

Desire.

The girl-child you carry is Mine, through your goddess.

Once again, my passion blinded me to sensibility. All I could think was to rise up in anger, ready to shout: *You will not have my daughter!* The flame of my rebellion, never truly doused, flared even under Her eternal burden of time, power, and sorrow. Nearly crushed beneath the majesty of Her titanic awareness so poorly contained in the swirling woman's body She wore, I still had to laugh. Or tried to. By the Wheel, this was difficult.

"Blackblood told me . . ." I gasped. The words were birthing hard. ". . . that I would bear . . ." Another gasp. This was like lifting stones. ". . . a boy-child." My mind leapt right past the obvious answer to those rare unfortunates born both man and woman in one conflicted body. Fool that I was, I did not want to know then what would come in time, what choices these prophecies would bring me.

Then She was gone without ever having been there. The wreckage was full of shouting men and crying women, while boys tugged at the beams and people swirled around me. No one seemed to take note of me, though several bent to attend to the two women I had rescued from beneath the rubble. I felt spent, as if a lover had used me hard through all the watches of the night, and forced me to orgasm far beyond the limits of either reason or passion. I knew I *reeked* of sex.

And fear. Sweat poured from me, even in the cold.

I could see why a woman might want to be a priestess of *that* goddess. I could see more why a woman would run screaming.

Laris, the survivor, opened her eyes and looked at me. She could not gain enough of herself to speak, but I saw that she knew, and that she understood that I knew.

I nodded to her, and touched my cap, mouthing the words *We shall meet again.*

Wrapped in the last of Desire's glamour, I walked away unnoticed. My plans for the Eyes of the Hills were forgotten now, set aside in the rush of thought about what sort of power it took to slay a goddess. No wonder Erio had feared.

Anyone who could make such a death magic as to shatter the divine could just as easily have shattered this city were they of a mind to do so. The fault lines that would likely issue from Marya's fall might do it for them.

I found myself deeply disturbed by Desire's intervention. Familiarity with the gods had lent me a dangerously casual attitude, but still, I have never grown easy with such encounters, then or in the time since. All through my life I have learned over and over the lesson that there is an order to the existence of the gods, just as there is an order to the lives of men. *That* I had known since my grandmother's funeral at the beginning of my memories, and I would recall it until the day I was laid out with the white and the red painted upon my own face.

Having Her come to me so was as daunting a violation of the world as having my grandmother return from her burial platform in the sky to correct my words and deeds. Or worse, *her* grandmother.

The *world's* grandmother.

This was not *right*.

During my time at the Factor's house, I had been exposed to any number of books on the divine. They largely contained views of the gods as some historical aspect of the life of the city and its people. In those days the gods were still sleeping away the years under the somnolence of the Duke's magic, so I suppose that had been deemed safe enough.

But even then, the Dancing Mistress had introduced me to the boy-priest Septio, who would later father my child. And Mother Iron, that chthonic force who seemed to me to perhaps be the soul of Copper Downs. Like Desire, a larger being wrapped in a smaller body. A woman sees a goddess much as a fish sees the fingers that drop food into its bowl—with no notion of the vastness looming beyond.

I did not deny the divine. For the love of all that was holy, I held regular conversations with the divine. I had *made* a god.

Desire had been something more. She was to the godhood of the Lily Goddess or Blackblood or Choybalsan or Endurance as they were to my personhood. It occurred to me just then how very odd it was that I had been on a first-name basis with *four* different gods and goddesses, when most of the priestesses in the Temple of the Silver Lily prayed all their lives for the simplest visitation from Her.

Still, the titanics were so far beyond human experience. Their roots were back in the deepest time, before cities and farms and the very tongues of men. To see a titanic manifest . . .

The sheer thought boggled me. I risked sainthood if anyone knew of this. If these visitations continued, I risked my own sanity.

I needed counsel from deeper in time. Previously I'd rejected the Factor's ghost, when contemplating how to move against Blackblood with the Eyes of the Hills in my possession. But he was the oldest person I could talk to in this city. Erio was tied to his tomb in the High Hills, so far as I knew, and besides was only a whispering voice in the shadows. I had known the Factor in life, at least a little, and held power over him in death, as it had been me who pushed him through the black door in his guise as the Duke.

Further, when I'd last seen the Factor, he'd been standing with Mother Iron. I knew *she* was much older than any of us. Possibly older than Copper Downs itself. Deeper in time, indeed.

A titanic had touched the city. A goddess had died. I still had my worries, but I strongly desired wisdom as to the meaning of *these* signs and portents.

If Surali and her plots had brought about the death of Marya through some illicit alliance with the pardine Revanchists, that signified very ill indeed for the Lily Goddess. And the Bittern Court would little concern itself with my goddess' fall. Quite the opposite, regardless of the consequences. No, I could not send the Selistani embassy home. I needed to stop them *here*.

Thank the goddess I now carried the Eyes of the Hills. Surali and the Revanchists could not seal whatever bargain they'd made without these, I was confident.

My thoughts were circling again. I slipped into an alley and located an entrance to Below.

I strode through an echoing gallery I had visited only a few times. This was not among my usual precincts, from the years when I ran beneath the streets of the city nightly. Coldfire gleamed in abundance on rough-chiseled walls, and I could see wide, irregular pillars holding up the roof atop which this part of the city squatted.

One of the old copper-mine galleries, before those ancients had delved deeper and opened tunnels into the darkest places as they played out their seams. Not that any place beneath the stones wasn't dark enough to drive any thoughtful woman to the edge of terror.

I listened, as one does Below. Water dripped in a dozen places or more. The air seemed to breathe slightly. No footfalls, no clink of metal, no shallower breathing of meaty lungs. That didn't rule out ghosts, avatars, or the other supernatural detritus that clung to the underside of this city like currants in a scone.

But then, it was ghosts and avatars I'd been searching for.

Long experience suggested that calling out names was an invitation to unpleasantness. So I headed toward the machines that bulked oily and rusted in the spaces beneath the Temple of Endurance. The Factor or Mother Iron either one could find me far more easily than I could find them.

And right then, to their perceptions, I must have reeked of the scent of divine magic. Even without the touch of Desire, the Eyes of the Hills would draw them like a fire on the ocean at night.

Traveling Below was very much a matter of listening, smelling, and thinking with senses other than the eyes. There was a lesson to be drawn from that process, which was surely part of the reason the Dancing Mistress had taken me Below in the first instance. I walked with lids half shut, hearing how my careful, soft footfalls echoed in the velvety darkness beyond the pallid, witchy glow of the coldfire. The damp, luminescent moss clung mucky to my fingers. I knew that in the complete, natural darkness of Below my eyes would soon enough invent terrors of their own if I did not give them soft shadows to see around the corners of.

When something sparked beyond the pale shell of my coldfire, my heart lurched. I'd been expecting a visitor, wanting one, but still . . .

Mother Iron's eyes as always resembled distant furnaces, fires banked on a hillside at dusk. I had never seen her face, only her cowl, but I still felt as if I could reach past the hem of her garment and touch another world. Relaxing my pace, I slowed to meet her.

The Factor's ghost was not about. This surprised me slightly. They'd been together the last time I'd seen them. Others moved through this place, but the usual practice was to avoid if possible, or pass quickly and quietly if not. Only those of us who had business here met on purpose.

"Greetings, Mother Iron," I said as politely as I could. The Dancing Mistress had made it very clear to me that this was one of the old, great powers of Copper Downs, for all that she kept herself cloaked and damped down to nearly a cinder.

"Green." Her voice carried that same rustiness I had always associated with Mother Iron, a sense of something vast breathing from far away. And hot, as well.

"I had hoped to meet you here." I could not decide if I was a supplicant, a petitioner, or even in some strange way a peer to her. Mother Iron always moved to her own will, and seemed utterly indifferent to whoever and whatever surrounded her.

"You bear the weight of history."

My right hand strayed to my belly. For one odd moment, I thought she meant the child. Then I realized she must be referring to the Eyes of the Hills.

"History threatens to return and weigh upon us all, Mother Iron."

She huffed. A sigh? I waited, to see what else she might say. Speaking with her was something like playing the traveler's game. Finally: "That price was already paid. More than once."

"I would not know what was paid before, Mother Iron. I only know what is balanced in the scales this day. And this day I have a problem older than the time in which it comes to me."

"Older time comes for you. The elder days of Copper Downs seek to return."

That made some sense. Erio was stirring for reasons beyond the latest problems in the succession of seats on the Interim Council. Of course, that kingly ghost could have been yapping his head off for centuries and I would not have known the difference. Somehow I suspected that Ilona would have understood, and mentioned it. "I have taken these gems from a fool, who would have used them to bribe greater fools. But they are not of this city."

She rumbled again: "That price was already paid."

Softly, I said, "I know. And Desire rises here. Her daughter Marya is slain."

"Another power from an older time. Only the oldest wisdoms can save this city from its oldest threats."

With that nearly pointless advice, she turned away and vanished between one step and the next. Whether it was only the darkness swallowing her and the black cowl she wore, or a more ghostly disappearance, I could not say. Most of the time, ordinary folk in ordinary bodies were sadly outnumbered Below.

I wondered how it had been for the miners, back in the morning of the world. Had they broken open the crust of the world only to find a population of haunts and legends already awaiting them? Or had they brought their fears with them on first creating the Below?

Musing so, I nearly ran into a man who seemed altogether flesh and blood. My short knife flashed into my right hand—it was rare for anyone to achieve such a complete advantage of surprise over me. I kept my point from his throat, though, for already I knew this was no attack.

"Excuse me." His nervous voice was thin, reedy, as a boy not quite grown to his prime, though he seemed tall enough in the glow of my coldfire.

That was such an unlikely response to having a blade pulled that I had to laugh. Stepping back, I gave him room, and looked at my involuntary captive.

"I am sorry," I said. "You startled me. This is unusual."

His head pumped vigorously as he nodded. I was pretty sure he was male. For one thing, no woman with any decent sense of herself would wear such a hideous mask. His head was wrapped in bands of leather over which were affixed two goggle-eyed lenses and a tiny, sputtering lamp between them so faint I could not see the use of it. His mouth was covered with a verdigrised brass muzzle with needled teeth set into it, that last detail seemingly just for the look of the thing. He wore musty dark robes and a heavy leather belt creaking with tools and devices.

Had I seen him before hearing his voice, I might have found him threatening. Instead I realized I faced a man dressed as a kind of mummer. A boy, really, with a man's height.

"Y-you are Green?"

I didn't think he meant that as a question. "Yes, I am Green." Now he was making me nervous. "I do not know you."

"Mother Iron called me to y-you."

The tulpa had just left me moments ago, but that did not mean she had not spoken to this boy-man, perhaps hours ago. Or even years. I'd long since understood that her rules were not my own.

"Who are you?" I asked gently, hefting my short knife for emphasis.

"I am Archimandrix."

Now there was pride in his voice. Pride of place, pride of purpose, pride of self. I could hear it. I knew that pride, from when I had been a Lily Blade. *Only a Lily Blade*, I corrected myself.

"And what does an Archimandrix do? Besides heed the call of Mother Iron?" I was not so sure I would, or could, ignore her call should Mother Iron choose to speak through me.

"I lead the oldest guild," he squeaked. Archimandrix cleared his throat and tried again. "I am the master of the sorcerer-engineers."

Frankly I would have doubted if he had mastery of a bathtub, but I'd long given up on judging people from their seemings. How many had failed and died owing to wrongly judging me on *my* seeming, after all? And how many more yet would?

But the sorcerer-engineers? I was to learn that they were in truth guardians of ancient wisdom, but at that moment I did not know them from dunny divers. "I do not recognize your guild. And I have studied the old Duke's lists." Thanks to Mistress Danae's careful instruction and endless books during my days in the Factor's house, I could name even of some of the most obscure guilds, such as the Brotherhood of Lens Grinders, and the Worshipful Order of Loom Mechanics.

"You know us from the brass-ape races." There was that pride again.

"I know of those races," I said cautiously. "I'd always assumed them sponsored and designed by men in little workshops about the city."

"Well, of course." His tone was quite reasonable. "Those men in little workshops are us. The sorcerer-engineers. Our true craft is much deeper and older. The brass apes are how we enter into the life of the city. The work excuses and covers up many of our other tasks."

That I could imagine. That work could excuse and cover up almost any other task. Still, this Archimandrix was not an easy man to speak with. As if he followed a script in his head that had not been written to include me. Further patient prompting was indicated. "Why did Mother Iron call you to me?"

"Sh-she said I might need you."

That he *might need* me, I thought. Not the other way around. Curious. "That may well be true." I kept my voice slow, in order to trail behind my thoughts. Was this about the Eyes of the Hills? "I might need you in turn." Perhaps. "Tell me more of your true craft."

"Those are secrets closely guarded down the generations," he said dubiously, still speaking from his place of pride.

In those words, I realized Archimandrix would not be turned by threat of force, weak as this one sounded in other ways. He possessed a steel core beneath the tissue of confusion that wrapped his surface.

I could admire that.

"There is nothing I can say to you," I told him, "which would be convincing of my credentials if you do not already believe in them. I do not know how Mother Iron calls you, or what that call means to a sorcerer-engineer. I can hardly claim to understand her myself. Only that I know Mother Iron has guarded this city down those long generations over which your secrets have been kept. And that she accepts something of me into her domain here Below."

He scratched his chin through the leather wrappings, nudging one dark nail up beneath the needle-toothed brass muzzle. "You have the right of it there. You speak with the sharpness of a logic-chopper, but the sense of your words is not so pointed toward tearing into my argument."

"I can chop logic well enough," I demurred. "I was in the custody of sharp-minded teachers for a long while. This is not my day for the razor of truth. Please, either tell me what you will, or bid me farewell, so that I may pass about my urgent business."

Archimandrix sighed theatrically. "Fair enough." He turned half away, facing my direction toward the gallery beneath the Temple of Endurance. "Walk with me?"

"Of course." I slipped my weapon away and wondered precisely what it was that Mother Iron saw in this ungainly youth with his core of power and pride.

"The sorcerer-engineers are the oldest guild, but we have been undeclared since the fall of the kings."

Eight centuries past, in my understanding of that history. "You were driven underground?"

"We took ourselves there," Archimandrix said distantly. I had the impression that if I but asked he would burst into recitation, chanting a list of kings and guildmasters like a memory man in the Dockmarket. "Once our guildhall was the proudest in the city. Where the Ducal Palace now stands, on Montane Street. Some of our old walls are still contained within those newer ones."

Ah, the gnostic entanglements of conspiracy and architecture. "Ancient secrets wrapped in modern confidences."

He glanced sidelong at me. For a moment, the trembling, foolish youth was in abeyance. "Some secrets are never unwrapped by those who follow later on. The Dukes were not always as the latest and last was."

Is he aware of my central role in the assassination!? "I would know nothing of the late Duke," I lied, the memory of his death at my hand blooming painfully in my mind.

"When the last king was pulled from his throne by the Varingii raiders and their pardine allies, the master of our guild at that time allowed himself to be taken as well in order to give out that the rest of our order had been eliminated. The banners were burned then, and our name stamped out."

I could well imagine that scene, unfortunately. Which led me to wonder where the Royal Palace had stood, if the Ducal Palace was on the site of their old guildhall. Or had they been one and the same? "Even the bravest men will fall before a surging tide of swords," I said, quoting the historian Benefactus.

"But the most patient will wait for the storm to clear," Archimandrix responded unthinking.

Obviously we'd read the same books.

With an audible effort at realigning his thoughts, the sorcerer-engineer continued: "Even then our guild was very old. Our earlier . . . functions . . . had grown dormant. When this city was called Cupraneum and men with a different color of skin and eyes lived here, we were great. The Years of Brass were our time. The mines grew ever deeper, as secrets were imparted by the gods above and the powers below."

It seemed he meant "powers below" literally. I would receive my litany whether I wished it or not. Mother Iron had urged me upon this strange man. It was incumbent on me not just to listen, but even to draw him out.

"We built machines to work the mines, to provide air and light and wondrous goods to the city. Though they are long since abandoned, most of their purposes forgotten even by us, still our guild tends those machines." His voice was sad now, tinged with the twinned losses of history and time. "Now in these late days, we sorcerer-engineers mine the old ways for scraps of knowledge. Steam-kettle ships cross the oceans on the wings of the learning of newer, lesser men. Some of them even bear light as we once did. All our city can do is buy goods over their sides and stare longingly at the iron hulls and the growling power to sail against the wind."

He was pushing me into the precincts of my own memory. "I have traveled aboard those steam-kettle ships," I told him.

"They were not built by us as we might once have done. Our pride is in our past. The future comes speaking another language, seen first by foreign eyes." That sadness had taken him over completely.

"And those are your deeper mysteries? Care of machines whose purposes you have forgotten?"

"Yes."

The sheer, simple grief in his voice moved me. I was seeking wisdom from the depths of time. Mother Iron had delivered me into the hands of an odd young man who quite literally saw himself as the warden of those depths.

We had arrived at the gallery below the temple. Light filtered in from above, but much more dimly than recent memory suggested. I looked up the ladder that led to the surface. The acolytes had built a platform over the hole in the middle of their temple yard.

I bristled. There had better flaming well be a door set in that platform, or they'd see some divine wrath.

"We keep many old secrets, but those are our core." Archimandrix sounded despondent now. He looked up, following my gaze. "You will need us soon. I am sure of it."

I of all people understood the weight of history, but I was not ready to submit myself to the depressed recollections of this holdout from another age. He was probably right. I would need them soon. But I did not need them today. Lost knowledge of ancient mines and kettle ships from another age would do little to address whatever had passed between me and Desire in the ruins of Marya's temple. I was looking for wisdom in the fruits of the wrong tree.

Neither would this one's metallurgy and delving relieve me from Blackblood's demands. Whatever magic these sorcerer-engineers carried with them, it had nothing to do with the Eyes of the Hills. I was certain of that much.

This was not divinity, nor even magic. This was tool using, elevated to a mystic rite then buried as all mystic rites are wont to be.

"How will I find you if I need you?" I fought the urge to dismiss Archimandrix and his obsession with ancient, rusted lore. It was important for me to trust Mother Iron that much, to believe that I would need this man and his guild again. She did not flow through the world as Archimandrix or I did; she might have seen a requirement years in coming, or moments away. I could only hope that I would know when.

Just not today.

"Return Below," he said slowly. "Touch any of the great machines with your power. We will know."

With my power? "Of course," I murmured. "But for now, farewell." I placed one hand on a rung, then turned back to him. "I thank you for the lesson in your history."

"It is not mine," Archimandrix mumbled, embarrassed. "I only recall it on behalf of those who have passed onward."

With that, I climbed, wondering how much I would have to work to break out at the top.

Someone had been clever enough to build a trapdoor. Not only that, they had been wise enough to leave it unlatched for me. The true dangers of Below were far more intangible than night stalkers surfacing to rob and to raid. I had never heard of a gang of thieves using the network of sewers, tunnels, and old mine galleries for access around the city. Any that tried would be made short work of. *I* had been introduced with great civility and care in my day, so I supposed that I counted as one of the dangers of Below myself at this point.

Archimandrix was not so much a danger as a puzzle. I was most unclear on what aid he, his brass apes, and his derelict machines would bring me. But I trusted Mother Iron and her word. I just didn't *understand* her. I had my counsel from deeper time, for all that was worth in the question of goddesses and city-killing power.

The temple construction was idle, which seemed curious. The afternoon had not finished slipping away. Chowdry's acolytes should be at their laying-out of the foundation. Though I understood something of architecture, construction was not a skill of mine. Still, it seemed to me they were nearly at need of digging the trenches for the stonework courses.

Had this been *my* work gang, shovels would already be in hand.

I followed the buzz of voices into the tent camp. They were raising and fitting a new kitchen tent. That I could excuse.

Slipping around the edge of the busy crowd, I headed for the tent that I'd been using. I wasn't sure who'd been dispossessed, but I wouldn't be here much longer. Every day I spent here was a danger to the temple and Endurance. The god might grant me divine protection, but that hadn't stopped murderers at the gates. Since Chowdry would neither set nor hire guards—*And is that his foolishness, or the word of Endurance?* I wondered—I needed to take myself somewhere that could be closed off, or much better hidden.

I paused around the canvas corner of my tent at the sound of voices. Something familiar but out of place. Listening, I realized I was hearing a muttered argument in Seliu between Chowdry and someone whose voice I recognized but could not in that instant put a name to.

Whom?

". . . this is not a matter for these pale folk."

"I will not be having any of this," Chowdry hissed.

"It will be worse for all of us. That other one slew the entire ship but me! *Chittachai* lies burned beneath the ocean."

The other man was Little Baji!

Chowdry grunted. "Good riddance to Utavi, I say, though I am sorry for the rest of them. But my answer is still being no."

"I am making no threats," replied Little Baji mournfully. "But the rest of them *are* threats. Those Blade women are mad as dogs in the market. Even the girl Samma. And that other one, the bitch from the Bittern Court. She frightens them all."

"This is Copper Downs, not Kalimpura." *Good man*, I thought, mentally urging Chowdry on. "Those powers hold no fear for me."

"Your ox god is Selistani surely as Green herself."

I knew my cue when I heard it. I slipped around the corner, short knife in my hand, and laid the blade edge at Little Baji's throat. "Looking for someone?" I asked, also in Seliu.

Chowdry glared at me. "I won't have you drawing weapons in my temple either, Green."

"This isn't a weapon," I told him, my free hand tugging Little Baji's short-cropped hair back to expose and tighten the skin of his neck. I eased the blade along as if shaving him, or stropping it on a piece of inferior leather. "This is a sacrament of the Lily Goddess."

Little Baji whimpered but did not answer. Chowdry appeared incensed. "I would not sell you to him. I will not be selling him to you, either. Let the man go, and both of you take your troubles elsewhere."

I shoved Little Baji away from me. I was angry now at both of them and perhaps at myself. "If your mistresses want me, they can seek me out. I'll cut their throats as easily as I will cut yours. And take more pleasure in it. Tell them I said that, and also that I'm done with dancing to the tunes of others."

Not god nor goddess, nor mistress nor politicians. I realized I meant what I said—I *was* done. Between my time in the High Hills and the rubble of Marya's temple, ambitions for the paths of power had truly fled me.

I lived now for me and for my daughter.

Somehow I doubted that was what Mother Iron meant by the oldest powers, but there was no power older than the bond between a mother and her child. Even the titanics knew better than that. Desire perhaps most of all, with Her brood of daughter-goddesses scattered across the plate of the world like so much smelt.

Chowdry's old crewmate rubbed his neck and stared at me. "You're all madwomen," he muttered. "That girl Samma killed us all and burnt the ship."

"Samma?" I laughed. "If *she* took all of you on, then you were worse than useless. Return to your kennel, fool, and tell Surali and Mother Vajpai that I am done with them."

Nodding brusquely at both men, I paid them the insult of turning my back and entering my tent. *You cannot strike me down,* I said, in the language of angry men. *You dare not.*

And so they didn't. When I emerged a few minutes later, both Chowdry and Little Baji were gone. Only Ponce stood there.

"I am to escort you from the temple grounds," he said, looking as mournful as he sounded.

"Chowdry is angry with me, but the god will not cast me aside."

Ponce shrugged. "This I do not know. I just wish things were different."

"All my life I've been wishing things were different." Patting his arm, I continued, "Besides, you are safer without me. I must solve some problems that have sharp edges behind them. A public ejection of me from this place may spare you further turmoil."

He walked me to the doorless gateway, but refused to shout down a banishment as I urged him to. His last words to me were "That big priest-killing pardine is back. I heard he was looking for you."

"Good thing I'm not a priest." I walked away whistling, pretending to far more cheer than I felt.

Once again I sought the roofs. They were among the safest places for me to think, and my likelihood of unfortunate incidents seemed minimal. A glance to the south suggested heavy squalls rolling in. For now the air was pale and quiet, with that tension which awaits a coming storm.

I knew all about coming storms, was quite capable of throwing more than a few lightning bolts myself at need.

Thinking wasn't always so productive, unfortunately. That forced me to concentrate on my worries, which had a tendency to multiply one another like mice in a pantry. I wasn't ready for more of Archimandrix, the Eyes of the Hills were heavy and sparking with tension within the inner pocket of my canvas shirt, and the rest of my troubles had not seen fit to take themselves away either. I could hardly search for the Rectifier with the Eyes of the Hills in my possession. Both good money and bad said the Revanchists would sense their presence. Besides, neither Mother Vajpai nor Surali was any kind of a fool—the two of them would have men among the Selistani refugees at the Tavernkeep's place, even if they hadn't already on my last visit.

The idea of simply taking to my heels and returning to Ilona's cottage in the High Hills had a certain appeal. But fleeing had never been my style, not when turning to fight was any option. It was just that not even I could fight *everyone* at once. At the moment the whole city was starting to feel like my enemy.

Besides, back in the High Hills, Erio would surely stir up whatever trouble a ghost from past ages would be able to. Ilona would welcome me, but she would not accept me if the graves were made uneasy by my continued presence. The old king was a vivimancer, a power among the dead who called the living to him to do his bidding. I did not believe he wouldn't seek to bind me further through Ilona.

The worst was, he had the right of the business. Danger presented to me and to my child. Walking away from Copper Downs not only betrayed the city, it betrayed my daughter.

Everyone had stakes in this game, and they all seemed laid against me.

With a strange reluctance, my thoughts circled back to the twins Iso and Osi. We'd spoken before about how gods came to be, and found their power. This knowledge in turn would suggest ways that gods might be checked. Common sense indicated that a woman would sooner stand sword-armed against a storm as deter divine intent, yet gods bore a relationship to their worshippers nothing like the violent indifference of a seaborne cyclone. The twins' studies uniquely qualified them in this regard. Besides, if everything here went so badly against me that I simply could not carry on, their pilgrimage was a vehicle by which I might escape both Copper Downs and my ever-burgeoning role as Blade to this fractious city.

As for Desire, well, the farther away from the ruined temple and Her presence I was, the less did I know what I felt there. I could identify a residue of overwhelming grief for Her daughter Marya, mixed with an intense personal urge to not experience the emotions of a titanic ever again in my life.

I was sick of being god-touched, and tired of being the point of contention.

Iso and Osi represented another avenue of ancient wisdom, should I wish to examine that question further. And somewhat more sensibly articulate than either Mother Iron or Archimandrix. Even better, the wandering twins could help me protect myself from Blackblood. As strangers to the city with only polite interest in our factions and their fates, the two of them could also possibly counsel me on how best to pit the Dancing Mistress' pardine Revanchists and the Selistani embassy against one another—surely my securing the Eyes of the Hills from Samma would allow me to dictate the terms of that balance, if I could best puzzle how to use the gems.

In truth, all that wondering pointed to only one reasonable conclusion. I must unravel one thing at a time, or determine that the knot was so tangled I had no choice but to cut it and move on.

Stated thusly, my plan was simple to the point of elegance. Short on useful details, perhaps, but those sorts of things tended to appear as needed.

Day was coming to an end by the time I'd fully sorted my thoughts. Iso and Osi followed their meditations and evening rites—this was the hour at which they had turned me out previously for the sin of being female. I skulked across rooftops until I found a rented room being vacated by a night worker, some clerk bound for an evening counting out the day's receipts, wearing the suit he carefully pressed before dressing and taking his leave. It was the work of moments to quietly force open his window. Within, I blocked his door with the lone chair, washed myself in his little basin, ate of his small bowl of dried fruit, and slipped into his not too grubby bedclothes for a few watches of comfortable rest. I did not neglect to leave an overgenerous silver tael on the washstand for the stranger's troubles, though I hoped he would not be too fearful and confused by my break-in.

Even in those days of my youth, I understood the value of small kindnesses in life.

I awoke in the later hours of the night, to judge by the lowered, glowering moon above the swift-moving clouds. The forced window rattled with the fast, nervous air. The squalls I'd seen the afternoon before had taken their time, but were still on their way. The impending rain rendered seeking the rooftops now an unlikely choice. I felt a bit guilty about appropriating my host's tiny rented room, so I took some time to straighten and clean. I even mended the torn shirt he had set out in his clothespress. Leaving the room better than I had found it, including the silver tael on the washstand, I headed to the cobbles and into the city before the rains that seemed likely to arrive with the dawn.

The baby hungered me, and tugged once more at my incipient nausea, so I ignored the roughening weather to slip around to the bakery near the Textile Bourse for a fresh cardamom roll and some kava. The woman there smiled to see me. I knew I'd risen in their estimation, because this time I was invited to sit in the kitchen and eat while two large, silent men worked the ovens. They were stripped to the waist, and their reddish-gold skins sweated in the heat like the demons of baking. They kept themselves clean with towels and wore long padded gloves to handle the breads.

The woman sat with me a little while once I'd tucked in. "We know you," she said shyly.

That was worrisome, but it could mean anything. "You are kind," I mumbled around a mouthful.

"You called the ox god, and spared the city." She nodded her head. I looked up at a sudden gap in the gentle noises of baking to see both the men—her brothers?—standing at attention with the butts of their long wooden paddles grounded to the floor. They nodded as well.

"Endurance called himself." I found myself embarrassed. "It was only my voice that made the prayer."

That brought a shrug from the woman. She handed me a small fruit with a ribbon tied to it. "Offering. For the god, for you. Our thanks."

She would not let me pay, either. I ate the cherry—a single one at that, strange offering though it seemed—and tied the stone into the ribbon to slip within my pocket. I bowed, took my leave, and went to find the twin pilgrims. Avoiding any chance of being viewed by prying eyes from within the Textile Bourse was my first step. After that I slipped into the burgeoning morning traffic of the city along with the beginning of the serious rain.

Iso and Osi were unsurprised to see me. So unsurprised, in fact, that they had already laid out a third setting for tea before my arrival.

"A fortune told?" I asked lightly. Their warehouse echoed with the drumming of the storm on the high, flat roof.

"Our rites are thorough," said Osi.

Iso nodded. "Sometimes common sense is enough. Even for old men such as us."

Common sense and good finger on the pulse of rumor, I'd bet. Anyone who made it their business to learn their way around the local gods of necessity learned their way around much else of the local life as well. And these two certainly had long practice at both.

"I thank you." The Eyes of the Hills seemed to crackle inside my shirt, as if their velvet bag were alive. Likewise I fancied the twins' attention drawn toward the hidden gems. Once more my memories of the encounter with Desire loomed large.

One thing at a time. These two had no place in my troubles, but I did not yet know them well enough to trust them with everything that had befallen me. How I wish I'd listened to that thought more carefully at the time.

"Tea first," Osi said.

Iso: "Then we will speak more of gods."

So tea we took, amid some very polite and inconsequential talk of local foods and the fall harvest and the inadvisability of eating shellfish that had not been bought off the decks of a boat just in. Always they passed the sentences back and forth between them as if in some private game. I had to strain not to hear them as one man. I knew that would be a mistake.

In time the tea service was wiped clean. They were fastidious in handling what I had used, and avoided my immediate presence with an almost eerie grace that was both fascinating and irritating. Once again ignoring my own inner wisdom, I laid aside my feelings on the matter in the interests of my larger needs. We had taken seats on mats laid in a circle so that we made three even points. I sat watching them as they watched me.

"You have been touched," said Iso.

Osi added, "The gods follow you as a dog will follow a cat in an alley."

"I am not bait, nor prey, for them."

"No," Iso agreed. "But once a way has been opened from the divine into a human mind, it is easier for the divine to follow a second time."

"Though far more often," his brother added, "whatever god opens the way guards his prophet with jealousy."

"You are most unusual, Mistress Green. You speak with several gods, and for none of them."

"We know priests who would give all to be touched as you have been."

"They can have it!" I almost shouted. These two certainly knew how to spark my fears and anger. "This is worse than being swarmed by beggars. You can kick a beggar, or outrun her. No door can be locked firmly enough to deter the entry of a god."

Iso shook his head gravely. "Though they often manifest as human, and we speak of them so, you would be better served to think of the gods as forces."

"As you might think of a storm, or an earthquake," Osi added.

That, I could understand.

Iso continued. "But directed. And with intelligence."

Osi touched his brother's arm, as if for emphasis. "To call them beggars does not properly describe your experiences, or characterize the nature of the divine."

"But they *are* beggars," I protested, realization dawning within me. "The gods demand attention and sacrifice and devotion. If enough people turn away from them, they fade. All the power of a goddess is in her followers."

Iso leaned close, so that I almost thought for a moment that he might touch me, ritual cleanliness or no. "We have learned much. Wisdom passed down from older times, that was once used like swords in the hands of warring priests."

"When the titanics fell," Osi said, "the world was wounded. How could it not be so? Just as when a mother dies the child's heart is stricken, even if that child has grown to be a general of armies."

His brother picked up the thread again. "This hermetic tradition has prevailed since the time of the titanics. For even now one or another of the oldest, deepest gods may sometimes emerge into the workaday world."

I almost spoke of my meeting with Desire in the ruins of Marya's temple, but held my tongue in the face of their unfortunate views on women. Instead I offered, "Choybalsan was a new god emergent on the strength of an older power requiring a vessel."

Osi nodded gravely. "Hear this, one of the greatest secrets, a secret so great that it abides in plain sight for any who wish to pluck at its wisdom. All gods are the same, beneath even their bones."

Iso: "There are magics and magics in the world. You already know this, in your life. You have told us of petty miracles, finding lily petals in the wake of a great moment."

His brother continued, "Or the small readings the arbogasters perform in the market for a bent copper tael and a handful of beans. Their price may be mean, but their power is no less to those who scrimp to purchase such seeings."

"I understand something of these matters," I protested. "There are layers in all the world. This does not surprise me. How could it, unless I were a fool? There are layers in this city. Layers of class, layers of politics, layers above and below the streets."

"Do you understand," Iso asked, "that all those layers are but the same? As if you folded a piece of silk, and looked at each fold separately, but then spread it flat again."

Osi added, "The gods worshipped in the temples of the city are to the titanics as the avatars of those gods are to their temple masters."

"Tulpas," I breathed. "The ghosts below."

Iso nodded vigorously. "You already know something of this lesson. But even the great titanics themselves are as the ghosts below to the Urges who first made the plate of the world and directed the string of suns in their course across the endless sky."

"All layers," his brother said. "The silk folds endlessly ever upon itself."

As silk did, ringing softly with the voice of thousands of bells. I could see in memory my grandmother's silk flowing down her shoulders, her last voice in this world. Each bell like a little god, planted in the folds of life?

Still, coming from the twins, the words seemed to border on sophistry. Yet at the same time, their description resonated with much of what I had experienced firsthand. "You ask who made the garden in which Father Sunbones and Mother Mooneyes first waked the birds and beasts of this world?" Desire, when She'd manifested to me, had been so *large*. Even a fraction of Her emotions, Her grief and pity, had threatened to batter my soul to shreds. "So you say the gods are all the same at their bones, as with this unfolded sheet of silk. In your conception, there is no difference but that of degree between the Urges and the titanics and the gods of a city and the ghosts that haunt the high graves or the dark sewers." Like bells of different sizes, ringing together.

"Precisely," the brothers said in unison. A shared expression of smug triumph passed across their faces. I wondered what point it was they thought they'd scored, beyond sharpening a small facet of my education.

Yet, even though the idea appealed with a symmetry that was pleasing to my mind, and echoed nicely with my own memories, it could not simply be so. Otherwise, what was the *purpose*? That everything turned upon itself, and was the same, again and again?

Osi spoke, as if turning aside my question as yet unasked. "If you comprehend this hierarchy among the gods, and how it is not so much rungs on a ladder as points on the grade of a hill, then you understand the gods and their relationships to power."

"A ghost, or a weak avatar, survives on his own power," I said slowly, setting aside the larger question in favor of their example. Now I was thinking of the two ghosts I was personally acquainted with. Both the Factor, whom I knew well, and Erio, whom I barely knew at all, had been mighty persons in their life. In the case of the Factor, his continued presence seemed to have been driven more by strength of purpose than sheer, simple birthright. Or any supposed place in some divine order of the world. I knew nothing of Erio's rule or his life history, but the arrogance of his tomb suggested much.

The twins nodded in time with my thoughts.

Fine, I knew how to follow a lesson. I considered the hierarchy. "An avatar, a strong one at least—" Here I thought of Mother Iron and Skinless. "—survives from energy of place or purpose, usually lent by a god. Or perhaps a modest following of their own. People might offer small sacrifices. While a god, for example, Choybalsan or Blackblood, must have the prayers and pieties of priests and a congregation. But a god writ large enough, a titanic such as Desire, lives off the strength of other gods." As wolves live off the strength of deer? "Urges would be an expression of the strength of the entire world taken as a whole. Do I have the right of it?"

Osi stirred, but Iso spoke. No look passed between them, but as so often was the case, I felt as though I'd witnessed a shared thought. "A fair summary. In your terms, the worship of men falls at what seems to us the midpoint of the scale. We can glimpse larger forces as we see distant storms on the horizon. We can take smaller ones almost in hand as if they were aspects of the natural world, like morning mist or shells on a beach."

I tried to imagine taking Mother Iron in hand. Their model of the universe certainly did not account for every possibility. Which was all the more of a pity, as it possessed a certain elegance of form.

Osi: "The titanics are mostly departed. Sundered, shattered, lost to us back in the time when the lands on the plate of the world were first peopled with men and beasts." His voice slowed, as if he thought carefully to see forward through his words. "Yet you mentioned Desire."

His interest in the mother-goddess bothered me, though I could not yet say how. "I was raised for a time in the Temple of the Lily Goddess, who so far as I understand these things is a daughter of Desire. She was the first titanic who came to mind." I reached for another example, from the stories I'd read. "We are all slaves of Her brother Time, for example, but I do not treat with him, or do his bidding."

Iso quirked a smile. "Every one of us does time's bidding. You are not exempt, Mistress Green."

"As may be." I resolved to change the subject, for this conversation had gone far deeper into the seductive trappings of theory and principle than I'd intended. Certainly I would not be discussing Desire's manifestation with these twins. Not until I understood their fascination better. "I am here today to seek very practical advice from you in the matter of Blackblood. Surely he is a splinter of some titanic god, but I could not name his theogenitor. He makes a claim upon the child I carry, a claim that I deny as false. I would deter him and avoid his scrutiny. That would be a great gain for me. Can your hermetic knowledge teach me to protect and shield my child?"

Could it serve to cloak me in divine benison, like my belled silk?

The twins exchanged another glance. This one was long and slow, and I received the impression less of a shared thought than of an entire extended dialogue passed wordless right before me.

Their sheltering warehouse bulked large and silent, and this morning, cold. The rain outside was a harbinger of the increasingly foul winter weather of this city, though autumn was not yet completely fled from the rooftops and gutters and ragged-leaved trees. A storm or two from now and the very air would be worrying at the building's corners like a dog gnawing a bone. Today it was merely a cloak of wet and stolid quiet, tingeing the harbor-scent of the wind and undermining my own hopes.

Finally Osi spoke. "Our rites are our own. You know that we share little with women."

Iso sounded embarrassed as he added, "Never in our pilgrimage have we before experienced the least temptation to open our wisdom to any female."

"Never before *now*," his brother added. "You are different."

"We will show you some of the ways of shielding yourself from the eyes of a god." *Or goddess,* I thought, as Iso went on: "And we will think on how to turn aside this Blackblood's thrust of divine will."

No one would claim my child. Not Blackblood, not Desire. No one but me. Even my claim as mother was only proxy on my daughter's eventual claim upon herself.

I spent several productive days with Iso and Osi. Even now, after all that later took place, I recognize that they stand among the greatest teachers I ever knew. Before sundown I would leave them and find quiet corners in which to sleep about the wintering city. The warehouse district offered possibilities for protected rest among untended burlap sacks or just above the musty warmth of stables. I was just as glad I'd placed my silk in Endurance's care for a little while. It was bulky, delicate, and not always so silent as I required.

I did not need to seek out food, as the twins were kind enough to provide for me, though we never shared directly. In regard to my being absent from the affairs of Copper Downs, it suited me that Mother Vajpai and Samma and Surali might think me plotting against them with hidden forces. Sadly, I had no such forces, but the fears of my enemies were ever my allies. As for Chowdry, he could manage Little Baji on his own. Whatever the pardine Revanchists were about did not concern me until they chose to make it my affair. Which they would, soon enough, if Samma's theft of the Eyes of the Hills and subsequent loss of them to me were to become known.

This education was different, more focused than what had taken up earlier years of my life. Instead of spending my days fighting, or learning the finer points of some household art, I labored at understanding the mechanisms and foibles of the gods. While this warehouse was neither the Pomegranate Court nor the Temple of the Silver Lily, I was back in the schoolgirl's seat again by my own choice.

I enjoyed the process immensely.

Iso and Osi taught just as they spoke—with shared voice and overlapping movement. Again and again I was struck by their almost eerie closeness, and wondered how they would have fought, if their rite had called upon them to be so trained. I resolved that if I should ever have the raising of children beyond my own—a possibility, given my eventual ambitions in Kalimpura— that I would school them much as I had been, across a broad range of skills and interests, save without the bondage and petty cruelties. And I would pay very special attention indeed to any twins who came into my care.

Gods tended to settle into their temples and places of power. That was obvious enough. The mechanisms were not so clear. Newborn, drunk with the energy of their creation, as both Choybalsan and Endurance had been, they could walk the world. Older gods like barnacles became not so much senescent as sedentary. Their miracles grew quieter. Here I thought of the Lily Goddess and how She spoke to the Temple Mother back in Kalimpura. Much like the difference between a maple seed spinning on the wind and a tree rooted and grown large.

"But," I asked, "a god cannot grow *into* a titanic, right? They were possessed of the power of their place and time at the morning of the world. This gradient of rank you speak of does not flow smoothly in both directions."

Iso smiled at me, the broad, quick grin of a teacher's pleasure in their student. "The world changes. A flower cannot grow on hard rock, or salty sand.
In these later ages, the plate of the earth no longer offers fallow soil rich
enough for titanics to take root."

"So only those titanics such as Time"—*and Desire*—"who survived from
before the sundering of the gods are still about."

"No one raises temples to them," Osi said quite seriously.

"They are woven into the fabric of this crowded world." I wondered what
those words of mine said about the titanics. Was stifling your siblings from
returning to their power blessed foresight or the worst sort of betrayal?

Iso frowned. "Fair enough. For now."

We continued to pursue related matters. How worshippers affected a god.
Why altars might be broken, and even a little of how; then far more of why
not and how not to do such things. What the true role of priests was—not
intermediaries for divine favor, as I'd always understood, but serving to
shield people who might follow the god from the raw force of divine regard.
Which explained some of Chowdry's behaviors. He had been changing.
Even the diffident, reluctant pirate Chowdry I'd met aboard *Chittachai*
would have thought it the height of idiocy to leave a gate unguarded, or at
least unbarred. The new Chowdry infected by Endurance's almost overwhelming mute nonviolence had done exactly that.

"Gods are like an ague or a grippe," I argued. "A plague of faith spreads
about a place. It rages early and strong. Soon the people most subject to be
taken by it have been infected, while the rest make their accommodations. In
time faith subsides, mostly affecting travelers and newborns and those with
a sudden change of circumstance. Priests carry faith the strongest. They
spread the complaint, while also shielding the worst of its effects." I wondered
how this explanation squared with, for example, the betrayal of Blackblood
by Pater Primus and his hierarchy.

Osi shook his head. "I would not have thought to explain it so, Mistress
Green, but it seems that you have a grip upon the question."

"So the gods need us to carry them through the world, as fleas need the
rats who carry them from ship to ship and port to port. What do we need
them for?"

"You of all people should be able to answer that," Iso replied sharply.

In the course of our instruction, I'd told them more of my own history
and the various events that had brought me to this point. Judiciously edited,
of course, to protect the guilty. I also continued to avoid any reference to my

encounter with Desire. I'd come to appreciate that while these two did not have personal interests in the disputes of Copper Downs, they certainly had purposes that might not be fully aligned with mine.

Choosing my words carefully, I ventured a reply. "We need them for protection from ourselves, I suppose."

"Go on," Osi said.

Somehow, in my readings this question about our need for gods had always been assumed to be a basic condition of humanity. "Blackblood is a pain god. He relieves suffering, in a sense. That is his rite and sacrament. I know there are temples in this city devoted to the rites of death, and others to healing. There are gods for sailors and shepherds and to watch over women. But such a view renders our gods into little more than guildmasters, parceling out skills and favors for those who petition correctly at need."

"Some gods are small," Iso replied. "To meet small needs."

"Faith," said Osi, "any faith, charts a course through life. Sets a purpose. If one's life has enough room in it to look beyond another meal and a safe place to sleep, one begins to ask questions. Questions faith, and a god, can help answer."

I thought of Shar's unquiet desperation on my father's poor sliver of land back in Bhopura. Her life had no room to look beyond her next starveling meal. By contrast, the Temple of the Silver Lily was packed full of fractious, well-fed women who asked questions all the time. And demanded answers. Was it fair to say that we there had faith and Shar did not? "Not so much faith," I answered, finishing my thought aloud, "as a framework for living."

Iso pounced. "Consider that the Urges gave a framework for the titanics, and the titanics gave a framework for the splintered gods, and the gods give a framework for their avatars."

"And people give a framework for the entire spectrum of the divine," I pointed out. "This is a circle, not a slope. If they help us with our purposes, surely we help them with theirs? How else will a sailor's goddess know that the sea is her domain if sailors and their widows do not bring her their prayers?" Surely drowning men saw *someone*.

"Yet some purposes are higher and deeper." Osi again. "And stand outside the small needs."

"Our rite is such a one," Iso added. "We pursue a map of the dispersion. In doing so, we seek to redress an ancient wrong so that the world might be better balanced."

But they would speak no more of that. Foolishly, I let the matter drop.

In the course of three days we ranged across theory, practice, and purpose. Along with the rest of my abbreviated lessons—such a syllabus, to cram into so few words and scant hours—they showed me how the view of a god into the world is colored by his worshippers and his purposes, and thus how one might hide oneself away from a god's eye with crafty misdirections. A certain symbol scratched upon a wall might draw aside the mystic power present in a place. The one who placed it there could pass through unobserved. A prayer or rite, if known, could be turned in on itself and to a degree the effects would be reversed. A gathering-in of both the spirit and the body, following certain signs, could make one as silent and small as a shadow on the wall. Walking in curves provided no angles to reflect the attention of the divine.

Strange and useful lore, much of it with applications in the more mundane world of Blades and runs and street violence. Further proof to my thinking that the gods were not so different from us. Just . . . *more.*

We also talked directly about how to thwart Blackblood in his purposes, given the manner in which I understood them at the time. Or at least we did so as directly as Iso and Osi ever spoke of anything. "Even gods may be trapped, stopped."

Killed, I thought, recalling Marya, and Desire's grief amid Her ruined temple. Who would cry so for Blackblood should he depart the world? The fall of Choybalsan had not riven the city both because he was so new, and because his power had been preserved in the form of Endurance. In a sense, this was true of Marya as well: The grief of the titanic Desire served to focus Her attention, likely providing the energy that kept the death of Marya from echoing far more widely. Who would hold Blackblood's place in matters divine?

I knew from my readings in my younger years that the cost of god killing was high, not necessarily to the killers, but to those who lived on after. Nothing Iso and Osi had said now led me to believe otherwise.

At that price, would I be willing to strike Blackblood down if he did not give me and my daughter his leave to pursue our lives as we would? This is what my newfound teachers hinted at.

"I have much to do in this city," I said. "And soon. My enemies abide, plotting and awaiting the plots they expect of me." Or simply the attack. I laugh to think of it now, but I was late to subtlety. "You aid me in understanding Blackblood's needs and purposes. I suspect he will not be turned aside by suasion, no matter how cogent the argument. Better that he be stopped and directed away from me permanently."

It occurred to me that I did not wish them to strike Blackblood down like some bandit on the road. God killing was not the answer. As I'd said, I merely needed to twist the god's attention from me. Likewise the entire trail of divine affray that seemed to follow me through my days.

I craved the ordinary.

"What would you sacrifice to reduce a god?" Osi asked.

"I have nothing worth so much," I replied, "except my own life and the life of my child. Those I will not lay down. Not even for this."

"Think on it," Iso said.

The Eyes of the Hills burned hot in the inner pocket of my shirt, and for a moment I imagined that the canvas smoldered. "I will, but I do not see much changing."

"We shall think, as well," Osi replied.

The evening of the third day, I bid them farewell. "I take a pause from our lessons and discussions tomorrow. I need to spend time seeing how far out of control my other fires have burnt."

They promised to meditate further on the matter of Blackblood. I promised to return with such additional insights as my explorations brought to me. I believed I'd intrigued the twins, given them a pretty problem against which to exercise their theories.

That night I kept to the streets. The weather had grown sufficiently wet that I'd stolen a rather nice dark blue oilcloth coat from a banker's coach. The broad collar I turned up against the cold, steady rain that had taken over from the squalls of earlier in the week. Gas lamps hissed and burned along some of the wider thoroughfares. The rest were lit haphazardly by house lights, carried torches, or were simply embedded in wet shadow. In the dreams Archimandrix had spoken of to me, the bottled lightnings of the kettle ships would snap and spark from each corner, until Copper Downs might have seemed some great trading metropolis of the Sunward Sea.

Listening to the city, I wandered up to Lyme Street to see if I could secure another cardamom roll. The little teahouse with its bakery was already closed for the day. That meant I would have to find something else to feed the baby. The last few days of living on lentils and flatbread had maintained me well enough without satisfaction. I wanted more. I would have given much for a well-stocked kitchen just then, that I could prepare myself a feast.

Likewise my balance had gone off a bit further just in a few days. Growth of the baby, growth of the woman carrying that child within her. "You will *not* pull me down," I whispered in a low voice, patting my daughter before I trotted on into the night.

I would have loved to find the Rectifier now, but I was still not ready to simply barge into the Tavernkeep's place again. Especially not with the Eyes of the Hills close against my breast. Still, absent a cardamom roll, I'd seek out such food as I could, then set myself to finding the old rogue on the sly. He'd not be too hard to locate. Surely he was looking for me by now, given the gossip to be had. And if anyone could triangulate the twins' advice for me, it was the Rectifier.

I once again took my leave of Lyme Street, my back turned toward the Textile Bourse. Trotting through the rain in search of a chophouse, I twice thought I spied Skinless, but that did not seem likely. The avatar bulked far too large to be out in the streets unnoticed. His very size would have ignited a panic, let alone his rather gruesome aspect. Shadows at play? Or some trick of Blackblood's seeming?

In time I found a laborers' kitchen with a single shared stewpot serving duck soup, alongside brined eggs and a hard, dark bread that was not the most usual local style. It was outrageously cheap, in part because the ducks were actually pigeons. I did not care so much. They served from a small cart meant to be drawn by two people. That pair worked their little kitchen—an old woman and her much older mother. The mother tended the pot, took in the copper taels and half-taels, and ladled out the rations of soup. The daughter, still old as my grandmother had been, at least to my eye, wiped out the bowls and restocked them for use, kept a regular supply of dark braided dough shoved into the little oven at the base of the cart, and more or less continuously chopped vegetables and plucked pigeons to replenish the soup vat.

I resisted the strong urge to take over from her.

This was the common food of the sort I would have been forced to turn my nose up at during my Pomegranate Court days. Even now, in a different mood I might have questioned the wisdom of my choices. Still, crowded against the eaves of a tack shop in the rain among a dozen large, silent men who mostly reeked of horses and drank down their soup with a dull-eyed intensity, I knew again what it meant to be of Copper Downs.

What it meant to be human.

To these folk, the sundering of the gods and the laddering dependencies of the divine world were not even rumors. The men around me lived in a small world of rented pallets stuffed with straw and bedbugs, of food from a corner cart because there was nowhere to cook in the places they worked and slept, of working fourteen days out of every fortnight and never sitting down to rest their weary bones.

Who were the gods to these people? The only thing they had faith in was the price of the night's meal. If it had been in my power to grant miracles, I'd have left them all with a pocket of silver taels and a happier future on the morrow.

As it was, I just left them. Even the Eyes of the Hills tucked deep within my clothing had fallen silent.

I was feeling chastened when I scrambled up to my overwatch by the Tavernkeep's place. The rain made the roofing tiles dangerous, but it was nothing I could not handle so long as I moved with some deliberation and took sensible care of myself. The baby had definitely upset my balance, and my abilities continued to shift in unexpected ways.

Surely I would not care to be pursued across wet rooftops in this condition. Even so, I could find a watchpost. That thought made me wonder in turn if I shouldn't attempt to ensure I wasn't likely to be pursued in the near future. *I am working on it*, I promised myself.

The High Hills kept looking like a better choice, that much was certain.

The Tavernkeep's place was being overtly watched this evening. Two men loitered by a garbage fire near the alley mouth, but they weren't begging or eyeing the passersby for someone to roll. The glances they stole were aimed toward the Tavernkeep's door. After several minutes, as a lone man turned down the alley, their outbreak of studious inattention was as good as a flare telling me what it was they waited for.

I scanned the rooftops around me. Nothing moved in silhouette. The day was on to dusk now, and the rain obscured much of everything in dull, glittering curtains. I was not willing to trust that I hadn't missed a watcher. Samma, or Mother Argai, for example. They had my skills and my training. Though in truth any of us Blades would have tried for the nest I currently occupied before seeking another post.

Anyone else who watched was hidden in one of the other buildings, or simply drinking comfortably inside the inn below. Smarter than I, in either event.

The rain was wearing down my earlier reluctance to approach the pardines with the Eyes of the Hills in my possession. I'd carried them in the presence of Iso and Osi, after all. Inside would be warm and dry, and offer good Selistani cooking. My resolve melted at that last thought. Especially in the face of simply crouching here in the wet, watching for the Rectifier.

I debated drawing off the two by the alley mouth, as opposed to the merits of simply slipping into the building unnoticed. Neither plan was completely without risk. The question was where I wished to place my emphasis.

The wet weather being what it was, climbing cornices did not appeal to me. Instead I scrambled along the tiles until I was right above my watchers, though still on the opposite side of the alley from them. A few minutes' scrounging turned up some broken bricks. I then waited for my opportunity, confident it would not take long.

My patience was soon rewarded when a clot of longshoremen approached, heading for a round of healthy drinking after their work. They'd already begun at the dockside, that much was clear from their singing and their collective erratic, rambling gait. I laid three brickbats out before me and considered my timing carefully. Just as the group rambled past my alley-mouth watchers, I lobbed my brick ends one by one. The first came down in the trash fire with a satisfying thud, sending a shower of sparks twisting up into the rain. The second, already launched, landed among the longshoremen, cracking someone a good hit to the noggin, while the third bounced at the feet of my watchers as if dropped there.

Provocation committed, evidence in place, and yes . . . attention drawn. The crowd of drunks didn't even bother with the usual shouted obscenities, choosing instead the swift vengeance of an offended mob.

As I hurried back to my descent and quickly slipped into the Tavernkeep's place, I wondered whose men I'd just set up for a beating. My money was on the Selistani embassy having hired poor local talent. The Interim Council would have found better people to do the job, while the pardine Revanchists would simply be waiting within. As for Blackblood, well, if I *had* glimpsed Skinless earlier, that would have been the god's effort to monitor my movements.

Inside the Tavernkeep's place, I brushed the water off my coat. I might have hung it up, but I preferred as many layers as possible to keep the Eyes of the Hills closely guarded. Especially here.

Besides, someone might steal it. There'd been a rash of clothing thefts lately.

The crowd of Selistani men still occupied the inn as if it were their own, but quite a few more pardines were present this evening. Including, I was delighted to note, the substantial bulk of the Rectifier. He was recognizable as always by his fur knotted into little square mats secured with the knuckle-bones of priests. Much as a Lily Blade's leathers did for us, his unusual grooming advertised—loudly and with an alarming bluntness. I admired the Rectifier for his sense of presence, and wished for myself his utter fearlessness.

Swiftly I eeled through the crowd. The room had that familiar fug of too many men spending too much time in close quarters, overlaid with the homey scents of Selistani cooking and the sour odor of spilled beer. The Rectifier was deep in conversation with two pardines I did not know. They showed off the cultivated wildness of the Revanchists that I'd previously noted among the Dancing Mistress' companions. When I approached the table, I realized Samma was seated there as well, her place hidden from me before by the Rectifier's looming so large.

Samma?

So, all the pieces were coming onto the board again. I thought quickly. She knew that I held the Eyes of the Hills. So did whomever she might have told of my forcing them from her. This game could already be blown, at least that far. I was unsure how committed the Rectifier was to the Revanchist cause. He was a traditionalist, to be sure, but I simply didn't know if he was that sort of traditionalist.

Nothing to do but play it through.

I stepped in between the Rectifier and Samma. "Hello." I tried to keep my voice from being overtight with tension.

She jumped slightly. Samma had not seen me enter, then. I thought she might have been hiding from my line of sight behind the old pardine rogue. I'd certainly used her hard enough the last two times we'd met.

The Rectifier's huge head turned slowly toward me. He looked me up and down twice, with almost exaggerated deliberation. His lips curled to show a bit of fang. I understood pardines probably better than most humans, after all my time with the Dancing Mistress, so I knew to watch his ears—they did not lie flat. I smiled back, letting him see my own modest fangs in turn.

Then the Rectifier jumped up, sending his chair over backwards to skitter into a table full of men betting at some fast card game. I leaned away, but restrained myself from palming my short knives as he bellowed "*Green!*" and swept me up into a rag-doll hug.

When I extracted my face from the matted, musky fur of his shoulder, I realized the entire tavern was staring at me. *Mark the exits,* wailed a futile voice within. But I was too busy to play the spy as well, even in my own defense.

"My old friend," I said in my warmest tones. To my surprise, the feeling was genuine. The Rectifier was the only person besides Ilona who had always dealt completely fairly with me. Even when I'd thought we might be fighting to the death in front of the Textile Bourse, the day we brought down Choy-balsan, the Rectifier had been utterly straightforward.

He put me down, then turned with a growl to look for his chair. It was handed respectfully back by an abashed man in a linen kurta. The Rectifier gave a sharp nod, which was the height of courtesy for him, before sinking to a seat once more. I leaned on the table between him and Samma, giving her a bright smile.

She cringed.

Not so good, that. She had reason to flinch from me. Even so, I sensed that something was afoot. More to the point, something *new and unpleasant* was afoot.

"You part the waters of trouble as claws gut a deer," the Rectifier rumbled.

He was the biggest pardine I had ever seen—tall, broad, and barrel-chested, unusual for a folk who ran to lithe and lean in their form. I was pretty sure he was the biggest pardine most *pardines* had ever seen. Sheer size gave him a voice that sounded as if it came from a well.

If the Rectifier wanted to drive straight to the point, I was happy to oblige. "Trouble parts me like a comb through hair, I am afraid." I stole another quick glance at Samma.

She still looked guilty, not angry. Whatever counterbetrayal was in the offing would be close at hand. *I've earned it,* I thought with regret, but I had no time for such games.

"Some persons seem to believe that making more trouble lessens it." *That* from a man who killed priests for a hobby. On saying those words he glared at the Revanchists with whom he shared the table. I recognized one of them from my previous visit.

"And how is the Dancing Mistress?" I asked that one sweetly.

The half-wild pardine gave me a cold stare. Or as close as he could manage—I'd been glared into submission more times in my life by harder-hearted women than he'd ever be. "She has not asked after you," he finally replied.

If Samma were not here as, what, witness? messenger? accuser? I could have begun the negotiations right now to direct the Revanchists against the Selistani embassy. The lie of the Eyes of the Hills hung heavy in my pocket, but no less real for all that. "Give her my regards. Our mutual interests have not lessened, as I am sure she is fully aware."

The Rectifier's enormous hand pressed heavy upon my shoulder. "Green, do not bargain with those who hold history more dear than the present. I warn you—"

His warning was lost in Samma's startled gasp. The Rectifier and I both looked up to see what she was staring at.

Mother Vajpai and Surali had entered the Tavernkeep's place. Some watcher had done their job. Mother Vajpai had donned her full street leathers, something I had not seen her do in a very long time. The Bittern Court woman was dressed formally in a salwar kameez of watered dove-gray silk and white linen. The clothes she'd worn the day she'd asked the Temple Mother to grant her my death.

They approached through a widening wedge of silence.

Why had Samma been surprised?

This threat I would not meet seated. I pushed to my feet, all too conscious of my impaired balance, my slowed reactions, and the unfortunate fact that I'd spent much of the day in the chilly autumn rain. My muscles were tense and I was not sufficiently warmed to be prepared for a fight.

Mother Vajpai's face was slightly flushed. Had she run here? To limber up? Though I could not envision Surali doing such a thing.

All around the room the Selistani stood and stepped back, crowding the walls to be away from the tables and us. The pardines did not react so. Few of them realized what they might be seeing next. A handful of the humans darted for the door, but most watched.

Not only would there be a fight, there would be a show.

"I doubt they mean to kill me here," I whispered to the Rectifier, "but the one in leather is capable of it. The other has already called for my death, offering both funds and favors in return."

"Are either of them priests?" he rumbled.

Technically Mother Vajpai was, but then technically so was I. "No," I said shortly, with one last, sidelong glance at Samma. By herself she was not especially troublesome to me. As I'd recently proven, she'd never been half the fighter I was even on my off days, let alone when I was in the full flower of my practice. But as a foil for Mother Vajpai, Samma was still quite dangerous. And Mother Vajpai knew Samma and I were old lovers—first lovers, in fact. That fact could well cause me to hesitate at a critical moment.

Samma looked as if she would throw up right there at the table. *Good,* I thought viciously. Whatever plot was afoot had passed her by. I hoped she did lose her stomach. It would keep her out of the fight, which would be important should the press of conflicting loyalties grow too strong.

Back to Mother Vajpai. I slid my toppled chair farther away with my foot, keeping it close enough to hook again with my ankle. Surali was a different kind of danger to me, but I had to leave this room with limbs and liberty intact before I could work against her effectively. Seeing the Bittern Court woman here now, a smug smile of triumph on her face, confirmed my resolve to foment dispute between the Revanchists and the Selistani embassy. That smile also suggested to me that it was she who had engineered this setup. Though in truth there were candidates aplenty, including my erstwhile friends on the Interim Council.

They could all carry one another down to the Smagadine hells so far as I was concerned. As for the Rectifier, I would keep him in reserve against Blackblood, as intended.

"Hello," I said to Mother Vajpai.

"Green." Her voice was sad, gentle, almost sweet. "It is time for you to come home."

"I *am* home." I backed a little farther away from the table and kept its width between me and her. The Rectifier and the two Revanchists remained seated, all three very much alert with claws extended. I wondered briefly if the Revanchists had any idea that humans existed who could stand toe to toe with their kind in a fight.

Mother Vajpai walked briskly around the left side of the table toward me, passing behind the Revanchists as well as Samma. Because this was my old teacher, for the second time in a few minutes I fought the urge to palm my knives—let her be the first to bare steel, if we were to be at blades. I kicked my chair back up and balanced it before me. Hours and hours of exercises with the Dancing Mistress had taught me much about how to use furniture as weapons and armor both, though some of that skill was useless now that I was pregnant.

Did Mother Vajpai know? She must, I realized, after raising and training more than a generation of Blades. The question was whether she would fight to kill my baby, intentionally or otherwise.

"Enough, Green," she said in that teaching voice again. Still in stride, Mother Vajpai reached for my chair to toss it aside.

We were committed to the bout now.

As her hand grasped the chair rail, I lofted it with my foot, so the chair came up off the floor more swiftly than she had expected. Her arm followed. I stepped in with the momentum of my kick to land a strike with the side of my hand along her left ribs.

First touch!

Mother Vajpai took the blow with an audible crack, let herself slip away from me on the motion transferred from my hand to her body, and spun a low kick toward my ankles.

A cheap move, but effective. I had to jump off my already compromised stance to avoid tripping. As a result, I could not back away fast enough before she landed hard blows on my shoulders, trying to batter me down. I ducked below that and did a quick backwards roll. My impaired balance took me off target, which surprised both Mother Vajpai and me. Her next foot strike passed through the space where I should have been, while I bowled into a knot of watching men.

Hands grasped at me as I bounced to my feet. To stay on the floor would have been surrender—or death, in a slightly different fight. I swiftly tracked Samma, standing now as well; and the looming bulk of the Rectifier. Where *was* Surali?

In this room I had too many enemies and not enough allies. Spinning away from Mother Vajpai, I blurted to the Selistani watchers, "She would bring down the god Endurance!"

That was a weak arrow with which to move them to action, but I had no better ready and no time to think of one.

Even then, I'd distracted myself too long. Mother Vajpai was upon me with a swift rain of pulled blows. She meant to make me submit without actually disabling me. I ducked into them, accepting the punishment on my shoulders and upper arms, to drive my elbow into her hip.

That caused her to step back as the joint folded in reaction. I followed the hip blow with a feint to her gut and an open hand to her face. Much to my surprise, the face blow connected with a resounding smack and an arcing sheet of pain strongly suggesting I'd just seriously damaged a finger or two.

Mother Vajpai stopped moving to shake her head twice, sharply. Blood was running freely. Had I broken her nose?

Good!

I stole another moment to spot Surali. Around me the Selistani men were moving, though I could not yet tell if this was space-clearing, flight, or incipient riot. The Bittern Court woman stood just past the Rectifier, raising something in her hand to point toward me.

The only way to defeat someone about to shoot you was to run them down and hope they missed. I'd played this trick before. I kicked off, intending to smash Surali's face for her trouble—let her negotiate the purchasing of unquiet deaths with a lopsided nose and missing teeth!

Mother Vajpai had recovered faster than I'd realized. She grabbed my elbow to swing me off my intended course. I stepped into the grapple she offered in doing that, and butted her damaged nose hard with my forehead. Out of the corner of my eye, I saw the Rectifier's hand close over Surali's.

I pulled back from Mother Vajpai as she landed a slap on my ear that made my hearing echo dully. I tried for another head butt. She turned aside just slightly and I caught a shoulder in my sternum for my troubles.

That pushed me backwards, winded almost to the point of blacking out.

Mother Vajpai took advantage of my moment of incapacity to step away from the fight as well and put her hands to her face. Trying to set her nose, I presumed. A quick scan of the room showed me Surali on her knees. Tears streamed down the Bittern Court woman's face, her hand still in the Rectifier's grip. I owed him a thanks. Samma visibly nerved herself to step in, but I realized Mother Vajpai was waving the other Blade away with one hand even while the other still pressed against her own nose. My countrymen were hanging back to shout and wave fists.

By now most of the pardines in the room were on their feet. We were moments from a full-scale bar fight.

Wait. . . . Something nagged at me. Why was Mother Vajpai keeping Samma from the sparring? Right now my old teacher desperately needed a foil to help her take me down.

I glanced at Samma again, then back at Mother Vajpai. Over the line of her hand, her eyes crinkled, even with unshed tears of pain glittering within them.

She was *smiling* at me, out of Surali's line of sight.

Mother Vajpai had been fighting to *lose*. Already my body was in agony in half a dozen places, so her blows had been real enough. But she'd intended to lose to me.

Betrayals within betrayals. I nodded very slightly, just a tic of my chin, then rushed my old teacher hard. Her hand came down from her nose a fraction too slowly to block me, as I now knew it would. I slammed my shoulder into her chest, digging low and pushing up with the blow.

Mother Vajpai left her feet and slid backwards onto the now-empty table. Her head cracked loudly into the pardines' stone bowl. I winced, but turned away, ignoring her and Samma both.

The Rectifier had pressed Surali to the floor. She was openly sobbing. I heard popping noises from her hand still clenched inside his fist. "We must leave," I shouted in his ear.

"Should she survive?" he rumbled, his eyes flickering toward the Bittern Court woman.

"Yes," I said, not even trying to weigh the benefits of having him kill her right here. This was not the Rectifier's business. I wanted the Revanchists and the Selistani embassy to thwart one another, not launch an all-out war.

What if I gave him the Eyes of the Hills? Maybe, maybe, I told myself, but dismissed the thought for later consideration. Too much else occurring in the moment, too much else at stake. This was not the opportune time for important decisions.

The huge pardine dropped the Bittern Court woman's right fist and swung his arms wide with a growl. The surging brawl inside the tavern made space for him and his wicked claws. I stepped close and kicked Surali hard in the chest, then stepped on her unhurt left hand, grinding my heel into her remaining unbroken fingers. Having someone spoon-feed her for a week or two might teach this one some humility.

Samma grabbed at my elbow as I turned to walk away. She almost got a faceful of knife blade for her trouble before I realized who it was. Her expression nearly stirred me to tears.

I followed the Rectifier out into the rainy night, cowering behind that broad back as the sounds of fighting faded behind us. Only the chilly, wet darkness welcomed me onward.

We found shelter inside an old grain wagon. This was a wooden box about eight feet high, seven feet wide, and twenty feet deep, down on its frame amid a jumble of junk and salvage in a narrow yard behind a wheelwright's shop on Kraster Road. I'd never seen the place before in my life, but the Rectifier led me there by a steady, purposeful circuit through the puddled streets, obviously designed to allow him to spot and throw off any pursuers.

When we'd reached the little yard, the Rectifier was satisfied we were alone. So was I. Climbing through the collapsed stacks of old scaffolding and cart axles and warped lumber was educational. I had no idea someone as massive as he could so effectively squirm through such apparently tiny gaps.

Inside stank of mold and rot, but it was dry, and relatively clean. A small alcohol stove and a bedroll bespoke frequent occupation, though I wasn't sure the Rectifier was the sort to bother with such niceties.

"This is your place?" I was still breathing hard from the fight at the Tavernkeep's. My ribs were grinding with a sharp, discouraging pain. When had Mother Vajpai hit me so? I examined my right hand, which promised some marvelous bruising. All my knuckle bones were intact, somewhat to my surprise. I began idly exploring my mouth with my left index finger, wondering if any teeth were loosened from the head butts I'd delivered.

"I use it," he growled. He added a few words in the flowing language of the pardines, which I had rarely heard spoken. I could not say if it was a blessing, a curse, or something else entirely.

Mumbling around my finger, I answered, "I need to check myself for serious injuries. Then I must ask your patience to hear me out on something."

The Rectifier eased himself to the floor. He had not fought, much, but he moved as if something bothered him. Had he been in an earlier combat? "We will stay here this evening. My time is yours, until either one of us passes into sleep."

"Mmm." I finished exploring my mouth, then took inventory of my other hurts. Several good-sized lumps on my head, but the worst was definitely the damage to my ribs. There didn't seem to be much I could do now except wrap them. I proceeded to do that with fabric torn from the lining of my stolen coat.

Eventually I eased down onto the floor next to the Rectifier and covered myself with the bedroll he seemed to be ignoring. If there were bedbugs about, they would have to work very hard for my attention this night.

"I need your help," I finally said.

"Mmm." He appeared to be asleep, his breath wheezing through his muzzle in irregular time. I knew from the set of his ears that the Rectifier was still listening.

"I am trying to shut myself of the gods in my life. Blackblood has designs upon my unborn daughter. I am being visited by a titanic. I have even come to doubt the value of my connection with the Lily Goddess and Her servants my sisters, as they are allied with my enemies." *Or seem to be.* Mother Vajpai's fighting to lose weighed on my mind.

One pale eye flicked briefly open. "You are human. Those are human gods. I have no wisdom for you there."

"I am human, and they are human gods, but they afflict me like chancres on a beggar's mouth." I tried and failed to keep the bitterness from my voice. "I am no priest to be ridden for a god's horse."

This time both eyes flicked open. "No priest, mmm?" His tone conveyed laconic amusement.

"No. And I will be shut of their influence."

"I do not believe your gods can be shut out, like a door latched against the weather."

"Something must be done." My frustration bubbled. "I am taking my life back from the influence of the divine. Divine influenza, more like it. Gods slide into a person's thoughts until their choices fall away."

A long silence; then, in a slow rumbling, almost a many-worded sigh, "This has what to do with me?"

"Nothing. Everything." I paused, collecting my thoughts. Rain drummed on the wagon's roof, sounding like voices raised in the distance. "I ask not from responsibility but from friendship. You have dealt with more priests than I can count. As allies, as enemies, as targets, as obstacles to be overcome. I would deal with a god, remove his power from my life. It seems to me that you know something of this."

The Rectifier sat up. From the floor he gathered a rag and began carefully polishing his claws one by one, extending then cleaning them. "You are being foolish, Green," he said slowly. "Human gods are needed for those with human powers and human problems. Each people worships according to their needs."

I wondered whose needs the Urges had met, in the darkness before the morning of the world. I wondered whom in turn the titanics had served, besides their own prodigious appetites and strange lusts. A pardine theory of godhood, perhaps, for all that they didn't seem to have gods as I understood the concept.

"Human gods I have aplenty," I replied. "I wish fewer of them in my life.

You know I will not cast aside Endurance, could not do so even if pressed. I just wish to shut certain doors. Block certain powers. You possess that might and that talent."

"Might?" He snorted, an almost human laugh. I had never heard the Dancing Mistress do so. "I can stand to fight against a dozen men and walk away intact. I can scale cliffs, swim rivers, and bear down against the weapons of prayer like a warm spoon through cold grease. But I am not mighty. And certainly not against your human gods."

"You chop logic." I struggled to keep my voice from becoming sullen. It would serve me no purpose at all to whine at my hoped-for ally. "I know your reputation among priests is infamous. I have seen you stand before the wrath divine unconcerned."

He rumbled a low noise I could not parse. Then: "Do not confuse foolish bravery with might and power."

"Still, these gods do not touch you as they touch me."

"Of course not. You have a soul."

"And you have a soulpath." I stared at him in the glimmering darkness of the grain wagon, though all I could see was the flash of his eyes and the folded shape of his power. The soulpath was an aspect of pardine theology and spirituality of which I had only a tenuous grasp, even with the Dancing Mistress' various patient efforts at explanation. Their kind were born into a family or tribe or grouping—I did not even know *that* word in Petraean, translation for whatever they called themselves in their own tongue. Each new pardine was feasted into the soulpath of their people. A collective soul, perhaps. Or a herd soul, every individual contributing what was needful and taking what was required, while the whole never lost its collective identity.

Pardines shared a connection with one another and among their people that flowed much deeper than anything humans could lay claim to. Twins, perhaps, such as Iso and Osi, could touch something of the sort. Not the greater run of us.

"I walk a soulpath." His agreement was almost grudging. "Some among my people would tell you I have strayed."

"The Revanchists?" I paused, tasting my next thought before I laid it out for him. "They seem concerned with purity. I have known humans of their sort. It's a petty philosophy."

"They think me lost," the Rectifier admitted. "Too long I have hunted among your kind. Any longtime hunter takes on an aspect of their prey."

I tried to imagine the Rectifier as a human priest. The necessary focus and dedication to a god seemed so terribly unlike him. He did not have that strange gift for embracing contradiction that every priest I knew seemed to contain. To follow a god was to follow improbabilities. How could such a thing as Skinless walk the earth? Of what fabric did the Lily Goddess wreak the miracle of her appearances? How did Endurance manifest, even at my call and with the power I'd harnessed in that moment?

This was the true point of Iso and Osi's stories, of the Rectifier's strange ideas about godhood and need, of Desire's grief as She passed through the world of Her daughter-goddesses. The concerns of gods were beyond me.

All I really wanted now was to be beyond *them*, and to take my growing daughter safely with me into that refuge. "I have been hunted by gods," I told him. "I doubt they have much taken on my aspect. It is from their predations I would remove myself."

"You still struggle with Blackblood."

"Yes," I said, somewhat surprised that he understood this.

"Your gods mean little to me, Green." The Rectifier's voice was grave. "You risk being a great fool in acting so against your nature. But I will stand beside you against Blackblood if you ask it of me."

"I shall not stop you from your knucklebone harvest," I said.

He rumbled another almost-laugh. "No, that you shall not do."

With that we sank into a quiet that in turn descended into troubled sleep, at least for me, under the staccato rain on our temporary wooden roof.

Morning brought chilly air that recalled all too well winter's frosts. My hand was a bit swollen, but the fingers had retained their flexibility. The less said of my ribs, the better, though I doubted they were actually broken. I could breathe without screaming. My belly felt bigger, as if my child had grown overnight. Also, I was hungry beyond the point of ravenous. No food would be safe from me until I was sated.

The Rectifier roused as soon as I began to stir. "Do you have a plan to fight the gods?" he asked quietly. "Or will you simply continue to move faster than everyone else and trust your weapons as always?"

"I cannot carry a blade large enough to slit the throat of a god," I replied. "And besides, I must eat first."

"I have cured meat."

He sounded oddly diffident, which I realized was the Rectifier's way of being polite. "No, thank you. I feel an urgent hunger for cardamom rolls, actually."

Though I would not risk heading over to Lyme Street with him in tow. We would be too easily recognized—there were not two like the Rectifier, at least not in Copper Downs. Nor me, either. Surely I could find a bakery here somewhere in the brewery district where so much yeast was used that the air always smelled like spoiled dough, and secure some warm treat or another to carry me through my hunger. Once more I longed for a kitchen of my own.

"As you please." He began shredding long-shanked strips of meat with his fangs. I found myself curiously unwilling to ask what animal had been slaughtered and cured to make his snack. I was afraid the answer would be too unpleasant for even me.

When the Rectifier seemed to have taken his fill, at least for the moment, I told him I was ready to venture forth and find a bakery. We crawled from our shelter through the jumbled junk of the yard outside. No one noted our appearance on the street under the stark, clear sky. Faint clouds scribed frosted glyphs at the very top of the heavens, but I was not wise enough to read them.

He set a loping pace I was willing to follow, for the effort would only benefit me, whatever the pain in my chest. I let the pavement absorb the pounding of my feet. The distresses of my spirit slipped free in each glancing step. The air had enough of an edge to hurt my lungs, which made a fine counterpoint to the jarring of my ribs. *Ilona's house must be so cold,* I thought. She would have made a fire, but even amid an entire forest of feral apple trees and neglected lumber tracts, the woman was parsimonious with her fuel.

There were times when living in Selistan seemed like much the better option, regardless of my station there. I wondered how sincere Samma had been in saying she'd meant to find me and bring me home. Warm, those streets were warm, even when they were filled with enemies.

As if Copper Downs were not.

We skidded around a corner and I went sprawling on the cobbles. That multiplied the pain in my ribs, and struck me a hard blow to the jaw that made my teeth and skull ache. I managed to guard the baby, but the sheltering made the rest of my fall worse. The Rectifier spun and scooped me up before I could recover myself. At his hands, I was back on my feet.

"You are in litter," he said, sniffing at me. "You should not fight."

I was still trying to sort out how to respond to that when we fetched up before a bakery. This was a commercial establishment, turning out racks and racks of loaves for taverns, inns, chandlers' carts; whoever would purchase by the dozen or the twentyweight. It *smelled* like a bakery, all yeast and wheat. That was surely what had drawn the Rectifier. The scent was sufficient to distract my own attention from the fresh hurts of my body.

The thing was, he had the right of it.

Grumbling, I went inside and bargained for a basket of butterflake rolls. The two women behind the counter didn't want to sell such a small quantity to me. I pointed out that the Rectifier and I could make a day of loitering in front of their bakery discouraging customers while we waited for minds to be changed.

They relented quickly enough at that threat, though I was gouged on the price. I judged little point in overplaying my hand for that. Instead I took my rolls and left.

The smell was luscious. Still, these were not cardamom rolls. They tasted well enough and went down all right. I nonetheless wished for the others. Or possibly some pickled cabbage.

That last had to be the baby talking through my appetite.

When the two of us had finished gobbling down my acquisition—the Rectifier ate two of them, possibly out of some misplaced politeness—I took the lead in walking us toward the warehouse where Iso and Osi waited. The Rectifier followed along with studied patience, as if he were indulging me. Which might even have been true.

"Why do they call you the Rectifier?" I asked.

"Because it is my name," he replied in his rumbling voice. Nothing of his answer invited further inquiry, but I was feeling a childish rebellion against his obvious indulgence.

"I know something of pardine names. What do you rectify, that they should call you so?"

His claws flexed. "Troublesome humans for the most part."

"None so troublesome as me," I announced cheerfully.

"Few, to be sure," the Rectifier admitted.

I decided I'd won my point. Whatever that trivial victory might mean. We approached the warehouse, so I pulled him aside to lean against a wall in conversation.

"Now we shall visit a pair of human . . . well . . . ascetics."

"Priests?" A delight bloomed in his eyes. I realized this was surely as much to tweak my sensibilities as anything.

"Monks, more like," I told him. "And you *will* behave."

"What order?"

"Excuse me?"

The look he gave me was far less indulgent. I was thankful for all my years with the Dancing Mistress—most humans found pardines next to impossible to read, I'd been told.

This time his voice rumbled. "Of what god are they priests or followers?"

"I don't know." In that moment I realized how curious an omission this truly was. "They speak of their ancient rite, one which excludes women, but they have never named it. Surely because I am a woman."

"Surely." Doubt rang heavy in his voice.

"In any case, they are twins. Iso and Osi. These two are strange, even by the standards of the religious. But they know a great deal. And they are helping me to overset Blackblood, that he might cease hunting my trail."

The Rectifier shrugged, a dangerous, slow ripple of muscle and attention that meant he was focusing if anything too closely. "Even my help is dangerous to you. Simply because we are of different kinds, without respect to our regard for one another. The aid of those with an unknown purpose is likely to be a far greater trap."

"I know, I know. . . ." Everyone had to warn me of something, it seemed. The world never stopped trying to teach me. Maybe I needed to keep trying to learn? That lesson about lessons continues even now, years later. "I am willing to trust them, based on their own self-interest. I do not know their character or their history except for what they have chosen to display. These two brothers are among the few in this city without some hidden purpose for me."

"You know that, do you?" The sarcasm in his voice was downright human. "Who you choose to trust is your business. I pledged you my aid. Aid you I will."

The balance of his unsaid words echoed quite clearly in the chill morning air between us. I shrugged off a surge of frustration. The Rectifier would help me as he saw best. Surely he had even less agenda than the twins, unless he were in secret league with the Revanchists. The idea of the Rectifier doing anything in secret coaxed a reluctant smile to my lips.

"I trust you," I said. "For reasons stronger and older than anything offered by these two mystics from the deep east."

"Neither of us died when we fought." He chuckled, that slow grinding laugh of his. "That is rare. And trust-making."

The implications of that sank in. "I am glad I did not train in your school."

One great paw enclosed my shoulder. "If you had, the school would have been bettered."

I ducked my head to hide the foolish grin that tried to seize my face, and mumbled a thanks. Then I led him through a small side door into the dusty country where I'd left the ministers of my ambitions.

Iso and Osi rose to their feet at the sight of the Rectifier, once more reminding me of a pair of fighters ready for the sparring ring. How had they ever fooled me in the Dockmarket with the supposed threat of the local thugs? I had only needed look at their stance to know better, but I'd been blinded by their age and my willingness to believe in these two men who so reminded me of Lao Jia.

The great pardine settled his weight as if about to leap into a fray. Whether he was reading their stance or their saffron robes I could not say. Priest killer that he was, the Rectifier might well recognize the order or temple from which their rite stemmed.

For now, though, it was on me to speak, and quickly. "Revereds," I said sharply. "I bring friends together today, to pursue the matter that troubles me most." I bowed toward the twins. "Iso and Osi, I present the Rectifier. He is a warrior among the pardines, one who has stalked the shadows of the divine through the human world." Then I turned and nodded at the Rectifier. "These are Iso and Osi. They also stalk the shadows of the divine along a somewhat different path than yours. Each of you has given me wise counsel, and all of you have said you would grant me aid in this matter I now seek to resolve."

"Blackblood," rumbled the Rectifier. His ears were laid back but not flat, and his claws flexed. That could be a lie, or it could be readiness to do battle.

The twins stared back at the Rectifier impassively. No fear flickered on their faces, no doubt danced in their eyes. I had expected nothing else of these two old men, and was proud of them. The Rectifier was not easy to stand before even when he was in the best of humors.

"A god of this city," Iso said. "Who troubles Mistress Green without cause or purpose."

"I do not debate the purposes of gods," the Rectifier responded. "Only the intentions of their faithless priests."

The twins stirred at that. Osi spoke up. "You have the air of one who has broken a few altars."

The last broken altar I had seen was the Temple of Air, in the Eirigene Pass, and that from a distance. Still, the smoke and bodies had been terrible. Choybalsan had no altar so far as I knew. Just the temple of his ambition, wherein I had slain him.

Besides, I had not truly broken *him* either, so much as remade his power into Endurance.

The Rectifier shrugged again. This time it was definitely an act, the elaborate, showy ripple of his shoulders intended to impress with his might. "Altars are made for breaking. Are we proposing to do so here in Copper Downs?"

Iso: "Not as such. Just place limits on a fractious god."

"Erm." That noise was somewhere between a growl and a purr.

Osi spoke again. "If you can stand against the force of a temple ward, or a shielding prayer, we could make use of your powers in pursuit of Mistress Green's project."

The three of them grew close and began to speak of the mechanics of blocking a god's will, of invisibility and boundaries and how to hold the edges against an eruption. I listened closely, for of course this touched much on me. Their vocabulary and common experience passed quickly outside my knowledge. They descended into a deep discussion of threaded souls and power flows and ritual boundaries. The Rectifier had no trouble at all with the twins' strange style of conversation, and seemed quite comfortable addressing them both as one.

The worth of my strategy of neutralizing Blackblood continued to nag at me, especially in the light of the Rectifier's words about human gods for human needs. Was I making the right choices? Wisdom was slowly returning to me.

I cradled my belly—and truly, it had grown larger, as if my tumble outside was not evidence enough—and thought on how best to approach the problem of setting the Selistani embassy against the pardine Revanchists. Could I simply buy the attentions of the Dancing Mistress' new sect with the Eyes of the Hills?

No. She would not play that game with me.

I considered an appeal to her loyalty, but our bond was strained almost beyond credibility, let alone the passion we'd shared not so long ago. Choybalsan had damaged my old teacher badly. She was not the woman who'd spent years training me; neither the one who had passed a few hot, strange weeks being my silken-furred lover.

The baby fluttered at that thought as well, as if she could read my memories. "Hush, child," I whispered. "Your day is far, far away."

Even if I could turn the Dancing Mistress toward me, that said nothing of the intentions of *her* followers. I doubted she could bind the Revanchists to my needs.

What if I took the Eyes of the Hills back to Mother Vajpai? I dismissed that idea as well. Whatever game Mother Vajpai was caught up in served as an extension of Kalimpuri politics. That she'd fought to lose in our contest at the Tavernkeep's place was enough for me. I knew I should accept her passive support, but could not lean upon her given her active and official betrayal of me.

What had the embassy hoped to buy from the Revanchists with those gems? *That* was the true price and prize, and I simply could not see it yet. Neither group held anything in common with the other, except a very tenuous thread winding through me and my experiences in both Kalimpura and Copper Downs. Well, and whatever Endurance might symbolize to each of them. The pardines had played a hand in the birthing of the god. Their long-stolen power had been embodied in the ox.

Which implied that the Revanchists wanted to cast down Endurance and restore that pent-up power to their own people. The Dancing Mistress had all but said as much. She had not called for such a violent vengeance, though, only asked for their idol's gems to be restored.

Likewise, the Selistani embassy was here for me. Or so they alleged. Plausible enough that someone might send Samma or even Mother Vajpai across the Storm Sea on such an errand, if the need were large enough or the call sufficiently urgent.

But Surali? And the Prince of the City?

Not for me, not as their sole end. Even Surali's anger with me could not justify this expedition of theirs. Some greater game was afoot, that the entire Temple of the Silver Lily was enmeshed in, or Surali would not have whatever hold she already kept on Mother Vajpai.

It was up to *me* to free my Blade sisters.

This whole affair coiled round and round, though I could not see the center. I had forced Samma to give me the Eyes of the Hills. I did not yet know what purpose the gems filled for the pardines, nor did I comprehend what deeper thing might be guarded beyond that purpose.

Something essential was hidden from me.

And did that matter?

What if I just forced the two groups to open conflict? They would fight until even the Interim Council could not ignore the trouble. Let the twins and the Rectifier neutralize Blackblood, then bring my real enemies to force of arms. Copper Downs possessed no army as such, and no real law enforcement since the disbanding of the Ducal Guard, but the Interim Council now had Lampet's Lads. If motivated, the guilds here could muster quite a few men under arms even without a renewed effort to raise the vacant regiments. Chowdry quite possibly could conjure up elements of Federo's old bandit army just by trolling taverns and chophouses and dockside flops with the right words in his mouth.

If Jeschonek and the others wanted the Selistani and the Revanchists gone, they had the power to force the issue. All I really needed to do was create enough of a ruckus to call down that official wrath.

Creating a ruckus happened to be something I was very, very good at. Yesterday's fight in the Tavernkeep's place wasn't a bad start. I would continue the effort by sending a note to the Selistani embassy and informing them anonymously that the Revanchists had taken possession of the Eyes of the Hills. Whatever bargain Surali had meant to make with the gems was already overset with my seizure of them from Samma. This would make public what only she and I knew.

As for that, I was certain Samma had not yet betrayed herself. If she had, the affair yesterday would have run quite differently. Surali still played like a woman who controlled the highest cards. It was time she knew her hand had been stolen away.

I discarded the reflection and turned back to my allies at their work.

They squatted on their heels, drawing diagrams upon the blackened floorboards with dust and an old stub of chalk. Squinting close, I recognized a version of Ashton's Ladder of the Divine, a classic theological illustration I'd encountered during my time of enforced education in the Factor's house. They worked together to annotate it with notes that looked as if the Rectifier were propounding his notion of the utility of godhead.

Pardine theology meeting with, well, whatever rite the saffron-robed twins practiced. With a nod, I left them to it and slipped back out into the city's burgeoning day.

It was my intention to head for a scrivener's and procure the needed letter to the Selistani embassy. I did not want the missive written out in my own hand, for surely Samma and Mother Vajpai would recognize my script. It was possible that Surali would as well, depending on whether or not she had made a study of me in pursuit of her vengeance. With a small grin, I wished her ill of her injuries. I hoped that her own writing would always have a shiver in it to remind the vicious woman of the cost of crossing me.

The morning was still bright and quite cold. I found myself drawn toward the Temple Quarter. That impulse I followed despite my earlier plan, though I had no intention of marching up the steps of the Algeficic Temple. Black-blood would be fine without me, until he wasn't. That thought made me check my backtrail for signs of Skinless, whom I thought I'd spied the previous day. There were no nine-foot-tall flayed corpses rambling the streets behind me.

I could not *wait* to be well and truly shut of these gods.

Soon enough I was standing before the ruined Temple of Marya. The site was a jumble of joists and fractured bricks, just as I recalled. Whatever activity the recent rescue had stimulated was long gone. Scavengers had not yet crept in to clear the rubble for salvage or fill. Offerings had been left behind, too. A few flowers—in winter?—scraps of food, a little girl's smock.

I sat on a lump of masonry and stared up at the brick looming beyond. It was the back of some other temple's refectory or priory. What had been an interior wall of Marya's temple stood exposed, the last surviving piece of what was otherwise utterly destroyed. I saw a row of hooks, as if to hang pots, and a discolored square where some icon or image had long been displayed. Small chalk marks around the edges of the wall looked fresher, and oddly familiar.

Hadn't I seen chalk marks on the shattered bricks here before? On my first visit . . . I craned my neck to look about. They were familiar, too familiar. And not just from this wreckage.

The air thickened. I tasted metal again. My thoughts interrupted, I tried to gather myself close, as Iso and Osi had taught me, to render myself small as a mustard seed before divine regard. It was already too late. Two birds wheeling in the sky above slowed to a halt in place, their wings trapped between one beat and the next.

Desire, I was certain of it. Blackblood spoke to me in the flesh, so to speak, while the Lily Goddess manifested by different paths.

"You may as well show Yourself," I called out, my words braver than my heart. "My attention has been captured."

She stepped out of nothingness, and was indeed Desire. I imagined any woman would know this goddess simply by Her aspect. I tried to look close, but again She was of all shapes and sizes and colors in one body, so it was like staring at a crowd and trying to make them into a single person.

You were drawn to My temple. Desire's voice was a thousand women whispering on the threshold of their greatest passion.

"I followed where my feet led me." I would not admit to being Her creature, even temporarily. My purpose was to shut myself of gods. Not to accept more.

No, She said. **Your purpose is much greater than that.**

This time, the titanic was not driving me so close to the edge of reason. Had I grown stronger, or was She grown gentler with me? "You cheat by heeding my thoughts," I told Her. Defiance was ever my way, even in the face of all good sense. Or perhaps especially then.

Laughter now, a storm off the sea. **You would stand protesting before Father Sunbones himself.**

Having already raised the argument, there was no reason not to follow where it led. "I would sooner steal his spoons and find my way home again."

Your fierce will is what draws the divine to you, Green. Now Desire spoke in a voice I could swear was my mother's, for all that I had no memory of her. **You are a candle amid the vague shadows of so many other souls.**

"I am not Your candle," I said, struggling against the gentle temptation enfolded in Her tone. *Not my mother, You do not play fair,* I thought with a desperate urgency.

Fairness is such a human idea, She said, Her vasty power almost gentle now. **But I bring you something far greater than fairness.**

"What?" I let myself grow sullen, for that, too, is a kind of armor against temptation. Whatever came next was surely intended to woo my unwary heart.

I bring you magnificent opportunity. Though Her multiplicitous body did not move, I had the impression Desire knelt before me, to reach me on my level as an adult might bend down to address a small child. **This city will need another in Marya's stead. In time the women of Copper Downs would find their own goddess, and she will come together. If I might raise such a one now, much needless privation would be spared.**

My words failed me for a moment, two, three; a long gap of thought unrealized. Finally, I spat out a protest. "You do not mean to elevate *me* to godhood!"

You have experience of theogeny, Green. You have touched and been

touched by more of the divine than almost any priest or eremite. Marya's passing was no accident. A newly raised goddess with your powers and experience could do much to block another such effort at casting down.

"No!" I tried not to shout, but I was offended, frightened. "I c-cannot do this. I harbor no hopes of ever reaching such an estate. I can't even stand the thought of being a priestess of my own goddess. C-caring for myself and my child is t-too much. How could I look to the needs of generations of women?"

And their children, Desire reminded me.

I reined my voice in. "I have held too much fate in my hands already. I will not grasp more. Find Yourself another girl. Luck to you both when you do."

This offer will not be repeated, the goddess warned me. I felt the pressure of scolding, of deeds ill done, of poorly considered choices and the impulsive shame of youth.

"Do not do that," I growled. My knives were close, though none of them long enough for *this* target. "I will not be pressed even by You."

Those rebellions arise from within, Green. Desire's face came into focus, long with regret and sadness. **I am not here, in truth. You have only the least focus of My attention. Most of what you see and hear is your own words and feelings. That is how I know your thoughts.**

I wondered if She had just given me some great secret of godhood that I was too dense to comprehend. No matter. I would not play this game for anyone else; I certainly was not intending to play it for Her.

Besides all that, I was certain that I would be a *terrible* goddess.

"My thanks," I said, begrudging even the gratitude. "But, no. I have held enough authority to know that I wish no more of it."

She was gone with the sigh of a dying child, leaving me weeping atop a heap of broken stones and clutching at my belly to protect the baby within from everything.

After a while, Ponce, the pleasant young man from the Temple of Endurance, came to me where I sat listening to the breeze fuss among Marya's ruins. He was winded, as if he'd been sprinting across the city. A spot of ash was smeared across his forehead.

"Another attack?" My words puffed white in the cold. It was then that I noticed that the pain in my chest and hand were gone as well. Had Desire taken them? I could not decide whether to curse or praise. Divine healing was rank bribery to one like me, who was supposed to learn from her mistakes. Memory of pain is an excellent teacher.

"No." Ponce stopped, bent with his hands just above his knees. He drew in several deep, shuddering breaths that steamed harder than mine. The scent of him was strong and musky, and tugged at a corner of my thoughts in an echo of Septio better left untouched in this moment. Some lingering aspect of Desire still upon me. Or an unfortunate taste on my part for young men of priestly vocation.

"Worse, perhaps," he added as he straightened and focused his attention.

I looked into his brown Selistani eyes and wondered what he saw of me. Had the goddess left Her mark? The very touch of a titanic was like walking into a bonfire. Despite the evidence of my own experiences, I knew that in these latter days of the world, they were not worshipped directly. Or indeed thought to be present at all. I wondered if this acolyte could spy Her words yet upon me. "What is worse?"

"A woman cries for you."

A handful of responses crowded my thinking, none of them respectful or appropriate. I swallowed what would surely have been a smirk, settling for "What does she say?"

"She pulls at her hair and shouts your name, then bursts into tears." He appeared baffled. "None of us have ever seen her before. She is not known in the temple."

With a long, slow sigh I unfolded myself from my rubble pile. Whatever Desire had intended, that moment had passed, taking the goddess' plans with it. I found myself hard-pressed to care overmuch about divine ambitions. As for the crying woman . . . "Is this a trick? Did you spy bravos lurking in the bushes nearby?"

"No," said Ponce gravely. "And if we did, we would not offer up our fists. This is done as Endurance wills."

Endurance is an ox, I thought scornfully, then felt guilty over the words. When Ponce steadied my arm, I did not even notice. My balance was just strange lately.

I broke into a trot. Not a hard run, for my escort was already winded, but something to move my body with the newfound energy Desire seemed to have imparted to me. I could not help but be grateful for that. On the other hand, too soon these boy's pants would have to be let out or replaced. I might as well maintain what I could of my poor body in some useful shape.

Ponce kept up with me. I could hear the breath shuddering ragged in his chest as he ran, but his legs pistoned every time mine did and more. He proved to be a magnificent pacekeeper.

We ran down Whitetop Street and over Durand Avenue, straight into the Velviere District. I watched again for Skinless, or others on my trail, but saw only the business of the day.

I slowed down as we approached the area around the temple. Traffic thinned there. This was a part of town that named street runners "thief" without waiting to see if anything had actually been stolen. The temple surely already had unhappy neighbors, simply for drawing any traffic at all through those recently opened gates, where only a blank wall had for so very long guarded nothing but empty mine galleries rotting beneath a layer of brambles.

Still, our approach was brisk. The same old Selistani man sat on the chair outside the gate. Endurance already with an avatar? He nodded us in with no acknowledgment from Ponce and a bare answering nod in return from me.

Inside, the temple seemed to be in its usual state of disarray, except for the quarryman's low-bedded wagon with its team of four enormous draft horses. Foundation stones were being unloaded.

That explained the ash on Ponce's forehead—dust.

"She's at the kitchen. Asti is pouring kava down her, or was when I left to find you."

Something that had been nagging at my mind leapt to the front. "How did you know where I was?"

He grinned. "Endurance told me."

The god was *mute*. I wondered if my ox was manifesting new powers. More likely Ponce was very close to his patron deity's dreaming mind. That was where this god spoke—not in thundering visions and declamatory exhortations forced from the fumbling mouths of arrogant priests, but directly through the thoughts and deeds of his followers. I had to admit that this seemed an elegant solution to the corruption of priests.

We walked toward the kitchen tent. My heart beat cold and hard for the span of half a dozen breaths. Ilona sat at one of the long tables. Her orange dress was torn, soiled, bloodied. Her hair trailed in a madwoman's messy cloud, like dreams escaping from a mind overheated with confusion. A mug shivered in her hands, spilling steam and brown drops on the trestle tabletop before her.

I did not see Corinthia Anastasia anywhere about.

Shoving past Ponce, I raced to Ilona's side, full of unnamed dread. "I am here." I plucked at her elbow. "What has happened?"

She looked at me and dropped her mug. It bounced on the table, sending chips of ceramic and a spray of kava flying. "Green," Ilona gasped, then collapsed sobbing into my arms.

I looked across her bare head toward Ponce as I stroked her neck and back. "Have you gotten any more from her? Where is her daughter?"

He shrugged, hands spread wide, face a mask of wordless regret.

"Ilona," I whispered, holding her close. "Listen to me, Ilona. Where is Corinthia Anastasia?"

She mumbled something into my shoulder that ended in a shriek and a sob. My heart hardened in that moment. My enemies had gone hunting among my friends. I would pay them out in rich, hot blood.

"If you do not tell me," I crooned, patting her hair, "I cannot help you."

The older woman broke away from my shoulder to look me in the face. Her own dark eyes were rimmed with ragged red. One was bruised, as from a blow. "They took her." Ilona's voice was so plain and stark that it carried more weight of grief than an army of tears could have borne.

I gripped her shoulders tight, forcing her to keep looking at me. "Who did?"

"I d-don't know. Men. Dark-skinned. Selistani."

"Looking for me?"

"They didn't say." Tears pooled in her eyes. "They didn't say anything at all. Just beat me, laid Corinthia Anastasia across their saddlebags, and set fire to my cottage. Then they were g-gone."

My rage blossomed like oil burning in a scorching pan. Whoever did this would pay, body and soul. I would piss on their corpses instead of lighting the candles or painting them with the red and the white.

This was aimed at *me*, a trap laid with a single prey in mind, but it was sprung about a child stolen away to snatch at my attention. No one could have conceived of a harder strike to my heart, short of ripping my own babe from my womb.

I'd been attacked here at the Temple of Endurance, to the cost of two lives, and shrugged it off. I'd been confronted to the point of riot at the Tavernkeep's place and continued about my business. This, though . . .

The only question was whether it was the Selistani embassy behind this—Surali, to be specific, whose face I should have smashed instead of her fingers—or some other player.

Clutching tight to Ilona, I forced the fire of my thoughts to burn slower. If the Interim Council wanted me they would simply send for me. Blackblood might have hired the men who'd killed the girls, but I could not see that god causing his nervous priests to hire Selistani migrants—who could not possibly know these High Hills—as freelance raiders to commit such dirty work among the ancestral graves of his own people.

No, this was the work of whoever had been asking after me at Briarpool right before my return. Whomever Corinthia Anastasia had spied on that day, and showed herself to in the process. Possibly the pardine Revanchists. But again—why would they use Selistani agents? My mind came back to the embassy, Surali, and the people who would know how child stealing overset my heart.

Mother Vajpai.

No.

Not possible.

Not her.

Regardless of my banishment, or the political situation between the Temple of the Silver Lily and the Bittern Court, I could not credit Mother Vajpai, even now, with setting such a vile trap. But I could credit her with informing Surali of my feelings for children and the uses to which they were put. And the Bittern Court woman was quite able to make such a disaster for me, laughing all the while. They'd certainly brought their own bravos from across the sea. Little Baji and some other pirate toughs, or the Prince of the City's men.

I would bar the doors of their rented mansion and burn it to ash with everyone roasting inside.

All this pouring through my head, I leaned close to Ilona. "I know who has your daughter. I will see to her return."

"It was h-h . . ." Her news delivered, and accepted, she dissolved into tears, leaving her latest words unspoken.

Oh, the power of a child over a parent's heart. Though I did not know it then, I would be so weakened by that power in the years to come. At the same time, it is a different kind of strength. Ilona cried in my arms for a while. Eventually I coaxed her to the tent I had been using and got her to lie down upon a cot within. Someone else slept there these days, I didn't know whom, but I wasn't concerned with that. Instead I wrapped myself around Ilona's back and picked at her hair in an attempt to ease the horrid mess, while she wept herself to sleep. I realized from her messiness, and the sweaty reek upon her, that she'd raced straight all the leagues from her cottage in the High Hills to here.

As Ilona slept I cleaned her a bit more, then unbuttoned her dress and eased her out of it. She rolled as I tugged at her arms and legs. Beneath she wore a simple cotton shift that I did not attempt to remove. I could not see pulling it over her head without waking her. Instead I fetched warm water and a cloth to clean her face, her hands, her feet. In another time this would have been sensual, even sexual. Right now it was all I could do for her.

The whole time I cleansed her and wiped away the grime of the road and her suffering, I considered the problem.

Surali.

This whole business hinged in large part on the Bittern Court woman. Though I longed for hot, bloody vengeance, the child was far more at stake. Could I trade the Eyes of the Hills for Corinthia Anastasia? What would I be giving up? What kept the girl safe from another abduction afterward?

The only answer was that they must surrender the child and be forced to leave the city. Unburnt, though if I could find a way to trouble their ship . . .

No, I would not do that. I had known too many sailors by now to think that in pursuit of my wrath they could just be disregarded as furniture aboard their vessels.

Still, Surali would never run far enough to escape me, even if I was forced to let her slip my grasp awhile in this time and place.

As I watched Ilona sleep, my thoughts returned to the subject of Blackblood. Another child taker, in his own words. I still wondered how he fit in. He'd sent those men to me, killing the girls in the Temple of Endurance.

Or had he?

I'd assumed that, but had not yet proven it. Skinless had sought me not so long ago, yet I had persuaded him away with the open hand of friendship. The avatar and I shared a bond. Beyond that the god still must have been willing to let his pursuit of me lag awhile. After all, Skinless was little more than a finger from Blackblood's divine hand. If the god had chosen to close his fist over me, Skinless would have folded me in, despite the creature's dim regard for me.

If the raid on the temple had been commissioned by Surali—and I had to admit, that sort of action was more her style than Blackblood's—the deed was done with local bravos hired to find me. Their failure to do so might have prompted her to send a handful of Street Guild men out to the High

Hills in a side bet, a play to secure another hold on me should Mother Vajpai and Samma fail to tame me.

Which they in turn indeed failed to do. Mother Vajpai had fought to lose. Further evidence that it was unlikely to be she who had stolen Corinthia Anastasia away.

Here was the betrayal. Even Samma allowing herself to be forced to part with the Eyes of the Hills was a portion of the betrayal. The Lily Blades playing false to everyone. That was not our way, but these were perilous times with terrible pressures.

If Surali was behind the attack on the Temple of Endurance, then what *had* Blackblood done to me? In response to . . . nothing? . . . I had set not one, but two, enemies upon him. Iso and Osi were no friends to the god. The magics of their ancient rites would not be so easy for Blackblood to ignore. Not to mention I'd united them with the Rectifier, who was a mercenary in the purest sense of the word. He had no loyalty to Blackblood at all, nor to any human god.

In that moment, my focus finally returned to the chalk marks on the wall of Marya's temple. I understood how great my blindness had been. I did know what they signified. They were the same marks Iso and Osi had shown me in counseling me how to cloak myself from the attentions of a god. Wards, and boundaries. They were the same marks the twins had been drawing on the warehouse floor to the Rectifier's benefit.

Those two were on a more troubling pilgrimage than they'd admitted to me. Except they had. Their rite forbade eating with or touching women. I thought back to the stories of Desire and Her daughters that I'd read long ago. Both the men's and the women's version spoke of the daughter-goddesses always watching for a man at the window, just as a woman would with a drunken husband to avoid.

Sick with realization, I was near to throwing up. Iso and Osi had brought down Marya. Slain her. Not in open conflict over the future of a city and the fortunes of its people, but by stealth and guile and timeless rite in pursuit of an ancient grudge. The ultimate beating of woman by man, laying a death magic on her protector goddesses.

I had loosed a pair of god killers on the trail of Blackblood. They might just be warding him away from me, but what could I trust? The prospect made me ill.

My own doubts had tried repeatedly to alert me, but I had failed to listen to myself. *Fool, fool, fool!*

Worse, what if Surali was in league with *them*? No wonder the Lily Goddess had feared a fate emanating from here across the Storm Sea in Copper Downs. I could easily believe the Bittern Court woman to be plotting against the Lily Goddess Herself. It all made sense. And all of it tied back to the Eyes of the Hills. Even my old crime of slaying the Duke.

The truth fell upon me like bricks collapsing to spontaneously form a wall.

Having first used me to wrest the Eyes of the Hills from Michael Curry—and to whom had *he* meant to sell or give them, anyway?—Surali brought the stolen gems across the sea to buy off not the pardine Revanchists, but the twins Iso and Osi. All in pursuit of the Bittern Court's vendetta against the Lily Goddess. God killers pursuing daughter-goddesses across the plate of the world to satisfy an ancient vengeance would have any number of uses for such artifacts. Even with their power stripped away, like me, the gems were a conduit to the divine. As I'd been reminded so forcibly, much as small children who would not release a favored plaything, what the gods had once touched they would touch again far more easily than not.

No wonder Desire had pressed theogeny on me. She must have seen me as someone who could stand against the threat of the twins.

The sheer scale of the plot was sickening. Likewise my part in advancing it. Shame bloomed within me at being so readily gulled, until I myself had become a weapon in the hands of my enemies. Easing Ilona under a blanket, I hurried from the tent to see what I could salvage of both error and vengeance before the day grew any shorter.

I passed urgent words with Ponce about the need to care for Ilona, and keeping her quiet for a while. He was shamefaced as I lectured swiftly in a hard tone. When I finally wound down, his only response was apology. "I am sorry, Mother Green."

"For what?" Anger still boiled, but there was little point in allowing it to spill on him.

"That we do not fight." His voice was stark. "A man—a person, excuse me—should defend himself. Herself."

"A person should live in peace." My own words surprised me. Perhaps I had been listening to the god Endurance.

With those words, I took my leave. My heart had been seized with a burning desire to look into the house of my enemies. I knew *where* they were, and I knew more of their rented mansion than my countrywomen there realized, thanks to my studies of architecture. What I did not know was where within that place they were holding Corinthia Anastasia.

Below would not be a sensible approach. For one, I doubted that I could gain interior access to the house from the sewers. Neither did I want to do a reconnaissance from the street. The gate guards would see me, and report to Surali.

It came down to some sneaking by the back wall, and possibly grabbing hold of someone from within the household to question. Both of these things I could do.

The grounds of the embassy's rented mansion met another property along the back. These were not true fortified walls, such as had surrounded the Factor's house in my youth, just masonry courses designed to keep stray animals and undesirables like me from wandering across the lawns. No guards here, or even empty guard stations. I glanced around to be sure I was unobserved, then took a running leap to grab the top, using my momentum to hoist myself up and over.

The mansion adjacent to the Selistani embassy was in sore need of a groundskeeper. This was fine with me, as it meant the wisteria along their side of the common wall had grown quite wild. That is not the easiest plant to move through, but at least it only grips at one's ankles, rather than slashing with thorns or spreading poison from its leaves.

I skulked along the wall inside the shelter of the thin wooden whips of the overgrowth. The midpoint would give me the best vantage to study the rear of Surali's mansion. I already had some good notions of the layout of the front, and the public rooms.

Not for a moment did I imagine that Corinthia Anastasia would conveniently leave a banner or some other signal from an upper window, but I wanted to see whatever was to be seen. Perhaps certain rooms were sealed, or there would be balconies I could climb to—unlikely as that was in the Haito style.

Mostly, though, I needed to visualize a target for my wrath. I could hardly set fire to the house with the hostages within it. Though the idea was still tempting, especially if I nailed the doors shut first. The whole neighborhood could burn for all I cared.

When I reached the midpoint of the dividing wall, I scrambled up under the cover of the wisteria to see what I might learn.

The rear of the house opened in two wings flanking a paved court or terrace. Low windows among shrubbery and vines indicated a basement, likely servants' territory for kitchens, laundry, maids' quarters, and so forth. Two main floors with high ceilings rose above that, then a lower-ceilinged third storey that tucked into the roofline. The uppermost floor would be suites for senior servants and junior relatives.

If I were holding a hostage here, I would keep her in either the basement or the top floor. That would simplify the guard rota, as well as reducing the possibility of accidental exposure to visitors.

There were a number of paths to access the house. No balconies, unfortunately, as I'd figured. The grounds between the terrace and the wall were lightly wooded. Oaks and maples widely spaced, with cropped lawn and patches of leaf-covered loam between them. No cover. The only bushes were those in the beds lining the house.

Even worse, if we had more snow, my tracks would show up like lines on a map.

I very much wanted to know whether Corinthia Anastasia was in the basement or on the top floor. Good money would bet on Surali choosing to go high, but I couldn't tell from out here. And entering the house to gain the uppermost floor was probably beyond me acting alone in this moment. Surali would have dozens of Street Guild men in there. I could not fight them all by myself.

There were other ways to see inside a building.

I retreated down the dividing wall to the corner by the street, to watch in unaccustomed patience. I kept an eye on the front gate to see who came out. I resolved not to pursue a target should they turn left instead of right out of the front of the grounds. Instead I waited for someone to walk down Knightspark Street, past my watchpost.

Over the course of the next hour, a pair of servant girls came by. They carried baskets, giggling together as they went marketing for something needful that must not have been delivered by the purveyors who normally supplied great houses. They were Petraean, and I did not think they would likely have the information I wanted.

More to the point, I did not want these poor girls to pay the price I would be exacting for that information.

My patience was rewarded in the second hour when a Street Guild thug strode quickly out of the house, then chose to walk my way. This was someone with whom I could deal in whatever fashion I chose.

I chose to slip over the wall as he passed me by, and take him from behind with the butt of my long knife to the base of the head. Knightspark Street was fairly quiet, but I could not count on much uninterrupted time. Neither was I prepared to haul him back over the wall.

He groaned and slumped to the cobbles. I bent close, pressing my short knife into the soft skin behind his left ear.

"Where is the northern girl being kept?" Speaking Seliu, I kept my voice fierce.

"You will not—" he began. I sliced off his earlobe, then punched him in the mouth with the knife hilt when he began to scream.

"Be advised that I am short on time and shorter on patience."

"Green." The Street Guildsman made my name a curse.

That was fine with me. "Unless you want me to be the last person you ever meet in your life, you will tell me where she is kept." I once more set the blade against the spot beneath his ear. "Or I am done."

"They will be killing me." He almost made it a sob.

"*I* will be killing you now. Your choice." I poked the knife in until blood ran freely. He stifled another scream. "Three . . . two . . ."

"Upstairs," he gasped. "West end of the top floor."

I clubbed him harder, banging his face into the cobbles, and left him there unconscious with a bloody nose. "You may keep your life by way of my gratitude," I told him, though he could no longer hear me.

Feeling much better informed, I cleaned my knives then hurried toward the teahouse that had become my favorite. Once again I approached without passing by the Textile Bourse. I found my seat in the shaded table hard by the front of their little store. My friend the cinnamon-skinned woman brought me cardamom rolls without my asking, and a rich cup of kava. This time the dark beverage had been foamed with milk and cinnamon. I asked her politely for some meat and cheese to accompany it all, then applied myself to the serious business of eating and thinking while the afternoon of the city flowed past.

My angry fantasies aside, I could not simply snatch Corinthia Anastasia from the Selistani embassy. They would be prepared for any such attempt. This took more planning.

In any case, I had to be sensible. The girl was already hidden away behind stout walls and numerous guards. Rushing headlong to rescue her might have made sense if I'd known before her captors returned to Copper Downs, but not at this point. Far more significant now to stop what pieces of this plot I was able to, *my* pieces, and set in motion such counterplot as I could manage.

Did I dare try to speak to Iso and Osi? I suspected they would realize at the mere sight of my face that I had finally grasped a corner of their truth. Whether or not their graceful economy of motion truly reflected a battle readiness I had not been willing to see until now, I suspected I would not easily walk away from them if they were determined to stop me.

But I'd left the Rectifier with the twins. Not that he needed rescuing, not exactly, but the Rectifier in possession of all the facts as well as my informed speculation was a far more useful ally to me than the Rectifier plotting the downfall of a god I'd wrongly set him against.

My next step would be to spy out whether the pardine rogue was with the twins now. I would not by myself beard Iso and Osi in their warehouse den, but I might be able to approach them if the Rectifier was there.

If I did not see him with the twins I'd have to go hunting at the Tavern-keep's place. Given that I'd last left there under the cloud of a riot, my welcome back might not be as open as I would have liked.

Still, one thing before the next. As always.

I realized that before I headed out on a new round of potentially deadly errands, I would be needing my leathers back. And my good fighting boots. Raiding wasn't so much an option in the corduroy trousers and canvas shirt of an errand boy, no matter what coat I wore. I dug my bundle out from where I'd hidden it amid the scattered stones behind the tents and tried to change right there in the field.

The tunic fit my shoulders but would not close over my belly. The trousers were impossible. Frustration nearly made me cry.

They smelled bad, they were in need of cleaning and oiling, and worst of all, they *did not fit*. The baby had stolen my body from me.

I went stalking off after Ponce, suddenly very conscious of how large I'd grown, how foolish and ungainly I had become.

When I found him, the boy was engaged in close discussion with a quarryman. Or at least, someone with a great sheaf of papers and a wagon-load of various small stone slabs in different colors and textures.

"Now," I said roughly, grasping at Ponce's arm.

"My pardon, Lucius," he told the merchant as I dragged him away.

Lucius just stared a moment before shaking his head and laughing.

When I'd gotten Ponce to a quiet space between two tents, I shoved the leathers into his hand. "If I were home—in Kalimpura at the temple, I mean—I could get another set."

"Of what?" He turned the leathers over as if he had never seen them before.

"Of *those*." I patted my belly, growling at him. "I have grown too fat for them. But I need working clothes."

"C-could they be let out?" He stopped at the look in my eyes, before gathering his courage and trying again. "We have nothing like this here. This is a temple, of a *peaceful* sect."

"I know whose temple this is." I narrowly avoided calling him a fool. "But I need something better, now."

"We could find sturdy canvas trousers," he said dubiously. "Some among the young men would have them to fit you. Sister Gammage could take up the cuffs. As for the shirt . . . more canvas? And maybe a leather vest?" In a careful voice, he added, "From among the men, obviously."

It was a terrible solution. But my other options were worse. I'd already learned the foolishness of working in a robe, and my borrowed boy's clothing would not suit for heavy fighting. "Dark as it can be, black if possible."

"We are not carrion birds, to dress like shadows."

"I am a night hunter." I almost snarled in my frustration.

Several hours later, I was off through the streets. My clothes were still damp from the swift, cheap dye job, and I had best not sit on any pale furniture for a while. At least I had something sturdy to work in.

Even so, my clothing bore its disadvantages. The Velviere District was no place to walk around looking as if one advertised for work as a housebreaker. Likewise, because of the wide lawns, roof-running was useless here. I needed the crowded parts of the city, narrow alleys, with little bridges where barrels or bales passed over traffic from one warehouse to another. There I could take to the roofs once more.

So I found them. Once I'd scrambled up a black iron drainpipe, I felt much safer. Atop a red-tiled roof that sloped down toward Theobalde Avenue, I crouched and watched the street.

My sense of being followed tingled. This was the same feeling I'd had when I thought I'd spotted Skinless. I didn't see how Blackblood's shambling avatar could move through the daylit city unimpeded. On the other hand, if the twins were able to cloak themselves from the eyes of a god, it was logical enough that a god could cloak his minions from the eyes of men.

I studied the scene awhile. People walked with a bit of an edge, something disturbing their movements without interrupting them. As travelers along a country road might circle round the reek of a hidden corpse without ever quite knowing why. Horses, though, being essentially stupid, were much harder to fool. None of the teams being driven down the street would have anything to do with an alley mouth a block up from me. They shied, they bucked, they stopped.

Staring for a time told me little except that my eyes ached, which was not exactly news. Still, something was in there. I was pretty sure it stared back at me, for all that I was a curved shadow among some chimney pots. I was almost certain Skinless was below. So certain that I flicked a wave of my hand before bounding away.

The avatar was welcome to try following me over the roofs if he pleased. We were not Below this afternoon. This was *my* country now, the land of water tanks and air vents and lopsided little sheds scattered with empty bottles reeking of gin or wine.

I led a merry chase, not bothering to see if he was behind me. Likely enough both Skinless and Blackblood understood where I was headed. The twins' warehouse wasn't difficult to locate from above. I'd been in and out of there the better part of a week without taking great care to obscure my movements.

Spying within would be a greater trick, for the building lacked convenient windows. I was perfectly confident that I'd solve that problem soon enough. When I reached a rooftop across the street from my goal, I settled in behind a decorative false parapet and simply watched awhile.

Of course no one came and no one went. We'd used a side door that from this vantage I could barely glimpse in the narrow close between their warehouse and the next. A watchman's entrance, that bypassed the great loading doors fronting onto Theobalde Avenue. I studied the grimy mouth of the alley until I thought I could spot my own footprints leading in and out. A pretty muddle, mine mixed with several others. Had the Rectifier been here recently?

An hour passed quietly. No movement, no evidence of movement. That was fine. I'd expected nothing more. Then I slipped back across my chosen roof and detoured several blocks so I could approach the twins' warehouse unseen from behind.

I would have bet good money they had the doors warded, but the roof might have received lesser diligence. At a minimum, it would not be seen as such a danger. Iso and Osi had taught me something of passing by scrutiny, things I had not known for myself before. For example, a curving approach to a numinal boundary provided no angle for the magic to act against. As with any weapon, magic requires leverage. Likewise, holding power beneath your tongue or within your fists could distract a warding sigil.

It was hard to cross roofs in that fashion. I gave the process a try. One of the Eyes of the Hills fit into each hand as I stepped drunkenly along the roof of the building behind theirs. There was a gap of about eight feet. Their roof stood a few spans higher than the one I was on.

This was the first test. Could I make the jump without alerting the twins either magically or through sheer misplaced balance? I patted my abdomen, whispered, "Not yet, baby dear," took a deep breath, and sprinted into the leap.

My takeoff was perfect. I'd trained for this over the years, both with the Dancing Mistress and among the Lily Blades. My kick and follow-through, and the arc of my jump, were all as should be. My mistakes were being over half a dozen pounds heavier and off my usual center of balance.

Feet scrabbling, I struck the edge of the opposite roof shins-first. Momentum brought my torso past the edge but I muffed the fall trying to protect the baby. It was a flat roof, and so I did not immediately slide off, but two of the half-rounded tiles on the edge did. They landed in the narrow space four storeys below with a shattering crack that betrayed my presence.

Forcing myself to move against the intense pain in both shins, I rolled all the way onto the roof, tucked flat and small. All I could do for a while was breathe, deep and hard. If Iso or Osi had thought to check just then I would have been a dead woman.

I had not blown a jump like that since . . . well, ever. I'd done better in my first childhood sallies with the Dancing Mistress. Shamed, I took a few more moments to collect myself. Flecks of snow eddied across the sky, dotting me with tiny, frozen kisses as I lay curled around my regrets and tried to will my legs back into motion. The damp of my borrowed clothing threatened to turn to clinging ice.

Bless you, winter, I thought. I'd always hated the cold. My old loathing was sufficient to get me moving again.

I stumbled to my feet, slipped the Eyes of the Hills back into an inner pocket, and went in search of a skylight or a stairway down.

Eventually I was confronted with the prospect of dangling from the building's front and slipping through one of the fourth-storey windows that let into the offices within. Had there been a ledge? I tried to recall that much detail from my earlier observations. After the ugliness of my missed jump, I lacked my usual confidence in such maneuvers. The alternative was to climb back down and walk in the side door.

That appealed even less.

I waited for a lull in the traffic below—most people don't look upward as they go about their business, but it only takes one—then slipped over the cornice along the street facing.

Ledge!

This time I was very careful of my balance, and managed to slip into the second window I tried. The small office within was vacant, furnished only with scattered junk and scraps of paper. Not even the rats had found anything to do here.

Now to creep fog-soft until I could listen downstairs. My shins still ached terribly, and I worried about how well I could hold a silent position, but I was committed to my course. With overdone caution I crept along the upper hall. I was wary of canary floorboards singing out my steps. Stairs carried me down to a landing on what would have been the third floor, in the ceiling of the cavernous warehouse. I was able to cautiously observe Iso, Osi, and the Rectifier crouched around a much larger and more elaborate version of their earlier diagram.

He *was* here. Now, how to get him away. I'd figured earlier that if I found the old pardine, my chances of walking out free and intact were much better than being caught alone with Iso and Osi. The question was whether I was willing to put that theory to the test.

Or I could create a distraction and meet later, after I'd separated the Rectifier from the twins. Setting fire to the building suggested itself. But I doubted I'd fool any of those three. Likely I'd create larger problems that I might later regret.

Such forethought still felt odd to me, but I had a child to consider now.

Though I did not realize it then, finally I was coming into a measure of wisdom.

I was cold, I was tired, and my legs were killing me. The direct approach held a stronger appeal with every passing minute. Seizing the initiative, I clomped down the stairs, shouting out a greeting as I went and wishing I had something of the pardine language.

All three of them looked up, startled at my approach. At least I'd gotten into the building unnoticed. I knew the significance of me entering from *upstairs* would not be lost on either my newfound enemies or my old friend. "Rectifier," I called out. "We must be away now." I nodded to Iso and Osi. "Gentlemen. Always a delight to see you."

The twins flowed into a stance that once more suggested violence, with the muscular aura of a fighting pose. The Rectifier simply stood, shrugged, and extended his claws. I knew what that meant. With luck, the other two did not.

"Green," Iso called back to me as I reached the floor. I briefly lost sight of them through the jumbled maritime supplies, which should have scared me, but I trusted the Rectifier. I *had* to.

"Welcome," his brother said. I realized from the cast of his voice that the two of them were on the move.

"Hold," rumbled the Rectifier, but I could not tell to whom he was talking. Hopefully not me. Palming both my short knives, I vaulted up onto a stack of spars covered by cargo nets.

Osi's head bobbed about two rods to my left, beyond several hummocks of crates. I could not see Iso. The Rectifier stared at me from a position almost directly in line with the side door. His ears flicked back once, he nodded, then he ducked.

He *was* on my side, then. I'd hoped to bluff my way out of here, but it appeared we'd be playing blade tag for our exit rights this afternoon.

This I could do.

A quick, short leap to a pile of deck grates, which shifted beneath my weight. I swiftly rolled off the back down into a little grimy walkway between the grates and a row of coiled hawsers. That had made some noise, and left a spiral of dust. I kept rolling into a space between two coils and slid backwards.

Silent for a five count, I heard footsteps moving very softly. A saffron-clad leg passed so close I could have stabbed a calf. Instead I tossed a piece of nautical debris, some chunk of brass, over my shoulder so that it sailed back toward the stairs with a clatter.

The twin, whichever he was, slipped onward quickly. I wriggled out and followed him.

"Green," someone whispered, but not from behind me. I checked. I slid around the next corner to come upon either Iso or Osi craning their neck to look over into the next narrow walkway.

Flipping my remaining short knife around handle-first, I struck him hard at the base of the skull. He collapsed. The other brother shrieked nearby, then cursed in a language I did not recognize. At least I assumed it was cursing, from the tone and volume.

I had finally touched one of them after all.

The Rectifier roared, something shattered, and more cursing erupted.

I bent to cut this one's throat when I heard the pardine shout out, "Do not kill them, Green. Leave with me now."

Point against skin, I stopped. Did I trust him? These men were dangerous, hideously dangerous. But the Rectifier knew *something*, or he would not have spoken so.

I patted the fallen twin's cheek instead. My fingers trailed along his papery skin. Let him cleanse himself of my feminine depravity. Still, being a Lily Blade, I also left behind a single ruby drop beading the twin's neck as my calling card before I raced swiftly toward the door. There I followed the Rectifier out into the late afternoon's snow flurries.

With a giant like the Rectifier alongside me there was small point in skulking, so we swaggered as if we owned the streets. A night of hard freeze—the season's first, if so—seemed to be coming on. That drove most people indoors earlier than usual. Still, dozens marked our passing.

I looked over my shoulder to see if we were pursued. Nothing behind us but the pale shadows of snow swirling through city air.

"We should go Below," I told him. "It will be warmer, and we will be hidden."

"Prefer the open air," the Rectifier growled at me. "Underground is too far from the trees."

He led me instead to a tiny bar off a grimy alley near the Dockmarket. No sign here, any more than the Tavernkeep's place was marked. Inside nine tables were drawn up knee-and-elbow distance apart. The ceiling was so low the Rectifier was forced to duck his head. The walls were crowded with broken weapons, rusted blades and shattered wooden poles—the aftermath of a battlefield or a dueling ground had been scoured to fit this place out. An odd assortment of characters lurked there, including a few more nonhumans. The world was vast, I knew, but where was the land of the very tall, very narrow-bodied blue-skinned man in pangolin-hide armor? His eyes were as mournful as last year's graveflowers.

I avoided his stare, and the stares of the others, while the Rectifier wedged us into a table at the back of the room.

"No one comes here," he said against all evidence. The place smelled of sweat and ferment and the odd undercurrents of unfamiliar people. There was no fire, not in this room, just the close, stale of air being breathed by too many lungs.

"Why did you not let me kill them?" I asked, moving straight to the point.

"They were. . . ." His voice rumbled, a pardine word being swallowed. "Bound, I should say. And much older than you realize. They carry the same weight of time as gods may do. Slaying either brother by yourself would release enough power to kill you."

I knew that effect perfectly well from brute experience. Accumulated power didn't simply leach away harmlessly into the air. "Fair enough," I said, for again, I had to trust him. "But how will they be stopped?"

"Stopped from what?"

Feeling foolish, I answered, "Attacking Blackblood. I have declared myself their enemy. Surely my errand is of no account for them now." Though abandoning my wrongful attack against Blackblood would just return the twins to the hunt for Desire's daughters. Including the Lily Goddess. Which was no improvement at all. I had laid quite a trap for myself.

"Their work feeds their bond. You have put the brothers on a trail. They will hunt that trail until they make their kill. Or until they are thwarted."

"Iso and Osi are not human, are they?"

He shrugged. "Neither am I."

That was difficult to answer. Instead, I focused on the problem at hand. "I must now oppose what I have begun with the twins. Then I must find a way to turn the Selistani embassy from attacking the Lily Goddess."

"Let them all kill each other."

"No. There is a child at stake."

He favored me with a curious stare. "You would upset the fate of cities for one child?"

I felt myself grow hot. "If not for one child, then for whom? How many count? If we stop at one, we may as well never try at all."

The Rectifier raised a hand. Claws gleamed just at the tip of his blunt, furred fingers. "That is a matter for your people to decide. I merely point out how the costs hang in the balance."

He had the right of it. For the same reason I could not simply charge into the Selistani embassy with blades drawn, neither could I exact my vengeance in a swift series of back-alley killings, nor set the will of two cities against one another.

Some prices truly were too high.

And some were already paid in full.

"I can perhaps solve this problem of Iso and Osi, and also protect Blackblood from my own worst impulses." I reached within my clothes and pulled out the small velvet bag that contained the Eyes of the Hills. "I must ask you to take something from me, but only for safekeeping. You are specifically charged not to bargain the worth of this."

He took the sack. "Should I look?"

"As it pleases you. In any case, I wish you to hold them for me."

The Rectifier closed his eyes a long moment, fingers twined around their small burden. "I know what these are," he said softly. "You carry a key to a lock you do not understand."

I was startled at how precisely his words echoed my earlier thoughts. How had he known? Was I that transparent? "And you know where that lock may be found, yet I trust you to carry this key. People will try to take those from me. My position will be improved if they cannot be shaken out of me or seized while I am under restraint."

"You should not do this, Green." He slipped the bag inside his own ragged manleather vest. "But I will hold them for you, for the sake of what you did with the ox god."

A narrow-faced woman brought us two tankards unasked, interrupting our conversation. The Rectifier glared at her until she wilted from his gaze and turned to glare at me. "How much?" I asked, surrendering to the inevitable.

"Two coppers."

I fished a pair of the smallest taels from my diminishing cache of money.

"Enough," I told the woman. She drew her lips back as if to spit, then wandered away.

The smell was vile. Beer brewed from milling waste was my best guess. I did not touch it. "I bound your people's ancient power into a human god."

"Not all pardines agree with the Revanchists," the Rectifier said mildly. He took a deep draught of his tankard. "Some sacrifices are better left unredeemed."

"Here," I told him. "Have mine." With my fingertips, I shoved the questionable stuff across the little table. "Somehow I would not have expected you to see the world that way."

"Yet you trust me."

"I trust you because you fought me until the need had passed, and not a moment longer. You never lost sight of who I am."

"You have never lived wild."

I thought of my first days in Selistan, after leaving Pinarjee and Shar behind—my father in his dementia and the woman who was properly my stepmother, however I chose to think of her. I'd lived as close to wild then as ever I would. But I didn't think that was what he had in mind. "No, I have not. Not as you mean it."

Another long sip. "I am the greatest warrior of my people in this age, though we are a small echo of what once was. I understand as well as any of us what has been lost. Very few realize what was gained in return when that power was given away."

Even across the table, I fancied I could still feel the crackle of the gems. I was certain the Rectifier could do so. "I thought it was stolen from you."

"Could someone steal your spirit without your permission?" His eyes seemed to deepen as he stared at me over the rim of the tankard. "Some things can only be given away, not stolen. However that might be recalled later."

"The Factor told me that as the Duke he had fought a great war against your people."

"We are still very dangerous. Once we were far more so." He took up my tankard. "I would not see those days return. It will be the end of us if they do. In their terror, your people would hunt mine until nothing remained but pelts, bones, and travelers' tales. Even so, I will guard your treasure, not for that reason, but for your own sake."

"Thank you," I said simply. "I must go Below and seek further aid. When I want those back, I will find you."

"If you need to tell someone where the Eyes of the Hills are in order to spare your own life, that does not trouble me." He grinned, his mouth all teeth for a moment. "I could use the exercise should someone come searching for them in my hand."

I took my leave of him then with no more ceremony than a swift farewell. Outside, I knew what I must do next. Mother Iron had already handed me this answer. I found a large sewer grate with an inspection ladder and slipped Below, out of the ever heavier snow and into the dank, sheltering darkness.

Winter cold had begun infecting the uppermost tunnels. I felt as if I wandered through ice. I was tired, while my rooftop adventuring earlier in the afternoon had left me with horribly aching shins and a deep sense of lassitude.

Still, Archimandrix had offered his services to me, and therefore presumably his guild's entire strength. Mother Iron had indicated that old problems required old solutions. I was coming to appreciate how old a problem Iso and Osi truly were. Not to mention Desire . . .

I wasn't sure exactly where I was Below, but I knew the direction I needed. A swath of coldfire in my hand, I headed for the great machines. Archimandrix would be somewhere near there. That was his world. I was only a guest here, far from the lost time in which he and his sorcerer-engineers still dwelt.

Which was fine with me.

The sewage tunnel opened into a larger gallery. Here the flow had been routed through masonry guideways—low walls containing the muck, in order to keep the runoff from flooding into the old mine tunnels. I stepped away from the shallow filth I'd been splashing through and reoriented myself toward the Temple of Endurance.

I walked, noting landmarks such as a great skeleton covered in moss and mold, some eldritch creature that could have served as a mount for Skinless. My thoughts continued to range through the issues bedeviling me. I wondered what the Rectifier would have me do about Endurance, if he could. He'd certainly intervened at the death of Federo and the casting down of Choybalsan. Had the wily pardine rethought his desires? Or perhaps the realities of the situation had simply passed the old rogue by.

Power moved in circles, in circuits. Like a rooftop tank of water released, it had to go *somewhere*. Bleeding it off would be as slow and cautious a problem as draining the tank through the smallest pipe.

Endurance was a safety valve on the ambitions of the pardine Revanchists and the rogue twins alike. The ox god was a safety valve on me also, in truth. He had already served this city well.

Soon I found myself among the machines of the great gallery beneath the temple at the old minehead. They were colder now, leaching what little warmth might be in this room to leave behind only the chill. Seen glittering in my coldfire, they looked as if frost had settled upon them.

Winter. That curse of cities and people alike. A blanket of quiet, white death to put us all to sleep.

I touched one of the old machines and thought of Archimandrix. The metal was so cold my fingers threatened to stick. My warmth would pour from me, I realized, to be absorbed within those brass and copper and iron angles. Time seemed to congeal here in the chill beneath the world. The ancient men in their leather masks who'd built this thing were waiting just beyond the line of shadows for their chance at trying yet again for whatever aims had first driven them.

"What purpose?" I asked the machine. It was large and inscrutable, with bolted hatches long since corroded to a single mass. Multijointed arms folded against the higher reaches of its body, where once they might have swung free to service some distant, unknowable need.

"What purpose ever the past?" asked Archimandrix from behind me.

I swung about, startled, short knife in my right hand. "Who's with you?"

"You are," he said reasonably. "I knew you'd be back."

Again, the young man—or to be more accurate, the man with young voice—had wrapped his head in leather bandages except for the brass oculars. His robes covered the rest of him.

"I am back," I responded. "And I do need your help."

"As Mother Iron foretold." He tipped his head toward me. A nod? A bow?

"Foretold or not, the moment is here. I have caused a problem you may be able to sort out."

"Explain, please."

I got the impression he didn't very often remember to say "please."

We squatted on our heels in the cold presence of the machines while I told him about Blackblood, about Iso and Osi, about Corinthia Anastasia and the Selistani embassy, about the pardine Revanchists. I left out nothing, and did little to alleviate my own sorry role. I had gotten the entire affair wrong almost from the beginning. As a result of my own poor judgment I'd placed two deicides on a god's tail.

When I was done, Archimandrix remained quiet for a while. From the set of his head, I surmised he was squinting thoughtfully, as very smart persons will do when confronted with an idea outside their notions. Intelligence could be so limiting at times.

"You want my sorcerer-engineers to oppose these divine twins."

"I do not think them divine," I replied quietly. "Very old and very powerful, yes."

"The fall of Marya is being spoken about the city," he said. "Her loss troubles Below, and imperils women everywhere. That these ones should claim another god from Copper Downs is unacceptable."

"You will block them from Blackblood?"

"I can do better than that." Now I could hear the grin in his voice. "Much better."

"Then I leave you with this problem. I have more to do, and time is terribly precious for me right now."

Archimandrix touched my shoulder. His heavy leather glove was as cold as the machine beside us. "See to your people and the missing child. My sorcerer-engineers will see to the gods of our city."

It was all I could do in this moment. "Thank you."

I knew who my next contact would be. Blackblood needed another line of defense. Arranging chessmen on the board, Skinless was my next play.

The best way to find the avatar was to head for Blackblood's temple from Below. Unfortunately, I knew *that* path all too well. Following it reminded me overmuch of Septio, who had brought me here, and up through the labyrinth that joined Below with the sacred precincts. I passed into a familiar corridor of carved, screaming faces—homage to the pain god, or an ossuary of souls, I could not say.

As I walked, I whispered the avatar's name. "Skinless . . . Skinless . . ." In the unquiet tunnels, that sound carried to blend in with the drips, the rivulets, the groaning of the earth, the occasional distant knocking and banging. I felt as if I were calling a lost goat. "Skinless . . . Skinless . . ."

I continued to suspect that the avatar had been following me for days. Surely he would be found now, here, close to his home.

At one point I stopped and turned to look behind me. A great, gelid eye peered back from a muscled face. He was so close I could have touched him with my tongue. A shock of surprised fear coursed through my veins before quickly settling.

"I bear a message for your god," I told Skinless.

Great hands flexed, tendons sliding over fat, along muscle, as veins throbbed. I had fought this one too—was that true of all my friends?—and knew how difficult he was to even check for a brief moment. Never to be defeated, not by me.

"I have wronged Blackblood, grievously. A pair of hunters are on his trail now." Slowly, carefully, I detailed my missteps with Iso and Osi, and my fears for what they planned.

Skinless listened, nodding, with as thoughtful an expression as that great, flayed face could manage. When I had spun my entire tale, I finished by saying, "I have asked Archimandrix and his sorcerer-engineers to deal with the twins before they ever reach your temple. But the god must make ready."

Another long, slow nod. Then one great hand reached out, finger extended, to delicately brush against the not-so-gentle bulge of my belly.

"Yes, I'll be careful." I tried not to think of my missed leap to the warehouse roof this afternoon. I needed to stop acting as if I were a Blade in prime condition, and start behaving like a pregnant woman.

If only everyone else would *let* me do so.

He mimed picking me up, carrying me, as he had once done when I was wounded.

"No," I replied. "I shall make my own way. But thank you."

We parted then Below, uneasy friends, he to his god of bitter dregs, me to my plotting.

My next step would conveniently bring me to a resting place for the night. I had need to raise a great noise against the Selistani embassy but it would do me no good to run through the streets decrying a stolen child. Who would believe me? More to the point, who would care?

Children were essentially disposable, unless they happened to be heirs to a great fortune or the objects of great love. My own life was sad testament to that truth.

And in the scheme of the fate of cities, well, the Rectifier was right. The matter of one child was irrelevant. Even counterproductive. It was up to *me* to save Corinthia Anastasia. By saving her, I could make things a little safer for my own daughter-to-be. By saving her, I could do what no one had ever done for me.

Not even the Dancing Mistress or Federo had saved me. They had only used me for another purpose. No more.

The world could be repaid one shred at a time. In the meanwhile, I still needed to create some opposition.

I climbed back up to the streets and walked briskly through the falling snow to the Tavernkeep's place. My last exit there had been amid riot, so my welcome was uncertain. That was also the place where I could most easily find disaffected Selistani. *They* were the ones I could rely upon to raise that great noise and be heard. Most of Copper Downs, if they cared in the slightest, already saw the Prince of the City and his embassy as masters to the refugees. If I could mobilize these same men against that authority, I could bring wider attention on the embassy and slow their departure whenever they made ready to leave.

Anything to keep Corinthia Anastasia in the city until I could rescue her. Or force her captors to release her. Anything to shine the light of the public's dubious regard on Surali and her betrayals. Like all roaches, she prospered best hidden in the shadows.

A man watched at the mouth of the Tavernkeep's alley. I simply walked past and backhanded him without breaking stride. He stumbled away from me with a curse, so I spun to follow up with the short knife in my left hand and my right fingers clutching his throat.

"Who ordered you here?" To my surprise, I realized he was Selistani.

"N-none," he gasped.

"You just happen to be sheltering from the snow by standing in an alley mouth." I closed my fingers on his throat. Any moment now he would realize he outweighed me by at least double, and I would be forced to either kill him or take to my heels.

"Y-you are c-crazed." His voice was cracking, probably from my pressure on his Adam's apple.

"Go home," I growled. "Hide for a few days. It won't matter after that." I stomped hard on his instep to give him something to think about as he limped away. Then I left him standing there with the gift of breath still in his lungs.

I realized that while I was no longer in a red rage, my anger at the people who were bedeviling me had not diminished in the least. Still, I could be generous with the lives of others.

Inside, the Tavernkeep's place was as quiet as I'd seen it since returning from across the sea. For a moment I was taken aback, wondering if my countrymen had departed. Very few pardines were present. The endless round of gambling men was reduced to a few diehards.

The Tavernkeep, however, was at his bar.

"Greetings," I said. "If you have a cook working tonight, I would enjoy some curry."

He put down a narrow yellow bottle he'd been examining. "Welcome, Green. Do you bring chaos on your sleeve again tonight?"

That brought a smile to my face. "Not unless it already lies in wait for me here."

His lips pursed; then he turned to look back into the kitchen. Moments later he returned with a small stone bowl of the pardine bournewater. "This will serve you well."

Grateful, I took the bowl. "I am rarely certain what serves me well anymore." I sipped at the drink. It went down much as its namesake—clear and cold, tasting of rocks in the high thin air, but also of the stuff of life. "Where are the Dancing Mistress and her Revanchists?"

"They pursue an errand."

Something deliberately oblique in his tone caught at my ear. "In truth? On this night?"

"I cannot say why."

What or where, he might be able to tell me, but the pardines were not *my* errand. Not right now. "I wish them well of it."

That brought a snort of amusement. "If you do not carry chaos on your sleeve, what does bring you here this evening?"

"Looking for chaos elsewhere." I nodded over my shoulder at the room—heavy wooden pillars, beams overhead, a low fire, quiet voices scattered about. "Where is the Selistani wrecking crew which has been occupying your dining room of late? I have need of their services."

"Some are here. Some have gone off with the Dancing Mistress. Many are upstairs sleeping."

"Already?" It was barely dark outside.

"They drank away their sorrows after your last riot, I believe. There is always a price to be paid for such." He glanced back at the kitchen again. "The boy is out on an errand. Can you abide awhile for your food?"

"May I prepare it myself?" I hated the diffidence in my voice.

The Tavernkeep stared a long moment, then flicked his ears. "Of course."

Commanding a kitchen again, however briefly, was a taste of the peace I'd been longing for. One always knows where one stands with food. Ingredients, cookware, time, and skill could be combined so that the only surprises were whatever the cook planned.

Chowdry had never been trained as I, but he'd lived all his life with Selistani cuisine, and so had substituted long experience for my refined knowledge in stocking this kitchen. At least the portion of it dedicated to human cookery. I ignored the dry-cured game haunches and bins of desiccated flowers that served the needs of pardine cuisine. Instead I attended to the paneer cheeses, the strong spices, the tubs of spinach and chickpeas and beans and rice that were the building blocks of what I sought.

Curry, of course. The *sambar podi* was readily identified. I sniffed at it. The pungency was clearly from the sun-warmed south—no Stone Coast greenhouse could have grown this. I smiled, carried by the spice's scent back to better days in the Temple of the Silver Lily when I had traded recipes with the cooks and been allowed the run of the kitchen.

I found coconut-milk stock already prepared. That I set upon the iron stove to warm while I hunted vegetables and meat to furnish the curry with. Most of what I could locate was the carrots, cabbage, and suchlike of northern cooking, but there were some good, honest onions. And of course the spinach. I did not attempt the pardine larder in my pursuit of meat. I did find a slab of fish in a stone cold crock—from the texture of the flesh, a redfinned shark taken out of these northern waters.

That was sufficient.

I spent a very happy twenty minutes chopping, sautéing, and blending, with several wide-ranging trips through Chowdry's spice selection until my curry was powerful enough to blister a dead man's lips. Once the dish was simmering nicely, complete as I could make it, I cleaned the knives and boards I'd used, wiped out the pans, then served myself a generous bowl. I left the pot warming for any others who might hunger soon.

Cooking was better than prayer. Maybe even better than sex.

I tucked in, surprised to discover how hungry I was. Another thing I'd soon have to take more care for. I needed to keep myself and the baby fed without racing through the entire day on nervous energy and anger. I touched my belly again as I ate, apologizing to my daughter. She seemed to have nothing to say in return, so I left her to her peace.

When I was done, the Tavernkeep took my bowl. "More?"

The pot I'd left on the stove beckoned, but I was satisfied. "Enough for now." I looked back at the room. What I wanted could not be done in this evening's storm, and besides, getting men out into the freezing wet dark would require a greater cause than I could likely argue right then. "I would ask a favor. May I engage a room for my night's rest?"

"They are all full." A deliberately human regret tinged his voice. "I can find you a blanket if you want to sleep down here on a bench or the floor by the fire."

"That will do." I concealed my disappointment. The idea of an actual bed had been very tempting. "I plan to rouse these men early. I'd like to borrow a decent-sized pot and a metal spoon."

"Do not come up to the third floor with those," he growled.

I nodded and thanked him. In time I took my kitchenware and the proffered blanket and made myself comfortable near the heat. I was as safe here as anywhere this night. At least people watched the door in this place. Still, I slept with my short knife in my hand.

The common room was fully dark except for glowing coals when I awoke. The oil lamps within were long since wicked down. Not even their scent remained in the room's close, stale air. The Tavernkeep's place had no windows on the ground level, but I was sure dawn had not yet stolen into the skies outside.

A number of my countrymen slept on the floor—more than I'd seen last night. Either the Dancing Mistress' delegation had returned, or some of those upstairs had descended once more to the common room. I'd have woken up to any raucous party, though.

The door was barred when I checked it. *Interesting.* To the best of my knowledge, the Tavernkeep didn't really keep closing hours. At least he had not done so in the past.

I slipped the bar, cracked open the door, and peered outside. My breath steamed in the air. Several inches of snow blanketed the ground, the last of yesterday evening's tracks filled in to soft hollows. The sky above was crystal sharp, stars glinting like knife points through velvet. No one watched. The whole city might have been asleep.

Perfect. This quiet morning would find me making trouble in a very public fashion.

It did not take me long to visit the privy at the back of the tavern. Then I put some fresh coals on the quiescent fire, poked it to life, and took up my pot and my spoon. I was not much for speeches, the Lily Goddess knew, but I needed these men. And I would be shameless about their need for me, or at least for Endurance. *Mother Green, indeed.*

I began walking among the sleeping men, banging the implements together and shouting in Seliu:

"Up, up, up! You are my army for today. In the name of the ox god Endurance and all good men of Selistan, up, up up!"

I went on in that vein for several minutes, until three dozen bleary, hostile faces glared at me.

"You know who I am."

Nods and mumbled agreement.

That was inspirational. I continued, glad I'd never thought to train for a Temple Mother. They had to *speak.* "You also know the Prince of the City is here, to oppose my work and snatch me back to Kalimpura."

Those words brought a more puzzled blankness.

"They are here," I said, "to take us all home. Whatever brought you to Copper Downs will not matter to the Street Guild. This embassy is rounding up strays. I am the most famous of Kalimpura's runaways, but I am far from the only one they seek to box and take home on the hold of their ship."

Now I had their attention, along with murmured discontent and more eye rolling.

"We're going to take the fight to the popinjay and his bastards." Once more I whapped the spoon against the pot for emphasis. Grasp their attention, keep it. Like sheep after a goat, men would follow anyone with strong words and a bright sword. "*All* of us. For your sake. For mine. For the god Endurance. And for everyone who came here because they could never find their way out of one life into a better one back in Selistan." My voice dropped, I almost hissed the next words. "I know what this means to you. To all of us. And we will not be pushed."

Bleary, confused, the gathered men muttered agreement as they adjusted their clothing and scratched their nethers. I was the only woman here, but they all knew me. I was *famous* among my countrymen here in Copper Downs. Every one of this group had somehow found the gumption and resources to cross the Storm Sea. I wondered how long it would take them to open shops, or locate a trade they could work their way into, then send back for brothers, wives, children, cousins. In that moment I could see half a generation into the future. A wave of dark brown faces would be living *here* because the social powers of this place could not force the lowborn into a lifetime of hard labor for tiny reward, as did the guilds and courts back in Kalimpura.

Copper Downs relied on force of habit and the shame of class to keep people down. To someone from a caste society, that was an open door.

"*You* will not be pushed," I said, keeping my voice low. "*You* left our home for something better. Are you ready to be forced back on someone else's whim?"

"What do you want us to do?" shouted one of the men. He could just as easily have been my father's brother, from the set of his nose and eyes. A Bhopuri.

I smiled at him. "Stand before the Selistani embassy. Follow them in a group when they venture out. Do not let the Prince of the City and his lackeys pass back and forth unnoticed. *Embarrass* them." I did not want the embassy to take ship yet—they *could* not—but this group were not the ones to stop them. Slow them, yes. "If they look to be packing out to the harbor, send swift word to me. Let the Rectifier know. They cannot be allowed to leave without first being called to account."

That was as close as I dared approach the truth of what I wanted. I could scarcely raise an army here, but I could and would harass Surali and her minions.

"Remember," I added, "you will not be pushed." That was not much of a slogan, but it was what I had that morning. Mother Vajpai would have done much better. Mother Meiko would have just terrified them into submission without a word. Me, I had to argue with an eloquence borrowed from only the gods knew where.

So far as arguing went, it took me another half hour of chivvying and tea and cold rice to cozen them out the door into the snow. I finally sent my ragged band marching toward the Selistani embassy. Let Surali and the Prince of the City deal with *this*—two dozen grumpy men who would just stare morosely without raising a fist, standing with the quiet, sullen anger of the poor and disaffected, while their Velviere District neighbors watched nervously from behind lace curtains and rang for their own guards.

I wanted to betray their stealth. Therefore, their stealth I would betray.

The street in front of the mansion housing the Selistani embassy was a mass of slush. Some fairly large group had passed by here overnight. My heart caught a moment. Was I too late?

But two Street Guild men remained stationed at the gate. This morning their blades were naked. One bore a strung crossbow, which was not the best idea in the damp. They looked terribly uncomfortable in the freezing light of day. The Prince, or at least some of his household, were presumably still in residence.

"Gather in the street and watch the gate," I said. "Don't block traffic." It was winter, and miserable, but if this little picket lasted even a few days, that might be enough. I tugged at the elbow of a man who could have been my uncle. "What is your name?"

"Harun, Mother Green." He stifled a yawn.

"Keep this up three days, and I will make it worth your while." I had no idea what I meant by that, but right now my promises were worth more than my purse. "I must slow them down. And if anything unusual happens, for the love of Endurance, please let me know." As if anything were *usual* here and now.

He made his right hand into the horns of an ox. "Of course, Mother."

"What was that?" I imitated Harun's gesture.

The ox again, flashing and gone. "The sign of the god Endurance. We make it that we might know one another in the street."

I couldn't decide whether that was worrisome or inspiring. In either case, I let the business pass. "Observe as I talk to the guards. Then I'm off again. I'll check back here. If you need to, send word to me at the Temple of Endurance."

Harun looked dubiously at his huddled mass of watchers. "Three days? The city guard will run us off."

"I'll take care of the watchmen," I said. Another promise. The actual street patrols, such as they were, reported to the Interim Council. The Conciliar Guard under that snake Lampet were another matter, of course. I didn't think they'd turn out in force for something like this. As for the hired guards here in the Velviere District, they were small, independent units unlikely to pick a fight with a large group so long as my lads didn't start freelancing about the neighborhood.

If the Interim Council wanted me to solve these problems, they'd better stay out of my way. I'd pop around and talk to Nast this morning before checking again on all my various chessmen in their positions. Then I'd figure how best to winkle out Corinthia Anastasia.

Ilona's stolen child was within shouting distance of me right now. But I could not outrun that crossbow. And once I was within, behind obscuring walls, Surali and her people could do anything to me.

I needed a Blade handle, and a run.

Which led me to wonder where Mother Argai was. I should have asked the Street Guildsman I'd mugged for information about Corinthia Anastasia's location.

At an easy walk, unhurried, relaxed, telegraphing no intentions at all, I approached the gate guards.

We were all Selistani here, dark-skinned people in a pale-skinned place. Even the whitebellies. Our country was never this cold—I had not seen snow once in my four years in Kalimpura, did not even know the Seliu word for the nasty stuff.

"Long way from home," I said in their language. *Our* language.

The man with the crossbow rested the weapon in the crook of his arm and pointed it at me.

"Last fellow who did that to me met with an accident." I smiled, my most raffish, wolf-toothed grin. "Permanently." With any luck, they knew of my earlier foray. With more luck, they were smart enough not to try to kill me.

"You're not supposed to be here," said the other man. "They're out looking for you around the city."

"Shame I came around on my own then, isn't it?" I flipped my short knife in my left hand, tossing it in small loops through the air. "But you're not supposed to be here, either. Cold, don't you think?"

The crossbowman snorted. "How these ice people can be abiding their city I do not understand."

"We should all go home."

"We all will soon," said the swordsman with a glare at his friend.

"So where is Mother Argai? She stood watch the last time I was here."

"You will need to be asking Lady Surali," said the bowman, ignoring his fellow.

Interesting. And they were quite relaxed, given my previous interaction with one of their fellows. Had my chosen victim not returned? "As I am hearing the story, Surali has to have someone else hold her spoon right now. Not much with the leadership, is she?"

The crossbow steadied on me. "I shall not be pretending to take you prisoner," the bowman said. "You are too dangerous. But if you are surrendering yourself, please to do so now. Otherwise move on." He glanced over at Harun and the other Selistani protesters, huddled together. Someone had started a fire along the curb with broken-off branches. "And be taking your rabble with you."

"That *rabble* is your people, too," I reminded him. "For my own part, I am moving on. But please to be telling Mother Argai that Green was asking after her health."

"Every word," the other Street Guildsman replied cheerfully. "We're to report every word."

Every word. *Hah!* I had a few choice words for Surali, and for that matter, words for Mother Vajpai and for the Prince of the City. This did not seem to be the time to offer them.

With a nod to Harun, I turned my back to the crossbow and walked away. My shoulders itched, expecting a bolt. Not out of the question, depending on how angry Surali was, but those two had spoken to me easily enough. They were not sufficiently nervous for men with orders to kill on sight.

Opportunism came easily, though. Especially to an ambitious Street Guildsman.

Once around the corner, I indulged in a little opportunism of my own. I knew that at a minimum I should be speaking to the Interim Council, checking on Archimandrix, spying on Iso and Osi, and sorting out what the Rectifier had gotten up to since I left him, but I *had* to try to find Corinthia Anastasia. Despite my misgivings. And I was curious whether Mother Argai was being held against her will.

The idea of having my own Blade handle, here in Copper Downs with me, seemed a convenient way to solve so many problems.

Back to the walls for me. I boosted myself up again, as I had before, but this time my uncertain balance defeated me. My vault took me to the top of the wall and right over the other side into the Selistani embassy grounds. My right ankle trailed and caught, banging my too-sore shin against the icy stonework and twisting at the joint. I tumbled with a sharp, whispered curse before smashing to the ground.

A mere seven-foot drop, I thought. Flat on my back, without touching down properly. Only luck that I hadn't hit my belly, and the baby. My shin was on fire. My ankle was complaining as well. At least I was wearing the right boots.

There was nothing for it but to keep moving. If I sat and waited for someone to investigate the noise, surely I'd be found. If no one came, sitting and waiting would be pointless anyway.

I hoisted myself up and trotted along the base of the wall. Small purpose in running the top of the wall. Too icy up there, and I didn't trust myself to stay on my feet now in difficult balance.

Hoping that I hadn't misinterpreted Mother Argai's relative friendliness, or Mother Vajpai's reluctance to take me on in a straight fight, I approached the back of the house. The plantings around the base of the walls were hummocked with snow, the stretches beneath the trees powdered thinner. I could do nothing about my tracks here—no one had ever taught me how to remain stealthy in this stuff—so I left off dodging and walked purposefully toward the arbors bordering a terrace at the back of the house. Skulking was so much more obvious. So long as no one looked too carefully, I might make it.

I paused again at the side of the terrace.

Now that I was out of line of sight of the windows, and could safely sneak along again, I felt much better. Listening for a count of thirty, I detected no sound of alarm. In fact, I detected no sound at all.

Was the house empty? That would explain both the churned snow and the upbeat guards. Perhaps Surali had put one over on me after all. That thought rekindled my anger.

The terrace was actually a built-up structure, I realized, topping a hollow space beneath with small windows peeking from behind the arbors. I eased up to a window and looked inside. Dark, so dark I could barely make anything out, but it appeared to be a tool room. Perhaps the space down there was for the gardeners? Or storage?

I'd take that.

Some work with my short knife and my arm strength forced the little window to pry open. It was hinged to swing up, a popular choice here in Copper Downs. I sniffed at the stale air within. Rust, a little bit of oil, soil, clay.

Definitely a garden shed. A very elaborate one, but a garden shed.

I wriggled through the window and dropped down into the darkness beyond. Carefully I pulled the glass shut behind me. Then I stalked with slow deliberation across the room to the door leading inward.

Locked, of course. From the outside. But the hinges were on my side.

That took more work, and the borrowing of a few tools along with a liberal dousing of oil, but I got myself out the door into a narrow, stone-floored hall. The lock was just a latch, so I undid it, stepped back in, and re-hung the door.

No point in making Surali's life easier later.

From there I followed the hallway into the depths of the basement.

The first person I saw was a pale-skinned scullion humming as she dragged a basket of linens to some basement laundry. Stone Coast servants, then. That probably pleased Surali to no end. It was possible that she would not be able to tell me from the other Selistani here, but I had already wasted too much time wandering to try the subtle approach.

Instead I raced up to the servant and cracked her against the wall. She started to squeal, until I stuffed my short knife butt into her mouth—no chance she'd bite my hand that way.

"Silence," I said in my most flawless Petraean, straight from the Pomegranate Court.

The scullion's eyes rolled. Pale green, like Federo's. This wasn't a woman. I had captured a girl my own age or younger. The hot smell of piss cut the air between us.

Captured and scared to death. Sometimes I could hate myself.

"I won't hurt you." I kept my voice low, hoping I hadn't already damaged her teeth. Whom to ask for first? "But I am very short on time and even shorter on patience. Where are the Mothers?"

She squeaked, her eyes rolling. I pulled the knife hilt out. A few chips of tooth came with it. Oh, well.

"That h-hurts," the girl sniffled.

"A lot of things hurt," I said roughly. "But not you, if you talk."

"What m-mothers?"

"Southern women, dressed in dark leather."

"Oh." Her eyes glanced upward. "The priestesses. Jayce s-said there'd been a fight."

Who the hells is Jayce? Squeezing her arm hard, I whispered urgently, "Where?"

"S-second floor. South w-wing. In the Azure Room." She closed her eyes. "Kill me fast. I don't want to hurt m-more."

Oddly brave, this one. "I'm not going to kill you," I told her. "Just hide for an hour. Then quit this household. It will not stand much longer in any event." I put my knife away and fished out one of my last silver taels. "That's a week's wages at least. Walk out of here."

She closed her hand over the coin and gave me a strange look.

"I'm a terrible villain. I don't do evil very well." I shoved her away and trotted up the hallway from where she'd come. There'd be stairs, maybe a lift, some way for the servants to move the laundry about without bothering the lords of the house. Finding Mother Vajpai, if she wanted to leave, would make freeing Corinthia Anastasia much easier. The Blades could help me fight my way to the girl much more readily than Corinthia Anastasia could help me fight my way to the Blades.

With a bit more scouting I located a laundry chute. No screaming echoed from behind me, so the girl had taken at least some of my advice. I didn't mind killing men under arms, or sometimes even men in general, but my heart just wasn't in murdering girls younger than me merely for the sake of silence.

The chute was inside a little closet with several large baskets piled to one side. The only stairs I'd seen so far were fairly wide, with kitchen noises echoing from their head. That did not strike me as my best option.

Instead I stuck my head into the chute and peered up. Miracle of miracles, it was angled. And small without being impossible. Whoever had built this had assumed that drapes or carpets might be sent down it someday. I touched the insides with my hand. Wood, lacquered with age and regular use. The panel joints were tacked over with slim laths.

That was enough for me. I'd easily make the second storey this way, and stay clear of both servants and masters. If the scullion kept her mouth shut another twenty minutes, I could find my fellow Blades without an alarm being raised, and possibly even Corinthia Anastasia.

Unfortunately, I still didn't see breaking the child out. Not by myself. Certainly if I could persuade Mother Argai, and even better, Mother Vajpai, to my cause, Samma would follow them. The four of us would be only a half-handle of Blades, but I'd wager that nothing in Copper Downs short of a pardine Hunt could stand against us.

I braced and climbed, keeping my boot toes wedged against the laths as I went. A slip would not kill me, but I'd make a racket, and lose my progress. Belatedly it occurred to me that such a fall would be terrible for the baby as well. I could not touch my abdomen, but I whispered an apology. This wasn't *balancing*, which pregnancy had begun to steal from me. This was *strength*, which I still had. I not yet gained sufficient weight to lose my ability to pull myself up.

I climbed past the first-floor trapdoor into the chute. The room beyond smelled of oils and soaps. I heard two more girls chattering about some boy as they worked. *Do* not *open the laundry chute*, I thought. I didn't want to threaten more children. Thankfully, they were at some other task. I reached the second floor undiscovered. The chute went another flight above me to where I thought Corinthia Anastasia was being held, but I stopped at this trapdoor and listened.

Silence beyond.

Carefully freeing one hand, I checked both my short knives and my long knife. What was I doing burning away my morning skulking about inside the walls here? The city was stirring toward more fighting, if everything I'd schemed for came true. I didn't need to be creeping like a mouse.

Except for Corinthia Anastasia. The Blades were my path toward her. She was my true goal. I was the only one who would make her rescue a priority.

Resolve steeled and weapons checked, I pushed open the trapdoor and slid into the second-floor maid's closet.

No shrieking girls greeted me there. The room was small, painted stark white gone a bit grubby with age. Except for the laundry chute and the door into the hallway beyond—I assumed it led to a hallway—everything was shelving and equipment. A person couldn't even sit in here to ease her aching feet. I looked around at the stacked linens, the mops, the buckets, and briefly considered grabbing an armload for disguise. But in a house with pale-skinned servants and Selistani masters, I would fool no one. Likely I'd slow myself down in the bargain.

Now was the time to stand straight and walk knife in hand into the throat of whatever awaited me. Still, I wondered where everyone *was*. The place was strangely quiet. The presence of servants about their business made me less fearful that Surali had stolen a march on me and simply decamped overnight. I worried nonetheless.

Worrying, I darted into the hall.

Thick carpets, probably from Selistan, I noted with some irony. The walls paneled with insets in a blond tropical hardwood. Honeytree, from the look of it. Smagadine art sat on small plinths every six feet or so—broken heads and hands, fragments of larger statuary. Someone had been making a political point when they'd decorated this hallway. At least two centuries past, I estimated, based on the details in the woodwork and the framing of the scattered paintings depicting traders and markets. The oils were all mediocre imitations of the style of Fechin during his Commensalist period. The ceiling was relieved in a line of low vaults, with a kerosene lamp flickering within each vault. Otherwise there'd be no light at all. This was an interior hall, connecting sitting rooms or suites.

South was to my right. Long knife bare in hand, my remaining short knife loose in its wrist scabbard, I walked that way, counting doors so as not to lose my place. Of course the owners of this house had not been so kind as to *label* the rooms. I could not readily tell which was the Azure Room. Double doors at the end of the hall would open into a larger space, perhaps a ballroom. I put my ear to them and listened.

More voices. Several men. Street Guild guards? Was the Azure Room behind this door? Or more likely their bivouac?

I thought a moment about the typical architecture of the great houses of Copper Downs. That could not be a conservatory—we were not on the uppermost floor—but it would be a ballroom or a gallery. Surali couldn't keep prisoners in such a place. Too much space. She'd confine them instead. *That* was much more her style.

Stepping back, I tried the first door on my right. It opened to a dusty sitting room, drapes closed over the windows along the far wall. Furniture bulked awkwardly under white sheets. Even the paintings were covered over.

Not here. Unless they'd been stored as corpses. With that thought, I glanced at the floor. No sign of anyone being dragged through the dust, or walking in here.

Across the hall, I tried the other door. A bedroom that had been in recent use. The bed was stripped—I knew where these linens had gone—and the fireplace smoked slightly. The occupant had forgotten to open the damper.

"Idiot," I whispered.

Back out in the hall, I was reaching for the next doorway when someone opened it from the other side. A Selistani clerk stepped out, clad in a well-tailored green silk kurta of a very traditional cut. He looked up at me in surprise as I thumped him hard in the side of the head with the butt of my long knife.

A man in the room behind him called out. I jumped over the body and charged, blade already swinging forward, only to meet another clerk.

This one yelped and tried to dance away.

I caught him a long, shallow slash to the arm that sent blood spilling widely. He drew a breath to shout, so I slapped him hard across the face. "If you want to live, *be quiet*," I barked.

My words had been in Petraean, I realized, as he screamed, "Help, housebreaker," in Seliu.

My next blow took him on the neck, right across his vocal cords. The clerk collapsed in choking surprise. I swept a dish of water—for soaking nibs and brushes—off the desk and dumped it on the one I'd laid out. "Help your friend breathe," I barked into his unfocused face as his eyes flicked open.

Out in the hall I threw open the next door. Surprise was lost. My time advantage would be gone in seconds. Corinthia Anastasia was already beyond my reach. I'd need to find my Blade sisters quickly, or the entire run would be a total loss. The latest door yielded two men already moving to investigate. One clutched a fireplace poker, the other had his hands spread wide.

Not Street Guild then.

"Stay back," I shouted. "Invaders, you won't be safe." I slammed their door and spun around.

The door across the hall opened. This time it *was* Street Guild, two of them with swords out. I hoped like the hells that my sister Blades were somewhere behind them, because I was about to be outnumbered.

Yelling wordlessly, and spun a kick that took the lead man in the side of the knee. I'd used a similar move on Mother Vajpai once, the first time I'd ever counted a touch on her—and the last, for quite a while after that memorable day. He collapsed with a howl. His fellow came right over him, leading with the point.

Long knife at the ready, I stepped back and right into the poker swung by the idiot from the other room. He connected hard enough across my shoulder that something cracked audibly. I felt the pain like a stabbing.

So much for the healing that Desire had bestowed upon me.

Spinning half to my left, I backswung my short knife into the fireplace enthusiast's side. I caught him just below the entangling ribs. As expected, he had no parry, and fell away sobbing.

I completed my spin in time to sidestep a sweep of the long knife from the more capable fighter. "I'm one of you," I shouted in Seliu, in hopes of confusing him.

He was not fooled.

Another of his brethren came out the same door. If that wasn't the Azure Room, I was deep in the cesspit. I gave back two more steps and palmed my long knife to grab and hurl a nearby marble head at the swordsman. He dodged that as it cracked into the wall, but my short knife came right after and caught him in the cheek.

The man howled, then swallowed the point of my long knife. He vomited blood around my blade before collapsing with a puzzled expression on his face.

The next one was more wary, which was fine with me. Unfortunately the door at the end of the hall flew open as half a dozen more Street Guild raced pell-mell toward us.

I knew my exit when I saw it. Cursing, with no more knowledge of Corinthia Anastasia or my Lily Blade sisters than I'd had before, I snatched up my weapons and shoved through the door to my right before the mob could reach me.

This was another bedroom, double length for a suite. Four tall windows overlooked the patio and back lawn. Slamming the door behind me, I sprinted through the shadows for the glass. I intended to dive and roll, taking the fall into the arbors with whatever momentum I had and to the Smagadine hells with the splinters.

"Green!" snapped a voice in Seliu. The familiar tone caught at me. I swerved, bounced off the wall, and turned around with both blades bristling. Already they were arguing in the corridor about who would follow me through first.

Mother Vajpai sat up on the bed. Mother Argai was springing from the chair beyond her, on the other side of the bed from which I'd passed. Samma was not in sight.

I could have blessed a thousand goddesses in that moment. "I came for you."

"Fool," Mother Vajpai replied. Mother Argai just shook her head sadly.

"They'll be on me in seconds. If you want to be shut of Surali, come with me now." My sense of my own failure about Corinthia Anastasia gnawed at me, but I had no time to dwell on it.

The Blade Mothers exchanged a fast look in a familiar, unspoken negotiation. I turned my back on them and kicked open the window.

I was above the terrace. No pursuit was yet visible outside. Looking over my shoulder, I asked, "Are they more afraid of me or of you?"

"It does not matter," Mother Vajpai replied. I realized she was still in the bed.

"I am coming," added Mother Argai. They glared at one another—more silent argument—then Mother Argai dove out the window, tucking to land running eighteen feet below.

"Samma?" I asked.

Mother Vajpai shook her head.

The door burst open.

I flipped over the smashed windowsill backwards, knowing I had enough fall length to right myself. On the way down I remembered what pregnancy had done to my balance.

Thank the Lily Goddess Mother Argai spotted my landing, taking much of my weight and keeping me from pancaking into the tiles of the terrace.

"That way." I pointed toward the back wall.

Stealth abandoned, we raced through the snow-choked garden, trying to outdistance the crossbow quarrels I was certain would be fired at any moment.

Twenty minutes later I stopped to breathe. Mother Argai and I had taken to the rooftops as soon as we cleared the Velviere District. Even that had been a project. Two women in dark, bloodied clothing were conspicuous, so we'd been compelled to stick to walls and alleys until I'd stolen a tarp off a wagon. After that we'd just appeared to be derelicts, homeless and wageless. Now we crouched in the lee of a water tank. The tiles sloped gently away from us, treacherous in the slick drip of the morning snowmelt. I watched smoke rise somewhere over near Lyme Street.

"What was that all about?" I finally asked Mother Argai.

She answered my question with a question. "How many did you kill?"

"One for certain, another if he is unlucky. I tried not to." And three of my own left behind. Failure by any measure.

"Hmm."

It wasn't clear to me what that grunt meant, whether she signified approval or disapproval. Mother Argai had run with me, trained with me, bedded with me. Though I'd learned much from her, she'd never been one of my training Mothers. I'd not learned to read her so well as some of the others.

All I could do was ask. "Tell me, what was that all about? Why were you staying in a room unguarded? Why did Mother Vajpai not rise from that bed?"

"Don't you mean to ask where Samma is?" Mother Argai's voice was soft.

Embarrassed at being caught out, I mumbled weakly, "That would have been my next question."

"No, Green, it was not. We all are knowing how you are." Mother Argai appeared sad. "But this is being your city, not ours. Mother Vajpai and I both realize how little of it we know. Not just a matter of buildings and streets. A matter of people and their discontents."

"Copper Downs is not kind to strangers," I agreed, "but neither is it so overwhelming and dangerous as Kalimpura. You do not know your way."

"No. And you do. So to you we will heed, even against our judgment."

"Then heed my questions. What took place back there?"

She glanced away a moment, embarrassed. "Samma is hostage. Mother Vajpai is wounded."

"Wounded how?"

Mother Argai's voice was flat with pain and anger. "Surali has cut off her toes. Mother Vajpai cannot yet walk."

I was shocked out of my impending funk over losing the girl again. "Who could cut off her toes? Who could hold her down?"

"You do not know the powers at stake in this, Green."

"No, I don't. Not from Kalimpura." I leaned close, growling. "But I know the powers at stake here in Copper Downs. Some of them have arms long enough to reach across the sea."

"Surali did this to Mother Vajpai to punish us for your conduct. Samma is now held against the good behavior of the rest of us."

Fighting down an urge to be sick, I glanced around our rooftop. "Which you have broken beyond question."

"Mother Vajpai will say you forced me from the room. Samma's life may be forfeit in any case, but I doubt quite yet."

I made a leap of logic. "She is with Corinthia Anastasia."

"The northern girl who is also hostage, yes."

With those words, Mother Argai lapsed into her usual silence. I stared across the city awhile, trying to parse what this all meant, where my deeds and intentions would come into play. How much I might have betrayed those who loved me through unwise action.

None of what she had just told me changed my plan of action. At most, Mother Argai had deepened my sorrows. Those I had plenty of already.

I bent to clean my weapons. "I regret that man's life," I told her.

"Never regret a death that keeps you alive."

"Perhaps." I restored my weapons to their proper places. Long knife on the thigh for the running and the fighting. Short knife on the right wrist for close work, short knife on the left wrist for stealth. That was drilled into Lily Blades from the earliest years of their candidacy.

I looked again at the pall of smoke from the general area of Lyme Street. This was not yet the time for regrets, not with so much to be done. "Where are the rest of the embassy? I saw half a dozen guards and two clerks."

"Most of them marched out under Surali's orders to deliver a demand to your Interim Council."

"It's not *my* Interim Council," I said reflexively. "Did Surali march with them?"

"She seems to be having some difficulty with her hands."

I glanced over at Mother Argai, suspecting her of humor. Her expression was bland. "Well, there is at least one glimmer of hope here."

"Her troubles have not improved her disposition."

"I should think not." I looked back out over the city. "We need to move on. I want to find out what is happening on Lyme Street, and I have business with the Interim Council in any case. Are you prepared to go Below and work our way through that particular maze?"

"You always did have a fondness for tunnels."

That was all the answer I was likely to receive. I took that for a yes, and led her back down to the street. We dodged through the alleys until we found a hatch that would carry us both into the stygian depths of this city's permanent, stone-walled night.

Mother Argai had never been a tunnel runner back in Kalimpura, and certainly not here in Copper Downs. I was not even sure she'd been off the grounds of the embassy's rented mansion since first arriving. Nonetheless, she climbed down a beslimed wooden ladder without hesitation or question. This entrance was over a running sewer line, but as I'd hoped, the rungs led to a board that stretched across the tunnel.

"Mind your feet," I whispered up to her. "Dead dark, you're landing on an uncertain plank. Step toward my voice when you reach it. I am standing upon a narrow ledge. Sewage flows beneath everything just here."

"Many thanks," she muttered.

I scooped the small trace of available coldfire off the wall as Mother Argai landed on the board. It creaked under her weight—perhaps forty pounds more than my own, allowing for her squat, muscular build. Her hand reached out in the shadows as she took a step toward me, when the board gave way. She dropped another four feet into the stinking stream.

Leaning down, I held my glowing hand over Mother Argai to check that her face was above water. Well, above liquid.

"Cold," she gasped.

"Snowmelt," I said. "Makes even shit frigid. *Don't* grab the glowing hand." The slime would keep her from getting a decent grip, and she'd wipe it off in the process. We'd lose our light. "I'm reaching down with my off hand."

"Understood." She caught my grip.

"Side walls will be slimed but rough underneath," I warned. "Are you ready?"

"Yes."

Trying to keep as much of my weight as possible back on the ledge, I grasped her wrist as she grasped mine. She kicked while I pulled, and scrambled up the edge of the channel. I felt myself leaning into her. To counter that I flattened back as best I could. "Have care," I hissed, then pulled her up with me.

Mother Argai wound up lying on her side, stretched away from me along the ledge.

"It's dangerous down here," I said.

Given only the dimmest light of the coldfire, I could still read her reaction to that comment.

I got her up and moving as soon as possible. Below was not so cold as above, even in winter's harshest grip, but it was still far too chilly and damp for anyone to lie about quietly in stinking, wet leathers. "Fifteen minutes to where we're heading, and I can probably find us a warm spot to clean up in." I was thinking of the bakery-kitchen behind my little teahouse.

Mother Argai followed me along the ledge until we came to a side tunnel that branched away in the general direction of Lyme Street. I knew this one. It was part of a series of cutoffs laid into Below by some builders with a fondness for arched brick vaulting. Also, and more to the point, the water flow in these tunnels was largely incidental.

Getting her away from the wet, chilly tunnel was sensible.

"I reek," Mother Argai said quietly. Not quite complaining—Blades did not complain—but definitely unhappy.

"It's a good masking odor," I offered. "And besides, that was at least half snow." Maybe. "You didn't fall into the slaughterhouse runoff, for example."

"One is always grateful for small blessings."

That brought a backward glance from me. This time I *definitely* suspected

Mother Argai of humor. Once again, nothing in her voice or in the ghostly-lit hint of her face cracked the least bit of a smile.

"Really, we should have run Below more in Kalimpura," I told her.

"Our tunnels are not so extensive."

"Even so, you learn much down here." I held up a hand; we were coming to a larger junction that the Dancing Mistress used to call the Station. "Quiet," I hissed.

We stopped so I could listen. No one was moving or breathing audibly up ahead, but some of the most frightening people and things down here didn't make noise.

She needed to be warm, but I had to understand what I'd seen back at the Selistani embassy. I'd been mulling all that over as I walked. Such knowledge might be critical to our own next moves. We were as safe as we might be Below, right here. And Mother Argai seemed to be in a talking mood. Turning back to her, I asked, "What was Surali thinking, to hurt Mother Vajpai so?"

"I do not know," Mother Argai said, her voice very serious. "I cannot imagine what she believes will happen back in Kalimpura over this. But Mother Vajpai forbade me to interfere."

What would happen back in Kalimpura was clear enough to me. If the Bittern Court planned to bring down the Temple of the Silver Lily and slay the Lily Goddess in the process, then there would be no consequence to injuring Mother Vajpai here and now. The point would be moot. "I don't understand why Surali didn't just kill her. Mother Vajpai wounded and angry is far more dangerous than Mother Vajpai dead."

"She would have been forced to kill all three of us," said Mother Argai flatly. "Even Samma."

"A foolish girl," I grumbled.

Something in the tone of her next words warned me. "Samma may be a foolish girl to your eye, and even to mine, but she is still a Lily Blade. As such, she is deadly in her own right to the rest of the world."

I picked at the problem, still disbelieving. "And you stood by while she, what . . . ? Snipped off Mother Vajpai's toes with a hedge clipper?"

"As Mother Vajpai ordered." Mother Argai's tone was wooden now.

"Why?"

The words poured from her in a rush: "Because we have to live to return home and carry word of all this. If none of us Blades return, the tale will entirely be Surali's in the telling. We who serve the Lily Goddess will be painted traitors and apostates and worse by the time that woman is done with us."

I could have shaken Mother Argai silly for her political obtuseness. "*What* makes you think you will live to see home? Surali has already waged war upon the temple with her suborning of Mother Vajpai into the embassy. She has enough Street Guild thugs with her to slit your throat a dozen times over before breakfast. There is no Death Right here. You would die unavenged."

"We were waiting for *you*, Green. That's why Mother Vajpai permitted me to leave with you."

Her words made me want to scream. I caught my breath, almost shuddering. "You're Lily *Blades*. You don't need *me*. You could have walked away at any time and taken ship home on your own. I did it as a girl of eleven."

"I know more now than I would have had we fled a week ago." Mother Argai's voice was a growl. "That was part of what Mother Vajpai made as an excuse; that we learn what we could of Surali's plots, and her affairs here. For my own part, I agree with you." She spat into the darkness. "We have given up too much to gain too little. Including, likely, the lives of Mother Vajpai and Samma. Thanks to your raid just now."

The words *But I saved you, at least* died on my lips. I could imagine the political pressures back in Kalimpura that had driven Mother Vajpai to join this expedition. And I could just as easily imagine the woman's political thinking that forced her to stay in the face of her own further torture and probable death. All for the sake of what she saw as the best chance to transmit the information about Surali's true intentions back to Kalimpura.

"You are all fools." I was caught up in the harsh judgment of youth. "This could have been handled better." Later in life, I would have been more kindly, and more wise, about such a thing. At the time, I should simply have been grateful for Mother Argai's regard.

"Samma was supposed to . . ." Mother Argai's voice trailed off.

Supposed to what? Does it matter? "Never mind." Trying to keep from snapping, I continued, "What if we find Surali here at Lyme Street? I presume we are both likely to be snatched or murdered."

"After what you and your pet savage did to her hands, I would recommend avoiding Surali." Again, that not-quite flicker of humor.

"I'll do that and more if I catch her again," I promised. "For now, we keep moving."

With a wave of my fingers, I summoned her onward. I wasn't sure what I expected we might find up there—Skinless, the Factor's ghost, Mother Iron. There were more possibilities than I wanted to consider. Mother Argai had just given me several additional scenarios, some nightmarish.

My life would be so much simpler if my enemies would just wait their turns.

In the event, we encountered nothing. Soon enough I brought her up in an alley near Lyme Street, not far from my teahouse.

Despite the sleet that was falling, the air was thick with smoke. Sparks popped nearby like small explosions, and I heard voices shouting. The odor tugged at my gut in a most unpleasing way. "No more rooftops," I whispered to the baby. "But I have to do this thing."

My gut flopped, but settled again. I took a long look at Mother Argai in the dim overcast of the day. She'd been telling a terrible tale down in the dark. Her eyes seemed haunted.

"Were you and Samma lovers of late?" My voice was soft, easy as the hissing of snow on quiet cobbles.

She looked away, which was all the answer I needed.

"Listen," I said. "As I told you, there is no Death Right in this city. You cannot buy a murder openly. But there is not so much law in this city, either. They have no Courts as we do in Kalimpura, only judges with little power. The guilds here are merely trading houses that train up boys. If we can punish Surali, or strike her down, there will be little consequence to fear. Just foreigners killing foreigners, in the local mind. No one will call for vengeance or justice."

"I follow you," said Mother Argai, her voice wooden.

"One more thing. I must rescue that northern girl from Surali. We will take Samma and Mother Vajpai when we leave the house next time." I had no idea how I meant to keep that promise, but I could not leave it unsaid.

We loped around the corner to see that the fire was not down at the Textile Bourse as I might have thought, but closer to hand. With a gasp, I realized that my teahouse had burned. It was still smoldering in the snowfall. A small crowd milled and gawped out front.

My blood ran cold. I pushed through the gathered people and looked. The cinnamon-skinned woman was laid out on the pavers, one of her brothers with her. Their faces were already crusted with icy drops, as if bejeweled for some exotic feast. I saw blood, not just burns. The other brother sat weeping beside them with his hands around his knees. A dirty rag bound his head, soaked almost purple with more blood.

I bent close and touched his shoulder. "Who did this?" I asked in Petraean.

He looked up at me, eyes unfocused, then at Mother Argai. A trembling hand rose to point at the two of us, then sweep down the street toward the Textile Bourse, where another crowd was gathered.

I ignored a flare of rage. First Corinthia Anastasia, now this. The reason was not so hard to guess, given the nature of my enemies. "Not us, but people who resembled us?"

A nod, then he went back to staring at the pavement.

Mother Argai touched my shoulder. We stood and looked toward the Textile Bourse. I had wanted to speak to the Interim Council, but apparently Surali wanted them even more. What I had taken for another group of onlookers was in fact an organized group of Kalimpuri Street Guild. The two huge Conciliar Guards normally at the door were nowhere to be seen. The interior would be defended only by clerks.

Not after today.

"Can the two of us drive off a dozen of our countrymen?" I asked Mother Argai in Seliu.

"These people have no guards of their own?" She sounded incredulous.

"Not as such. There is a Conciliar Guard, but I would not look to it for any service or protection. Politics are involved. The Interim Council also commands the city guard. They are just old men without a captain or a barracks, who roust street drunks. We stand together far better than they."

"Who keeps the streets safe?"

I shrugged. "No one, really. Not since the collapse of the old Ducal Guard. There is less fighting here than you might think."

She drew a long knife that was in truth more of a short sword. The little crowd that had been watching us with interest, as the latest entrants into the day's violent street theater, suddenly found business elsewhere. "Let us change that. We cannot defeat a dozen men, but we may well drive them off."

I pulled out my long knife and palmed one of my short knives. Blades of the Lily might mean nothing in Copper Downs, but seeing Mother Argai in her leathers, these Kalimpuri Street Guildsmen would know perfectly well who she was. Thugs they were, and mortal enemies of the Blades besides. But we controlled the Death Right at home, not they. So the Street Guild feared us for both our training and our relationship with the law. Whatever their purposes here, they were habitually reluctant to fight Lily Blades to the death.

We would use that reluctance to our advantage. With one long, shared glance at Mother Argai, I began to run.

Surali's men had found a timber baulk somewhere, which they were using to bash at the entrance to the Textile Bourse. Surali herself stood in the freezing rain flanked by two large Street Guildsmen. Her hands were bandaged. I didn't see any of the Prince of the City's popinjays here, but that didn't mean they hadn't simply switched clothing to turn out as ordinary thugs.

I wanted very badly to run down Surali. That was likely the most strategic thing for us to do, but stopping the rammers was more important in the moment. Pointing with my short knife, I indicated our targets.

Mother Argai nodded. She had a wild look in her eye. Ahead, we had been noticed. The battering ram faltered. Surali began to shriek orders.

"Clear now, or suffer the consequences," bellowed Mother Argai in Seliu.

Two of the Street Guild thugs dropped their grips on the ram immediately. The other six looked around in confusion, then did the same. Their baulk clattered down the chipped, stained marble steps.

Again I was putting my life at swordspoint for those fools on the Interim Council.

Then we slammed into our enemies, everyone's feet slipping on the icy steps.

Mother Argai bowled right into the two of Surali's men closest to the bottom of the steps. One caught her sword in the upper thigh, the other took her shoulder in his gut. His parry nearly blocked her, but snagged only leather before he tumbled into the much-abused rosebushes beyond.

As the first pair fell, I leapt up two steps higher. I cleared that even with the heaviness of the baby in my belly. Three blades were rising to meet me. Those I could handle. I danced close inside one's guard, using his arm and shoulder as a temporary shield, and boxed his ear hard with my short knife, reversed. The long knife I slid along his side, just above the crest of bone at the front of the hip.

He shrieked at the pain.

I used my momentum to turn my captive so his back was to his fellows. They obligingly stabbed the unfortunate in the shoulder and neck. My long knife snaked out to jab one shin—these fighters were not armored, as few Selistani ever were. That one yelled and jumped back to leave the other's flank open for Mother Argai to swarm past my shield.

She stabbed him straight up beneath the chin with a shorter blade, slamming his head back in a spray of blood. The weapon stuck there. Mother Argai released the man to tumble into the bushes as well, taking her knife with him.

Four left, but our momentum was spent and they had the advantage of height. I dodged a downswing to hiss *Street!* to Mother Argai.

She grunted, and we both jumped backwards.

That's a difficult move at the best. Much harder on icy, blood-slicked steps, and damned near impossible with a baby in your belly. Mother Argai landed on her feet, spun to check the position of Surali's guards, then finished her spin facing our remaining opponents. I bounced on my heels and went over hard to crack my head solidly on the cobbled pavers of Lyme Street.

For a long, slow moment, I saw only glowing red spots. Someone shouted. A foot caught me in the side. Reflexively my left hand went up, short knife clutched tight. I realized Mother Argai had jumped over me. She nearly stumbled in doing so. Another foot presented itself—not hers—so I focused my attention sufficiently to slash the muscles and tendons at the back of the calf.

The man came down weapon-first. I rolled away, but nothing quite worked. My chest and midsection were pinned beneath an angry attacker who pulled himself up for a clean stroke. He was crushing my baby. My left hand was free to stab him again in the right side, which distracted his focus sufficiently for me to push him off. I rose drunkenly to my feet and put a boot into his groin as hard as I could.

That would keep him down.

Mother Argai was at swordspoint with two others. The fourth man was on the ground, scrambling uselessly to find the rest of his fingers. Swaying, I stepped close behind her opponents and tried to stab. I succeeded only in falling over.

Something clanged loudly near me as I got back to my hands and knees. A large brass vessel rolled away. A wet grunt told me that someone connected with a weapon just then, but I still couldn't quite focus. Another clang sent one of the Street Guildsmen collapsing. He'd been hit in the head by a blue ceramic flowerpot.

The last one broke and ran. I rolled to my side and watched him follow the other two down Lyme Street, Surali racing before all three of them.

"Green." Mother Argai squatted beside me, touching my head.

"Hello," I said. My voice sounded dreamy, even to myself. I was very cold.

"Can you stand?"

She did *not* sound dreamy. "Oh, certainly." I struggled to my feet, and nearly tumbled again except for Mother Argai's vise grip on my arm.

"I suppose I should thank you," said a familiar voice in Petraean. I looked up to see Mr. Nast at the top steps.

"Hello, sir." I waved a bloody knife at him.

"We must go, *now*," Mother Argai whispered urgently in Seliu.

"I expect there will be more of Councilor Lampet's Conciliar Guard here shortly." Nast looked down his nose at Mother Argai, then turned his attention back to me. "You might prefer their attentions at a later time."

"Thank you, Mr. Nast." I waved again, then turned to Mother Argai. "We must go now," I announced to her, proudly.

"Where?"

"Inside!" In that addled moment, the Textile Bourse seemed safe to me. Tugging her behind me, I mounted the steps.

Nast appeared startled, the most emotion I'd ever seen from him, but he did not flinch. "Where are you heading?"

"Council chambers," I told him, then realized I'd spoken in Seliu. I tried again in Petraean. My head was clearing fast, but not fast enough. "Council chambers. I'll speak to Jeschonek there."

The head clerk looked as if he had some comment in mind, then shook his head and stepped back. "Inside, then, before they start counting bodies." As I passed him, he asked quietly, "Should the fallen live to be questioned?"

Is he intending to slit their throats? That thought cleared my mind somewhat further. Shaking off some of the melting slush that still clung to me, I asked, "How much trouble do you wish for?"

Nast nodded. "Upstairs, then."

Inside, the clerks and their assistants cleared out of our path like rabbits before a wolf. Wolves, in truth. Mother Argai, still clutching my arm, swore and put away her sword. As we wove among the desks and stacked files, she pried my weapons out of my unsteady hand.

By the time we mounted the steps, I was coming further back to myself, and wondering what the hells I had just done.

"Why didn't we depart?" I growled in Seliu, sheathing the knives as she returned them to me.

"I was hoping you could tell me that," replied Mother Argai.

Someone at the top of the stairs whispered, "Thank you," before darting out of our way. Behind us, shouting arose.

"Down the hall, now," said another young clerk. We were hustled into the Interim Council's meeting room. I flopped into Jeschonek's seat and found myself bleeding on his leather. Mother Argai sat in Lampet's chair.

"What now?" she asked in Seliu.

"We find out what that was all about," I said heavily. "Because I cannot imagine what Surali intended with such an attack. That was not enough men to overturn the Interim Council, but it was too many for a social call."

"Social call with battering ram."

We fell silent for a few moments, resting our shaking muscles. The surging tension of a fight takes time to wear off. After a little while I rose to my feet and saw to Mother Argai's hurts. She had taken two stab wounds in her thigh, which I bound by slicing up a priceless Hanchu brocaded silk runner from the sideboard where the Interim Council kept their wine and a bowl of withered pears. The rest of the silk I portioned out for us to clean our weapons with. Otherwise she had the usual assortment of bruises, cuts, scrapes, and aching joints.

When she looked me over in turn, even a light touch to the back of my head made me sickeningly dizzy. Mother Argai swore softly and explored the spot until I made her leave off.

"You need to be abed, or at least be looked to," she told me.

My head was down between my knees, my breathing deep and ragged. "Just check the rest of me."

It seemed I still possessed my usual inventory of fingers, toes, ears, nostrils, and so forth. I'd done more damage to myself the night I'd mutilated my beauty in the Pomegranate Court than Surali's team of eight Street Guild thugs had managed today. Somehow I'd escaped even any significant stab wounds.

"Two against eight," I gasped. "And no stitches after." Especially since we lacked needle and thread for those wounds of Mother Argai's.

"They were fools," she muttered. "And frightened of us."

We sat a little while and ate the withered pears. They were honey to my fighting-honed appetite. Even the baby seemed to appreciate the fruit. After that, we polished our blades, removing blood and muck and looking for nicks from weapons, belt buckles, or stone. When a ruckus arose in the hall outside the glass-paneled door, Mother Argai and I both slipped to our feet and stood against each side of the entrance with bared blades.

Jeschonek burst in, slamming the door behind him. He tilted his head back to avoid having his lower jaw sliced open by the points of our weapons pressing up into his neck.

"Green," he gasped.

"None other," I said. "You were expecting someone else? I believe I left a calling card in the street."

"Oh, yes." Jeschonek rocked back on his heels, trying to pull his neck away from the blades. "Could you put down the cutlery?"

I ignored him. "What happened out there?"

"Betrayal." His face flushed ruddy dark.

"What, *against* you for a change? I know how this Interim Council behaves."

Jeschonek grimaced. "I survived Federo's rule."

"A lot of other people didn't," I snarled.

Mother Argai spoke up, in Seliu, for of course she had no Petraean. "Tell him to be answering your questions or I am making certain he never answers any more."

"You understand Petraean?" I asked her.

"No. But I understand what it is being to stall a question."

"Huh." I switched back to Petraean. "Mother Argai here says to pick up the pace. She grows impatient."

"Take those knives out of my face," he snarled.

The man deserved credit for his sheer nerve, if nothing else. I pulled my short knife away, but kept it in hand. Mother Argai did the same after a nod from me. "Who betrayed whom?" I asked.

He gasped, rubbed his neck and glared at our still naked weapons. Then, with a sigh, he said, "Lampet. And Johns."

"They betrayed the Interim Council? Isn't that rebelling against yourself?"

"Don't be naive, Green. They've declared a Reformed Council. Lampet swore out a writ before an arbitrator over on Letterblack Street requiring the city seal and the treasury's records be turned over, then sent that Selistani woman of yours to serve the writ."

"She's not *my* woman," I grumbled. "I recall warning you about her. You told me she was my problem."

Clearly Surali had expected the writ to suffice, as it would have in Kalimpura. Nast had done the right thing in staving her off. For all the old clerk's fanatic attention to the details of law and process I could not imagine him being impressed with such paperwork from a rebel authority. Even if he had served both the old Duke and the new Interim Council.

"You were right." Jeschonek eased himself into his chair, then noticed the blood smearing the leather. With a moue of distaste, he wiped his fingers against the arm. "Worse, Lampet controls the Conciliar Guard. The city guard, such as it is, seems to have followed him as well. I tried raising the harbor patrol. The Harbormaster is claiming this is no affair of his."

I could hardly blame Jessup for not taking sides. Which had been his strategy since the fall of the Duke in any case. Still, somebody could certainly show *some* spine around here. "Two women ran off eight men attacking your offices. Surely your own could do better?"

He sighed. "I should have hoped. No matter now. Ostrakan and the bankers are sitting this out, protecting their money and waiting to see who they'll bow to on the morrow. I don't know where Kohlmann is. The Reformed Council is carrying the day by sheer default."

Leaning close, I spoke through clenched teeth. "I don't give a pickled fig for your councils, Jeschonek. Surali attacked me, tried to kidnap and tried to kill me. She has injured and murdered my friends, snatched a child I'm sworn to protect, brought my baby nearly to harm, and threatens my patron goddess. She even burned down my favorite bakery, and slew the baker. I *will* take care of her. And I *will* take care of the city in the process. But what happens to *you* . . ."

I let my voice trail off. He could take that as a threat or not. Mother Argai tugged at my elbow. I realized I'd placed the point of my short knife into Jeschonek's chest once again. *Where is my long knife, anyway? In someone's ribs?* Then I realized by the weight on my thigh that I still had the weapon. Mother Argai had just resheathed it for me. *Focus.* I needed badly to focus. I pulled the short knife away from the councilor and wiped the bead of blood off the tip, using the folds of his robe to clean it.

"I can't—" he began, but I interrupted. "We're not working for you anymore. I will address these problems. But the bill is coming to you. If I burn down any more buildings, if any weregeld is claimed, I will send the complainants to Mr. Nast for compensation. And when I'm done, *we* are done. If you are very lucky, I'll have rescued you in the process."

"Yes," Jeschonek said.

I hadn't actually asked him a question.

"Are we finished?" Mother Argai, in Seliu.

"I think so. I believe I've made my point."

She spat at Jeschonek's feet. "Fool," she said in reasonable Petraean, to everyone's surprise.

We walked out of the Interim Council's meeting room.

I expected further trouble in the street. For one, Surali had more men in the city. The embassy grounds had been nearly empty when I'd been there in the morning, and she'd had less than a dozen swords with her here at the Textile Bourse.

The sleet had let off, brightening the day, but the street was a mess of blood and ice and water. No thugs, though. Even the severed bits and corpses were gone. Wherever they happened to be at the moment, the Street Guild muscle were not showing themselves on Lyme Street.

I glanced toward the ruined teahouse. People still milled about. I could do nothing for that poor little family except seek some justice. I could do nothing for Corinthia Anastasia until I'd cut Surali further down to size. Preferably bite-sized chunks. I could try a raid to grab the child when they moved her out of the embassy compound, if I found no greater success before then.

Mother Argai and I scuttled away to locate a quiet rooftop where we could talk. It wasn't snowing today, at least, but the slushy, cold night had left its spoor on the buildings of Copper Downs. Misery fit my mood. We crouched among the copper domes and long clerestories of the Musicians' Hall. The wind plucked at us both, which made me realize that we would need very different attire for winter running. If there ever were a resident Blade handle in Copper Downs, the women would need seasonal wool linings to their working clothes, at the least.

Surali burned bright in my hatred, but she was not my sole focus. Spider at the center of the web, surely, but the web stretched far and wide. Of the problems left to me to solve, Iso and Osi were the more difficult. Even Archimandrix and whatever strange mechanical magics he brought forth were likely to be insufficient to them. I'd warned the god Blackblood as well. But I needed another approach.

Samma might be a more tractable trouble. I owed her goodwill, for what I'd done to her over the matter of the Eyes of the Hills. Turning that thought over, I said, "We know where Mother Vajpai is."

"Was," Mother Argai corrected me.

"Was," I admitted grudgingly. "Where is Samma, though?"

"Now you want to return for her?" Something hard and shrewd burned in her eyes.

"I would have gone for her before," I said, exasperated. "We were pressed for time."

"You will hardly get in there again."

"I promise you they have sewers." Though in truth I still thought that a most unlikely avenue.

That gave her a moment's pause. Then: "Your eagerness to roll in shit is commendable. You might have the beginnings of a plan. But I doubt even your ability to make this happen."

"Where is she?" I kept my voice mild. There was no threat I could bring against Mother Argai, nor cajoling.

"Locked in an attic of the house, I believe." Another long stare. "Not convenient to the sewers," she added helpfully.

If they'd put Samma in the basement, we would have a chance. Fighting up three floors against an enemy already disturbed was another question entirely. And there was no way over the roofs into the Velviere District, as I knew far too well.

"Fine," I said angrily. "It does not matter where she is. We'll get her out when we rescue Mother Vajpai."

"You are the leader." Mother Argai's tone was simple, final.

And she had the right of it. Under Blade discipline, on a run specifically, the leader was the sole authority. Every handle belonged to one woman and one woman only. If this wasn't a Blade run—albeit overextended, badly understrength, beleaguered and troubled—then I didn't know what was.

The discipline applied to me as well. I was responsible. Solve what could be solved, run from what could not be fought, and always clean up the mess afterward.

Besides, most things *could* be fought.

"We need to find you a robe or some such," I said as I reached a decision. "I want you to join the men I have outside the gates of the embassy. They're not likely to be reliable, especially if Surali goes on a rampage. But even the weather will be driving them away before long."

Mother Argai snorted with amusement. "You are setting a rabble on her and the Prince of the City?"

"I had nothing else to put there. My stones on this board are poor."

"You play Prince-and-Assassin without either your warriors or your walls."

It was my turn to laugh. That game relied on two basic strategies—fast-moving attacks, or stolid defense. The handicap she described would be like baking without an oven or a pan. "Indeed. I am asking you to be a wall for me. There are other worries, other tasks, but you do not have enough Petraean to perform them. And I don't want to be having you drag some stranded sailor around for a translator."

"I will do as you have bade me." She rose from her crouch.

Touching her arm, I stopped Mother Argai for a moment. "You are needed. Badly. This is where I need you, until I find you again. You know the Tavernkeep's place?"

"I have heard of it."

"If you must leave the area of the embassy, meet me at the tavern. We will find our way from there as required. Otherwise I will return to you."

"And Samma." There was that grim set in her eyes.

"And Samma. And Mother Vajpai." My feet ached in sympathetic pain at the mere mention of her name. "And Corinthia Anastasia." *Most of all.*

Mother Argai grabbed my wrist with her hand, then leaned low for a kiss. It was long and slow, with probing tongues, as we had done when we had been lovers back in the Temple of the Silver Lily. After that she was up and gone without asking further directions.

She'd come here from the embassy. She'd find her way back. Still, I wondered a moment how she'd fare among the streets of Copper Downs. I wondered a moment more how the streets would fare with her loose upon them.

I was no longer the single most dangerous human in this city. Not with both Mother Argai and Mother Vajpai around.

Even considering all that troubled me, the thought made me smile.

Climbing down, I went to make some purchases. I found my funds once more depleted except for a pair of corroded copper taels. That would not do. It was a serious problem, in fact.

Walking slowly, I considered my options. This was the last of the money I'd been given by Mr. Nast and his clerks. A private subscription, so to speak. In the past here in Copper Downs, what little I had needed had flowed from the Dancing Mistress, and thus ultimately from Federo when his writ had still run in the city. Jeschonek was unlikely to help me further at this point. That meant additional funds from the Interim Council were out of the question.

Chowdry might give me money, if I asked, but already he was chronically short of resources with his construction project and the general busyness of running a temple. And besides, I would be forced to listen to a long lecture about this thing or that if I approached him so.

I didn't feel up to a simple mugging. It wasn't my style. Besides, too much could go wrong. Housebreaking was more in it for me if I needed money in a hurry. With that thought in mind, I stole a robe from the rack just inside a tavern entrance and made off before anyone realized what I'd done. My borrowed clothing cloaked, and my body rather more comfortably warmed, I turned my feet toward the Velviere District. I didn't want to visit the Selistani embassy, or even approach too near it, but if I was to steal outright from someone, I'd much rather it be someone who could afford the loss.

I toyed with being ashamed of my decision. My life was too busy for such emotions just then. Someday soon I'd concern myself with turning an honest tael, but this didn't seem to be the time to begin.

Ghosting through the Velviere District, I soon realized how many optimists believed themselves protected by an eight-foot wall. Mindful of my earlier experiences breaking into the Selistani embassy, once I'd selected a likely residence I was very careful going over the top of my target.

Within, it was the work of twenty minutes to slip into the house, find the bedrooms, and liberate a modest amount of jewelry. On further deliberation, I took some silk smallclothes from the rooms of the lady of the house, and also a cut rose from a crystal vase on her dressing stand. That would save me the trouble of shopping for what I planned next.

On the way out I was forced to kick a butler, hard. I leaned over and whispered that the household should apply to Councilman Jeschonek for reparations. After that I strode through the garden and passed over the wall once more.

The hit had almost been easy. The effort and thrill put a bounce into my step. My spoils safely tucked away, I patted the baby bulging ever more and hummed a happy tune until I'd reached the Temple Quarter.

Sometimes, it was good just to be at work.

Marya's ruined temple was even more forlorn under the night's slush and ice. Older snow had lingered here as well, now glazed in glittering, frigid armor. Ragged offerings of food and children's clothing had been scattered by weather, dogs, and scavengers. The place had already taken on the air of a midden.

I climbed over the masonry chunk that had hosted me before and leaned against it. From one of my robe's inner pockets I removed some of the jewels, along with the flower and the silken smallclothes, and laid them out before me. Desire was a woman's goddess. Her greatest power lay within Her name. I had before me the conventional trappings of desire—wealth, beauty, sex.

To that, I added three drops of blood squeezed from a tiny cut in the ball of my right thumb. The goddess Desire had sought my service, had looked to elevate me through a private theophany. I was *Her* object of desire.

"You are everywhere women can be found," I said to the empty air. "You have been drawn to me as a bee is drawn to a new blossom." At my feet, the blood stained the dirty snow a strange crimson-black. "You asked something of me, and I refused. Now I would ask something of You, for You to refuse or not as it pleases You."

My only answer was the wind, which blew heavy and damp. A cat trotted across a nearby roof. It spared me a single, incurious glance. Even the birds had given up on the day, hiding wherever it was they went when the weather grew too raw to contemplate.

I stared at my offerings. A few green shoots poked frosty-tipped through the snow. Had they been present moments ago when I'd arrived at this place?

That made no sense.

Then I noticed the metal tang of the snow in my mouth. No, not the snow. The divine.

I looked up to see a woman looking back at me. Soulful eyes, hair that had been flowing until someone had hacked at it. With a start, I recognized her. The wounded priestess I'd rescued from this temple on its destruction.

What was her name . . . ? Laria? Raisa?

Laris.

"You are not the goddess," I said, more sharply than I'd intended.

"Do not be so certain." The voice was human this time, without that world-spanning scale of the divine I'd previously heard in Desire's words. But her eyes were doors into other years, longer than any human life could encompass.

"Welcome." I made my tone as simple as possible. "I am shamed that I did not know You."

"You did not know my vessel," Desire said. "Though you should have."

"Yes." I could give no more answer than that.

"You were told I would not make my offer again."

My head tilted back. I could not swallow down all of my pride. "I do not return to petition for Your offer."

Amusement, now, and a hint of the horizon-wide divine even in this woman's voice. "You would bargain with me? You truly are one of my daughters."

"A great-granddaughter, at the most," I replied. "But I come to tell You something, and ask You a thing in return for that gift of knowledge. I know who slew Marya. They aim to destroy more gods and goddesses. Blackblood here in Copper Downs. Then Your daughter the Lily Goddess in Kalimpura, to my certain understanding. They will shake the foundations of the world to serve their petty interests." *And their petty god,* I thought, *whoever he might be,* but I was not prepared to say that aloud.

She regarded me for a long, slow moment. Even in those human eyes, Her regard was a smoldering light that should have burned my skin from my flesh and my flesh from my bones. Then: "What of it?"

This was my moment, my time to reach for the entire prize. "If I tell You all, will You lend Your titanic might to stand against the agents of destruction here, before they can move on?"

The priestess reached a hand for me. In that instant, I saw not a woman's palm but something huge, the size of countries, with a map of all our lives graven upon it. I quailed to be struck down then and there with no more purpose to my life than what I'd brought to this meeting with the goddess.

But Her fingers rested on my arm. A deep spark passed through me, finding its way to the earth at my feet. Everything was warm, then hot, then screaming pain, then normal once more.

If you were truly one of My daughters, Desire said, with more of that soul-crushing sadness I'd heard before, **you would tell Me this thing and hold no hostages at all in the bargaining.**

Now Her voice had taken on that bone-wrenching solidity. Somewhere I found the strength to stand before this goddess. "I am a woman. But I am not Yours. Otherwise I would have taken Your offer. This is why I present a bargain between us rather than an offering."

Another of those long, slow goddess-smiles. **You misunderstand so much.**

"I misunderstand everything far too often." My baby moved within my belly, until I rested my hands there and calmed her. Something caught at my eye. I glanced away from the goddess Desire for a moment to see one of the twins' chalk marks high on a ruined wall, glowing with a faint spark.

With a dizzying suddenness, the true plot that was afoot became clear to me.

"You," I whispered in a slowly dawning horror. My gut threatened to spew. "They are hunting You." Surali might be playing a game of cities, but the twins were playing a much deeper game of time. And the fall of a titanic now, *this* titanic, would betray women across the plate of the world.

Now you begin to see it.

Someone nearby shouted. The voice caught at me. What would happen next? "I have been the bait in a trap for You," I told the goddess, almost driven to my knees by my sense of loathing for myself, for the enormity in play. "I have led them to You."

Green, the goddess replied gently. **I have been pursued across all the time of this world. They slay My daughters for the same reason one might kill the priests of a god: to weaken Me. Always I raise more daughters, but always they take from Me.**

Another shout. Was that a chase, coming closer? "I am ashamed of my bargain now," I blurted. "Watch for the twins, Iso and Osi. They may be with the Rectifier. But remove Yourself."

I cannot. The woman whose body the goddess had inhabited sagged so suddenly that I was forced to leap to catch her before she collapsed upon the ground. Once more merely human, she tried to stand. I could feel the weakness in her, as if all her power had fled with her patroness.

"We must move on swiftly," I whispered, my lips so close to her ear I might have kissed her.

The woman looked at me, her eyes soft and brown, pain lines etched upon her freckled face. "Leave," she said in a quiet voice.

"Not without you." Having rescued Laris once, I could not abandon her this time. Though she was most of a foot taller than me, I swung her arm across my shoulder and walked her away like a Blade aspirant being taken drunkenly to a corner sleeping mat.

Whatever the noise behind us, it did not catch up before we found a new alley in which to hide.

I sat her down on a bale of rotten straw that had been discarded behind some temple stable. The stuff stank, and was sticky with brownish rot, but it was relatively warm, sheltered under the eaves. The furred, thick scent of horses filled the air around us. Their nearby whickering served as counterpoint to our conversation.

"I know who you are," I said, bending low. "Laris. Priestess of Marya."

She nodded, eyes bright with tears. Or possibly fear.

How it must break a priest's heart when their god dies. Worse than the agony of a lover perishing of the crab disease, or even a child being taken by the flux. "I am sorry," I whispered. "Do you know what just happened?"

"She rode me." Laris' chin dropped, as if she were falling asleep just then and there.

"Desire, not Marya."

"Desire?" Laris sounded drunk, almost.

"Where *were* you?"

"In the lazaret on Bustle Street."

I'd heard of that place. Girls went there sometimes to lose babies, either before or after they were born. "A place where women can doctor women."

A faint smile ghosted across Laris' face. "Men will kill us all."

Perhaps they already have. I pushed the thought away. "Do you know what Desire spoke to me of?"

"Wh-when She rode me, I became light." Laris shivered and pulled herself back deeper into the fouled straw. "I-I'm cold. Can you take me home?"

"No," I said softly. My fingertips brushed her face, and I felt an upwelling of sympathy and pity for this broken woman. "But I can take you back to Bustle Street."

"They tried before, you know," Laris said as I hoisted her to her feet. I considered hiring a horse, but the remainder of my haul from the theft earlier this day wasn't in coin. Not yet. And I didn't feel like trying to bargain a jeweled brooch for brief use of a mount worth a fraction of its value.

"I'm sure they did." I *had* to return her to where she needed to be. Time was slipping away. At least it was not snowing now.

"Last time we stopped them." She took a deep, shuddering gasp, then clung on to me. "My sister and me, we stopped them."

"Stopped who?" I looked out of the alley mouth along the Street of Horizons. Where was Skinless when I needed him, anyway? The Temple of the Frog God rose to my right, faced with slick green tiles and vaguely disturbing sculptures along the roofline. To my left was the Sailor's House, a generic sanctuary dedicated to a dozen gods and goddesses of the sea—from the Hanchu ports, the Smagadine cities, Selistan, and farther beyond the endless horizons of the world's oceans.

The street had traffic, but nowhere near a crowd. I eyed a dung cart that presented some possibilities. A swift getaway didn't seem likely considering the two shaggy mules dispirited between its poles.

Off we went. Laris had found her feet, and stumbled along beside me. She the drunk, I the friend carrying her home to sleep off her misfortune. It was a simple enough guise, all too ordinary for the city. "The Saffron Tower," Laris breathed in my ear, returning my earlier semblance of affection.

And by the Wheel, my sweetpocket stirred at the warmth of her. *What a terribly foolish moment to be thinking of the solace of skin.* "Tell me about them," I said, to keep her talking. I knew a little—the Saffron Tower was both a place and a monastic order headquartered in that place. It was located somewhere along the channel connecting the Storm Sea to the Sunward Sea, well east of the Stone Coast. Religious contemplatives on some rocky headland, looking for their gods in the toss of waves and the glare of distant sunsets.

Or pilgrims, I realized, *searching the world for the pattern of the fall of the titanics.*

"Monks," she slurred. "In yellow robes. Except the last ones weren't monks, they were servants."

"Servants sent to kill a god." My mouth was running ahead of my thoughts.

"A Selistani red man and a sprite woman." She giggled. "He was . . . something to behold. Something more to fuck. A sturdy giant."

Selistani? Red man? Mythical beings of the Fire Lakes well south and west of Kalimpura. "What did you do with them? Where did they go next?"

"My sister and I took them carnally as a rite of the goddess." Her voice caught. "I believe they departed south across the Storm Sea after."

To Selistan. Had the plot been moving before this most recent surge of events? I tried to keep the desperation out of my voice. "How long ago?"

"Years . . ." Her voice slurred. "Years, and tears ago. Not long after the Duke fell."

I felt a brief surge of despair. Once again, the whole business seemed to trace back to me.

She stumbled again, and began muttering. I all but carried her through the slush and cold water of the streets. Together we wended toward Bustle Street and the lazaret there. My thoughts dwelled on old men in saffron brocade, whose wiles were generations beyond my own. How much like a god would a man become if he'd lived hundreds of years in health and sound mind? How different were these twins from the Duke?

Magic, divinity, the life of people and cities. It all played together. And I knew what to do about powerful immortals.

Of all people, *I* knew. Some lessons truly did last a lifetime.

A pale, heavy woman with a face scarred by pox and old violence peered at me through a narrow gap in the lazaret's front door. The place had obviously been built for a counting house or something of the sort, and was still fortified as it had been during its heyday. "What is she doing out there?" the doorkeeper asked with a gasp of recognition.

"The goddess brought her to the temple. Laris was not fit to return on her own."

"Come in, come in . . ." The door creaked open and I stepped into the shadows to face a pair of crossbows.

Crossbows?

I almost dropped Laris to reach for my blades when I realized the weapons were mounted on swivels, but untended.

"From earlier days," the heavy woman said. "Though they've been fired a time or two since. Not many here with the strength to string or cock them."

The winding gears were locked back with pawls, but those weapons should have been manageable even for a fairly small person, assuming the cranks were the right size. Probably no one in this women's house understood that. "You find yourselves under siege often?"

"Sometimes." A slow sigh escaped her. "A man has every right to his wife," she added cryptically.

I wasn't sure what to say to that, but something in her tone stirred my unease about stolen children. "Please," I said. "Take Laris and care for her. Again."

The woman reached for the priestess in my arms. "You're a killer, aren't you?" She grunted as I shifted Laris' weight over.

"Is that so clear to you?"

"Yes," she said, over the unconscious priestess' shoulder. "Return if you need shelter. We'll see to you, or give you a safe enough bed. Can't hurt to have a woman like you around."

If there were a Lily Blade handle to be raised in this city, I now knew of a candidate Blade house. "I will remember you," I said truthfully. "And I may have a few women to send here." Mother Vajpai. Samma. Corinthia Anastasia. I made a mental note to inform Mother Argai of this place, its location, and her likely welcome. "Some of those I send may not speak Petraean. They would be dark like me, and have my same manners."

"Marya help them if so," she said. "Go, go, woman. And be welcome on your return."

I slipped back out into the street and puzzled on what I'd just learned.

Wrapped in my stolen robe, I was not so conspicuous as I might otherwise have been. My feet were tired, and I would swear my ankles were swelling inside my boots. In fact, my whole body was exhausted in a way I didn't re-call it ever being before.

Pregnancy.

I had never asked for a child. I had also never considered seeking out some place such as the lazaret to rid myself of the baby. She was mine.

Mine. Not Blackblood's, nor the Lily Goddess'.

Mine.

Thinking about Desire, I could not say if She'd heeded my warning. I'd certainly failed to enlist Her. Most probably, I'd endangered Her anew. Iso and Osi were distracted from Desire for the moment by my co-opting them in an attempt to control Blackblood, but I could hardly hope they'd take him down.

The audacity of the larger plot was almost overwhelming. Plot-within-a-plot. Or more accurately, a plot-outside-a-plot. Much as in the twins' view of the divine, layers played into layers in this matter.

At the core, Surali was making a play for me to satisfy her personal ven-geance, and possibly the Bittern Court's, for the way I'd handled the killing of Michael Curry. They'd not won the Eyes of the Hills as they'd hoped. Even so, the gems had been secured with the key I'd thrown into the harbor back in Kalimpura. I pitied whoever had been forced to dive to recover it.

Wrapped around that was a larger effort to overthrow the Lily Goddess and shift the balance of power in Kalimpura toward the Bittern Court and their allies. Specifically including the Street Guild and its longstanding rivalry with the Lily Blades. That effort seemed to encompass an attempt to assassinate the Lily Goddess. Which would, among other things, well and truly put paid to whatever place of safety the women of Kalimpura could hope to find. Let alone those from the rest of Selistan with the courage to come seeking aid.

Laid around all *that* was a larger effort to stalk the daughters of Desire. The Saffron Tower sought to overthrow what it saw as the error made at the beginning of time when Father Sunbones had allowed his daughter Desire to exercise Her free reign in the garden. At least, that was the man's tale. As I'd first read it in *Goddes &e Theyre Desyres,* the story had concluded with a warning to women and their goddesses.

Passing another layer, wrapped around *that* was the effort to stalk Desire Herself. The titanics were long gone from the affairs of the world, or so we who lived in these lesser days were taught. But the old, old anger of men and their gods at the rebellion of women was very real.

Stop Desire from continuing to raise daughter-goddesses at need, and you would stop the thread of subtle power that united and protected women wherever on the plate of the earth the writ of the old titanics ran.

And to do all this, Surali and the Saffron Tower would casually overthrow both the political and divine order of Copper Downs. The sheer effrontery of this offended me. The intersection of a hunt as old as time and a political conspiracy of this generation of power in Kalimpura was deeply unfortunate. My presence at the heart was even more unfortunate.

Or had the Lily Goddess intended this all along? Had Her mother-goddess, Desire, intended this? Was I only and ever a weapon forged, honed and drawn for this moment?

Such thoughts brought me past the verge of illness. I stumbled in the snow, placing my hand on a wall as I toppled past the verge and spewed my guts. Not so much there, in truth—the pears from before, and whatever orts I'd snatched at the beginning of the day.

I was no one's tool. I'd fought and killed to escape being used. The idea that my entire life was of someone's making, even beyond the slavery of the Factor's house, was enough to set my heart racing and my imagination spinning until my head felt fit to burst.

With a chilled hand, I wiped the vile, stinging tang from my lips and moved on. While I'd been thinking, my footsteps had carried me back toward the Temple of Endurance. Why did I need Chowdry now?

But I didn't need Chowdry. I needed the god.

Despite my gloating earlier about slaying the Duke, there was no fire I could raise against Iso and Osi. Not at their age and power. Even the Rectifier might be crushed beneath the weight of their wills. Archimandrix would only be a distraction. At most, I'd warned Desire, though it was inconceivable the goddess had not already known. She was a titanic. She could surely see their every step.

Why She didn't just act against them directly was beyond me. All magic had rules—sorcerous or divine. I didn't suppose it was mysterious for a goddess, even a titanic, to be bound by those rules.

But Endurance . . . Endurance was not sprung from Desire, nor any titanic. My ox god had not even arisen from the human impulse to religion. I'd instantiated him with the stolen power of ancient pardine Hunts, their braided soulpaths filtered through four centuries of the Duke's iron grasp on the numinal affairs of this city.

Whatever magics and weapons Iso and Osi deployed would be less effective against my Endurance. I hoped.

I swept through the open gates of the temple to ask my father's ox to protect me one last time. And through me, so many others.

The afternoon brought a stinging trace of frozen rain by way of reminding me that winter was here. As if I could have forgotten. Also, more of that raw wind. Chowdry's acolytes had abandoned their construction project under threat from the weather. I heard singing somewhere inside the tent encampment, but I ignored the music. Instead I stepped up to the door of the wooden temple and passed within.

The bead curtain parted at my touch. The ox statue sat where I'd last seen him placed, amid his incense burners and guttering tapers. My belled silk still lay between his forelegs, an offering of my entire life, in a way. Which I supposed was a strange echo of the truth. The hangings on the wall had changed—more added and the rest rearranged. The air smelled of incense and oranges and the slightly rotten odor of rain-soaked wood.

I stood quietly before the ox, so close I could touch his muzzle. The impression of a stable was still overwhelming. And still more than a little amusing. Endurance in life had been a creature of the sun, the water, rice paddies and ditches and the stubbled margins of our little walkway back toward the road to town. Pinarjee, my father, could no more have built an enclosed stable like this than Endurance would have sheltered in it.

Yet I was coming to a renewed appreciation of the relationship of gods to place. Desire had shown me that, as had Iso and Osi in a different fashion. No one in Copper Downs would understand a god who stood in a rice paddy. But a stable was a meaningful symbol to anyone who lived in this land of cold winters and long spring rains.

Carefully I reached out and brushed my fingers across the ox's nose. I almost expected it to be warm and damp, as in life, but that was just an illusion of the moment. Prayers were tied to the horns as I'd seen them before. I hooked a few off, curious what I'd see. It didn't feel like snooping—in one strange sense, I was an avatar of the god Endurance. Or perhaps the god was an avatar of mine.

I laid that uneasy thought aside for consideration at some future date. It didn't need to trouble me now. Instead I read the prayers I'd taken.

I want for Nitsa to rest easy

That one stirred my heart, for Nitsa had died in my place. I gave the ox a long, thoughtful stare.

I am sorey for what I did to the Merchants' dautter

Please give me a better chance

Green needs peace, her world is too driven

The last one stirred me all over again. I found myself both angry and sad at the same time. I crumpled the prayers, each on a little slip of foil-backed paper, and bent to feed them to a fat, slow beeswax candle burning with the faint scent of oranges almost beneath Endurance's chin. One by one the prayers flared with blue flame. They curled to ashes as they reached toward the ceiling.

When I was done, I rocked back on my heels. Much as when I was a child.

"Do you suppose the god is hearing them better that way?"

Chowdry's voice, speaking Seliu. I heard the clack of the bead curtain immediately thereafter. I considered palming my knife, then realized that if Chowdry wished me ill, he wouldn't inform me of that by stabbing me in his own sanctuary.

"In truth, I am not so sure the god hears prayers at all," I answered as he came to squat next to me. "Intentions perhaps. Actions certainly. But what are prayers except packaged hopes? And what god will deliver hope when we are here to care for ourselves?"

"Endurance is not hearing the words," Chowdry said quietly. "But Endurance does hear prayers, I can tell you."

I favored the priest-pirate with a sidelong glance. "He was my god even before he was yours."

"It was you who placed me before the god. I will never be forgetting this."

"Do you pray in Seliu?" I asked him.

"Sometimes," he admitted. "But even the Selistani acolytes are wanting to worship and pray in Petraean. In half a generation, Endurance will not be a Bhopuri god at all. Just a Stone Coast god with a few odd words in the mouths of his temple priests."

I looked back at those blank marble eyes. "I should hope that Endurance would ever be too humble to fall prey to hubris." That was perhaps the point of seating the god in an ox in the first place.

"What are you wanting here, Green?"

I let that question wash over me, wondering the best way to answer.

He mistook my silence and continued: "You are not coming about to debate theology, or develop ritual. You are not being a builder to raise the temple. And for all your dancing with those terrible women back home, I am sure you were never being so much of one for the gods."

"I want to stop some plots, and set others in motion." Vague but truthful. "I have met another god—a goddess, actually—who I would never have thought to see even if I'd spent all the years of my life within a temple. Now I have returned to this god. To *my* god."

"He is not being your god." Chowdry leaned forward and tapped some ash off the end of an incense stick. "He is belonging to all of us, and to this city. You do not see the roots, but they are there already. Settling deep into stone so that he will never be removed except by great force."

"I know about roots, Chowdry." My right fingers trailed on his left arm a moment. "Endurance's roots and my own are in a sun-drenched rice paddy back in Bhopura. Selistan's sun is our sun. Yours as well. And now I will call upon the god for the sake of my memory and his. If he ignores me, well, I can hardly be worse off than I am now. If he heeds my call, then I will have once more raised a great ally."

"You cannot be summoning gods as if they were clowns for a children's party."

"No. But I can speak to Endurance as if I were still standing between his legs over a dozen summers past."

I stood and laid my hand flat on the ox's nose. Closing my eyes, I thought of my grandmother's funeral—that first memory of my life, before the days began to know their number. The bells of her silk sang the last song of her life. Endurance had plodded along, me held beside the ox in my mother's arms.

You were there, then, I thought. *You bore me up and carried me forward and preserved my history for me until I was ready to write the book myself. Walk with me now.*

I caressed the face, from the spot between the eyes down the length of the nose. The horns hung close. I remembered their near-pearlescence in the fiery Selistani sunlight, how on certain days Papa would tip them with woven red balls, one to each side.

I am here, I told the god. *Come to me.*

Chowdry murmured something, but I did not hear his words. The god was warm and close. As I had before, I could feel him. Wordless, of course, mute as any ox, but filled with intention and divine regard.

How have the pardines changed you? I wondered. *Do you feel their high, hidden groves; the violence of their Hunts?* Pardine power had twisted Federo well past the breaking point, and birthed the strange, short-lived war god Choybalsan. But if an ox was anything, he was a reservoir of calm. A sink for what might have boiled over from a lesser god. A more facile deity.

Sunlight wrapped me like a heated cloak. I smelled the warm mud of the paddies, the sweet bloom of the plantain trees. My eyes were shut, at least here, where the solid mass of the ox loomed close beside me. Flies buzzed, shit stank, and the air was hot and still, while bells tinkled from some place I could not see.

Very far away, Chowdry spoke once more. Again I ignored him.

I need you, I told the god.

Wordless, the answer came and I still understood it: *You will always have me.*

Too many mistakes.

There was no response to that. In time, I opened my eyes. Chowdry sat staring sadly at me. "So it is to pray to the ox god," he said in Seliu.

I bristled with defensiveness. "Endurance heard me."

"Of course. He is being very . . . awake. For a god."

"You have obviously not met Blackblood," I muttered. "Or Desire."

"When I was a boy, the gods of my village were safely quiet. We prayed and made offerings of fruit and money, but they never came looking for us."

"Welcome to Copper Downs. This place has been a nexus of divine power through the Duke's rule, at least. The new order has not yet settled in. Endurance disturbs that order. Marya's slaying disturbs it further."

He shrugged. "I know little of gods. Even of this god I serve." One hand strayed unthinking to the marble muzzle of the idol. "I am not believing in Endurance. Any more than I am believing in the weather. The god just *is*. Like the weather."

"That must be true of all gods." I stood, balancing my hands on my hips to stretch my aching back. No more rooftops for me. If further fighting was to be had, I'd best array my champions before me. I could no longer carry my own colors.

With that thought, my next steps fell into line in my mind. Inspiration from Endurance, or just the time spent praying serving as a meditative reflection? It did not matter. I must finish organizing my attacks.

Surali's other men were somewhere in the city. Possibly coming here. My little mob of sailors and refugees could barely be counted upon to watch the embassy, let alone influence its doings. Even with Mother Argai in their midst to lend them both spine and purpose. But if I entreated Archimandrix to set his brass apes onto Surali and the Street Guild instead of Iso and Osi, I could enlist my other allies, who were better suited to the task, to stop the twins. The Rectifier had been watching them for me. I would need him, and through him, some way to secure the temporary loyalty of the Revanchists. Sundering their alliance with the Selistani embassy would be a wise, wise move.

All of this would serve to save Blackblood. Even more so, it would protect the Lily Goddess. And through Her, Desire.

"I shall call upon you," I told the ox.

There was no answer, as befitted a mute and wordless god.

Outside the weather had reverted to sleet. Needles of icy rain whipped across the temple grounds as if a divine seamstress exerted her chilly wrath. I wrapped my robe close and walked through the construction project to the trapdoor covering my ladder. Chowdry trailed behind me. "You will be having a care," he said in Petraean.

"I will." Turning, I drew him into an awkward embrace. We had never been friends of the touching kind. "Surali's men may come here under arms. I beg you to make a defense."

"No," he said simply. "Our innocence is our defense."

"But you are guilty of so much," I whispered.

His smile was odd and sad.

I turned, opened the trapdoor in the temporary deck, and descended once more into Archimandrix's realm.

This time, Below was much warmer and noisier than my recent experience would have it. Perhaps that was only contrast to the dedicated misery of the weather above. Several of the ancient machines in this mine gallery hummed and clattered. Another thing I had not seen or known of before. Blue sparks wafted around the floor—coldfire, in many hands. Some had been set into gonfalons or lantern-topped poles.

The sorcerer-engineers were preparing for war.

I reached the bottom of my ladder to be confronted by two figures with leather-wrapped faces, eyes goggled and mouths muzzled. It occurred to me that with their guises these priests could be any race of human. Petraean. Selistani. Or something older and more furtive. They were accompanied by a brass ape that shivered and clicked. Though I was certain about the ape, I had to assume the other two were men. No woman I knew would allow herself to smell so.

Neither of them *appeared* to be Archimandrix, but that was hard to tell with the tattered robes and the leather straps and the brass oculae.

"I am Green," I announced in my most imperious voice.

The men nodded. The ape just clicked some more. When they turned to walk away, the ape followed them. So I followed the ape. Its great legs pistoned like the armatures of an engine. Something hissed within—however they had powered this thing, the magic or natural science of it was beyond me.

A regiment of these armored suits would have its uses in defense, but I could not imagine them being effective attackers at the best of times. Defeating them would not be easy work, but the tactics could not be too challenging.

Could they?

We arrived at a machine that glowed the color of coldfire. The faint blue light crackled along the device's brass and iron limbs. A man was strapped within. His body was gaunt, each rib as countable as a tooth, his penis dangling shriveled from a groin tattooed in concentric triangles that ran across his thighs and abdomen. His chest was tattooed as well, tiny letters in a script I didn't recognize scrawled across his body in a testament to . . . what?

Only his face was hidden, wrapped in leather with the brass eyepieces.

Archimandrix, of course. I stared up into the gleaming blue formlessness of his lenses. "I have returned."

"Ah," he gasped, then shrieked fit to split the heavens.

I covered my ears until the piercing noise dropped off. The two beside me did not stir, though the brass ape clanked and settled a bit in its stance. When Archimandrix was finished, he gasped again before licking at the blood trailing from the corners of his mouth.

"Your mysteries are deeper than those I know of," I said politely.

One of my guides reached up and began to unbuckle the bonds holding Archimandrix into his machine. After a moment he stumbled to the cold stone floor, dropping to his knees to retch. His back was covered with the same tiny scribing as his front. The skin there was spotted with welling drops of blood where a hundred or more needles had punctured him in the machine's embrace. Nausea grabbed at me. I turned away and tried to hold down a sympathetic lurch, but I lost my own battle.

When I turned back, mouth tainted with stinging bile, the sorcerer-engineer was pulling on a quilted robe. "I am sorry," he said in a strangely normal voice. "You should not have seen that." Fluid dripped from his brass muzzle. I reflected on how difficult it would be to vomit in such a contraption.

"I have decided I do not need to know." My fervor stained my voice. If Archimandrix noted it, he did not remark.

"We have brought all the apes out of storage." One of his silent assistants handed the sorcerer-engineer a small wire brush, which he used to clean his muzzle as we continued to speak. The rasping of the tool lent his voice a strange distortion. "Some of our best have been working on their punchleather instructions."

"Are you ready?" I asked. My fear that Surali might pack up her embassy and leave was growing stronger. They held three hostages of great import to me behind those walls.

Archimandrix waved one hand, as if brushing off objections. "We will never be as prepared as we might prefer, but we are ready."

I realized that his fellows were gathering around us as we spoke. Fair enough. They should all hear this. Time for my vision to begin falling into place. "We spoke before of the twins and the temples. But I have rethought my plans. Tonight, in the middle watch, I want your apes to surround the Selistani embassy. It is a rented mansion in the Haito style, at the corner of Richard Avenue and Knightspark Street. There may be some of my countrymen out front, watching the place; and a woman of my order named Mother Argai. She speaks no Petraean. Some of the men do. Together they are watching the gates for a departure. I must recover two other women of my order as well as a young girl from imprisonment by the embassy guards."

"We are to attack them?" Archimandrix asked. The flickering blue light of the place lent him eerie highlights.

"Almost certainly, though do not swarm the walls or break through the gates. Rather, stop them if they attempt to leave. They will seek to make their way to the port. I cannot have them taking ship until I have recovered my people, and put an end to . . . certain plans."

"Your god killers." His voice was flat now, flat as his machines.

"My god killers," I said, owning up to Iso and Osi. "I have other intentions for them now. More, well, spiritual. Along an axis of power where their strength does not lie." Pardines, and Endurance. And, by the Wheel, Mother Iron if I could find her and once more truckle any sort of aid from her. She was the soul of this city, I had come to believe almost literally so.

A strange notion was dawning about her. I wanted to let my deeper thoughts tease the idea out before I plucked at it. "The twins cannot be allowed to take ship either. Too much is at stake."

"We have not moved openly in the city for centuries," Archimandrix said. "And never against our own."

"These are not your own. I am asking you to take on my people, not Petraeans. Besides . . ." I could not help the grin that seized my face. "The Interim Council will bear all costs or charges arising from these actions. I am driving inimical forces out of the city at their commission."

That was about as far from the truth as I cared to venture, for all that it was not yet exactly a lie.

Archimandrix looked back at his gathered sorcerer-engineers. "What say you brothers?"

"Much is at stake," I put in. "If we do not act, the Interim Council will fall." *If it has not already done so.* Lampet had raised the Reformed Council to be met with an aggravated helplessness by the assembled sages at the Textile Bourse. "The Temple Quarter will be in disarray yet again. Even worse, the greatest danger to order which has been seen in an age will prosper here." Before passing onward to wreck my own city. *After* wrecking my own city. I was indeed a woman under two banners, however much I sought to deny either or both of them. I cradled my belly with my hands. "I want more for my daughter. Each of you wants more for yourself."

A rumbling arose, the sorcerer-engineers speaking a language unknown to me. Short, sharp gutturals echoed, offset by vowels that buzzed as if they used the cords deep in their throats without benefit of lips or tongue. I knew a chaffer when I heard one. The Blades used to do this on occasion. We would meet as a body to overwhelm a difficult decision with dozens of individual voices, separate opinions, smoothing together like rocks in a sand barrel until they'd reached a consensus as if by summoning it from the very air.

Much more quickly than I'd imagined, the muttering died down. Archimandrix turned to me. "We will be there. How will we know your hostages?"

"Two women of my order," I said. "Prisoners on the second storey, last I was aware. Everyone there but a few servants will be my countrymen, so do not assume that any dark-skinned female is your goal. The names of these women are Mother Vajpai and Samma. Also, a girl of about twelve, of your country. She is pale, with sandy hair in curls, and eyes somewhere between blue and gray. Her name is Corinthia Anastasia. The women will be expecting a rescue, and can be relied upon. The girl is not so wise or prepared, I should think."

"Will you wait with us while we ready ourselves?"

"No, I must sort my other allies." I glanced up the ladder, and decided I'd be better off heading for the Tavernkeep's place through Below. Too many up top knew me, might be looking for me. Besides, that way I could watch for Mother Iron.

Or Skinless.

I could not decide if I wanted to see Blackblood's avatar or not. That hand I would let fate deal to me.

"Farewell." Archimandrix bowed deeply. Behind him, dozens of his fellows followed his obeisance in a rustling of robes and a creaking of leather. Their lenses flashed with the faint blue-white of coldfire reflections as they rose again, each head moving in an eerie, precise unison with all the others.

"Farewell." I pushed through them toward a familiar passage leading east and south.

Several turns away, in the Station, I stopped and pulled out my short knife. I needed Mother Iron, and I could not be sure she'd find me of her own accord. Whatever ritual might call her wasn't something I knew, either, but I thought I could summon the Factor's ghost. And *he* was definitely allied with Mother Iron.

Libations are the oldest ceremony. Warriors had honored their dead from history's first battlefield, just as families honored their elders who had taken the longest sleep. The wine of a libation poured into the opened soil was nothing more than a symbol for blood spilled in combat to run into a freshly dug grave.

I had no wine, and the earth beneath my feet was stone, but blood I did have. The blade fit my right hand as well as ever it did, then turned around to slice across my left palm. I clenched my fist around the stinging pain. Blood filled the cup of my hand in a sickening rush.

When I opened my fingers, the red pattered down upon the floor in a slow, silken rain, black as old sin in this underground darkness. "Factor," I whispered. "You are never so far from me. You stand behind all the great conspiracies of my life. Even now in death the shadow of your power writhes through this city, drawing gods and god killers and assassins from across the sea. In name of my debt to you and in the name of your debt to me, I call you now."

It was no ritual, but the words felt right. I'd known the man in life, and I'd known him better in death, as he had passed over at my hand. We were bound as surely as any parent and child.

"What debt do I now owe you?" The Factor loomed next to me as if he'd been there all along. He still wore his semblance of living, though I could faintly glimpse the stone of the passageway through his body.

"You owe me your life," I told him.

"Which you took unknowing. I do not see that as debt."

"I released you from an ancient power not your own, and freed you into the next world."

He laughed gently. "You always were one with novel ideas about how things work."

"Where do you suppose I learned them?" In a strange way I felt almost sympathetic toward this man, the source of all my torments.

"We all make mistakes."

Nodding, I agreed, "I am doubtless making another mistake now. I need your help."

"You? Slayer of dukes and gods? I thought you ate cities for breakfast."

"No. I eat rulers for breakfast. Cities give me indigestion."

"How shall I ease the rumbling in your gut, Emerald?"

His use of that name very nearly closed my ears. I ignored the flash of anger that shot a tremor through my hands. "I am confronting another problem of the divine."

"God killing?"

"God saving, actually."

"You play both sides of the fence well enough."

I shook my head ruefully. "I would rather not have the fence in my life at all, but I am afraid it is too late for that. But now, on this side of the fence, I have need of Mother Iron."

He paused awhile, as if thinking through his next words. Erio was a ghost a thousand years older than the Factor, I was sure, but the Factor had lived centuries longer than any man might expect, which lent him an unusual substance in the afterlife. How that experience bore upon his thoughts, I could not say. It must have granted him an involuntary wisdom at the least.

Finally, the Factor spoke. "I will not bandy with you about Mother Iron. She is much older than even the farthest extent of my knowledge."

"I do not believe she is so much more ancient than the sorcerer-engineers."

"Tinkering fools," he said dismissively. "Boys toying with brass and wire. Mother Iron is something else. Older. *Deeper.*"

"I have seen you in her company."

"Yes . . ."

"I would speak with her."

"She does not respond when bidden."

"Unlike ghosts?" I asked, my voice nasty. "I never believe what people say. Not when they act the opposite. You can find her. Bring her to me."

"Even for me, it does not work that way." Something of a smile played across his face. "My powers are far more limited than you seem willing to credit."

"I have no idea what your powers are, in truth. Not here in this place, at this stage of your existence. I just know you have a bond to Mother Iron."

At this latest mention of her name, Mother Iron stepped up to my other side. Her furnace eyes glowed as if from a deep distance. As always, I received the impression that her cowl concealed immensities far larger than the space it enclosed.

"Welcome," I said modestly.

I received an indifferent stare for my troubles.

"I am hurrying to defeat a plot against this city."

The Factor snickered, I swear he did. Mother Iron only continued to stare. The fires in those deep-set eyes were not even shuttered by a moment's blinking.

"Another god will be stricken soon, if we do not move. And . . ." Here I took a breath, readying myself to play the strange card that had occurred to me earlier. "I know how to restore you to a portion of your former power."

That was a knife throw in the dark if I'd ever taken one, but all the same, not unreasonable. Something flared in her eyes. It was the opposite of a blink, as if the fires within had been unbanked to briefly rage beneath a rain of oil.

A hit, then.

I used my own silence. Not as a weapon against her, for I could no more fight Mother Iron than I could fight a storm, but as a tool. A lever, cracking her open.

"You do not have that authority," she finally said. As it had always seemed to do, her voice gusted deep from within a large, hollow place, bringing oven-hot air with the words.

"No, but I know of one who does. Here in Copper Downs, now."

"Her . . ."

The Factor's ghost looked both bemused and puzzled in the same moment. His lips parted as if he wished to speak, but at a sharp glance from me he swallowed whatever he had planned to say. Even the ghosts feared me.

"Yes," I replied to Mother Iron. "Her. And She speaks to me. You remember Her, from the beginning, don't you?"

Mother Iron sighed, a rumbling that reminded me of the collapse of a mound of coal. "Not the very beginning, no. But yes. I remember."

"The days of the titanics. You are no daughter-goddess, or splinter of that era." My thoughts ran ahead, dragging my words with them through fields of theory and foggy banks of speculation. "You are from another creation, spawn of another Urge. Much as the pardine gods were."

"You presume." Mother Iron's voice was hard, but carried no threat.

"I only speculate. But you have persevered, borne upon the prayers of sorcerer-engineers and existing within the echoing places of this undercity. Carried along into the currents of time without ever recovering your proper place in the depths."

"Vanity is for men." Her objection carried its own weakness embedded in the tone and power of the words.

"Vanity is for all things that carry self behind their eyes. Gods are vain, men are vain, cats are vain. But this is not vanity." I pitched my voice for her, ignoring the Factor's increasingly sardonic smile. "This is *opportunity*."

Mother Iron's tone changed. Words creaked as if bouncing down a mountain. "What would you of me?"

"Accompany me to meet Desire. Accept Her charge if She will lay it upon you. Then cloak Her power in yours and help me to stop the god killers that hunt Desire's daughters across the plate of the world. When we are finished, you will have stature again."

"Or my fires will be banked forever."

"All opportunity is risk." I opened the aching, stinging hand I'd slashed to summon the Factor's ghost. Blood dripped. "Everything worthwhile comes priced too high for our tastes. This is the way of the world, Mother Iron. Live in it. Or hide beneath the shadows."

I had no better offer to make her. Either she accepted my argument or she did not. In any case, my evening called me, a midnight appointment to be at blades with the forces of my chief tormentor.

Mother Iron made a slow, steaming noise, like a kettle on the hob. Then, to my surprise: "Take me to Her. I would see this power for myself."

"Of course." I glanced once more at the Factor's ghost. He mouthed the word *vanity* at me. I nodded at him as if accepting a compliment.

Even now, that would gall him. Being dead, his amusements were few. My refusal to be baited was salt in his never-healing wounds.

Walking Below with Mother Iron was very different. There was no sense of menace. I was one of the most dangerous human beings in the city, but the denizens of Below were their own class of risk. Nothing stirred when Mother Iron walked those dank halls.

I carried my coldfire always as any sane person did Below, at least any sane person who relied on her vision to navigate. Mother Iron's burning gaze swept the darkness ahead of her with a vague orange glow. That was a bit unnerving. The light caught on things I did not usually notice, given that I'd never been Below with a torch or open flame. Glittering compound eyes tucked into the vaults and arches beneath which we passed, for example. Narrow slits of shadow at waist and shoulder height, primed for traps or hidden bowmen to fire through. Chips of bone scattered along the edges of the floors, as if whoever had died down here over the years had lain too long for even the scavengers.

I ignored these things, for they did not threaten me this day. Even the close and stale air fled before her approach. We followed the Sheep's Head Cutoff, then picked up the Whitetop Street sewer line to approach the Temple Quarter from Below. I wasn't sure how comfortable or safe Mother Iron would be walking the street openly.

Which was, admittedly, not my trouble to resolve.

"We will emerge at the grate behind the Shrine of Indulgences," I said, breaking the silence that had followed us since we had left the Factor's ghost behind. "That's about two blocks from the ruins of Marya's temple."

Mother Iron turned her head toward me, but said nothing. I'd already begun to doubt my plan—fusing an old power outside the purview and descent of the titanics with Desire's daughter-descent. An analogue of how I'd called Endurance into being, really, sidestepping one set of problems by folding them into another.

But I'd *made* Endurance, for all practical purposes. Mother Iron came with centuries—millennia—of her own power, her own traditions, her own fate. For that matter, so did Desire.

I realized I was like a child who imagines two leaves and a stick to be the same as a boat, fit to sail filled with cargo and men down a rushing river to the infinite sea. I had done a simple thing, terrible and portentous as it was, in raising Endurance into the world. Now I proposed to do a far more complex thing.

We reached the grate I expected. I looked up into the gloom of late afternoon sullen through the bars at the top of the ladder. "Follow," I told Mother Iron, not knowing if that was a command, a request, or wishful thinking.

I climbed. These rungs were metal, sunk into the dressed stone of the shaft. Pitted, corroded, mossy, they stung slightly at the palms of my hands. Still I reached the top and clambered out. The sleet had given way to fat, slow snow once again. I could tire very quickly of winter, I realized. Especially when it was me forced to race about in all weathers at all hours.

Looking down, I saw Mother Iron climbing like a furnace on legs. It would not have shocked me had she simply *risen* up the shaft, but her hands—such as they were, hidden in the folds of her robe—and her feet brought her up into daylight just as anyone else's would have been forced to do.

When she came out to the surface, I noted how the snowflakes sizzled and popped when they landed on her. I'd only ever seen her in sunlight once before—the day we'd stood off Choybalsan and slain the god, along with my old friend and enemy Federo. One body, two minds. Or so I had told myself.

She was squat as ever. I imagined a walking stove, though Mother Iron certainly appeared to possess the usual number of arms and legs. That cowl was just as deep in daylight. It still seemed to contain far more space than its outside dimensions would suggest. Even the cloth of her cloak was oddly textured, as if it had been fabricated of metal, or at least pounded on an anvil instead of woven on a loom.

No one was about in the alley except for a three-legged dog rooting through spilled garbage. With a grunt, I flipped the grate back into place. Then we headed toward the ruins of the temple.

Mother Iron still said nothing.

As we approached the Temple of Marya, I noticed that the few other people out in the last daylight amid the increasingly foul weather avoided us. They passed by the other side of the street, walking in long careful curves that took no notice of who was approaching. Just as people will avoid a mad-woman in the road without remarking on her.

Or a Blade, trained by deicides, skulking to avoid the notice of a goddess.

They were stepping around Mother Iron, of course. I wasn't certain what her seeming was for other people. Sometimes the avatars and godlings of this city moved cloaked in invisibility, much as Skinless himself could apparently roam with discretion despite his enormous size and horrifying visage.

Unease, it could just be unease.

We reached the jumble of bricks and shattered timber. Snow and sleet had alternated sufficiently to make a gray-brown slush of the ruins. That was now being overwritten by more freezing rain dumping even as we stood. My earlier offerings were gone, no doubt scavenged by whoever had passed here since I'd taken Laris back to the lazaret on Bustle Street.

"Here," I said to Mother Iron, then stepped up onto my ragged chunk of masonry, which had served me as both lectern and altar. "Third time pays for all."

"Nothing pays for all," she rumbled.

A joke? Couldn't be. "Can you climb up here with me?"

Her joints popped with an audible metallic echo as she stretched to top the rock. Once again, up close to her, I was struck by how hot Mother Iron was. Snow and slush at her feet sizzled to water, then flowed away.

Looking back across the years, I now know that this was one of the better ideas I had ever had. At the time I was nearly panicked at the potential for disaster.

"Desire," I said, shivering. "Goddess." I reached into my vest and pulled out the last of the jewelry I'd stolen earlier. So much for hocking it for spending money. I scattered the rings and earrings on the ground. They disappeared into the snow, leaving only dark little holes. "I call You once more, this time the last. I have brought You an answer, someone who can stand against the Saffron Tower and those who would avenge the insults they have pursued since the first days of Time himself."

I closed my eyes and thought of Marya, the Lily Goddess, Laris, Mother Vajpai, the fat woman at the lazaret, Ilona, and least of all—or perhaps most of all—myself. Women. Goddesses. Desire's daughters and granddaughters.

Everyone who'd served Her, and needed Her, and been under Her protection.

A traitor thought demanded my attention, distracting me. *Is Mother Iron female?*

That was between the two of them. "Desire," I said aloud again. "I offer a solution to the problem which has dogged You down the generations. Raise up a goddess from a different path to power, and face those who persecute You with a different weapon in your hand."

I do not use weapons, She whispered more quietly than snow thunder. Her voice was the wind.

Not Laris this time. Though my mouth once again tasted of metal. "You are leaving us already."

It costs much for Me to appear.

"Then see this one I bring before You. An ancient protector of the city. A woman of a different era and kind. A power in this land, who can close the divine fracture in this place before it grows too wide. Mother Iron, I present the titanic Desire. Desire, I present the autochthonic Mother Iron."

I felt as if I'd gone to some dinner party of the gods, and made introduction between two rival thunderbolt hurlers.

Wind swirled around us, much as it had in the Temple of the Silver Lily when the Lily Goddess had manifested. Snow crystals flew up from the broken stones, or were drawn down from the sky, until we stood in the core of a frozen vortex. Mother Iron steamed as the stuff melted from her cloak on contact. I felt myself becoming buried. Strangely, my body was now blessedly blood-warm.

The wind took the shape of a woman—familiar, pulsating, shifting through all women, all races of human, all shapes and heights. **You would be My daughter-goddess?** She asked in a voice made of this private storm.

"No," said Mother Iron. In her word I heard rusted metal doors slamming shut, cutting off ovens full of screaming souls, burning charnel houses blocked from view. "I would protect this city."

The storm gusted, sighed with lungs the size of clouds, the shape of fate. **Do you deny Me?**

"No." Again, a clang of finality. But these were immortals bargaining over divine power. Likely their words carried meanings far beyond what my ear could understand. "I do not deny you. But neither am I a daughter of your line."

Not human. Not of the titanic descent.

Were we ourselves sprung from the gods? I laid that thought aside for future consideration alongside other troubling ideas.

The storm hummed further. Mother Iron reached out, her cloak slipping from one bony hand so that I saw fingers like metal pistons, a wrist motivated by chain and pin and axle. Was she quite literally a machine? Who had made her? Perhaps Archimandrix's first and greatest ancestor.

"I will take your charter, but I will not bow to your high place."

"Exactly," I hissed. "Step outside the ancient feud."

Now the storm laughed. The very air shook. The stones beneath my feet seemed to slip, ready to walk of their own accord. **So finally it is time for a change.**

They came together then, in that vasty place I had only barely ever glimpsed, where time echoed like a stone dropped in a well and the world was the size of a fingertip. I watched as the forces met. Goddess and tulpa swirled together as the water of two different seas will where they merge, until only ocean remains, ever changing and endlessly unchanged.

Finally, after seconds, after an eternity, the two pulled apart again. All the hair on my body smoldered. My eyes felt as if lightning had danced within them. I did not know if I would survive this experience, and found I did not care.

Instead I dropped to my knees. "Mother . . ." I whispered.

The hand that reached for me was not quite the same. I could see the mottled, corroded metal, but it flexed beneath a form that gained density even as I looked. Skin, the opposite of Skinless really. Though on Mother Iron it seemed to be just another cloak. Still, rosy nails and a hue almost as brown as my own showed where before there had been only in truth an ancient, creaking machine.

"Rise," she said. Her voice was still distant ovens and banked fires, but now it came from bowed lips that I could just barely glimpse within the shadows of her cowl. If she were to pull back her hood, Mother Iron would be both beautiful and terrifying in the same moment.

I stood. We were in the street, myself bone-cold and soaking. The bricks of Marya's shattered temple lay arrayed around us in a circle, like straw in a field after a whirlwind. No, not a circle. A spiral. With Mother Iron and myself at the center.

Already the joyous transports that had taken me up were fading. Already my sense of captivation was transforming to a sense of having been captive. *All* of this was about freeing myself from gods, not binding myself closer.

At least I had served the women of this city well, as a Lily Blade should.

"I am not yours." My voice was quiet.

"All women are mine," she answered. "But you serve others."

"I do. And I must rouse more of them."

"Do what you need. This is my temple now. I shall abide until it is time."

Reluctantly, I walked away. A part of me wanted to hate her. I imagined nursing a resentment and a sense of blind folly that would push this force away from me. But another part of me wondered how it might feel to have the whole of Below, the entire undercity, as your sacred place, then be folded down into a smaller and smaller package until you fit into a spiral of bricks in some back alley.

Like a bird descended from the high airs and a wide view of the plate of the world to sit in one tree and think small thoughts. Would I have chosen the same?

No, of course not. I had refused this exact choice, turned away from this opening of the mind and soul. It would have torn me apart surely as any coney in the talons of some great falcon. Mortal women were not meant to be vessels of such power.

I hurried through the evening's sleet and freezing rain. It was a proper storm, too, much to my disgust. The Tavernkeep's place abided, awaiting my small pleasure as my choices narrowed toward nothing. The midnight hour would bring me to some end.

No watchers lurked in the alley. I sighed at that, realizing that I'd been looking forward to taking my frustrations out on someone properly deserving. On the other hand, it meant I would be out of the nasty weather all the sooner. Pushing within, I saw that almost no Selistani remained in the tavern. I wondered where they all were. Then I realized that Mother Argai had likely chivvied more of them out to stand watch. A rescue was needed, and I was sending them, if not real troops, at least walking armor under the leadership of Archimandrix. That boy knew this city far better and deeper than did either my allies or my enemies.

Pardines there were in plenty, though. Revanchists, from their half-wild look, and city-bred alike. Somewhat to my surprise, I did not glimpse the bulk of the Rectifier. Perhaps the old rogue was off haunting the twins' warehouse. That thought distressed me.

One thing at a time.

The Rectifier might not be present, but the Dancing Mistress nodded at me from near the fire. She knew me as well or better than anyone alive. I imagined that she could read my entire errand from the set of my shoulders, the cast of my mouth. I found I no longer cared. Stepping to the bar, I sat myself heavily in front of my host.

"I am short of funds tonight." Nothing remained to me except my weapons, the clothes on my back—the outer robe itself stolen—and the child within. "But if you can see your way to a bit of credit, I could stand a good bowl of whatever curry is on the fire in the kitchen."

The Tavernkeep gave me a long, slow look, with a secretive smile at its heart. "Your word is always good here, Green." He stepped into the kitchen, his tail flicking back and forth.

Binding my slashed palm with a bit of rag, I found my mouth watering to the smell of Selistani cooking. Even the pardines seemed to have taken to it. But there was a musk in the room tonight, something stronger than the odor of wet fur and winter on the backs of these strangers. Was it the scent of a Hunt coming together?

Did I care about *that*?

I turned to scan the room. The Dancing Mistress caught my eye. Between us, pardines shifted their chairs, or stood to find other places in the room. A lane was being cleared. Perhaps we were to fight.

On my best day, I could do no more than battle her to a draw. Now, pregnant, bruised, battered, and tired, I would not even think to stand to the combat. If she wanted to take me down, she could. Rangy strength and an intimate knowledge of my own weaknesses as a fighter were a combination I didn't care to challenge.

Besides, I held secret what she most desired. The Rectifier still carried the Eyes of the Hills for me. The old rogue, priest killer and historian of his kind, was as close to an unbeliever in the human sense as I had ever known a pardine to be. He understood the power in the Eyes of the Hills. He simply did not care.

Was all of this what Erio had feared? The larger circles of plot that spun around me were so vast, the entire fate of Copper Downs was but a cog in their gearing. I could fight only one battle at a time.

Well, perhaps as many as three or four.

The principle was the same.

A bowl clicked on the bar beside me. I turned away from the burgeoning challenge and began to eat my supper.

Behind me, the noise of the tavern resumed.

The door banged open. Wind howled for a moment, pushing a frosty gust through the room before being cut off again. The murmur of voices did not die this time, so I was willing to take it on trust that no maniac was charging me from behind with a naked blade. Besides, the Tavernkeep had not lowered his ears.

The meal was hot, and spicy. Someone had found a selection of actual Selistani vegetables—roots and peppers that could have been harvested from any garden in Kalimpura, though here they must have traveled across the Storm Sea in the hold of a ship. Wasteful but delicious. The meat was Stone Coast mutton, unfortunately.

Still, it was a taste of home. Of my other home.

I realized all over again that I would never settle the question of home. Not in my mind, not in my heart. I promised my child she would not ever be so beset by confusion. Even to my own thoughts, the statement seemed hollow, for all my intentions.

First, survive the night. Second, stop these plots and counterplots. Third, keep my child disentangled from them all. Fourth, free Corinthia Anastasia and my fellow Blades. Perhaps my priorities were backwards.

Or perhaps not.

As I finished my bowl of bastard stew, I resisted the temptation to put aside my knives. I would not fight the Dancing Mistress, not now, not ever. And it was not in my desire to battle anyone else tonight. But there was violence to come. Some of it would surely be directed at me. What could I do but respond from my place at the heart of the storm?

I wiped my mouth on a bar rag, smiled at the Tavernkeep, then slipped from my stool and turned to face my old teacher. As I did so, the gentle buzz of voices died once more.

They'd all been waiting for this, pardine Revanchists and city pardines. Likewise the Selistani onlookers. I suppose I had too, ever since that day when she and I had defeated Federo, our co-conspirator from the earliest times.

Now was a time to pass over our differences. I did not need pardine power loose in the city, least of all a Hunt. But I badly wished to give her a reason to return to her groves and mountaintop meadows.

And I had one.

I walked toward the Dancing Mistress.

She rose from her table, stepped around her supporters, and stood before me.

"Green."

I nodded sharply. "Dancing Mistress."

Her tail whipped back and forth, but her ears did not lie flat. This evening she was wearing loose leather, almost armor. So unlike her city ways from the whole time I'd known her and held her as my teacher, let alone our brief period of being lovers. That bond had fallen dormant under so much else that had passed since.

She spoke next. "We search."

"I know. And I have found." I let a smile slide across my face. She would understand the expression. The Dancing Mistress had been as citified a pardine as I'd ever met.

"What?" she almost whispered. "What have you found?"

The silence around us deepened. So many in this room were Revanchists.

"Back in Kalimpura," I said, "I killed a man named Michael Curry for the gems that he carried. I did not know then what stakes were in play. Surali of the Bittern Court brought those gems back across the sea here to Copper Downs. She had planned to barter them for more power, but I have taken them away from her." I looked around the room, catching in my own gaze glittering pardine eyes with their barred pupils. "They were not hers to sell."

"Nor are they yours," breathed the Dancing Mistress.

"No. Neither are they mine." I sighed. Here was the play I needed to make, the edge I had been forced to approach. "So I gave them away."

The sigh ran around the room as if one breath from several dozen mouths. Muscles rippled, chairs scraped. It seemed the whole pardine nation was ready to spring upon me.

"I gave them away," I continued, interrupting whatever words were forming on the Dancing Mistress' lips as her claws flexed, "because I gave them back to you."

"Do not toy with me," she snapped. Her ears had lain back flat. The Revanchists at her table were all on their feet, tails flicking.

"No. I will tell you of the meaning of my actions, but I ask a bargain."

"None will bargain in ill faith," growled a male beside her.

"This is not your soulpath." I bared my teeth at him.

"What bargain?" The Dancing Mistress ignored her fellow.

"This one: That you take the Eyes of the Hills . . ." I paused, to let another sigh ripple through the room. I had their attention even more fully now, if that was possible. "Take the Eyes of the Hills back to their shrine and trouble this city no more with dreams of lost power. Every measure of that dance has long since been trodden. You will not find your elder days amid our ruins, nor in the promises of southerners bearing lost treasures."

"You make promises now," she said.

"No." I spread my hands. Empty, weaponless, softly blunt-fingered as any human being's. "There is nothing I promise. All I do is deliver. Deliver, and ask you to walk away from a fight that was never yours."

"They stole . . ." the male began uncertainly.

I focused on him. "They did. How shall I redeem that theft now? How can more death reclaim what was lost? Besides, what I have heard is you gave away power as much as it was stolen from you."

"We could not be who we were," the Dancing Mistress said. "We can only become who it is left to us to be. If that is a twilight people, so it is for us."

"Have we a bargain?" I asked.

"Show your terms."

I waited a long beat. "Have *we* a bargain?" I stared intently into her eyes, willing the old trust between us to spark back to life.

"*We* have a bargain," she said slowly. I knew she'd taken my meaning.

Another long, quiet moment passed. The musk in the room seemed to thin a bit. A few pardines relaxed; one or two even took their seats again.

"The Eyes of the Hills are safe." I looked around at all of them. "I gave the gems to the Rectifier. He will guard them for you. What you make of the Eyes of the Hills is between you and him."

The Dancing Mistress shook her head, then snorted, that almost-sneeze that passed for laughter among the pardines. Amusement, self-mockery, a lightening of the heart, I could not say. "You gave the most sacred stones of our people to a priest killer?"

"Who better? He of you all knows best the weaknesses of that sort of faith." And they were *welcome* to try to take the gems from him. I could not have found a safer hiding place in a bank's strong room.

"You spin the divine the way some people spin wool."

"Never!" I took a breath, calmed myself. "The divine clings to me the way wool clings to some people, perhaps. It is my business now and again to brush it off."

Her amusement melted into sadness. "And so we depart, taking our power and our anger with us."

"Well, yes. You have achieved what you came for. There is no need for further threat."

"All well, Green, all well." Her eyes narrowed, her ears flicking. "But for one thing. *Where is the Rectifier?*"

Every plan had a flaw. She had found the flaw in mine.

"He dogs a pair of god killers for me," I said, speaking honestly. "I go now to resolve that fate."

Her voice was cool now. "You sent the Eyes of the Hills into the hands of god killers?"

"I placed the Eyes of the Hills into the hands of the Rectifier." My ground felt less certain now. My foolishness was laid clear.

"We will depart when he comes to us and shows what he carries." She sat down, her stare narrow and emphatic. The tension melted from the room to be replaced with a wary waiting.

"Then I shall see to him."

I had definitely outstayed my welcome here. Glad I'd eaten on my arrival, I slipped back into the driving sleet of the evening.

The time had come for me to confront Iso and Osi. I had broached all the allies I could. The Rectifier was dogging them or he was not. Archimandrix would succeed in overwhelming the Selistani embassy or he would not. Mother Iron, in her new guise, would support me or she would not. Endurance had given me as much blessing as I might have hoped for from my ox god.

Later on, if need be I would turn my face away from Blackblood, and even the Lily Goddess. Tonight I would defend them, so that when I did walk free of their influence, my escape would be on my own terms. With my child free as well.

Such foolish hopes I had then.

The storm was breaking up as I hurried toward the twins' warehouse lair. The clouds spread ragged across the sky, and a tired moon glimmered down. My feet slipped on icy cobbles, and I felt so huge, so unbalanced, like a tree on the edge of falling. I had no idea what I hoped to accomplish now—all my plans seemed to have flowed out of me, leaving only a curious admixture of determination and fatigue.

But I knew that I must face down the twins, and trust Mother Iron and Endurance to stand at my back when I needed them most.

Nothing moved on the streets. The wind still knifed. All sane persons were long indoors. By the time I reached the warehouse, stars stabbed the night sky, and the moon had found a sliver of her usual courage. If anything, the air was even colder.

I didn't bother with the roof. I recalled all too vividly what had happened the last time I tried that route. Not so many days ago, but the baby kept changing me. Robbing my lithe balance to feed her growth. What could I do but honor that? I could hardly postpone protecting her.

That left the side, where I'd exited from my previous raid here. And where *was* the Rectifier? I'd expected him somewhere around the area, since he hadn't been at the Tavernkeep's place.

Or there was always the front entrance. Big, rolling doors meant to admit heavy freight wagons. I wished one or another of my little divine interventions had left me with some pyrotechnic magic, but the gods seemed far more interested in annoying me than gifting me.

Such an entrance would certainly make an impression.

I looked up and down the street. Several unloaded wagon rigs were parked for the night, but their teams were safely stabled out of the horrid weather. While I could in theory roll a wagon through the doors, the practical mechanics of accomplishing that were a bit beyond my current resources. Still, the idea of a dramatic attack certainly appealed to me far more than breaking in through the entrance they'd be watching most closely.

No one left cargo in a wagon overnight, not unless they were sleeping atop it weapon in hand, but what was in the warehouses around me?

A quick fifteen minutes invested in peering through windows—no roof climbing here either, not on this icy night—confirmed that the second warehouse up Theobalde Avenue from Iso and Osi's lair supplied at least some portion of Copper Downs with candles, wax, paraffin, and lamp oil. If I couldn't make trouble out of a couple of barrels of high-grade lamp oil, then I might as well give up and open a restaurant.

Forcing entry was trivial. Their locks were simple, meant to discourage vandals and children. On a night such as this, the watchmen were off drinking with the thieves, or huddled over a stove somewhere in the back. And there were no stoves in *this* warehouse, I was certain of it. The air inside smelled like an accident waiting to happen. No one smoked tabac here either, I'd guess, or hempweed. Or anything else involving sparks and flame.

Surely these people have heard of vents?

But not when the air was freezing. I'd guess it might grow cold enough to gel some of their oils.

The interior was a bit lower-ceilinged than the twins' building, surrounded by catwalks near the top. I thought I saw a crane up there, but sorting out its mechanisms was more trouble than I cared to take right now. Rows of shelves and racks and wooden footings held the seeds of destruction that I sought. This place was a pyromaniac's delight, better even than a fireworks factory.

I smiled.

Working only by the moonlight from the high, narrow windows—and who would hoist a loaded barrel of oil up and out a window?—I found a rack of exactly what I was looking for. Lamp oil, with taps already placed in three of the barrels. I wasn't about to shift that kind of dead weight around, but the collection of ramps and levers meant to load barrels on and off the rack were stored close by. How thoughtful.

I worked the first two barrels off. One of them was decidedly light in weight, so I pushed it aside and fetched the third out. It made a nice, heavy slosh. I had to be careful not to knock the taps off. They weren't meant to roll about in this condition, but I didn't need to move them far. From the inside, I opened the streetward freight door, and trundled both barrels outside. Slipping back in, I secured the freight door, then chocked the office door shut on my way out. No sense in *inviting* criminal behavior to follow me wherever I went.

The barrels rumbled on the cobbles outside as I shifted them one at a time to the front of Iso and Osi's warehouse. Fine, if they heard me, they heard me. I was too involved in my plan to stop now. At any rate, that noise was nothing like what someone alert for me dropping through the skylight would be listening for.

I positioned the second barrel so the bung was almost at the top of its rotation. This rendered the side-mounted tap useless, but meant I could break it off at need to set a fire. My last step before doing so was to scavenge some relatively dry wood from the bottom of a junk pile in the alley beside the warehouse. Using one of the short boards, I knocked the tap off.

Oil spilled. Terrific.

I let the stuff soak my lengths of dry wood, then stacked them against the still-sealed barrel. A few moments later, lucifer matches had a flame started that the oil took nicely even in the whistling, cold wind.

I figured I could not lose. Either the barrels would burn, which would spill flaming oil under their front door; or they would blow up, which would shoot flaming oil under their front door. That the Interim Council would be seeing a substantial bill was a bit of a bonus, so far as I was concerned. Or even better, Lampet's Reformed Council. As for myself, I was cold, hungry, and tired. And I had not yet begun to fight.

Let someone else suffer a bit.

The oil caught and bloomed. I scooted away fast, keeping upwind in case the barrels decided to explode and spray. A doorway across the street and one building over beckoned me with a deep vestibule. I'd noted earlier that the floor there was an imitation of a Sunward Sea mosaic, done either by someone homesick or a student of the foreign art. It wasn't bad, really, and a fine place to rest my feet while I waited to see what might erupt at the twins' warehouse.

I hadn't counted on the doorway being occupied on my return.

"Green," said the Rectifier. He loomed close. His fur stank of wet weather and drowned cat.

I stifled a shriek. "What are you doing here?"

"Looking for you." He glanced up at my little fire, which was burning merrily. It seemed the flaming leak was going to be the answer, as nothing had exploded yet. "What are you doing?"

"Trying to smoke out Iso and Osi."

"They have gone to the Temple Quarter. Apparently this was an auspicious night for them to challenge your Blackblood."

I was in the wrong place!

Everything was at risk. As he fell, so fell the Lily Goddess in time. "By the Wheel, I need to be there."

One enormous hand lay heavily on my shoulder. "Have a care." Claws pricked, even through layers of my leather vest and canvas shirt. "I do not think you should walk alone."

"I have you," I said recklessly. Behind me, one of the barrels went "whoosh." The Rectifier's face was suddenly a study in glare and chiaroscuro.

He shook his head. "Can you call your ox god? Or one of your friends Below?"

Sighing, I turned to look back on my act of pyromaniac vandalism. The barrels were burning ever stronger, the warehouse door was smoldering, but the wind was whipping both the flames and the spilled oil away faster than they could spread.

Apparently it *was* time for me to open a restaurant, because my two barrels of lamp oil weren't even serving as a distraction. Let alone as the opening movement of any attack I might have intended to pursue.

"I will call Endurance," I said. "But I do not know if he will respond to me." The ox god had already given me his blessing, after all. Had always protected me. Would he not now? I was too far from the Lily Goddess. Besides which, I would not dream of exposing Her to these two.

"Where will you do this?"

"Nowhere. Here. Now." I sank to the cold tile, wondering how long I'd last freezing my buttocks. "Watch over me." Blinking, I looked up at him. "Oh, I did sell you to the Revanchists, in a manner of speaking."

"Mmm?" His voice was a rumble that struck deep into my bones.

"I told them they could have the Eyes of the Hills back so long as the gems remained under your control."

There was a long, strained silence. Then the Rectifier snorted. "You trust me?"

"Yes," I said simply, then closed my eyes and began to pray.

The ox god was never my god, but he was first and foremost my ox. Always. I did not try to imagine Endurance in his temple as a marble statue hung with prayers and ringed with incense. Rather, I took myself in memory to my father's fields, the mud-filled wallows of my youth.

Insects buzzed first. Despite the intense cold, I had no trouble recalling the warmth of the sun. Selistan was an oven, this place an icebox. Somewhere in the world lay a land at the pleasant midpoint between the two.

Mud. Rice. Flowers. Fruits. A great, patient ox, standing close on tall legs, brown eyes rolling to follow me. Always overhead, always a presence, always my anchor to call me home.

Was it any wonder I'd placed Choybalsan's power in the ox god?

"Are you with me now?"

The great, long face turned in my direction. The eyes were deep, deeper, the deepest things I'd ever seen. Wells of glossy brown light fountained forth.

The god was with me.

"Bear me forth to meet those who would slay my patrons."

The ox shifted toward me. He shook off the flies around his ears and eyes, tail flicking. I slipped over his back, to ride him as only the dead had done. And once, the Dancing Mistress.

A jangling weight settled over my shoulders. I opened my eyes again to find the Rectifier arranging a length of belled silk across my shoulders. I sniffed at the cloak—it was mine, indeed, from the temple. Mine, and yet also my grandmother's in a very real way. No stranger that the god should bring his relics with him than that he should appear himself.

Endurance lurched forward into the cold, cold night. My grandmother's bells jingled, the cloak wrapping me in an envelope of warmth brought with the god from some other realm.

I gave the ox god no directions, and he asked none. We simply plodded through the silent, frozen streets. The Rectifier padded close at our side.

What, I wondered, was in all of this for him? Not loyalty, surely. Interest, perhaps. Or possibly the idea of a herd of unattached priests running about in the panic sure to follow a divine battle featuring Iso and Osi.

Cradling my belly in my hands, I wondered if I was bringing my child where she needed to be in this world. Surely this was not the path.

The Street of Horizons seemed even colder than the rest of the city. It was broad, almost a plaza in its own right, with fewer windbreaks. The old sacrificial pots lining the roadway did not host so many trees as to deter the cold knives of the air.

We plodded toward Blackblood's temple. Each strike of Endurance's hooves was the dull tolling of a muffled bell. My cloak shook a gentle counterpoint, a silvered rain. I could see the twins standing before the steps of the temple. They flanked a brazier balanced on a tripod and were casting something . . . what?

Did they care about Blackblood at all? Or was this all part of the larger plot against Desire and Her daughter-goddesses? It didn't matter. In either event, they had to be stopped.

I did not know if the Rectifier would draw blood for me in this matter. I did not know if that would make a difference. Endurance and I would face these men down, though I had no plan anymore. I already knew I could not slay them out of hand without releasing great, destructive power. What else could I do? The gods of this city, of whom I was going to some trouble to shed myself though they stuck to me like spilled honey, deserved better than what I'd helped bring down upon them.

"If you are not safely born here in Copper Downs," I whispered to my belly, "you will at least be safely dead with me."

The twins turned to look at us. The light of their fire caught at their faces, twisting them from sallow, foreign men to leering demons. Their saffron robes seemed to glow. The cold didn't billow from their mouths in little clouds, or redden their skins. Rather, it encased them, bejeweled them, armored them distant from me as the uncaring stars.

This would never be solved at swordspoint, even if I'd been moved to bare blades against these two. But I knew from the warehouse fight they would be a difficult match. And too dangerous to kill, besides. Pregnant and freezing, I would not resort to arms.

All I had was a god between my legs. And a priest killer at my side.

"I bid you good evening." My voice whipped thin upon the chilling wind.

They glanced at one another. Then, out of one mouth, "More of a foul evening, Mistress Green."

The other: "Come to see justice done?"

The shared smile that passed across their faces was deeply unpleasant.

"Yes," I declared. "It is time for you both to return to an honorable retirement in the Saffron Tower."

The Rectifier slipped away to my left. One twin's attention turned to follow him. The other's remained focused on me.

"A remarkable theory," that one said. "But alas, of little interest to us." He turned back to the fire while his brother stared off in the shadows, a slightly puzzled expression on his face.

This was it. My bluff was being called. All I knew was violence. There were no other tools ready to hand.

I could pray to Endurance, but the ox god had already manifested. This one would never take the attack. He stood beneath me, defending me by his very presence, but he had no fangs or claws or flaming sword.

Mother Iron? Her power was women's power, if she'd begun to fit properly into the role Desire wished of her. The example of the Lily Blades notwithstanding, women's power was like water. It flowed around obstacles, it did not shatter them.

Blackblood himself? He'd promised to take my child. My misguided overreaction to that threat—serious as it was—had started the chain of events that had led us here. His temple was dark and silent as a cenotaph on this frozen night. The building loomed high, offering little more evidence of occupation than such a cenotaph would have.

I trusted the Rectifier was up to something worthwhile, but I could not count on miracles from him. The only person I could count on was me.

Always back to me.

And my child.

Well, ever was I trained to be a sacrifice to this city's need. The oldest lessons were the deepest.

I slipped from the ox's back. If only I could seize the power I'd held when I'd stood against Choybalsan.

And so what then? These two knew how to fight that particular power.

My belled silk rang as I walked toward the fire. The twin who wasn't scanning the dark—Osi, I thought as I drew close—looked up at me again. "If you will not be gone, we will make you go," he said, as if speaking to a troublesome beggar.

"I will not depart." Hopefully the cloak, an artifact of the divine, would protect me from whatever blast his hands could unleash. Or Skinless? Where was Skinless now?

"Do not disrupt our rite," Iso said, turning away from his study of the Rectifier to glare at me.

Their fire flared. Osi held a cone of powder that he trailed into the brazier even as he bandied with me. Iso wielded a small, silver knife—a ritual implement I would not have used to peel a pear.

I reached for the brazier's tripod with a jingling swipe of my arm. Iso swung around behind his brother, flowed into a motion so smooth and fast I could barely see it, and launched a cobblestone that struck me in the chest. That forced me to stagger back, all air in my lungs lost as pain radiated with a starburst of cold, miserable sharpness.

It took almost a dozen, deep, whooping breaths for me to begin to recover. My cloak rang faintly with each gasp, distant silver rain. The twins paid me the insult of ignoring me. Iso scanned the darkness, seeming vaguely worried. Osi had begun to chant. The night air curdled, a mist being born around us.

I longed for Endurance's envelope of warmth. Looking back at the ox god for comfort, I saw those great, brown eyes shift as he tossed his head to call me back to safety.

Trying once more, I made a run at Osi. One, two, three swift steps and a leap into a knee-breaking kick. My misbalance on the icy street again marred my attack, but even so, Iso was faster. This time the cobble took me in the pelvis, just below and to the right of where the baby rode.

I crashed onto my chest in a cacophony of music, scraping my hands and chin on the road. No time to think of it now, no time to worry about what that had done to my child. I was up and moving, spinning in the dark even as another cobble whipped out of his hand. As if they'd ever needed my rescue that day in the Dockmarket.

This stone I managed to dodge. But I could not both defend and attack. And something was wrong with my right leg. That last missile had injured me to the point that I could no longer move with my usual strength and purpose.

I'd known I couldn't fight them, but I wasn't even trying now. I just wanted to disrupt their ceremony before that curdling darkness came completely into being, focused on the chalk marks on the steps of Blackblood's temple, and subtracted another god from this city.

Let alone what these two will do to the Lily Goddess in Kalimpura.

That thought roused me once more. I *had* to win a different way.

"Women's power," I whispered. Slipping to my knees, though I nearly toppled from the weakness in my right leg, I prayed to Desire, to the Lily Goddess, to Mother Iron. "These two have stolen much from You, and threaten so much more. Bring me a regiment of women to oppose them."

Out in the darkness, the Rectifier growled. Something murmured. Both twins looked now, the rhythm of their rite on the verge of being broken.

Did Archimandrix's brass apes approach, despite my orders?

No.

A light sparked.

My prayers, being answered.

Then another light.

In moments, a thousand candles, lanterns, and torches were aglow despite the plucking, grabbing wind. A thousand female faces stared at me—no, not at me, at the twins. I turned my head. They'd filled the Street of Horizons from both directions. Desire's women. Marya's women. *Mother Iron's women.* Ragged. Wealthy. Thin. Plump. Young. Old. Pale. Dark.

Acolytes of Marya—traders' wives and maids from the great houses and fishmongers and whores and animal trainers and midwives and chiurgeons and mothers and daughters, Copper Downs women of all walks of life gathered to stand against the masculine, jealous power of the Saffron Tower in the form of Osi and Iso. I could sense Desire there as well, and Mother Iron, not in a direct manifestation, but through the breath and body and words of their followers.

Like the sea, women surged forward.

Now not even Iso's cobbles could stop me. Finally I had my way. Women's power, indeed. An elderly lady in the dress of some great house of a century past handed me a white candle. An angry, muttering Hanchu child offered me a black candle. Funeral rites. The only death magic I knew, the simplest one of speeding a soul upon its way. So I lit the two wicks from the fires gathering around me.

Then I waited for the tide of women to sweep toward the twins.

No cobbles flew this time, but Iso and Osi stood close about their fire, their rite abandoned in the moment. Not even *they* could slay a thousand women at once. I let myself be pushed forward until I was an armspan from them, candles burning in each hand.

"We choose life," I said, mindful of the Rectifier's warning about the cost of slaying them out of hand. "Not vengeance and death. Embrace us."

They both bolted up the steps toward Blackblood's door.

The tide of women followed, some pushing in to each side of the stairs, the rest flowing up, still buoying me along. Iso turned with two last cobbles in his hand while Osi banged on the iron doors.

"You will not live to regret this," Iso snarled. He took aim at my head.

Skinless reached out *through* the door, tearing the metal, to crush Iso's cocked fist in his own much larger meat-fingers. The other hand trapped Osi by the neck. I closed on the twins, whispering my thanks to Blackblood's avatar, and drew my two adversaries into a close embrace beneath my belled cloak.

Their kicks and blows were as those of angry children, while the avatar held them both trapped. The women behind me reached beneath my silk to touch as the twins' hands and feet slowed. Iso said nothing, but Osi began to keen in a thin, anguished voice.

"Know the power of women," I told them.

Skinless released the two. I twisted with them, handing them down into the crowd. A mob now, female hands clutching at the twins' saffron robes, tearing at their skin, prying their fingers back, clawing at their eyes. These two ascetics, for whom the touch of a woman was the ultimate unclean filth, were passed shrieking down into a seething female mass. They vanished as the murmurs of the mob rose to shouts and then thundering prayer.

The ox god was there with me, at the top of the stairs, and I slid beneath his belly and let him shelter me while death stalked the crowd below.

What one woman could not do, a thousand could.

Whatever power was bound into the death of twins was diffused by the touch of the divine and shared murder by a myriad of hands.

Eventually I cried.

Later, the Rectifier came to me. I looked up. The moon was strongly westering, but sufficient light flooded the Temple Quarter for me to witness a scene filled with the debris of a crowd—dropped scarves, hats, a shoe. The women were gone. Two sodden lumps lay unmoving in the middle of the Street of Horizons. There was no sign of their brazier or their rites. Behind me, Blackblood's temple was silent.

Also, Endurance had vanished, as had my cloak of bells.

"Hello," I said absently through chattering teeth.

"Your work is not complete, I do not think."

No, there was a whole different battle being fought elsewhere in the city. Still, I had triumphed sufficiently to assure some safety for the Lily Goddess.

Why doesn't it feel like victory? Another lesson I did not want to learn. In time I would, but not that night.

"Have you any word from Archimandrix or Mother Argai?"

His expression wrinkled oddly. "How would I? They do not answer to me. They do not *know* me."

"Then I should leave." I stood, profoundly exhausted. My hip joint felt ready to fold. "I could use that mount now." The joke fell very flat, even to my own ears.

"Here." The Rectifier offered me his arm. "I will aid you."

He led me stumbling down the steps, then up the Street of Horizons to Pelagic Street and on toward the Velviere District. I could not imagine going Below in my current shape. The wind had died, at least, leaving the night crystalline cold and still somewhere the far side of miserable.

I wondered if Corinthia Anastasia was safe. If Mother Vajpai and Samma yet lived. If I had done the right thing. Should I have gone to the embassy first and freed the prisoners? Who else would have found a way to remove Iso and Osi from this deadly game?

Except it wasn't me. It was Mother Iron and Desire. They could have done the very same without me.

Wrong, wrong, I'd guessed wrong again and again. How many lives had my error cost?

The night was too cold for self-pity. I needed to concentrate. At least in holding on to the Rectifier's arm, I was able to find my feet. Feel almost a little balanced.

Our first idea of how things were proceeding came when a team of heavy horses cornered from Ríchard Avenue ahead of us, running too swiftly. They towed a large drayage wagon, one of the dockside haulers. Selistani men hung off the sides with bared swords.

A motley mob of more men and three or four armored figures—no, brass apes—appeared behind them at a dead run. It was a small riot, fast-moving.

Some of the embassy were escaping.

I looked at the Rectifier in panic. There was no way I could halt four big horses. "Can you stop them?"

"Get out of my way," he growled, then stepped into the center of Knights-park Street. Arms wide, claws out, the Rectifier *roared* at the oncoming team.

The leads spooked, trying to turn though there was nowhere to go and they had no freedom to head there harnessed into their traces. Still, they forced their teammates to stumble. The wagon slewed, throwing off two of the defenders. Of necessity, it lost speed, though the drover still whipped at the horses.

I threw a short knife that caught him in the side as his arm was upraised. He shrieked and dropped his whip just as the Rectifier leapt onto the neck of the right-side lead horse, clawing and biting like a mountain lion. The leather harness straps snapped under his attack. The panicked horse bolted again, this time breaking free. Its fellow, in a similar frenzy to escape, headed for the opposite wall. The rest of the team and wagon followed, the box smashing into the stucco to shed more bodies before the whole thing tipped over with an enormous groan, scattering the last few Street Guild clinging to the wagon's right side.

Half a dozen clerks and servants spilled out of the back, shrieking and gabbling. Most of the defenders were down, or dazed. The pursuit overran them with a shrieking vengeance.

I kicked the injured driver hard in the head to shut him up, retrieved my short knife, then sprinted toward the scattered clerks before they were over-run or beaten. Selistani, all of them.

Amid the scream of horses and the shouting of the small mob, I grabbed at them. "Where is Mother Vajpai?" I shouted in Seliu. "Where is the girl Surali holds prisoner?"

Several of my witnesses rolled their eyes in terror. One young fellow bab-bled. The fifth one I took hold of, an older man, had maintained his compo-sure. "We are being only clerks," he said. "Everyone you want is still behind."

That I could believe. I looked around for the Rectifier. He was lining up stunned and wounded Street Guildsmen along the wall, throwing them like stale loaves. There would be many broken bones tonight. "We have to keep moving," I shouted in Petraean.

The Rectifier must have been listening for me, because he left off his work and shoved through the milling crowd of Selistani and the three now-silent apes. They stood still as their clockwork ticked away the energy of their fierce brass hearts.

We raced after the wagon's backtrail. The next turn found us on the same block as the embassy. Two more wagons rumbled toward us from the front gates. Men were down in the street beyond, but more continued to fight. Some of them were brass. Not enough, though. I thought I saw arrows flying.

Too late, by the Wheel and all its turnings.

I could have cried.

Then I saw Mother Argai clamber over the top of the lead wagon. She dropped down onto the drover and his guard—had the other one been guarded?—sending them both off with a pair of solid punches. One hand on the reins, the other on the brake, she tried to stop the vehicle. She suc-ceeded only in oversetting it. This foursome broke free and ran, trailing their harness.

The horses behind were not so lucky, caught between the overturned wagon and their own. A horrible, wet splintering was followed by more animal screaming.

Mother Argai staggered toward me.

"They s-still have Mother Vajpai inside," she shouted, too loudly. She must have hurt her head.

"What about the stolen girl?" I shouted back.

"In-inside!"

"Check the wagons," I shouted at the Rectifier, then ran toward the battle, wishing I still had my balance and my strength and my confidence. I'd have settled for a good meal and a night's sleep.

The night air had grown still and dry, though ice still crusted many surfaces. Closing, I realized that what unfolded before the embassy walls was not so much a battle as a brawl. Even as a brawl it did not seem to be succeeding. Wherever Archimandrix might be, he was not here with his apes. I had just seen that they fought, powerful and merciless, but without initiative or intelligence. My Selistani were no army at all. Without Mother Argai to harry them on, they were already fleeing. Arrows pelted out of the night to land among them—purely a weapon of terror at this point, for the archers could see no more from behind their walls than their victims could from outside.

I did not waste my breath trying to reorganize my men. I didn't know much of leadership and less of armies. Instead I raced for the front wall and swarmed over it without thinking, slipping at the slick top to drop down the other side in an acanthus bush a dozen yards in front of a foursome of archers. The Prince of the City's men, not Street Guilders, though that hardly mattered now.

They did not even notice me, so intent were they on their officer directing their fire from a place up in a nearby tree. The fighting outside had masked me. Fine, I had a moment to consider. There were at least four more archers nearby, judging from the arrow flights. Even with that thought, they released another round, and drew again.

I couldn't very well rush four prepared archers. They'd skewer me.

The answer was obvious enough. I altered my crouch, checked their officer, and threw my blade into his armpit as he raised his hand to call another volley.

Peacock-pretty silks make for lousy armor.

He shrieked and fell from his tree, grabbing at himself until he slammed into the ground with an unpleasant crunch barely more than an arm's length ahead of me. Some fruit is never out of season.

Two of his men dropped their bows to race forward. A third bent to pick up the discarded weapons. This wasn't likely to become any easier.

Roaring, I sprang from my crouch with my long knife already swinging. I landed one archer a solid sweep across the gut, then elbowed the other in the face before stabbing him hard enough in the thigh to make him forget about me. Momentum intact and freshly blooded, I ran down the third, who was busy grasping at bows. He took my knife point in a raking gash down his chest, then sat, very surprised and no little unhappy. My long knife was snagged in his ribs. The last archer released his arrow with a twang that echoed far too close, but I broke his bow and both his wrists for him.

No time to retrieve the weapon right then, not with four more archers nearby. I sprinted toward the house. Screaming behind me seemed to indicate something of a change in fortunes. Then the thwock of more arrows fluttering by, but I was already running away in the dark, toward another big wagon being loaded with crates of something. Papers? Bodies?

They were unguarded on this side, though two servants gaped at me. I slashed away all the straps I could of this team's harness, then slapped their rumps with the flat of my remaining short knife. The horses needed no further encouragement to race back down the drive toward the gates.

I chased around the back of the wagon, trying to avoid any more arrows, and bowled over the servants.

"Run!" I shouted. Then I stared at what they had been loading.

Furniture, goods. Not prisoners or people.

I glanced back to see the Rectifier racing toward me. Two arrows protruded from his shoulder. He yanked out the shafts as he ran.

"Charged the archers head-on, did you?"

"It worked," he rumbled.

"Barely."

We looked up the shallow steps at the fortress of our enemy, took a deep breath together, and kept moving.

The front doors stood open. A Street Guildsman in a borrowed leather coat—no Selistani tailor ever sewed those lines—stood just within, staring about in obvious exasperation. His expression changed quickly as my blade came up. He was alert enough to parry with his own weapon. Unfortunately for him, the Rectifier grabbed his parrying wrist on the blocking swing and tore his shoulder out of its socket.

Disarmed, the man went down howling.

"Upstairs," I shouted. Samma and Mother Vajpai first, if they were here. I knew *where* to find them, or at least where they had been. And they might be able to help with Corinthia Anastasia.

Scrambling up the marble steps, I stumbled. Fatigue, injury, the sheer lateness of the hour. I narrowly avoided impaling myself on my own blade as it tumbled away, bouncing down the stairs with a dull ringing, spraying thin arcs of blood behind. The Rectifier swept me up and carried me the rest of the way. My knives were gone now. I was naked, by Blade standards.

I led on, aware that I was fading. A Lily Blade never lost her weapons. *Never.* Could I be *this* tired? Three servants came out of a side door with armloads of baggage, saw us, and darted back in.

"End of the hall," I gasped. "By the ballroom doors." A whooping breath. "That's also the guard barracks."

We burst through a pair of doors partway down, opening into a wider lounge. The hall beyond held half a dozen more guards, mixed Street Guild and the Prince's men, hammering on a familiar door.

The Lily Blades were still in here. It looked as if they were not being pried out.

Startled faces glanced up at us. I charged them screaming, my hands empty. The impression I'd made on my last visit must have been strong, because four of them scrambled back from me to make a stand by the next doors. The other two turned to see what the fuss was.

I let the Rectifier hit them first. That almost immediately made several weapons available, which in turn helped me feel much more dangerous.

"Get them!" I hurled someone's sword end over end at the four cowering from me. They ducked, then opened the double doors behind them. The Rectifier charged and bowled the whole mess into the room beyond.

Kneeling by the besieged door handle, I shouted, "Samma, can you hear me?" Smoke, I smelled smoke. *Smoke?*

Something crashed—a dresser, maybe?—then a horrendous scrape. The door cracked open and a bloodied blade stuck out, a frightened deep brown eye just above it. More smoke oozed around her.

"Green?"

I hated the quaver in her voice, hated what they'd done to her. "I'm here to rescue you," I said as calmly as I could.

"The room's on fire."

"Yes, I smelled it." A deep breath. "Open the blessed door, Samma! And where is Mother Vajpai?"

Blade and eye disappeared. To my left, in the ballroom, people howled, while something very large broke with a shattering crash. Had there been floor-to-ceiling mirrors?

Another scrape, then the door jerked open. Samma stepped out. She was in her leathers, but they looked slept-in and thrown-up-upon. She dropped her weapon and tried to hug me. Right now, I was less frightening to her than our enemies were.

"Mother Vajpai," I growled into her ear.

My old teacher emerged next, dressed in her leathers. She was walking with two crutches—no, canes—made from bed slats. Her feet were bound in bloodied rags.

"I am afraid I cannot run so well, Green," she said.

"Can we escape out the window?"

"A-archers on the back terrace," Samma said. "With fire arrows."

"An effective discouragement," added Mother Vajpai.

I glanced back down the hall. Another handful of discouragement was creeping toward us, bristling with crossbows. "Rectifier," I shouted. "Our time is up." Then back to the Blades, "Where is Corinthia Anastasia?"

"Who?" asked Samma blankly.

Mother Vajpai just shook her head.

"Local girl," I said. "Being held hostage. I thought she was with you, Samma."

A flight of quarrels skimmed past me with a buzz to thunk into the wall around the ballroom doors. Several skipped into the room beyond.

The Rectifier had better return soon, or he wasn't getting out.

He arrived as if summoned by my thoughts, carrying a kicking, bleeding Street Guildsman for a shield. I pushed the Blades ahead of me into the smoky room. The Rectifier followed, throwing his man behind him like an old fruit peel before blocking the door again with the big dresser that the Blades had used earlier. The smoke was almost blinding. Curtains were on fire, and the carpet seemed to be smoldering.

"Out the window," I ordered. "It's a goodly fall to the terrace."

"Archers?" asked the Rectifier.

I nodded. "With more fire. We must move fast."

"Not me," said Mother Vajpai.

By the Wheel!

Pointing at the big pardine, I snapped, "You first. I'll drop her into your arms. Samma third. I'll be last. If we are forced apart, look for Mother Argai out front and meet back at the Tavernkeep's."

"We are not splitting," Mother Vajpai ordered.

I snarled, "This isn't your handle."

The Rectifier grabbed a chair from the dressing table, yanked down one of the burning curtains, wrapped it around the chair legs, then hurled the mess through the window. Arrows flitted and buzzed outside. He followed his own missile right after that with a yell that ended in an unpleasant crunch.

Trust, I thought, and cannoned into Mother Vajpai to shove her out the window. She fell backwards with a yelp, tumbling away from me. "Now, Samma," I shouted, and gave the girl a boost with my hands. "Tuck and roll!" I called after her.

Another flight of arrows came. Two more flamers sailed through the gaping window to embed in the far wall. I poised to jump, then paused.

Corinthia Anastasia. I could not leave yet.

I turned and looked back at the door. It was shoving inward. A large closet loomed behind me. Pondering for a brief moment the principles of Stone Coast architecture, I darted into the closet. At the back, viewed by the ruddy firelight from the room behind me, one set of panels was darker and less well-fitted than the rest. I aimed a kick.

It *was* a door, passing into what would have been intended as a small servants' chamber. Thank the Lily Goddess for ladies' maids. Stepping through, I saw a storeroom, now filled with chairs stacked high and a number of large white furniture covers folded away while the rented house was in use.

Grabbing up several of the furniture covers, I wrapped myself as a crude form of armor. I regretted my sneering at the officer in his silks. Once I heard the crash of the dresser toppling, along with shouts of triumph, I darted out the storeroom door into the hall and ran like crazy back toward the central stairs, borrowed sword in hand.

Corinthia Anastasia was up, either on the third floor or in the attic. I wasn't sure precisely where, but I knew she was *up*.

To my amazement no arrows found me from behind. In the central stairs, I met two more local servants. They cowered from my bloody blade. *Whose blood?* I wondered irrelevantly. "Is the hostage still upstairs?" I shouted. "The Petraean girl?"

"Yes," said one. "Gone," said the other.

They might both have been telling the truth.

I sprinted up the stairs again, slipped once more, and sprawled facedown for a moment on the marble. This time I held on to my sword. Gods, that hurt. And my gut . . . *the baby!*

Pulling myself to my feet under the frankly amazed stares of the servants, I walked more slowly to the top.

Lower ceilings up here, and less ornate decor. As I'd thought, this was a section of the house intended for minor relatives, or senior servants perhaps. Not for the quality intended to be lodged below.

I could see all the way down the hall in both directions. No guards. That wasn't good. Carefully I trotted to my right, passing above the scene of the recent fight. She had been above, right? *Above.*

This was a nightmare. I went door to door, opening them—after the first two I stopped kicking. My foot hurt too much. And I was definitely slowing down.

Surali and the Prince of the City had already moved their people out. Despite my hopes, we'd caught the tail end of the evacuation. It was cold up here, no fires in the hearths. The smoke from downstairs was growing thicker. The air bore the heavy odor of burning house—carpets and paint and the varnish from furniture all burn differently from firewood. I wondered how fast the fire was spreading below, but I had to keep checking.

Leaving Ilona's daughter here to burn would have been even more hideous than allowing her to be borne away by Surali.

I wondered if my Blades had gotten out. I wondered if they would make it to the Tavernkeep's. I wondered how Mother Argai was doing. I wondered how *I* was doing.

Finally reaching the end of the entire floor, I admitted defeat. I had failed. Corinthia Anastasia was not here. Long gone, to the docks, to sea, to wherever that bitch Surali had taken her. Tears welled in my eyes.

No, not just tears. Irritation. The smoke was even thicker, and I realized that I'd heard no shouts for a while. Firelight flickered in the stairwell behind me. This wasn't looking well for me.

Then I remembered the laundry chute. The one I had climbed was on the other wing of the house, but it might well have a mate down here. I'd seen a linen room already. I ducked back in there and found, yes, a trapdoor for the chute. Wrapping myself more tightly in the furniture covers and holding the borrowed sword close so it wouldn't bang against me, I slid feet-first into the hot darkness. I rattled downward with increasing speed, bumping against the laths that held the panels of the chute in place, until I belatedly wondered if I would smash into an iron door deep within the bowels of the mansion.

I landed with a hard jar to my ankles and shins. Nothing worse, thank the Lily Goddess. After rubbing my legs a moment, and soothing the baby, who had not liked the sudden descent, I checked my surroundings. This chute ended much as the other had, in a hallway. The laundry room was back to my right. Given that Surali had stationed archers on the grounds, emerging into the backyard alone without the Rectifier for a shield seemed dubious at best. The plumbing was a far better bet.

Sewers ran beneath the Velviere District. In most houses you'd have to be the size of a rat to climb up and down the pipes, but in a building this large, anything was possible. Perhaps there was even a cistern to draw from.

I cast about the stone-floored basement. The smell was just as bad down here, but the smoke not nearly so thick yet. Fire preferred to climb. I found laundry tubs, filled from a pump. They drained into a trough, then through a grate in the floor too small for me. So there was a sewer. I just wasn't getting in that way.

Ovens, too, fires banked now. No evidence of cooks or scullions. No handy open sewer pits in the bakery.

Pantries. Tool rooms. Maids' dormitory. Guards' dormitory. Room after room, none of them filled with what I needed.

Finally I took a mattock, rather too heavy for me, and dragged it back to the laundry room. The ceiling was getting hot, and I could hear the fire roaring. At this point I might not be able to depart by any other route.

The edge of the tool allowed me to lever the grate off. I stared doubtfully into the darkness. How far down did this reach? Did it branch or split, or drop straight into a sewerway? There had to be a tunnel to the street, at least, as the mains didn't run directly under most buildings.

Below was complex enough from within. I'd earlier deliberately avoided using that as a path. Guessing a route from above . . .

Outside held fire, archers, killing cold, and by now, a dearth of my allies. I'd been too long within the house. Taking a deep breath, I uttered a formless prayer and began to hack at the stonework edge supporting the grate.

The flags came up with quite a bit of strain on my part, peeling away to reveal a somewhat fatter pipe than the grate had implied. Straight down about six feet from the look, then opening into a horizontal run.

And wide enough to send a boy down to clear the drains as needed.

Plumbers' boys did not usually work pregnant. Unfortunately, I did.

I dropped the mattock down the drain. It thumped rather than splashed. That was fine with me. I took a deep breath, slid feet-first into the hole, and prayed again, that the horizontal run crossing below was large enough for me to continue. Otherwise I'd spend the very short balance of my life cowering under this house while it burned down over my head.

Halfway down I got stuck. The blessed thing *narrowed*. I almost cried, then cursed, then raged in fear. Wriggled. Moaned. Cursed again. Sucked my gut in, pressed my already-burning arms against the walls, and lifted, before I dropped a handspan or two. Something slipped. Something else caught. My pants?

Another heavy breath out, another sucking in, another lift and drop. The baby didn't appreciate it, I could tell. "You won't enjoy being rump roast, either," I whispered.

I pushed again, feeling my hips scrape even through the canvas trousers, and my belly crushed. Panic closed in on me, darkening my shadowed vision and pimpling my skin. I was going to die here.

Then I slid the rest of the way down in one ragged slump, nearly turning my ankle on the mattock and landing on my ass in the circle of light from above. Everything hurt. I'd slowed down too much, and my exhaustion was catching up to me. My gut was aching, my throat burned with the need to throw up.

Instead I grabbed the mattock and stumbled in the direction of the street, under an arch so low I had to either bend over or duckwalk. Two stout iron grates later, broken open with my trusty mattock, I was Below, safely beneath Ríchard Avenue, and away from that damned fire.

Operating only on faint hope and dim instinct, I headed toward the docks. I left the mattock behind. Still I carried some poor bastard of a guard's bloodied sword.

I emerged beneath the Mendicant's Well in the Dockmarket. A narrow tunnel opened into the shaft just above the water level of the cistern that supplied the well. A roof overhead blocked the night, but the wind howled just fine.

Up, into the cold. My entire body cramped at the thought. I was so tired I wanted to vomit. Every part of me felt bruised, some bits broken, and I was leaving a bloody trail as I walked. I didn't know why something large and hurtful hadn't already climbed out of Below and claimed me.

Up, up.

What was I chasing?

Up!

I don't know who spoke, but I could hear her voice.

The climb was so difficult, I almost didn't make it. My hands shivered on each rung, my arms stretched like clay. *It's only water below me,* I thought, and envisioned falling into that cool embrace.

Then I thought of Ilona, and kept climbing.

Over the lip of the well and into the little shelter where it stood. This close to the harborfront, the wind was biting, toothy and vile. I'd lost my furniture covers somewhere, and had no idea what had become of my comfortable stolen robe.

March on, march on.

An awning flapped nearby. I paused to cut it down, wrapping myself in blue and gray striping.

March on.

Even the waterfront taverns were shuttered. Though the storm had faded to clear skies, still no one was out in the raw, blustery weather. All we lacked was more snow or rain to complete my misery. The wind-driven spume along the docks was freezing in place. Ships creaked dark and ominous at their moorings, a few faint lights showing even lonelier than deepest shadow would have been.

No barking dogs, no whores' come-ons, no drunken singing. It was as if the entire city had been frozen into its grave. Copper Downs, brought to this. Though I'd be willing to bet things were quite warm inside the Selistani embassy.

That thought made me giggle. Giggling turned into laughter, and the laughter very nearly turned into whooping hysteria. I had to stop and sit on a pile of cargo nets until my breath ran out and I could rediscover my sense of purpose.

A few more ships farther down, stumbling under the starlight, I saw a vessel lit up with the pale orange-yellow flicker of bottled lightning. The steam kettle thrummed. She was making ready to sail. A few figures moved along the dock. One of those big drayage wagons was just pulling away.

Surali.

The Selistani embassy.

Corinthia Anastasia.

I tried to run, stumbled, slid on an icy patch and fetched up hard against a barrel. Climbing to my hands and knees, I staggered on. There was no running left in me.

Could I call them back? I opened my mouth and croaked. Damn me for carrying a sword but not a torch. These people would *want* me, if they knew it was me coming for them. I couldn't fight a sick chicken in my current state, but I could catch up. Later I'd find a way to escape with the girl.

The dockside figures withdrew up the gangplank, weapons still at the ready. In careful order. A rear guard. Watching for *me*.

If only they knew.

To all the hells with staggering like a drunk. It was time for one last run. Time to catch them. I took a deep breath, lurched forward graceless and heavy as I had ever been of late, and was caught up in massive hands. Screaming, I turned to look into the face of Skinless.

He shook his head, *no.* One massive, meaty finger touched my lips for silence.

A bell clanged. Water churned as the ship slowly backed away from the dock. I didn't even struggle. What would I have done, except be a prisoner? And who knows what Surali would have trimmed off of my body, the way she'd taken Mother Vajpai's toes?

Still, I strained to retrieve the girl. I wept, until the tears froze on my cheeks; then the lumbering giant carried me away through the crystalline spaces of the winter night.

Defeat, and Another Sort of Triumph

To my surprise, Skinless took me not to the temple of Blackblood, or even the Temple of Endurance, but rather to the Tavernkeep's place.

"How did you know?" I asked as the avatar gently placed me swaying on my feet before the door.

He shook his great, flayed head as if to deny any complicity, then lumbered once more into the darkness.

I was standing. Barely. For a moment, I was tempted to simply walk away. But that I could not do. I had allowed a child to be stolen to Kalimpura, home of the same child trade that had once sold me away. The two Blades who should be in here now were my key to following Surali, following that ship, and retrieving Corinthia Anastasia before . . . what?

I did not know.

So I staggered into the firelight.

My entrance was marred by my stumbling at the threshold. I hit the floor once more. This time I just stayed down. Something I'd never done. I felt too heavy to even move.

Strong hands—furred, as well as homey Selistani brown—picked me up off the floor. I was carried to a flat spot. A table?

Noises of crowding and moaning and the sweaty, bloody smell of recovery. Flickering light. Someone pouring pardine bournewater down my throat. Wincing as fingers probed for broken ribs.

Eventually I cried.

When I stopped crying, Ponce from the Temple of Endurance was holding my hand. "You need to sleep," he said softly. "And perhaps to eat as well."

"I need to know." Then, one of the hardest things I'd ever asked: "Sit me up." I *had* to *see*.

With the help of one of the acolytes, he propped me up, then they slid me into a chair. I looked around. Crowded, indeed. Rough-furred pardine Revanchists stalked among Selistani refugees with broken noses and bandaged wounds.

"Where is Mother Argai?" I asked. "And Mother Vajpai, and Samma?"

Ponce shrugged. "I am not certain."

He slipped off, to find me food maybe, leaving me to wonder if he meant he did not know who I meant, or he did not know where they were.

No one else I knew well was close by. I half-recognized most of these people, though in my current state of fatigue and confusion, I might have thought to recognize anybody. Or no one at all. But where were any of my people? Corinthia Anastasia was gone, lost to me. My fellow Blades should be here somewhere. The Rectifier with them. Of course, the last I'd seen those three, they'd been leaping into a fiery night, while Mother Argai had been stumbling wounded in the street.

Even the Dancing Mistress, alien and alienated as she had become to me, would be a welcome sight.

Have I lost them all?

The thought chilled me. The idea that I might have only the gods for company now seemed more than I could bear. I rolled onto my side and curled up with my arms cradling my belly. When had I grown so large?

Ponce came back with a bowl of dhal, Chowdry in his wake. The priest wore an apron spattered with grease and sauce—he'd been cooking, then.

Was there a better ministry for him? I wondered, though, who stood with the god, and wished mightily that I might spend more time in his kitchen.

Me. I'd stood with the god most recently.

My mind was wandering, I knew it was. I forced my attention back.

"You are being alive," Chowdry said in Petraean.

"You don't have to sound so damned surprised." I didn't mean to be peevish, but the words came out that way.

He glanced at Ponce. "I am not being surprised. You are never surprising me." Then, in Seliu, so the whitebelly could not understand us, "The embassy is gone. Little Baji went with them. So did some of the regulars here."

"Spies," I hissed in the same language.

Chowdry nodded. "But at least they are fled."

"The girl hostage is with them," I growled. "I have failed."

He smoothed his apron, dirtying his hands in the process. "I am not thinking you have failed so much. This could have been a far more difficult night."

"The gods live, but my sister Blades are missing. A child is stolen across the sea." I briefly closed my eyes, blinking out my tears. "I cannot name this a victory."

Chowdry took my hand. "Accept what success you can." With a nod to Ponce, he turned back toward the kitchen, pushing through the crowd.

I realized that as we spoke, pardines had begun to surround me. A momentary stab of fear traced through my heart, which I laid aside. These were practically my own people. Even the Revanchists held little terror for me now.

The Dancing Mistress stepped between a pair of tall, furred shoulders to approach me. Her water-pale violet eyes glinted as she stared. I sat up to meet her, though it cost me much to move thusly. Back and belly protested.

"Where is he?" she asked.

That was not what I had expected. "Who?"

Her voice was hard. "The Rectifier. You gave our heart's treasure away, but you have mislaid the bearer."

I realized the room had fallen quiet. The Dancing Mistress' ears were stiff, her tail flicking back and forth. "If you wish to punish me for losing track of your people's greatest warrior," I said, "lay into me and have done with it. I did not send him away or put him to sword. And he has two of my own with him."

Where can the Rectifier be? With my missing Blades?

My gut flopped. What had happened?

She shook her head, sighing, and for a moment was my old teacher again. "Green, I will not strike at you. Not now, not ever again."

A strange promise, I realized, but held my tongue.

The Dancing Mistress continued: "Much stands at risk here, missing."

"I *know* that. If I could search for them, I would." Instead, I could barely move. I did not then realize how much one is tied to children, whether they are in one's belly or at one's side.

"Where might they be?" she asked softly.

Not the Temple of Endurance or Chowdry would have known. With

Blackblood? He was a god of men, not women. Besides which, Skinless would not have borne me here if my people had been lying in his god's temple.

The answer came to me. "Archimandrix," I whispered. "They are Below. With the sorcerer-engineers."

"Ah." She turned swiftly away from me. I heard the door crash open and then swiftly slam shut again a moment later.

Better she than me, I thought. Ponce came to spoon dhal into me until I could take no more. I asked for a room, and they let me rest.

Daylight glowed red against my gummed-shut eyes. Someone had opened a shutter. I blinked, but it was too bright.

Closing my eyes again, I realized my belly was swollen and painful even beyond the pressure of the child within me. Too many tumbles onto my face. One hand strayed to stroke my skin there, trying to send comfort to the baby. I was still over two months from my due date, though it felt as if she wanted to emerge right now. When had I grown so enormous? I was unwieldy as any clay oven, potbellied and thin-legged and never the right temperature.

"Green," a voice said softly.

I tried opening my eyes again, just a squint. I didn't recognize the room— small and spare, with words painted on the plaster wall in some script I could not read. The smell of Selistani cooking told me I was above the Tavernkeep's place.

Ilona sat beside me. She took my other hand in hers. Her face was red and swollen, puffy with tears, with grief.

"I . . ." The words would not be said.

"You did so much," she whispered.

"Not enough." My own tears poured forth. "C-Corinthia Anastasia, th-they sailed away with her." I began to sob, to blubber as an ill-trained child might. "Sh-she's gone . . ."

"Green." Ilona gripped my hand tighter. "She's been gone since they took her from my cottage. We will find a way to get her back."

"That's my promise to *you*," I almost shouted, my voice mounting in anger.

"It is." Ilona leaned close and kissed my forehead, then my tears, then my lips.

That quieted me a little. But not for long.

"Where are my sister Blades?"

"Those terrible women in black?" Humor rode in her voice.

"Yes. They were with the Rectifier. Th-that big pardine warrior."

"Your Dancing Mistress brought them here this morning."

I gave fervent thanks to the Lily Goddess. "Where are they now?"

"Both are recovering."

Both? "I had three sisters here."

Her face fell. "Two came in. In the arms of brass apes that followed the pardine woman."

The next question made me very afraid. "Which two . . . ? And, and . . . where is the third?" Dead?

"I don't know their names," she said. "One could not walk. Something was wrong with her feet."

"Mother Vajpai." I was unsure whether I was relieved or disappointed.

"The other would not wake up. A woman who had been hit about the head."

"A woman, or a girl? My age, perhaps?"

"No, much older than you."

Panic tinged my thoughts. I could not keep *anyone* without losing them. "Then where is Samma?"

"I don't know, Green." She leaned close to kiss me again, but I turned my face away.

"Don't be too near me. You will suffer."

Ilona slid into the bed. "I already have suffered."

I let her curl her body around my back, and her hands clasp me just beneath my breasts; then I slept awhile with her breath warm upon my neck, safe in the circle of her arms.

Later I awoke again. At first I was too stiff to move. The light held a golden tinge, like honey glaze on a fresh-baked bun, suggesting the day was nearly at an end. Ilona was gone. I was alone.

No matter how much my body ached, I had to pee. I pulled myself from the bed, at the cost of no little pain and some lumbering misbalance, and found the chamber pot. Water came pulsing out of me like a countryman spitting durian seeds, urination so hard and deep that it was painful. How long had I lain there?

Pissing left me parched and hungry, but not so weak I couldn't walk. Someone had removed—or cut away—my ruined clothing. I was naked.

I found a tattered robe on a hook behind the door. Left for me, surely, for no pardine would need such a thing and especially not in so small a size.

Slowly, carefully, I stumbled into the hall, then crept down the stairs that opened into the back of the tavern. I kept one hand on the rough-carved rail. I could no longer see my feet, nor tell where they touched down. This pregnancy was like being aged, or ill. How did women stand it over and over?

The common room was much quieter, almost normal. Gaming tiles clacked, voices murmured, a fire crackled against the winter chill. I followed the sounds and smells to find Ilona sitting in close conversation with Chowdry and Mother Vajpai.

Most of the pardines were gone. Among those remaining, I saw none whom I could identify as Revanchists.

Mother Vajpai noticed me first, and pointed. Chowdry jumped up so fast he knocked his chair over. Ilona still reached me quickest.

"Green." Her voice was urgent with concern. "What are you doing about?"

"Hungry," I muttered, the first explanation that came to mind. A moment later I realized it was true.

She and Chowdry helped me to a seat at the table, then he darted off to the kitchen.

I stared at Mother Vajpai. Her cheeks were blistered, but she still possessed her dark, lustrous hair. "You are here," I said in Seliu.

"Yes. I am being here." Her tone remained somber. "Mother Argai sleeps upstairs. A real sleep now, not the stone-stillness of yesterday. We will be seeing what is in her thoughts when she awakes."

Blows to the head could be among the worst of wounds. Everyone feared that loss of mind and spirit that threatened with a cracked or dented skull.

"And Samma?"

Mother Vajpai did not flinch away, though her eyes were clouded. "She stood and fought so that your great cat and I could escape. The Prince's men wounded her. Then they took her down."

This was how my bullying of her was repaid. Guilt flooded me once more. "Dead?"

"I do not know. Dead or alive, she is departed aboard their ship."

My first lover, in Surali's vengeful hands. "So when I failed at the docks," I said bitterly, "I betrayed both Samma and Corinthia Anastasia." *Again.*

"Green." Ilona took my hand again. She was speaking in Petraean, of course; she had no Seliu. "I know what happened to your friends. You cannot blame yourself."

"All of it is my fault!"

"No," she said. "Others chose their own path."

"Not your daughter."

The haunted expression in Ilona's eyes cut me to the quick. I wished mightily I had not said those words. "Not my daughter, no."

"I will take ship," I announced in Petraean still, then repeated myself in Seliu. Looking at Mother Vajpai, I continued in that language. "I will follow them across the ocean, and I will burn down the Bittern Court. I will sift the ashes for Surali's bones. I will break them all one by one, then dance on the shards. I will cut the throats of every member of the Prince of the City's household. I will feed them all to the pigs." Brave words, given how badly my body was overset just then.

"No." Mother Vajpai's tone held the finality of a rusted chain around a man's ankles as he was thrown overboard. "You will stay here, and bear your child. Mother Argai and I will heal as best we can. Then we will return across the Storm Sea together and petition the Lily Goddess for guidance."

I opened my mouth to protest, to argue, to claim a right of violence and revenge. After a moment, I closed my mouth without speaking. I had sworn that my child would be born here on the Stone Coast. Why begin a war just now, when my balance was gone and my abilities compromised? I could not be timely—that opportunity was already lost. I could instead be prepared, and ensure the safety of my own child.

Turning to Ilona, I said, "Will you care for my daughter while I am gone retrieving yours?"

"Hush," she replied. "I am not so good at keeping little girls safe."

"Will you raise her," I demanded fiercely.

Ilona nodded, her eyes large and serious and grief-ridden.

Switching back to Seliu, I turned to Mother Vajpai once more. "I will follow your plan." *For now.*

My job was to bring my child safely into the world. *Then* I could do what needed to be done.

Chowdry returned with a plate of lentils and some saffron rice. "Here, you must eat more."

"Where is the Rectifier?" I asked him.

"Gone, with the Dancing Mistress and all those mountain pardines of hers. They were leaving at dawn."

"He must have taken the gems back to the Blue Mountains." I wondered what would come of that, and decided it was a problem beyond my resolving.

Chowdry shrugged.

I looked at him closely. "I'm feeling a bit god-raddled at the moment. Speaking of such things, who governs the city?"

Another shrug. "That new council, it is said, though the Textile Bourse still flies a flag."

"Oh, joy." Yet one more problem people would probably expect me to solve. Jeschonek, for one. To the Smagadine hells with all of them.

"Return to the High Hills with me," Ilona said, reading my expression.

That served to distract me from my newest line of worry. I was appalled by the suggestion. "In the dead of winter?" Not to mention that in my current state I was probably not fit to walk or ride that far, nor would I be until after the child came.

"They set fire to my house, but it can be repaired," she said. "Many at Briarpool will aid me. You can bear your child there, away from the gods who would trouble you."

The thought of all that cold was too much for me. "I cannot stand to live among such snow," I told her. "But when my daughter is born, take her there yourself. Please. And keep her safe until I can claim her once more."

Ilona nodded. So did Mother Vajpai, which made me wonder how much Petraean she had learned in her time here. Or before.

That, I decided, did not matter.

In the end, I chose to have my labor in the Temple of Endurance rather than the Bustle Street lazaret. The competing prophecies of Blackblood and Desire were overwhelming to me. Distracted by pregnancy, failure, and grief, I had been too much the fool to unravel what they truly meant. I wanted the protection of my own personal ox god. Wiser and more patient and more powerful than I, he had always stood above me. Ilona had slept with me those nights of the last two months—sadly never in passion, though my ever-bulging body would have made a frustration of that even if we had—but Endurance protected me always.

Ilona was as sweet and right for me as ever I'd hoped for. I grieved that I could do nothing to heal the crack in her heart that was her missing daughter.

Mother Vajpai and Mother Argai took their rest and recuperation in the lazaret, under Mother Iron's protection. The lazaret was under their protection also, as I had more or less foreseen. Already they were training some of the women in basic weapons drill, instilling them with the courage to stand and fight. Being so hugely pregnant in my last months, I had done little but watch them at their work. Not even so much of that.

The night of the birth, Chowdry filled the wooden temple with candles. Or his acolytes did. Mother Iron's priestess Laris came to attend me, Desire riding behind her eyes. I was not afraid Laris would claim my child, whatever her patron might intend. The priestess was aided by Ilona, and Mother Vajpai and Mother Argai, whose mind had come back into her head well enough, though her hearing continued difficult, as well as her thoughts strangely slowed. I lay amid the scents of incense and beeswax and tallow, swallowing waves of pain and strangeness.

I focused on the prayers tied to the ox's horns. They glinted in the flickering light as if coming alive. Every time a contraction seized me, I put my own pain and worry into those prayers. Over and over, while the women around me sponged me with wine and gripped my hand and offered whispered counsel I could not hear and would not heed.

Eventually my child slipped into the world on a flood of blood and water and a surprised wail. "A daughter," Laris announced. I wondered even in that red-hot moment how Blackblood would see this abrogation of his prophecy.

But something else came, I could feel it. Her. *Another child?*

Laris exclaimed wordlessly, while Mother Vajpai said, "He grasps at her ankle."

A second baby, sliding from me with another rush of heat and pain, close behind the first.

"A boy," Laris said this time. Then I knew how the prophecy was made. I should have seen it long before, but as with so many other mistakes, I had been blind.

"Do not," I said, straining, "do not *ever* give my children to the gods."

My own life lost to being ridden by their hideous strength was enough.

Crying, I lay back in the shadow of Endurance as they placed the babies on my swollen, sore breasts. Words and blessings and warm cloths touched me and my two children, but they would never be enough. Larger shadows loomed in the temple as well, as if Blackblood and Mother Iron and perhaps the Lily Goddess looked on.

Divine favor? Divine fear?

Even now, in this moment, I knew Kalimpura awaited me, and my two lost promises there—Corinthia Anastasia and Samma. Were they so different from my two new responsibilities here?

No matter what I did for them, my children could not be safe. Not safe enough. Nothing would ever be enough. Still, I would try, because that is what I do in this life, from the first days, through the birth of my children, and down the years to follow with all the sorrow and pleasure they have brought me.

I sobbed all the harder. My friends around me mistook this for joy.

After all that has happened since, I can say in truth that they were not completely wrong.